This Book Belongs To

dpInk
DonnaInk Publications, L.L.C.

Nocturnum's Muse

THE SPIRITUAL SOCIOPATH

Published in the United States of America

Nocturnum's Muse

THE SPIRITUAL SOCIOPATH

MITCHELL ALLEN

Nocturnum's Muse Imprint
Publishers Since 2012
An imprint of **DonnaInk Publications, L.L.C.**
601 McReynolds Street, Carthage, NC 28327
1390 Chain Bridge Rd., #10029, McLean, VA 22101

Library of Congress Cataloging-in-Publication. 2021932136

Allen, Mitchell, author.
Title: "The Spiritual Sociopath" / Mr. Allen Mitchell. 328 p. cm.

Subjects: FIC069000 FICTION / City Life, FIC050000 FICTION / Crime, FIC045010 FICTION / Family Life / Marriage & Divorce, FIC027200 FICTION / Romance / Historical / 20th Century, FIC027430 FICTION / Romance / Workplace, FIC031080 FICTION / Thrillers / Psychological, FIC031010 FICTION / Thrillers / Crime.
Identifiers: ISBN – 13 - 9798812653606;
ISBN – 13 - 978-1-947704-75-6 (alk. hardcover).
Printed in the United States of America

First Edition: 12 11 10 9 8 7 6 5 4 3 2; 2022.

For more information contact:

DonnaInk Publications, L.L.C.
601 McReynolds St., Carthage, NC 28327
1390 Chain Bridge Rd., #10029, McLean, VA 22101
www.donnaink.com

DEDICATION

MITCHELL ALLEN

This book is dedicated to my daughter Sarah. Not a day has gone by when she has not been in my heart.

Mitchell Allen . . .

INSPIRATION FOR

THE SPIRITUAL SOCIOPATH

The life story that was the inspiration for this book belonged to a certain Eddie Chapman, who was also known by MI5 as . . . Agent Zig Zag!

Eddie Chapman was a high functioning sociopath, serial womanizer, and a safe cracker. He was also an extremely brave and intelligent man, who saved many lives during WW2 by deceiving the Nazi's who then, misdirected their V1 rockets that were targeted over many parts of Britain.

But for Eddie Chapman's extraordinary guile and courage; the number of casualties could have been so much higher. I wish I possessed just 1% of the spirit Eddie demonstrated at that dark time.

Most bizarrely, Adolf Hitler was completely fooled and actually honored Eddie with the Iron Cross for bravery . . . you couldn't make it up!

RIP Eddie Chapman

THE SPIRITUAL SOCIOPATH
MITCHELL ALLEN
dpink
WWW.DONNAINK.COM
nook
available at
amazon

CONTENTS

The Spiritual Sociopath

EPIGRAPH

MITCHELL ALLEN

"They'll often break rules or make impulsive decisions without feeling guilty for the harm they cause."

BASED ON A TRUE STORY . . .

PROLOGUE.

THE KNIFEMAN

My story begins with my writing about a man who has had the most profound impact on my life. A man whom I never met, and someone whose life I will one day write a book about. His name was Frank Mitchum. My Uncle Frank. His claim to notoriety was as a criminal associate of the Krayford twins and as 'Britain's Most Wanted Man' in Christmas 1966. He was known as Frank 'The Knifeman' Mitchum, a ghastly rubric, which was bestowed upon him by the British Sunday newspapers.

Frank Mitchum was my mother's older brother. She sadly went to her grave never once speaking of him to me, or my two siblings. In fact, I can only ever recall having one discussion about him when I was in my mid-twenties, and that was an awkward and stilted conversation with my father. All conversations with my father were challenging, and I will address that particular 'Freudian Paradox' later in my story.

My only recollection 'something odd was going on' is the fading memory of when I was around eight years of age, when men in grey overcoats - who must have been CID Officers - were ushered into our front room to peer through the net curtain. I later discovered this strange behavior was due to the fact when Frank was 'on the run' he would bizarrely endeavor to make his way home to visit my grandparents, who in those days, lived just two doors along from my family home.

My father revealed finally to me, Frank habitually escaped from various secure prison institutions - such as Broadmoor - which was by no means an easy endeavor, as he would have had to survive extreme weather conditions to make his way back home to Old Ford, in Bow, east London. He would endure such an attrition just for a most brief taste of family love and comfort from his elderly parents. What is more, the police would apparently go through the charade of allowing Frank to have a cup of tea with my grandparents and then, they would escort him back, and return him into custody again. Hey, it was very different in them days, that's for sure!

Shortly before Christmas 1966, Ralph and Rex Krayford, sprang my uncle from the high security prison located on Dartmoor, in the county of Devon. The escape sparked what was then, the biggest manhunt in British criminal history. So was Frank the brutal psychopath of legend, or was he - a gentle giant, who was naively drawn into the fatal arena of the underworld.

Frank became friends with Ralph Krayford when they served a sentence together in the 1950s. During Frank's trial for attempted murder, Ralph hired a lawyer for him and paid for him to have a new suit fitted. The Krayford twins were keen on breaking my uncle out of prison, thinking it would help Frank to publicize his grievance and earn a release date, as well as enhance the Krayford's standing in the underworld.

Rex Krayford was more restrained than his twin, but finally reasoned that 'if nothing else it would stick two fingers up to the law'. So, Rex visited Frank at Dartmoor - in disguise - and informed him of the plan to help him escape. On 12 December 1966, while with a work party on the moors, my uncle asked the only guard on duty, for permission to feed some nearby Dartmoor ponies. Incredibly, his request was granted, and he simply walked over to a quiet road, where a getaway car containing associates of the Krayfords were waiting for him, and they drove off to London. The twins put Frank up in a filthy flat in East London, and even more bizarrely, it was over ten hours before my uncle was reported missing.

As I have alluded, Frank's escape made the national news and was featured daily on the main national TV broadcasts. The episode led to a political storm over the lax security around a man described in the press as 'Britain's most violent convict' and was even debated in the UK Parliament. A large fugitive hunt ensued, with over five hundred police officers, three hundred Royal Marines, and a R.A.F helicopter searching the moors.

With the aid of a sympathetic, and brave, journalist, Frank wrote to the UK national newspapers. His plea to be granted a release date was printed in two of them. However, the home secretary, was simply unwilling to negotiate with an escaped criminal and would not review his status until Frank was back in custody.

My uncle soon became a problem for the Krayfords, largely owing to his physical strength, and terribly short temper. Frank was difficult to control. He was unwilling to give himself up and return to prison. So, it was down to his handlers, who were given the near impossible task of placating Frank to prevent him from leaving the flat in case he was recognized. So, they resorted to providing him with a string of local prostitutes, who he could satisfy his frustrations with, and it is the stuff of legend, Frank's exertions were so loud and raucous, his handlers were concerned the noise would attract unhelpful attention.

The Krayford twins found themselves in a 'Catch 22' and feared releasing Frank or turning him in as he could implicate them both in his escape. Frank felt more than insulted Rex had only visited him in person once and was particularly upset he could not visit my grandparents, despite them living so nearby.

The prostitutes could only distract Frank for so long and he grew increasingly agitated and soon began making threats against the twins. Somewhat inevitably, the Krayford's decided the only solution to their problem was to have my uncle . . . killed.

My wonderful grandfather - and my namesake, Samuel - made a last-ditch attempt to persuade his son to give himself up to the authorities, by appearing on national television news. Sadly, despite my grandfather making a heartfelt appeal to Frank, his efforts bore no fruit. I have played back recordings of that appeal so many times. Samuel's heartache at his son's dire circumstances still resonates deeply within my very soul.

On Christmas Eve 1966, Frank's handlers led him into the back of a van, in the belief, he was about to be taken to a safe house in the countryside where he would meet up with Ralph. There was almost another argument when he realized his favorite prostitute Lil, would not be coming with him, but they managed to persuade him it was safer for her to follow later-on. Waiting in the van were several men, and among them; Frederick Workman - a notorious gangland assassin - who was armed with a revolver.

Once the van doors were closed and the engine started, he opened fire on Frank, killing him. Six shots were fired before Frank Mitchum died and his body was never recovered. Workman later revealed my uncle's body was bound with chicken wire, weighted down, and dumped in a Scottish Loch. Rex Krayford later admitted springing Frank 'The Knifeman' Mitchum from prison was his biggest mistake. Frank's murder must have utterly devastated my grandparents, and I just wish my mother had not covered up what was going on.

Indeed, the stress my parents must have put themselves under, to keep me and my brother away from news story of the day, must have been horrendous. Long term it would prove to be counterproductive, for it gave credence to the unhealthy mindset of being both secretive and lying by omission.

In fact, I only became aware of Frank's existence, when I was dating my first serious girlfriend. She was absolutely astonished to discover, she was far privier to details about my family's most infamous son, than I was. In fact, I hadn't even heard of him up until that point. My first girlfriend was called Lorraine, and she was just sixteen years of age.

Lorraine was also the lucky girl to whom I would lose my virginity - whilst screwing her on the stairs of the maisonette where she lived along Cambridge Heath Road - on the borders of Bethnal Green and Stepney. Looking back, she vehemently claimed she lost her virginity at the same time; although, I never believed her. Neither did I really care. As with the majority of oversexed and spotty adolescent lads, all I cared about was that first real fuck. You know, being able to back up all the bullshit and bragging young men tend to lie about to their pals - long before they ever get to truly 'lose their cherries'.

I can also recall, how we fucked like a couple of rabbits for the next eighteen months or so, until the illusory love we feel for each other at that age inevitably began to wear thin. Fuck me, we were at it so much and so fast, if it had been on film, my butt would have been just one fast blur!

My mind went into an utter state of disarray and confusion, when Lorraine began to tell me just how much she knew about my uncle. It also became very clear just how much detail everyone else close to me knew. Even now, after all these years later - I am still at a loss as to how no other member of my family, school friends, or my own parents indeed, had managed to keep Frank's existence from me and my two siblings.

Apart from anything else, Frank was a bear of a man at 6' 4" and never out of the national newspapers and TV news broadcasts of the day. So, it was pretty difficult to miss the man, bless him. RIP . . . Frank.

However, as I grew older it became increasingly plain to me, the hiding of Frank's existence, was only one of many things my parents had a habit of withholding from all three of their children. Not a healthy example for an impressionable and developing mind; a dysfunction, which would have dire consequences for them and so many others.

It would also be proper to say how eternally grateful I am to my little cockney lover Lorraine, wherever you are nowadays sweetie, for the manner she managed my sensibilities in those days. And for the sensitive manner she went about firstly revealing what she herself knew. Then the later research we embarked on by visiting local libraries and unearthing archived newspaper material, still available about Frank's life. As many years passed by, it was also telling, at no point did I ever feel comfortable enough to approach my parents - nor any other family member for that matter - to inquire about what I had discovered of such a powerful and tragic man's life, and the manner of his murder.

Lorraine did her level best to encourage me to confront my both of my parents about Frank, but 'secrets and lies' best described the dynamic in the Kirkham household. Most certainly, this created the environment, psychologically and socially, that began to shape a mental blueprint, which would eventually cultivate my fledgling sociopathic tendencies. In turn, I would become completely out of control and to a point of total self-destruction.

As I have already alluded to, it is my desire and ambition to finally write a concise, and most importantly, accurate account of the life of Frank Mitchum. From time to time, I will make various anecdotal references about him in this book, but for now at least, I will park 'Uncle Frank' until another point in my story.

THE SPIRITUAL SOCIOPATH

CHAPTER 1.

THE EAST END HAS CHANGED SO MUCH

Samuel Kirkham was born in St. Andrews Hospital, Bromley by Bow, on the 11th of May 1958, around 2 am I believe - which makes me a 'Sunday child'. So much then for the holy and self-righteous influence that would apparently have been bestowed upon my soul from the heavens above. Moreover, the christening that soon followed, did not seem to do the trick either! Or . . . did it?

My father Henry was always known as Harry, and my mother was Marie pronounced the 'Gaelic' way . . . Maree. I labor the point about my dad being named Henry, for I would have also carried the name if it had been left up to my grandparents. All first born males in the clan, had been called Henry. no doubt going back to William the Conqueror or some such bollocks. The fact my old man had some kind of aberration and refused to follow this arcane tradition, does have a tremendous bearing on later events.

11th May is a birthday I happen to share with Salvador Dali, Jeremy Paxman, Margaret Rutherford, Phil Silvers (I was always a huge fan of his hit TV show, Sergeant Bilko) Pam Ferris, John Parrot, Natasha Richardson, and Eric Burdon.

To give credit where it is due, both of my parents were hard working and discerning people. Although it would be fair to say, their experience of growing up in the post war years of austerity Britain, had definitely left its mark on both of them - as it did of course - for many of their generation.

Just as I had never heard my mother speak of Frank, neither can I recall either of my parents telling me that they loved me. In recent times I confirmed with my brother and sister my recollection was so. Both my siblings concurred, neither had experienced any form of loving affecttion from either parent. Their lack of nurturing would also have a long-term dramatic impact which resulted in my self-destruction . . .

My father Harry was an immigrant to the UK and came to these shores at the age of just two. He was born in Kingston Jamaica to my grandmother Enid, and allegedly, my grandfather Henry. I say allegedly, because I had my suspicions in later years Henry, or Bill, as he was known, was not Harry's real father.

My grandmother was clearly mixed race. For some weird reason I never became aware of that reality until I was in my mid-twenties. Enid spoke with a strong Caribbean accent, but I seemed to be in some kind of denial about it. My younger brother and I are very Caucasian in appearance. My late sister Cheryl, most clearly had mixed race features.

Enid was an amazing effervescent lady with a heart of gold. Unfortunately, she was also a gambling addict with a penchant for copious amounts of Guinness stout. Two dysfunctional traits I clearly inherited from the old girl! My memories of her are only fond ones, but she was utterly irresponsible and reckless with money, another inherited trait. Much to my father's consternation, she apparently would prefer to bet on two flies racing up a wall, rather than putting food on the family's table. She absolutely adored her time at the local bingo hall. If she ever managed to actually hold on to any winnings, she would love to spoil her grandchildren with small gifts, and bags of sweets, during her many regular visits to our humble home.

Whilst Enid was generous to a fault, my grandfather was a miserable old bastard with a gambling addiction of his own, so their union was a disastrous financial cocktail. Apart from my father, they had four more children, all boys. The youngest, David, was only four years older than me. He was much more like an older brother than an uncle for me and my siblings. He was also a comical genius, highly intelligent but profoundly lazy. His elderly parents did not impose any discipline and spoilt him rotten.

It is such a great shame my own dad, who David adored, did not get to grips with him and try to encourage his massive comedic talent. I remember he once adlibbed an entire football commentary that my father taped on his 'reel to reel' recorder. David was an incorrigible mimic. He was able to describe one hilarious episode after another with comic characters and 'Goone-like' names to match.

David's life tragically tail-spinned out of control once he joined the Navy at the age of sixteen; having found it difficult to hold down a steady job he invariably found too mundane. He was soon introduced to drugs. As a somewhat naive and unworldly character, David was easily led astray, which resulted in his predictable dismissal from the Navy. He continued the pattern of drifting from one job to another and his life began to really deteriorate. Inevitably he turned to harder drugs and developed an eventual life sapping heroin addiction.

David ended up in an institution because his mental health was compromised. During one drug crazed episode, he set about viciously attacking a doctor and nurse who were attending my infirmed grand-parents who at the time were living in sheltered accommodation.

The scene was akin to something out of a Stephen King novel. He first dragged the nurse, then the doctor, who was frantically trying to protect her from his knife welding savagery, across and over the grass adjoining a local playground. In front of screaming children and their horrified parents, David repeatedly stabbed both the doctor and nurse. Only the bravery of intervening local residents saved the lives of both of them.

David was admitted to an institution for the rest of his years. He died at the age of forty-five. His life was tragic. He harmed many. What a wastc of a fantastic vibrant mind. RIP . . . David.

Despite such a family tragedy, outwardly I had a fairly conven-tional childhood being the eldest of three siblings. My brother Terence, nearly three years younger than I, provided me with my earliest memory of my standing at the end of my parents' bed, looking at my doting mother cradling my shiny new brother in her arms. It was a further four years to the arrival of my sister, Cheryl. I remember both of my siblings being born at home, which was quite a normal practice in the 1960s.

Awwww . . . Cheryl. My baby sister passed in 2010 aged just forty-four, after losing her lengthy battle against a rare form of a bowel myopathy. The last time I saw her was in 2004/ By that time her health had already seriously deteriorated. I embraced her in floods of tears. As I write, her tender words of forgiveness still resonate deep within my soul. RIP . . . Cheryl.

Growing up in the old 'East End' of London in the 1960s, was great fun for us kids. We lived in the Old Ford Road at number 678. My grandparents lived two doors along at 682. Our road was in the small East London hamlet of Bow, which had been originally found in the traditional county of Essex but became subsumed by the capital of Great Britain following the passing of the Local Government Act of 1888. Bow is an abbreviation of the medieval name 'Stratford-at-Bow', in which Bow refers to the 'bowed bridge' built near the 'Ford' - from which, the name of our road was derived in the early twelfth century. Bow nowadays has parts of both Victoria Park and the Queen Elizabeth Olympic Park, which was developed for the 2012 Olympic Games.

The house I was raised in was a Victorian three-bedroom terrace with an outside 'lavatory'. I use that nineteenth century term, because that's how most old school Cockney's would describe a toilet. Oh, and by the way, so does the Queen!

Number 678 was dark, dingy, and cold most of the year. There were leaks everywhere with no heating, only a couple of open coal fires, which for several months of the year my mum would rise early to stack old screwed up newspapers, chopped kindling, and nutty slack coal. 'Nutty Slack' was a cheap fuel consisting of 'slack' coal dust and small lump 'coal nuts', which unlike other solid fuel, was not rationed during the period after World War One (WWI).

The house was a downright health risk because it was teaming with mice, even the occasional rat! I recall my old man sitting by the coal fire with a shovel in hand, smacking mice over the head when they peeped from their hole in the 'wood beetle' ridden skirting board. In one slick and practised action, Harry would whack the mouse, scoop it into the coal shovel, and flop the tiny carcass onto the fire. To make matters even more environmentally unfriendly, many of the roof tiles were missing. Whenever there was a typical London downpour, out came half a dozen tin buckets which would be positioned strategically by mum. Successfully catching the cascading rain was essential, which otherwise, would have soaked bedding and furniture.

It is hard to believe this was little over fifty years ago, when many today feel they are living in poverty. What with their smart devices, designer clothes, and UK benefits safety net still seem to find money for booze and fags. They are actually quite well off, compared to a typical working class East End family back in the early 1960s.

We also had a 'backyard', which wasn't even close to resembling a garden, believe me. Among the weeds and rough dirt, was our own microcosm of beetles, birds - mostly sparrows - and the most magnificent hairy caterpillars, the likes of which, you just don't see today. Chris Packham, where have all the hairy caterpillars gone?

The streets in our area looked very similar with the dilapidated terraced dwellings owned by private landlords, which had clearly once enjoyed a more prosperous past. I know this because our coal cellar was crammed full of old dusty medicine bottles left over from a former doctor occupier who apparently lived there in the interwar years.

Many lower middle-class professionals had lived in the East End; so, it wasn't quite all Dickensian squalor you know. The house was sadly demolished in the early 1970s as part of the East End Slum Clearance Program. Unfortunately, it wasn't just the house they knocked down. My mother's soul also crumbled in the brick dust.

The 'Old House' was the term my mum used to affectionately describe what was, without doubt, the happiest time of her life and in many ways, mine also. The object of her nostalgic memory stood in a main road that was, indeed, barely a stone's throw from where the 2012 Olympic stadium now stands. For my money, - that structure is in Bow, and not Stratford! The organizers just played fast and loose with the post code, so American visitors thought Shakespeare had lived nearby!

Bow in the 1960s still bore many of the scars of the Second World War (WWII) German Luftwaffe bombing raids, and the resultant adventure playground that remained for us kids to play on was simply a dreamland. We would shout out to our ambivalent mothers', "We are going to play on the 'debris' today Mum". Just like most of the other mums, she didn't even raise an eyebrow. Could you imagine the over-protective paranoid 'Snowflake' parents of today, contemplating the freedoms we all had as kids? Not to mention the politically correct 'health and safety Mafia' we must endure these days. They would have a bloody fit! So, throw in the uncertainty and restriction of our freedom, which the state imposed on the masses as result of the manmade Coronavirus, and it's no wonder our young are suffering from a 'collective anxiety syndrome'.

After school, we would all play out in infant gangs and would not return home until we could hear the collective yelling from our mothers of . . . 'time to come in'!

Never at any time did we feel at risk, and neither did our parents ever have concerns for our safety. The only caution being, 'don't accept any sweets from strangers'. That said, I am sure there were all sorts of weirdo's and perverts around back then, but thankfully, I never met any of them and neither can I remember any of my pals doing so.

So, this was a child's perception of a world, against the backdrop of The Beetles, Thunderbirds, Engelbart Humperdinck, the World Cup win of 1966. I can recall doing endless felt tip drawings of the England team mascot World Cup Willie, black and white TV repeats of Watch with mother, culminating in the 'Moon Landing' of July 1969! On that particular subject, I am still uncertain as to whether the whole thing was one big deception? Truth will out, I guess.

There were, however, two significantly negative episodes for me during this period. Firstly, was the gradual dismantling of my confidence by the incessant mental intimidation of my father. Secondly, something my mother did, which to this day, and over subsequent years, has become clear to me both of these episodes led to the seeding of sociopathic flaws deep within my psyche. The resulting insecurities would increasingly torment me and in turn, lead to a pathway of self-loathing, self-sabotage, inflicting so much pain and suffering on numerous others. I know this is difficult to digest, but as I have already said, it was actually meant to be that way. You see, I now understand, we do not have freewill!

My father Harry was one deeply flawed man, who died in January 2015 having suffered several mini strokes. It is always wise to have an insight into our own background to find the reasoning for a parent's dysfunctional characteristic traits and try to understand how they could have had such a powerful influence on another person. Who will then, impose inherited flaws through 'cause and effect', which can result in ruining many other lives . . . even decades after?

CHAPTER 2.

How Did It All Begin?

Harry was born in Kingston Jamaica in 1935 and came to Britain at the age of just two. Due to the WWII, he did not have any contact with his father. Remember, questionable parentage until he was ten years of age. For sure, that wasn't particularly unusual for many of his generation, but the estrangement created abandonment issues acutely marked him for life. That in itself wasn't the sole reason for the 'control freakery' Harry took beyond any reasonable limits into his adulthood. Many insecure people develop such traits, and his insecurities were compounded from vivid experiences he suffered over a six-year period from the age of four.

It was September 1939, and as we all know, Germany invaded Pol-and sealed the fate of millions of small children. One of them my dad, who found himself evacuated from darkest Bethnal Green in London to sunny little village of Wetherden in Suffolk. From what I was able to glean from the anecdotal references Harry made of those dark times, he was shipped out from Liverpool Street Station wearing the obligatory raincoat, short trousers, grey towelling socks, and scuffed shoes. I believe it was a brisk farewell from my grandmother and his two younger siblings - Lionel and baby Michael. He then morphed into the sea of the other traumatized evacuees being herded onto the steam train bound for the county of Suffolk. I could not ever imagine how those children felt at the time, what with all the chaos, uncertainty, and feelings of abandonment.

Just for one moment, try to imagine how the molly coddled kids of today, would cope if faced with such upheaval. Just . . . imagine it. It would have been bad enough, but what with the events of 2020, the state sponsored fear induced 'crises of the Coronavirus', and children of today will be evermore suffocated by paranoid 'Millennial' parents.

Harry would only see his mother five times over the next six years. Yet, Enid was only two villages away from where Harry was living! I never did find an explanation for that, so come on Enid, what was all that about? It would go a long way toward explaining why Harry would become an insecure, overbearing, and control freak of a husband and father.

Harry's first destination was a Barnado's institution which had taken over a commandeered stately home near Elmswell, Suffolk. At the beginning of the war, Barnado's were life savers on the one hand, but the sanctuary they offered sometimes came at a severe price. My dad had some very painful and embarrassing experiences. One might think of a stately home as a luxurious setting, but many had fallen into disrepair and the plumbing and sanitation, was no longer functioning properly and water had to be pumped from a local well.

As a child, my father was very private and self-conscious. So, pissing and shitting himself through sheer terror and fear, together with the draconian discipline, which was probably rather necessary during times of national crisis, utterly broke him. So, it was the fortuitous arrival of two 'guardian angels' in the form of Mr. and Mrs. William Clarke, who rescued Harry. No doubt just in time. They were the only souls my father ever trusted unconditionally. I truly believe that was his reality and certainly not my mother's or any of his so-called adult friends who were ever afforded his true confidence.

Harry would often recount how his luck really came in when Mrs. Clarke arrived at the Barnado's home volunteering to foster two London evacuees. One being a young chap named Jimmy. The other being my father. Indeed, the pair could not pack their meager belongings quickly enough to escape the austere regime of Barnardo's - to appreciate some homely creature comforts once again. No matter how frugal they might turn out to be, it had to be a vast improvement on the short time they had spent at Barnado's.

Mr. and Mrs. Clarke were, of course, lifelong villagers born in Victorian times. They have lived through the national catastrophe of the Great War. They were very devout Christians of the non-conformist

'Methodist' variety. I believe Mr. Clarke was more ambivalent regarding his duty to God, but for Mrs. Clarke, it was fire, brimstone . . . the lot!

The Clarke's did indeed, live a thrifty, but comfortable and secure life in rustic Suffolk. Bill was a farm hand all his life. I have extremely fond memories of boarding a train in London with my father and being met by Mr. Clarke at Elmswell Station. The country smell was then so alien to this London infant, it has been embedded in my cellular memory ever since. Frustratingly, I could never recreate the odor of 'pigs and barley' even when I was to later spend a number of years living in the country.

On the occasions I visited as a child, I was introduced to lifelong friends of the Clarke's. One in particular being Maude, a roly-poly old lady with thick 'Norah Batty' stocking clad ankles. Her image still resonates with me today. I never met Mrs. Clarke, who had died from cancer fairly soon after I was born.

Mr. Clarke had a laconic 'old Suffolk Boy' way about him. A kinder soul has never walked this earth. With his hunter watch glinting in the sunlight, he always wore the stereotypical flat cap, tweed waistcoat, baggy corduroy trousers with turn-ups, and old weather-beaten brogues. He wore what seemed to be a permanent angelic grin on his ruddy completion with only a few teeth to speak of. I can see him in my mind's eye right now, bless him.

Harry was idyllically happy going to the local school in Wetherden with just a dozen or so other children. That utopia was nearly scuttled; however, when Mrs. Clarke first became unwell. She was faced with having to make a heart-breaking choice, between which child she would have to give up and return to Barnado's.

My father had to endure standing paralyzed with apprehension next to his new little friend Jimmy, as Mrs. Clarke explained to them both what a near impossible dilemma she was faced with. To the huge relief of Harry, he was the choice of Mrs. Clarke. With a very heavy heart, the good Christian lady had to let Jimmy go. It was just as heart wrenching for Harry as it was for his foster mother. Harry never saw young Jimmy again. He would often wonder whatever became of Jimmy and in later years tried to find his whereabouts, but sadly, to no avail.

Over the next five years, my father was securely happy in the cozy world of wheat fields, cricket on the village green, one water pump serving the entire village population, and 'Suffolk Punch' heavy horses.

That majestic breed is the oldest in the country, and is seriously endingered, with barely four hundred left in Britain today.

As luck would have it, there happened to be an American Air Force base nearby. With his school chums, Harry enjoyed the bragging camaraderie of American GI's; although I might add, the pious Mrs. Clarke totally disapproved of their 'lack of morals and showboating behavior'. Harry often recounted how he would read by candlelight and at the same time count the number of Lancaster Bombers leaving for bombing sorties over Germany. In the early hours, having had very little sleep, he would count how many returned, which was often accompanied by a sinking feeling when there was a clear deficit in the numbers landing on the nearby runway compared to the brave number who had flown out to bomb Dresden, Hamburg, Augsburg, and Berlin.

So, despite only having a child's perception of war-torn Britain and a complete disconnect with his parents, all was well in Harry's life largely due to the discerning and secure foster parenting provided by the Clarke's. Unfortunately, such a stable environment was about to be derailed by a karmic juxtaposition as he approached his eleventh birthday. The kind of fateful series of events that can befall so many of us but often passes as a 'coincidence' or just unfortunate timing. Without doubt, the episode I am about to describe, whilst initially appearing to be just rotten luck, has created a chain reaction still playing out around me today, which has affected so many unfortunate souls.

As I understand it, in the 1940s the '11+ exam system' for gaining entrance into a grammar school in Suffolk was undertaken in two stages. At that particular time, the Clarke's were in the middle of moving house from Stowmarket and back to Elmswell. Harry had taken the first part of his 11+ exam and passed with flying colors, but due to their move, was unable to take the second stage at Stowmarket.

Mrs. Clarke had a very keen interest in Harry's academic ambitions and naturally assumed he would be able to take the second stage at the school in Elmswell. Unfortunately, when he had been admitted to the new school, it soon became plain the timing of their 11+ exams did not sync with the previous school at Stowmarket. To the dismay of all concerned, the new school had already completed the second stage of the exam, and despite sterling efforts on the part of the new school, they just couldn't accommodate Harry. That fateful disconnect of exam timing in 1946, has since cost many people so much money and heartache. It would turn out to be a fucking disaster for all our sakes, I can tell you! Harry, and his foster parents, were mortified. To compound everyone's agony further, his mother Enid, then decided he should leave the security of the Clarke's and return to Bethnal Green to be with the rest of the family.

To be fair, the Clarke's endeavored to persuade my grandmother Harry's future, and security was going to be best served by his staying in Suffolk. The East End had been ravaged by the blitz, and Mrs. Clarke, who thought Enid was a Godless, feckless, and 'everything else less' woman, was most anxious for the wellbeing of her pre-adolescent charge. She really believed his future, and character, would be wrecked if he again came under the influence of the wayward and contrary manner of his mother. Moreover, Harry had yet to experience any guidance whatsoever from the 'father' he had never even met and who had been at sea before and during the war.

Despite Harry's desperate remonstrations with Enid, she was steadfast and the Clarke's reluctantly acquiesced. Harry ended up attending a secondary modern school in Bethnal Green where he did very well. He had the stuffing and ambition knocked out of him at the age of just

11. And so, at every possible opportunity during the school holidays, Harry would jump on a train from Liverpool Street back to Suffolk to visit the two souls who, as far as he was concerned, were really his true 'mum and dad'.

I can remember him writing letters to Mr. Clarke and I would peer over his shoulder and wondered at his stylish looped handwriting. The letters were always headed 'Dear dad'. It was the only time I could ever sense a feeling of love and affection emanating from his repressed soul. RIP . . . Mrs. and Mrs. Bill Clarke.

CHAPTER 3.

THE MITCHUMS

I have previously alluded to the fact there were influences from my childhood that damaged me quite badly. I know its classic 'Freudian' stuff and we all have these dark tales, but mine can be described in one word . . . abandonment. Which explains how the events leading to my father's rejection issues had in turn, resulted in his lifelong control freakery. Which he would then impose on his offspring with such dire consequences for the future, and indeed, the sequence of events playing out around me, even as I am writing my story. My mother compounded matters, although it has to be said not consciously, by something that simply still confuses me to this day.

Harry had met my mother when she was just ten years of age. He was three years older. They were together for the next sixty years until Marie died of a heart attack in November 2008. To my eternal regret, I was not there for her and neither did I attend her funeral. I still have painful feelings of shame and dishonor for having let her down so badly during her later years of life. RIP . . . Marie.

I have no doubts my parents had love for one another, but on many an occasion, I witnessed a level of mutual loathing between them, that was just plain fucking weird. They would have made fantastic secret service 'spooks' because between them, they locked-down various family secrets, both from my siblings and many other members of the Kirkham clan. The controlled fashion by which they achieved such levels of ongoing concealment, would have even impressed the British Intelligence Services.

Harry had left school aged fifteen, joined the railways as a Capstan Boy and my parents' relationship developed from there. Interestingly, Harry's school headmaster pleaded with his new employers to send him back to school because 'such a bright student would be wasted working in manual employment'. Thus began the litany of missed opportunities would befall his life, which resulted in an increasingly cynical, insecure, and controlling personality.

My parents' relationship developed as only adolescent 'love' can do. At the age of eighteen, Harry inevitably received his 'call-up papers' from the War Office to commence his two-year stint of National Service in the British Army. A twist of fate worth recounting here, was those six weeks prior to my dad reporting for duty at the Army barracks in Aldershot, Hampshire, my parents experienced their only 'break up' due to a young lover's tiff. When later reflecting on the episode, my mother was adamant, had my father not visited to apologize to her prior to reporting for military duty, she would never have broken the silence between them. Mother, why, oh why, did you have him back? Must have been fated, eh?

Harry would reminisce about his two-year National Service Army stint, as an Army Cook, with great fondness and recited many anecdotal yarns about his experiences. One of which, to this day, still brings a smile to my face. Harry told me Army camp cooks would rise earlier than the other lads to prepare breakfast. They would open the cook house doors at 5 am and apparently kick the stacked bags of flour so the cockroaches could escape and scuttle across the tiled floors, how lovely. On the day of this particular story, the camp was due to have a 1950s equivalent of a 'health and safety' inspection. They needed to prepare the day's planned menu for display and inspection by 9 am. On the menu that morning were current buns! They went about their normal routines and by 9 am the delights of the day were cooked and ready for the keen eye of the visiting 'grub inspector' who, I understand, was the rank of Captain and accompanied by a junior civil servant from the War Office.

It was apparently like a scene from Carry on Sergeant. This sharp featured Captain who had an Estonian accent with a strut to match, barged into the cookhouse pronouncing . . .

"Cook Sergeant, we are on a tight schedule here this morning, so chop chop, let's get this over with sharpish, shall we?"

The Cook Sergeant, Harry, and the other three cooks, all stood somewhat nervously to attention, as Captain Fanshaw Chumley-Warner cast his eagle eye over the spread in front of him on the cookhouse tables. All seemed to be routine, until he checked himself, pulled the baton from underneath his armpit and pointing down toward one of the buns exclaimed in disbelief,

"Cook Sergeant-for god's sakes man, that is a cockroach!"

Harry craned his neck around the burly Cook Sargent standing by his side and looked down at the object of the captain's displeasure. Sure enough, poking out of one of the freshly cooked current buns was a gnarled, chargrilled member of the Blattodea family!! Harry thought to himself . . . fuck me, we're in trouble here! Without hesitation he shoved aside his superior, grabbed the bun from under the scrutinizing monocle of the warrant officer, and extracted the insect from the bun. HARRY then . . . ate the fucking thing!

"No sir . . . it's a current, just overdone a bit, sorry about that."

The astonished officer did not know whether to 'stick or twist' so after taking a few moments to compose himself, he then replaced his baton dutifully under his arm, and marched on whilst waving his approval. The cynical old Cook Sergeant crowed,

"Well done m' lad" as he put his beef-like arms around Harry. "But for your quick thinking, we were all well, truly fucked there. You are not as green as you are cabbage looking are you!"

Over the years Harry would tell us many Army stories. They may well have all been a load of fabricated bollocks, I don't know; but at lcast whcn hc was fondly rccalling happicr timcs with rclish, hc wasn't bullying my mother or his three children.

Marie was at her happiest when her children were young, and she could be just 'mum'. However, she was also totally dependent on her husband. This was quite 'the norm' for a married couple wedded in the 1950s. Boy, did that suit Harry being the insecure man he was. In those times, very few young married women had jobs. Even fewer had a full driving license. This meant the provider / hunter role of their men was still a cultural and social necessity. So, in turn, Harry was happy too. With a massive karmic twist, this balance would one day, completely reverse, but during the time our family lived at the 'old house' my mother was completely subservient to my father.

I once described my mother as . . . 'the loveliest person that I knew'. Not by any means a unique description for a son to use about his mother. When I used that phrase, I was about fourteen, and teenage boys do not tend to use such language about a parent.

Marie was the fourth child of my grandfather, Samuel Mitchum, who was born in 1903 and raised in Canning Town. Samuel had two children by his first marriage, Ethel, and Frank. His first wife died when Frank was just a baby. He remarried, and wed Mary, and together they had five more children. So, my mother was my Nan's second child.

I know a fair bit about my father's upbringing, but not so much about my mother's . . . for reasons I cannot honestly explain. I mean, it's not as if she was a particularly closed book or anything and we lived only two doors along from her parents. Yet, I heard many stories from my fantastic granddad and his exploits in the 'Boar War', which was hilarious when considering war ended several years before my grandfather was even born.

Marie was extremely close to her mother, but she had a conflicting rivalry with her older sister, Vera. She adored her younger brother Roy, who tragically lost his life when he drowned in a swimming accident during the sweltering summer of 1976 aged just thirty-two. She also had two younger sisters, Linda, and Maisie.

All I really know is she attended George Lansbury Junior School in Atley Road, as we all did. We never learned to swim. As a young child she was pushed in the deep end at the local Lido in Victoria Park, avoided being evacuated during the war, and started smoking at the age of only ten. Actually, many kids of her generation did that as well, it would seem. She was addicted to 'pie and mash', sausage rolls and jam doughnuts. She also came under Harry's spell at the same time. So, I guess that explains that then?

Marie would later enjoy a brief spell of independence when, in the early days of married life, she worked at the Bryant and May Match Box Factory. Yes, she slaved away for hours in the same place, as did many generations of women. That old red brick monstrosity is now a listed building converted to luxury apartments within a private gated community with the commensurate egregious prices.

So, the pattern I saw between the two of them growing up was set. Now, please do not get the impression things were always chaotic or depressing around our home, it was not like that in the main. We had a fun family Christmas. My father would spend most weekends 'lightening the load' for my mother, by taking my brother and me to visit many historic places of interest, and with days out at the seaside. However, when it did break down, it could be demonic. This is where we can really explore my parent's idiosyncratic and eccentric behavior that one day would have massive consequences.

I can recall my father speaking to my mother in such a disdainful and insulting manner I wanted to crawl under the very floorboards beneath me. A good example was when I was about seven years of age. The family were sitting around the dining table when my father would engineer the topic of conversation around subjects he knew in advance. He would challenge my mother simply because she was not as informed about current affairs and the like. So, he actually sought an adversarial exchange guaranteeing to bring a dark cloud over all of us.

My parents would sit opposite each other. My siblings and I were inevitably stuck in the middle of their verbal exchanges. An aspect of their linguistic sword fencing I found most uncomfortable. It was not just the language used by my father, but the seething and hateful tone he would use as he vented his dogmatic opinions in the direction of the woman he would profess to love. She never deserved to be spoken to like that . . . not ever.

My mother wasn't particularly well educated. Like the majority of her peers, she had attended the local secondary modern school, Bow Girls. But she was very intelligent in her own grounded way and did not warrant being subject to such insulting language.

"You are just so thick. You must be wooden-headed woman."

I felt nothing but disgust toward him for speaking to her like that. As children, my siblings and I would have to witness such invectives for years. My stomach would churn over with anxiety whenever he began his weekly round of verbal and mental abuse. Moreover, he most certainly didn't restrict the privilege of his scything tongue for the woman he apparently 'loved'.

Before I expand on how us kids were subjected to the attrition of Harry's mental torturing, it is worth examining the wider psychological point here. I am sure many of you reading this are already resonating with my experiences, probably not feeling too comfortable about it either. You see, the reasons I would have initially suggested were the cause of Harry's behavior would have fit neatly into many recognized 'Freudian' explanations.

I dare say more contemporary sciences, such as DNA and genetic hereditary coding, might go further still and throw in social and family conditioning for good measure. We could well be on our way to becoming an 'ologist' or three? No, that is not a good enough explanation for me. I just know there are other influences at work, and we shall explore such phenomenon later in this story.

Harry was such a paradox. On the one hand he was a charismatic manipulator and a highly intelligent charmer. On the other hand, he could be ice cold, aloof, vindictive and an incessant sulker. And boy could that man sulk! Far worse than Ted Heath - at his worst after being ousted by Margaret Thatcher as the Tory Party Leader in 1975. Seriously though, sulking is such an immature emotion, a classic trait of the insecure. I thank God that was the one real difference between me and him. While I have my flaws - and there are too many to list - I just cannot bear anyone who sulks.

As a child, without question, I was quite a dreamer and like so many infants I fantasized a great deal. Our backyard became a fictional world I embraced wholeheartedly. People reading this who are of similar age, will have been bought up on a diet of Gerry Anderson puppet shows such as Supercar, Fireball XL5, Stingray and my personal favorite Thunderbirds and Captain Scarlet! As I developed this dreamy character trait, it began to grate on my father, bigtime.

I can see him now, pointing his finger right into my face and demanding my attention by saying . . .

"Listen to me yon. Stop thinking about Stingray when I am talking to you!"

I wasn't at all, but he had this paranoiac fixation, if we as kids were not always pandering to his doctrinal mantra, then we must be tuning in elsewhere? Like all young kids or teenagers, when their parent starts nagging or berating them, they just kind of cut out the boring bits! RIP

. . . Gerry Anderson.

I was most certainly brighter than the average kid but by no means super intelligent, which was a real killer to my father's ego. Remember, he still carried the scars of missing out on the opportunity to attend grammar school and he was no different from so many controlling parents whereby he harbored an acute ambition, which he could now achieve through his children. Being the eldest, he naturally poured his efforts into my development and early schooling, as all good discerning parents should do.

What is more, he would go 'the extra mile' by taping the mathematical times tables on his 'reel to reel' for us kids to learn by heart and then recite it back to him. He also designed quiz games and educational trips were encouraged. I was a naturally gifted artist, and he would buy me fine pencils and Indian inks to create an effect and develop my own style. So, all really good stuff, wasn't it? But . . .

This is where his self-sabotaging mentality began to kick in and impact on my formative years. Successes were mildly acknowledged but failure, no matter how insignificant, was an absolute no go in his eyes. So, overtime, an inevitable element of fear and hesitation started to creep into my psyche when communicating with him. This in turn, would overlap into all the other aspects of my relationship with him. So, I found myself constantly seeking his approval to curry favor with him. I began to develop a flaw, a habit, a psychological defect, which would one day inflict so much pain and on so many others. I began to lie.

The other compounding influence that so panicked me as a child, which long term would have dire consequences, was down to my mother and something to most would have seemed totally out of character. She abandoned me.

Only recently, I asked my aunt Linda as to why she thought my mother did it. She was completely at a loss. In fact, she wasn't really aware she had even done this to me. I did have to remind her this was a woman who had kept me in the dark about her own brother Frank, throughout her entire life.

I have previously described the house I grew up in as a Victorian Terrace built around the mid-1850s. The austere front door would open into a dimly lit passage (never referred to as a hall) and it had a front room with an open fire, which was only really used at Christmas and the odd Sunday. Most of the time, the entire family huddled into the kitchen no more than twelve by ten feet I recall, which was central to the house and where during winter months, my mother would painstakingly make up a fire every day. A tiny black and white TV was stuck in the corner of the room and my dad's 'Telly Chair' would be strategically positioned in front of it, and like most families at that time, we only watched the programs my dad wanted to watch.

The kitchen would lead into the 'scullery', which was where women of my mother's generation would create fantastic traditional meals. She cooked fresh ingredients bought locally at the Roman Road Market, the wondrous smells were akin to a culinary nectar. We all did a pretty good impression of the 'Bistro Kids'. Mumm . . .

To think my mother prepared these meals on an old gas stove with just a tiny front oven was miraculous. The results were just mouth-watering!! No ready meals, no frozen stuff. We barely had a fridge with just a tiny ice compartment. No cooking technology, other than a hand cranked mincer. No blender. Not a recipe in sight!! Just like her mother before her my mum, she just chucked it all in a mixing bowl and happily became a 'cookery alchemist'! Could you imagine modern mothers coping? Nope! To be fair, my father was an even better cook, so we were really spoilt in the cuisine department.

Getting back to the house, it was dark, begrimed, and basically falling down. The roof leaked. We had mice everywhere. It was always bloody freezing. You know, with ice on the inside of the windows during the winter. It wasn't my parents' fault either the house was in such a dilapidated state. There was no hot water, just a lead tap precariously plumbed above a white butler sink. When my parents moved into the house in 1956, they were told by the private landlord they would only need to reside there for a couple of years, due to impending slum clearance plans. However, successive governments reneged on any deals with landlords, so they had no incentive to maintain the properties. The 'couple of years' then turned out to be another thirteen! We finally moved out of the old house in September of 1969.

This all resulted in a very bleak dwelling, which even as a child, I was embarrassed to bring friends back to. Although to be fair, most of their houses were in no better order. It was obvious why my father refused to spend any of his savings on decorating the house, other than slapping some cheap and nasty 'flower patterned' wallpaper on top of several other layers of cheap and nasty wallpaper.

So, bearing in mind how cold, depressing, and unfriendly this abode could be; why did my mother repeatedly leave me alone for hours at a time? I can clearly remember feeling cold, lonely, and petrified to compound matters all the doors were locked? Now she may have locked them, so I couldn't run off. What was stranger still, no one had their doors locked in the 1960s. We had nothing of value to steal after all.

I would wander around this uninviting prison screaming continuously and crying for hours on end. Mum, mum, mum! I can hear it now. Where was she? Where was my brother and baby sister? This would happen habitually, and when she would finally return, I was in such a state of trauma and so relieved to see her, I never asked where she had been. Even more heartbreaking neither would she hold nor comfort me. She never explained her absences. Later in life, I have obviously often wondered if she had been seeing someone.

Matters were made even worse, when it was time for me to be picked up from infant school, which I had attended from my nursery days to the age of seven. For some inexplicable reason, she was repeatedly the last mother to collect me, and this went on for an age. As the other children grabbed their coats and rushed out to the playground to be scooped up by their mums; the sense of rejection I felt was demoralizing. So, I would slouch back to the school building, sit on a chair, and would wait and wait . . . asking a teacher or classroom helper . . . "Where is my mum?"

They would dutifully smile and pat me on the head, and with a condescending,

"She will be here soon luvvy."

Yes, eventually, but again when she finally arrived there was no hug, no comforting, and no explanation for her lateness. Of course, there always has to be a kid who will be last to be collected. For me, it was regular occurrence. The long wait was confidence shattering.

So, between my parents 'conscious and subconscious' behavior, they created insecurities within me, which I would battle with to this day. Moreover, I observed similar traits within both my brother and sister. It is often the case the eldest sibling will bear the intensity of such idiosyncratic parenting.

My father's horrendous sulking continued to affect me. It was worsened still, by any lack of tactile affection. Without doubt, that man's ability to make me feel isolated, worthless, and lose any self-respect was relentless. Furthermore, when looking back, the sustained attrition, whereby he would invariably be subjecting at least one of his immediate family to being 'frozen out', still haunts me. I first became aware of it as an infant, when I would observe him using such a ploy, as one of his repertoires of 'mind-fucking' weapons against my mother.

Being so young, I didn't know why he was acting in such a manner. I recall long periods of silence when he simply would not communicate with her. I don't just mean orally either. He just acted as if she didn't exist. Again, not for a day or two, but for weeks at a time!

Inevitably, as we grew older, he had more than one target that would feed his insatiable need to dominate the weaknesses around him. Weaknesses he had actually created in the first instance. Here was one of my first lessons in sociopathic behavior, which is to project guilt onto everyone else for your own flaws! The sulking simply got worse. There were many episodes where it not only caused great trauma for my mum, but eventually cost him all respect from children and his long-suffering spouse.

The feeding of my father's ego, in terms of his visceral need to attend a 'grammar school by proxy' manifested as I approached my eleventh birthday. I was not exactly top of the class at junior school, but I always featured in the top five in any subjects the class was tested for. So not too bad, I guess? My parents were desperate for me to attend the Coopers Company Grammar in Bow, a school that had notable former pupils the likes of actors Bernard Bresslaw (carry on films) Jack Warner (Dixon of Dock Green), Jack Watling (many 1960s TV roles) and err.

. Richard Madeley, no less!! Ha!

I was fairly relaxed Coopers was going to be my educational destiny as well. My best friend Danny was also up for it, so it suited us all. Unfortunately, however, a spanner was thrown in the works - almost history repeating itself - because by 1969, the London County Council was inflicting its social mantra on the grammar schools and shutting them down with alacrity. Coopers was going to be one of the first, but the Governors held off, and decided the school was best placed to be relocated to Upminster in Essex. My parents had a collective fit!

And so, after conversations between my parents and my loveable Headmaster Mr. Gordon, it was agreed, along with a couple of my classmates, we would be going to Parmenter's Grammar School in Bethnal Green. It was the school which my dads' younger brother Mick, had attended in the 1950s.

CHAPTER 4.

GRAMMAR SCHOOL

Along with two of my classmates, Danny Roberts and Kevin Newman, the three of us passed our 11+ exams with flying colors and set off for interviews with the Headmaster of Parmenters Grammar School - the phlegmatic Graham H C Waterhouse. I still clearly recall being absolutely paralyzed as I waited with my mother outside his study. I find it really intriguing, in 'his hour of victory', where was my father? My two friends had both their parents with them in attendance, but no, he did not make it. I am certain my mother was equally in need of his support. The git!! Upon reflection, I have now been able to identify why. He was beginning to demonstrate a pattern where he needed us to succeed to satisfy his ego, yet his jealousy surfaced once again, and he began to resent us for the very achievement - he had personally missed out on.

Anyway, once I was finally sitting in front of 'GHW' (as he was affectionately known) I had composed myself. By the end of the interview I was much more confident. As my mum and I were walking home, we were both quite content with the proceedings. A couple of weeks later, that confidence was justified when my Headmaster at George Lansbury notified my proud parents, along with my two classmates, we had won scholarships to Parmenters.

Grammar schools are a divisive subject today. They most certainly were during my childhood growing up in the sixties. I am a fervent believer in the benefits of state-run grammar schools. I find it incredulous that in our current (and ridiculously politically correct) society, politicians will go to such great lengths to distance themselves from their reintroduction. Yet, will fall over themselves to devise alternatives such as free schools, academies, and the like, which overtime have all proved inferior educational models to something that worked brilliantly. I do appreciate there is the tired old liberal outcry that says, '11-year-olds shouldn't be thrown on the heap', if they have failed the grammar school entrance standard the 11 plus. So, bearing in mind the experience my own father had succumbed to, I do have a solution.

Academically, many children develop later than the age of 11. So, I would like to see the introduction of a 13 plus . . . whereby those kids who progressing and developing ahead of their peers at a comprehensive school can have a second opportunity of a grammar school education. Equally, if any children who are at a grammar are finding the academic curriculum too challenging, they can then have the choice of switching to a technical or comprehensive education. I realize there is the temptation to say these children could also be labelled as failures, but I know from personal experience it never did my confidence much good always being at the bottom of the class. Having said that, my defense of the grammar school system hasn't changed one iota.

The grammar school I attended was a voluntary aided school, which was founded by philanthropist Theodore Parmenter in the 17th century. Theodore was a wealthy silk merchant in East London who died in 1681. He left two farms in southwest Suffolk in his will, to supply $30 per annum for six alms houses, and $100 per annum for one free school-house or room for ten poor children in Bethnal Green, London.

The school was based there until the 1980s when it was moved to Hertfordshire as a mixed comprehensive. To this day, as a stipulation of Theodore's will, the school keeps placements each year for six East End children. I attended the school at the same time as big Tommy Walsh of TV's Ground Force fame. In more recent times, another infamous former pupil, who attended the Hertfordshire school, was Nick Leeson who single handily bankrupted Barings Bank! Must be something in there worth analyzing. RIP . . . Barings Bank.

I am a huge fan of Lord Sugar and when I read his excellent memoir recently, I picked up on what was for me, an amusing little anecdote, worth mentioning. He recalls in a rancorous fashion, how he attended an interview to gain entrance into the 'grammar school in the Cambridge Heath'; now bearing in mind there has never been any other grammar school in that area, I think it is safe to assume it must have been Parmenters who turned him down. He then churlishly goes on to say how he was pleased he had attended the local comprehensive instead . . . who is he kidding!! You can just tell how it still pisses him off, even after all this time.

I was part of the autumn intake of September 1969 and left the school in 1975, after having to retake my 'O levels'. I had failed them miserably the previous year because I had simply not taken my studies at all seriously. I spent that critical 5th year attending discos, getting drunk, and developing my fledgling womanizing skills rather than revising. I barely did any. Upon reflection, I was already beginning to demonstrate feckless and hedonistic tendencies that would eventually blight my life and prevent me from fulfilling my true potential. I did manage healthy grades and passed seven 'O levels' at the second time of asking.

Now I can understandably hear you thinking . . . If this chap did so badly at a grammar school, then why does he advocate the selection system so strongly?

Well, as I have already alluded to, I chose to be lazy, and life is about choices. But the 'comprehensive system' actually prevents choice. They were only introduced in the first place to satisfy the socialist doctrine of the day under the then socialist government of Prime Minister, Harold Wilson.

It was a deal struck with the teacher's union leaders to bring the salarics of thc sccondary modcrn tcachcrs up to and in linc with, thcir counterparts at the grammar schools. It actually had nothing to do with benefitting children. In reality, our educational standards have dropped year on year ever since. To prove this point, educational experiments have been undertaken from time-to-time whereby modern teenage students have been asked to sit GCE exam papers (the then general certificate of education) from the 1950s, with fairly predictable results. They struggled like crazy and in most cases failed the exam standard of yesteryear.

Moreover, we now have the ludicrous situation where even UK housing demographics and prices, are 'shoehorned' into the areas where the few remaining grammars exist. It's a joke and always has been. The hypocrisy of it all beggar's belief, whereby the abolition of the grammars has been orchestrated by those who had a privileged education themselves, and indeed, many attended grammar schools. Jeremy Corbyn and John McDonnell are two such hypocrites. Furthermore, when will we finally realize that schooling in this country isn't about 'education'. The elite - who dictate and impose the education system on the masses, are well aware schooling is one thing. Yet, a decent education is something altogether different. Which is why their kids are nearly always privately educated.

'Schooling' is actually intended to keep the 'children of the masses' off the streets within a disciplined framework. Unfortunately, the agenda of the neo-liberal mafia has imposed a culture of political correctness, where their program of social engineering is preventing teachers from having any tools to impose the slightest degree of discipline. The system is failing the masses and modern 'progressive' parents actually now give our children drugs to get them to behave themselves. Then we wonder why the rise of drug addiction is befalling the nation! It's not rocket science. Call me a cynic, but the drug companies always seem to benefit.

On a lighter note, I naturally had the assortment of school experiences we have all had. In the early years, I was bullied and later-on, became a bit of a bully myself. There were some great friendships forged throughout my time there and not least of all, my oldest friend Danny who came with me from junior school and was as honest and dependable a pal as you could ever wish for.

I am sure we all recall funny episodes from our school days classroom pranks, and I would like to recount one of my own, literally left physical scars and I can't help smiling whenever I think about it over 40 years later. It was during a third-year chemistry lesson and our chemistry master (a certain Martin Rabeneau) was also the gym master and indeed, an old boy himself. At that time, nearly every sports record listed on the schools polished honors board still belonged to him. He was a fantastic bloke and really understood us kids. He was, however, utterly ruthless! But . . . no one screwed around in any of his lessons and the kids got on with their work . . . end of!

During this particular-lesson, I felt myself sitting next to a lad called Ivor Middleburgh (obviously Irish) and in those days, it was dead fashionable to strut about with a steel comb in your pocket. The class was conducting some experiment or other, which involved the igniting of the laboratories Bunsen burners. As usual, my attention span was 'zero'. Boredom was inevitably creeping in. I actually had a full head of hair in those days, so I asked Ivor if I could borrow his comb.

"Sure, here you go."

Now Ivor was a kid who actually wanted to learn things, so he then continued to concentrate on the task in hand. Whilst he was doing so, I winked at the lad sitting next to me, as I inserted the end of the comb into the Bunsen burner flame. It didn't get white hot, but it was glowing nicely when I grabbed Ivor’s attention again with . . .

“Thanks mate.” I handed the hot end of the comb back to him. “AAAARRRGGGGHHHHHH!!!! FUCKING HELL!!!!!!!!”

What on earth could he be shouting about?

Ivor leapt into the air. The rest of the class were pissing themselves! Mr. Rabeneau immediately charged over and realized straight away what had happened. He was only just holding back a grin as he grabbed me by both lapels and dragged my scrawny adolescent torso across the lab table. You could not have slotted a fag paper between our faces as he bawled me out for my stupidity.

After what seemed like the longest bollocking ever, he then asked me . . .

“So, you like Bunsen burners do you Kirkham?” “Errrrm . . . dunno, why?”

“Well, let’s see just how much then, shall we?”

He then instructed the class to part down the middle and create a gangway through the centre of the lab. With a sense of great anticipation, the kids dutifully obliged. All except for Ivor of course, who was still hopping about in the corner blowing on his stinging digits.

I was baffled by his request, but then my worst fears were realized when I saw Mr. Rabeneau removing the rubber tubing from one of the burners. He was clearly relishing the prospect ahead and I could feel a sense of nausea overcoming my very being.

“Ok Kirkham, stand at the end of the gangway, drop your strides and bend over lad!!!”

Fuck, this is not good!!

So, like any good, condemned man, I adopted a slothful posture and walked toward the intended target area. The rest of the class could not believe their luck and were clearly savoring every second of this equivalent of a public hanging!

Mr. Rabeneau then wound himself up to unleash as much thermo nuclear energy as any man could muster and charged toward all seven stone of me as I quivered like a wreck at the end of the lab . . .

THHWWAAAAAACCCKKKKKK!!!!!!!! Boy, he was accurate!

I flew across the room and collided with two lads who were standing expectantly at the other end of the lab. We landed in one heap. The rest of the class were obviously whooping and clapping and as I looked up, and there was Ivor, clapping as well, the cheeky git! So, the comb couldn't have been THAT hot!

For the next few days, I was the talk of the third year. I was constantly being stopped by lads from other classes with 'Oi Kirkham . . . show us your arse'!!! It did indeed resemble the colors of the planet Jupiter and took bloody ages to disappear. Did I mention it to my parents? Did I hell! In those days, if you reported an incident like that at home, you invariably received a second dose of the original punishment. Parents had a much greater degree of reverence and respect for teachers. Such regard has pretty much disappeared nowadays and why? Well, it's simple. Kids know they can get away with murder and will report a teacher for nigh on anything, which they might take exception to. The parents always side with their children no matter what they have done. In my day, they sided with the teacher and would compound the punishment to an even greater degree. The result was that kids behaved much better and were far more disciplined than now.

My school career was very undistinguished and apart from an early success at athletics - when I represented East London schools in the sprints at Crystal Palace. I left Parmenters' in 1975 with the under achievement of 7 GCE's. I remember picking up my report book, which had been signed off each year by our Headmaster, I ruefully reflected on a comment he had many years before when I was a first-year student. "Mr. Kirkham has made a somewhat lackadaisical start to his Parmenters education. Hmm?"

It was point well-made, and a lack of concentration would undermine my endeavors time and again.

RIP . . . the grammar schools - destroyed by a left-wing elite who thought they knew what was best for the rest!

CHAPTER 5.

THE CITY

Although I left Parmenters as one of their great underachievers, I did have a fairly good idea of what I wanted to do. It is here we see fate playing its hand. Again, I raise the question, do we have 'freewill' or is it just 'freedom of choice'? They are NOT mutually inclusive; I can tell you.

At the age of seventeen, I experienced a personal dichotomy that would be fated to influence the lives of many others. I have mentioned previously, I was a fairly gifted artist. It would be an understatement to say I was rather pissed off; I had only gained a 'B' grade for the subject at O level. Anyway, I still had opportunity to pursue a creative career and various college options put to me as I was coming to the end of my sixth form retakes. Indeed, my girlfriend Lorraine - of the stair shagging variety - was also looking to further an artistic vocation at art college.

I could have done with some guidance from the old man, but . . . nothing, which had been his entire pattern throughout my time at school. Once he had been able to get all three of his children through to grammar school, he simply washed his hands of any onward encouragement and guidance. The reality being, he actually resented us for achieving something he had missed out on and was still smouldering away about it many years later. How many parents do that?

So, I found myself gravitating toward a working life in the world of insurance or banking. This particular pathway appealed to the 'left side of my brain' we will explore that phenomenon later - because it meant just one word to me . . . money.

Growing up in an environment of abject poverty, money was really scarce. Even as a child I yearned to be rich and experience excitement just like American icons of Napoleon Solo the hero from the Man from

Uncle, or millionaire Bruce Wayne who I used to admire so much when sitting on the floor in my front room, glued to a black and white TV. There were only three TV channels back then: BBC channels 1 and 2, and the commercial channel, ITV. Yes, wealth would give me an exhilarating life, but as a child, I could never have imagined the path I would take to achieve that aim.

After a brief spell of a summer job helping out Lorraine's dad with his typewriter maintenance business. I was ready for life in the 'Square Mile' or 'the City', which is how many describe the historic financial district - the home to both the Stock Exchange and Bank of England.

Before I set off on that particular yellow brick road, my experiences working with Lorraine's dad, are worth just a mention if, for no other reason, it is a trade that has now disappeared. I guess there must be the odd specialist remaining. At one time these chaps were to be seen all over the city, and no doubt, in just about every business than had a number of typewriters.

They did a really earnest job, keeping the wheels turning of all those iconic 'typing pools'. I had a very heady six weeks or so being mesmerized by all those gorgeous 'little sorts' hammering away with a 'ratatatat' of their QWERTY keys, followed by the distinctive clunk of the 'line space lever'. Halcyon days indeed. As with everything else in this digital age, the soul is being destroyed in just about everything. We digress, yeah, I know; I do that a great deal, but it's all healthy nostalgia for the time being. The really dark stuff will come soon enough in this story . . .

So, let's get back to the city then. I applied for a number of junior positions with various financial institutions and a few Civil Service departments as well. Realistically, I couldn't see myself as a potential Sir Humphrey Appleby, so I half-heartedly pursued a line of work in public service. Anyway, the career path of senior Whitehall mandarins in the 70s was the exclusive domain of the 'Oxbridge-elite' and only lower departmental positions could realistically be achieved by the likes of a grammar school tyke! Even today, in real terms, that culture has improved very little.

The employment situation of the 1970s tends to be described in TV documentaries as really bleak, with endless strikes and the three-day week. I clearly recall such difficult times, not least of all because we would regularly be stuck in a lift between floors of our high-rise block of flats and in pitch darkness. Many poor working-class families of my generation found themselves being shipped out of slum clearance dwellings with the delusional hopes of moving to a modern and warm house. Only to find themselves on the twentieth floor of a two hundred feet slab-built tower block.

Such annoying inconveniences were due to power outages during the first miners strikes, under the then, Ted Heath government. However, I seemed to have no difficulty finding a job or indeed, a number of offers. It wasn't just the brighter school leavers either, I had numerous mates at secondary modern and comprehensive schools who seemed to just 'job-hop' with relative ease. Ok, they were not going to be industrial protégés or captains of industry, they mostly found 'honest endeavor'. Just wish that I had . . .

In the end, it was a choice between a junior position working in the agency department of Sun Life Assurance Society (now part of AXA insurance group), and ironically, a clerical assistant post at the Ministry of Defense (MOD). For reasons I have already covered, I decided against the MOD and headed off to 107 Cheapside in the City of London, where the then head office of Sun life was located in the guise of a 1950s eight story building. The structure is still there today having survived amongst numerous towering glass developments springing up everywhere, as approved by the then London Mayor Boris Johnson, to appease his many cronics in thc construction industry.

The recent Covid-19 pandemic will have had a huge impact on the multiple levels of palm greasing which goes on between the City of London's public official's operating in the planning departments and the crooked architects, developers, construction companies, and bent financiers. Hopefully they will all go to rot, the corrupt fuckers.

I was at 'Sun Life' for barely twelve - yet really enjoyable months. But I have vivid memories of my time there and learned a great deal about myself, gaining an early insight into machinations of the corporate world. I will never forget the impression my department head made on me. It may have been the mid-70s but the tail end of the 'old school' city dress code still existed around most offices. My department manager was Maurice Carlisle. He was attired with the stereotypical wing collar, bowler hat, pin stripes, and 'Captain Mainwaring' specs. What a different world it was back then. All I remember him for, other than his iconic city image, is that on my first day at work he lectured me to no end that I had to, at all times . . . 'remember to ensure a brass fastener had to be inserted the correct way round through a new case file! Otherwise, I might catch my thumb on it lad and THAT just will NOT be acceptable'!

Life was going to be tough at the sharp end! Errrm . . . sorry about that one! Likewise, I must mention two other characters in the agency department who I have never forgotten - Ted and Albert. They were already retirees when I joined. They had both previously worked for British Railways - some thirty odd years each. It was quite common back then for retired public sector workers to have part-time jobs as messengers or work in the post rooms of banks, insurance firms, and lawyers. The agency department seemed to have more than its fair share of them. These two though, stuck out like proverbial sore thumbs and they were doubles for the muppet characters . . . Stadler and Waldow. But what really left its mark on me was a level of wit and banter, which I have NEVER experienced since, in either a working environment or down the pub! I can tell you, even Paul Merton and Ian Heslop would have had difficulty keeping up.

Ted and Albert became a daily fix for me and the other juniors. They were 'comic dynamite'. They would quip and dig at each other all day long and didn't give a hoot about upsetting the austere office management protocols, which were the custom of the day. They also both possessed a magical old style East End accent, which I had only really heard elsewhere when listening to my mum's father - Samuel Mitchum. They would use old cockney phrases such as . . . 'Well, I'll be blowed', 'Gawd blimey', and pronouncing the word 'Yes' as 'Yus'. I adored them both.

In particular, I was also mesmerized by Ted's handwriting. Even though he would only be using a Bic Biro, he would write in a most perfect and consummate 'looped style'. He was always grammatically perfect, despite the fact, he apparently had very little education to speak of. That's maybe, but he was also highly intelligent. They both had to be to verbalize in such an incisive and adversarial fashion. I guess they must have passed away decades ago. I, for one, will make sure they are both remembered beyond their family's memory, by the success of this book. RIP . . . Ted and Albert.

I really had ambitions to become an insurance underwriter, but my options were fairly limited at Sun Life. The company was looking to relocate to Bristol, which after a quick visit with Lorraine, I didn't fancy too much. Not long after the trip to Bristol we had split up anyway. I swiftly started the task of searching for a new job. I had a brief and utterly boring spell at Liverpool Victoria Insurance. I still couldn't settle because it was just another agency role as an underwriter, where I felt my early aspirations would be best realized.

This was the cue for . . . Unicorn Motor Policies . . . an underwriting syndicate-based smack bang in the City of London. Thus, it was in the New Year of January 1979, when I found myself searching for a fresh start. I was a tad downcast about my relationship ending with Lorraine, for she had taught me so much. Apart from enlightening me about my uncle, she taught me how to kiss, how to fuck, and by default, how to move on from parting company with any woman without ever looking back and never wasting my energy on emotions or regret. I held onto that mantra for another decade until I would be stopped in my tracks. Anon . . .

I was pointed in the direction of Unicorn via a recruitment agency based in the city. They arranged an interview with two gentlemen who I still remember today with great affection . . . not. Arthur Ogley and Bill Roberts; not a more contrasting pair of characters will you ever meet. Arthur Ogley was an 'old school' city gentleman. Then there was Bill Roberts. How can I best describe this indefatigable character? Well, anyone who is a fan of the 1980s sitcom . . . Only Fools and Horses, will recall a character named, Detective Inspector Roy Slater, played by that great British actor - Jim Broadbent. Now, I am not for one moment suggesting Bill had Roy Slater's flaws, but his character traits, mannerisms, and attitude were scarily alike! Even the over deliberate use of distrustful witticism and blatant prejudices, they were all there.

I arrived early for the interview. Strict punctuality was another protocol instilled in my generation, which has completely gone out of the window. Whilst I was waiting in the reception area, I consciously took just a few moments to scan the open-plan office environment. I can clearly remember the visceral resonance I felt, which has never really left me. In those days, Unicorn occupied three floors in a 1950s built office block in Chiswell Street. So, it was really in the hub of 'city life' which I had craved. Moreover, a culture and atmosphere existed back then, which sadly, I feel has now pretty much disappeared. I will expand on the reasons for this later. It is not a case of 'moving with the times' as always being a good thing either.

I was summoned into a modest sized office by Bill Roberts, and I dutifully sat down in front of his desk, which was next to Mr. Ogley's. Whilst Bill was the assistant office manager, it soon became obvious the senior gentleman in the room had much less influence over the day-today office affairs than he had probably once enjoyed. Mr. Ogley, had grey and drawn features, wore horned rim and thick lens spectacles and was clearly winding down for his retirement.

Apart from my Roy Slater characterization, Bill also resembled a children's comic character from my infancy 'Mr. Pastry' (Google it), and I had to just pinch myself quickly to stop gazing a bit too long at him due to the association being conjured up in my 'sub-cranium'.

Now this was also going to be just about the most eccentric interview I would ever undertake in my entire working life. Indeed, to even refer to it as an interview would be really stretching the point. It went along these lines . . .

BJR . . . "You seem like a sound young chap?" Me . . . "Err . . . yeah, I guess so?"

BJR . . . "Arrived nice and early, smartly attired. We like that at Unicorn."

AO . . . "Tell me young man, do you know the meaning of . . . 'pro-rata'?"

Me . . . "Err. No, I don't actually sir'."

AO . . . "Well . . . it means this . . ."

Arthur Ogley then spread his copy of the Financial Times across his desk, took out what looked like an antique fountain pen (I had to double check it wasn't a quill nib - for it looked so bloody old) and he then scribbled away in the margin what appeared to me as just jumbled numbers and he rambled something under his breath that was completely unintelligible to my youthful Cockney mind?

AO . . . "So, that my boy . . . is 'pro rata'!!"

He prognosticated with such relish I just could not let my expression display the reality, which was I had not understood a fucking word of it.

BJR . . . "Right then, as you have demonstrated such a quick and alert mind, I think you are just the kind of young chap we are looking for." There was then a silence that seemed forever - in reality, it was just for a few seconds. "You can start on Monday."

Bill stood up, reached out, and shook my hand. Arthur Ogley did the same. I spun around feeling both baffled and bewildered, at the same time rather relieved, I had got the job. I was to start on the 22nd of January 1979!

There are a number of reasons why my start date at Unicorn sticks so clearly in mind. First, it had been snowing heavily that day and although it was central London buses and cars were struggling through a few feet of the white stuff. Most of Unicorn's personnel lived outside London. There were barely a handful of staff arriving on time. I was still living with my parents, just a bus ride away, so I still managed to get to work punctually on my first day.

What is more, the main reason why that particular date resonates with me, is because I also met a young chap who is still my best mate to this day, Graham Warburton. Indeed, that man has witnessed just about every twist and turn that has befallen this soul since, so he will be anecdotally referenced on numerous occasions from here on.

I doubt very much, I am going be able to cover the great times I experienced at Unicorn in just the one chapter, simply because of the voluminous episodes I had encountered. This was the time where my flawed behavioral traits had begun their destructive and emotional pathways. This, serendipitously, also coincided with me meeting my first wife Pamela and the birth of my only child, Sarah. It would also be fair to say, the young man who started there in 1979 was unrecognizable by the time he left in December of 1986.

When I joined Unicorn, the underwriter was an extremely charismatic 'Tour de Force' by the name of Don Fairly or 'DF', which was how everyone referred to him. He who was a charmer, a manipulator, a driver, and clearly a . . . sociopath! His womanizing was legendary. His long-suffering wife Miranda had to endure the torture of his numerous marital deceptions and the heartache which came with his indiscretions. Nearly all women who are either married or in a serious relationship with such men, seem powerless to prevent their philandering and very often even with the painful awareness such activity is going on behind their backs. They continue to suffer in silence. Moreover, they even apologize or make excuses to their peers for the behavior of 'their man' who 'just loves me so so much'. Much more to come on this subject. Anon . . .

Within so many regimes, such as religious organizations, corporations, armies, and dare I say, even many countries, sociopaths either rule or are in control. Indeed, Unicorn was no different in this regard. One of the other outstanding traits of the sociopath is 'control freakery'. Oh, for some reason, Tony Blair, Gordon Brown, and Peter Mandelson instantly spring to mind? I wonder why? 'DF' most certainly shared that particular characteristic in abundance.

Some may even argue, such a manipulative hierarchy is actually necessary for effective leadership. DF; certainly, had his many loyal sycophants. Like most who have such a mindset, they tend to develop the handpicked teams around them, so no other pretender can ever really challenge or usurp their position. In DF's case, he would disingenuously claim, as Unicorn continued to grow, he would be 'looking to develop talent and recruit people with the skills to be the future management of the syndicate'. But in reality, he didn't mean a word of it. Sociopaths never do, for insincerity is their middle name. DF would simply use this ploy as an ongoing manipulative device in order to divide and conquer. Ultimately undermining the ambitions of any future pretenders.

So, it is here, where I cannot resist telling you about a rivalry between two women who gave the rest of us the most terrific entertainment when they both curried favor with the main man. The two gladiitors in this contest were Lainey O'Brien and Maureen Rippon . . . I am afraid to say, there was only ever going to be one winner.

As it is often the case when recalling such an amusing and adversarial duel, it can only have been such a spectacle due to the two combatants having such contrasting characteristics. These two did not disappoint in that regard. Apart from anything else they both had such egregious and flagrant eccentricities!

It was early 1980, I had been newly promoted to an underwriting section reporting to a smug and self-satisfied section leader, John Browning. He was already being supported by two of the most rakish wits I have ever encountered, still not quite Ted and Albert, though more in the guise of Ian Ratcliffe and the late Andy Staff. These two were a few years older than me. You would liken them both to waspish prefects at a public school!

I was now in my early twenties and developing my own linguistic powers I needed; for these two would repeatedly ensure that I was being stretched to my limits. After a few months of my arrival on the section, Andy moved on to take up a position with an insurance broker in Berkshire. Over the years he married, had three children, and was just a super fella and a discerning father. He sadly died in his early fifties. My pal

Graham attended his funeral and gave a moving and humorous eulogy to the man. RIP . . . Andy Staff.

Andy's replacement was just about one of the most affected females I have ever encountered. She was to occupy a desk opposite me for the next eighteen months. This was the Sugar Bum Fairy herself, Maureen. Now how do I describe her? Hmmm?

Well, she was then in her mid-thirties, long brown hair, fringe, permanent beaming smile - I am always guarded about that particular disingenuous trait. She seemed to only wear pencil skirts, which she carried off quite cosily, to be fair, with smooth stockings and stilettos. She regularly wore low negligée style blouses with her heaving cleavage on constant display.

On one of those seminal occasions a young red-blooded male will never forget was when Maureen just happened to lean forward across her desk to recommend me on an underwriting query and her right tit fell out of her blouse completely! Now then, at the best of times, most women would have been extremely embarrassed. Not our Maureen. In just one casual movement, she scooped up the wayward mammary and seamlessly placed it back into her obliging 'D cup'.

"Oh luvvy, that keeps on happening . . . now, where were we?"

I was shocked to say the least. My emotional state did not prevent a sense of warmness in both my cheeks, and a definite arousal in my loins. The sexual tension was instant. Most women would have felt an acute sense of embarrassment following such an incident in front of a much younger man and in an open plan office to boot. Not Maureen though. That brief, yet memorable moment, simply floated past her as if nothing could possibly be amiss. Such an ambivalent attitude to my own discombobulation just added to the sense of outrage I was also feeling as I caught the eye of many colleagues who were sniggering away at my own imposition.

Jeeeez . . . that 'luvvy' phrase. She used it all the bloody time! It was a disingenuous habit that grated on the nerves of just about every member of staff except one, the governor himself, DF! This was, of course, infuriating to all of us, but none more so, than the 'poison obese dwarf', Lainey O'Brien.

I mentioned earlier there was only going to be one winner as far as the contest was concerned between those two. It wasn't for the want of trying on Lainey's part. It is often only men who are spoken of as sociopaths, but there are certainly many women who are burdened with this psychological flaw. Lainey, sure as shooting, was one of those.

Ironically, she was also to be the first member of staff I would meet when arriving to start my new job on that snowy January morning. Like me, Lainey was a local. She lived just a short bus ride away. Initially, she seemed so friendly and helpful. Fuck me, did I get that wrong! Like all skilled exponents of that dark art, whenever a vulnerable soul first comes within a sociopath's sphere of influence, their predatory instincts surface and masquerade as an inviting new friend. Typically, with a 'Trust me, I am only here to help' nearly always to help themselves.

From memory, Lainey had been employed by Unicorn as a school leaver. She had stoically worked her way up the promotional ladder. To be fair, she had thoroughly merited her middle-management post. Managing her own underwriting section was quite rare for a woman in the 70s. Over that period, she had been pretty much unchallenged as DF's most influential female in the office. Apart from some other rather eccentric stalwarts, like the deputy underwriter, Dan Dudd. There was a chap called Barry Carpark who was just a plain weirdo who insisted on tucking his tie into his trousers, Joe Sanders. And then, Norbert Turnbull. Lainey was just about one of the longest serving members of staff.

It was, however, unfortunate timing just prior to Maureen joining the firm there had been a departmental reorganization. Despite the senior management maintaining the illusion of Lainey's 'seniority', the section she had been assigned definitely had a smell of a sideways demotion about it. So, you can just imagine; how threatened this egocentric rotund female was feeling when a far more attractive contemporary joined the syndicate. Not only captivating, but she also obviously was going to be a very smooth operator in her own right. What is more, it took Maureen less than a day to figure out the level of DF's weakness for a well-turned slim ankle and a heaving cleavage. And so, how could she best use her well-honed 'eye lash seduction' technique?

I will never forget the thinly veiled scowl on Lainey's contorted face as she was introduced by DF to the latest object of his desire. A kind of expectant hush had befallen the open plan office as the greeting was being made. It is worth mentioning, it wasn't just Lainey who was feeling insecure by the arrival of this most unwelcome of interlopers. The assistant office manager Bill Roberts, who apart from all his other failings was an overt misogynist, was also present. It was clear from the off that this female was going to get right up his alcohol ridden purple hooter! So, the scene was set for the next six years. I will happily relish, re-visiting this battle royal as one of my many Unicorn experiences.

CHAPTER 6.

SEX IN THE LIFT

A phenomenon that occurs in just about every organization throughout the civilized world is the office romance, . . . ta da! It afflicts so many of us mere mortals. I have succumbed to its temptations on many an occasion, I can tell you. Thus, for the emerging sociopath, the open plan office environment offers a toxicity of pheromones akin to an irresistible nectar to a newly hatched honeybee! Ironically, the trouble with the office romance, though is in the vast majority of encounters there is very little real romancing going on. The illusion of romance accompanied by deceit, lies, betrayal, greed, jealousy, and just about any other human flaw you care to think of, inevitably comes into play.

Now, before all the feminists out there start throwing the kitchen sink at me for being a cynic, believe it or not, back then, I still harbored a notion of finding 'the one' who would be with me until the end of my days. Having experienced very little demonstrable love from my parents I also had a certain romantic ideal in my own mind. However, it soon became clear to me due to the sequence of events unravelling around me during my early days at Unicorn, the reality was some considerable light years away from such an ideal.

Before I was introduced to the 'low hanging fruit' Unicorn's surroundings would soon be offering me, my only earlier experiences were fairly conventional adolescent relationships. Lorraine had been my first real 'love' and after we broke up there were only two other girls who I had been casually dating.

To be fair, even before Unicorn I had seen small snippets of the shenanigans that went on in an office during my brief spells at Sun Life and Liverpool Victoria. However, during that time I was still so spell bound by Lorraine or more like naïve and just too bloody stupid to really savor any of the delights on offer. Unicorn would most certainly change all of that. Not least of all due to two women, the poison rotund dwarf Lainey, and Janice Moses.

Now between these two I was educated and seduced. Although I did, of course, defend myself most gallantly. Then they sent me on my way to become what many sociopaths aspired to be, a serial philanderer!

One aspect I discovered very early on, was the complete myth and misconception men only find good looking women to be most alluring. Indeed, time and again, and as this story will concur, I have repeatedly observed this phenomenon and any women who misunderstands such a reality, will do so at their peril! If they don't fear the threat of that 'plain Jane' who is working in close proximity to their stressed husband, they are going to be in for quite a wakeup call.

Sexy, doesn't necessarily equate to the most attractive looks. Not in the conventional sense anyway. How many times have you heard the misguided woman saying, 'Ooooh, why on earth was he fucking that old trout when he has such a beautiful wife at home?'

That observation isn't by any means restricted to women either. I have seen endless examples of 'Brad Pitt' lookalikes losing out to errmm

. . . me! I will be very happy to explore my many theories regarding such a contradiction and provide umpteen examples as we journey down the rabbit hole of the addictive and dark world of the sociopath.

Lainey O'Brien was highly manipulative, intense, and above all else extremely vindictive. She had surrounded herself with her many loyal sycophants where unquestioned loyalty is something all sociopaths crave, yet rarely give any in return. Her little band of followers reinforced her own powerbase in the office and her spiteful streak was the stuff of legends. Indeed, when I initially joined her team there was no shortage of painful anecdotes flying around about unsuspecting staff members who had, in the past, been savaged by her malicious revenge. Anyone who dared to find a fault with her own work would only enjoy a short-lived victory.

Lainey's responsibilities, once she had been 'shuffled sideways' was to double check all the administration carried out by the underwriting sections, which had given her carte blanch to pull the rug from under just about any member of staff who upset her. She would then snitch on them at the first opportunity in the most underhand and conniving manner. A 'woman scorned' is not just restricted to romantic relationships I can tell you. I have never really believed in coincidence and Lainey's new role appeared to be tailor made for a woman having her predilections which allowed her to inflict a great deal of damage on those within her radar like range.

Even worse, she then set about projecting her own brand of a retaliatory mantra onto those around her who were mostly quite young, naïve, and easily influenced by her seniority. Furthermore, she would actively coach and encourage us to follow her lead and undermine other work colleagues. Firstly, by identifying underwriting errors and then, at every opportunity, maximizing the effect by highlighting the mistakes to their senior managers. Lainey's 'brief' was to check for errors, not compound problems, and ruin careers. But ruin careers she did with growing pleasure.

Whilst she was spreading her vile school of thought, Lainey would embark on her other favorite sociopathic pastime, bedding men! In keeping with my earlier assertion good looking doesn't necessarily mean alluring, she was a classic case-in-point.

Lainey would have been in her early thirties back then. She was barely an inch over five feet tall and appeared to be the same in girth. Her huge cleavage jutted out from a weighty torso which was precariously supported by the spindliest of legs! She did, however, have dark 'continental-like' features and a radiant smile, albeit a scowl masquerading as one, which she used with devastating effect when seducing her latest prey. Her sidekick, Janice was twenty-three at the time with a dark complexion and long wavy brunette hair. She was married to a postman had a young daughter and was bored stiff. So, as I say, one would seduce me, and the other, was my first real conquest as I embarked on what would be a marathon lifetime of philandering.

Just to clarify, prior to my promotion to John Browning's underwriting section, I cut my teeth at Unicorn by reporting to Lainey and likewise, I met Janice for the first time. Together with four other colleagues who made up the numbers on the section, Lainey's team was complete. In the early days - we all just jogged along quite uneventfully other than to observe Lainey's constant sniping and plotting the downfall of various colleagues. However, this also coincided with a rather rare period in my life - when I was somewhat bereft of any real female attention. Cue . . . Janice.

I hadn't really thought of Janice as a prospective lover at all. I was generally otherwise occupied with a series of dates. I hadn't really fancied her to be truthful. So, it was quite an aberration, when on a day just like any other, I happened to catch her eye through the halo of cigarette smoke that was her constant companion. Hard to imagine today, offices up and down the country were smoke filled dens of direct and passive smoking. Never having been a smoker, the cleaning up the work environment by banning smoking was a most welcome one indeed.

Hello, what is that stirring? There was a very distinctive combo of pheromones and Woodbine in the air! So, I waited until she left her desk for a drink at the office water fountain, and I then took the opportunity to sloth up behind her. I pulled a paper cup for myself and uttered those fatal words that start 99% of all clandestine encounters . . .

"Fancy a drink at lunchtime?"

"Oh, hello. I didn't notice you behind me." Total hogwash of course.

"Yeah, you know me, always appearing from the shadows."

Never a truer word!

"Yeah, that would be very nice, but I will meet you inside the Pub, you know how people can talk."

Too right Janice, no one was a bigger gossip than . . . her!

We agreed to rendezvous at 12:30 pm. I should have twigged then, she was a real schemer, because she asked me to arrive 10 minutes after her. Funny, isn't it? For someone who would one day live by guile, and deception, it didn't actually occur to me she already had the psychological angles all worked out. 12:30 pm ticked to attention. I instinctively looked up from my blotting pad only to find Janice already peering back over at me with that 'knowing' look of a lioness who was about to devour her first kill of the day.

She had been to the ladies' room ten minutes beforehand to dutifully 'powder her fanny' or whatever it is females seem to instinctively do before putting themselves on display to attract a potential mate. She then left her desk and sauntered off into the direction of the pub. I impatiently waited about five minutes at best, because a sharp curiosity was already killing this cat!

Our agreed place of rendezvous was The Plough a typical 'city pub', frequented every day by city types ranging from spiv like wide boys, hooray Henry's, and old school 'chaps' who didn't know anything about anything, because . . . 'I have always been a banker'.

I pushed open the door of the sixteenth century Tudor built former coach house with a mixture of heightened anticipation, and a feeling of adolescent nervousness. As I say, I hadn't really been that attracted to

Janice but the allure of a slightly older woman, a penchant for that particular type of lady would most certainly manifest itself by my early thirties. The fact she was married had a delicious irresistibility about it. I scanned the bar area but then my eye level adjusted to that familiar smoky vapor hovering over a swarthy brunette who was dragging away on her already tenth cigarette of the day. The obligatory lunchtime tipple of 'white wine spritzer', who are they kidding with that one, was parked in front of her. She nodded back at me in acknowledgement. I picked up my pint of Hofmeister lager. Geez that stuff was like piss water! I slipped into a stealth-like posture and approached the object of my want.

"So . . . what are YOU doing here then?" Janice grinned. "Well . . . I hardly know where to begin really."

We embarked on the obligatory exchanges and as with nearly all clandestine meetings we conducted a disingenuous charade of asking after the wellbeing of husbands / wives / girlfriends etc . . .

"You know I have always fancied you, don't you?" I lied. "HAVE YOU?"

Beaming smile . . .

"God yes, I just didn't know how to tell you what with you being so happily married, and everything."

"Well, yes there is that cos you know I do love Denton, don't you?

I don't usually do this sort of thing you know."

Looking back, I do not believe Janice had actually crossed that particular Rubicon before. She had married Denton as a pregnant teenage bride. By the time she was in her mid-twenties, she was bored senseless and just didn't find her husband, who had 'green teeth' by the way, to be attractive anymore. What was left of the lunch break flew by. She again left earlier to avoid arriving back at the office together, as if we had not already been noticed. From here on, the outcome was never going to be in doubt.

We met a couple more times for lunch. Another obligatory aspect of the charade it would seem. Then we began to escalate matters. Now, because Janice was married, this presented a further challenge, because I had, until now, been able to have access to my woman without any restrictions. What is more, even if she had been readily available I didn't really, and I quote Michael Caine from the movie 'Alfie', want to be . . 'seen out with it'.

We then began to meet up in 'secret' on the walkway of the nearby Barbican, pretty much in full sight of the passing public. We would snog like mad as she pulled me into her inviting body. I am, if nothing else, known for a very passionate kissing technique, whilst false modesty doesn't suit me, I have over the years had a myriad of women who would complement me on the manner of how I kissed them.

I was not, however, going to be able to afford Janice the same compliment simply because of her addiction to nicotine. She didn't have 'breath like a lioness' but having never smoked in my life, the 'ashtray effect' did leave me with a feeling of 'how long can I keep going with this'? Well, as we all know, any prizes in life do not come to those who lack tenacity.

Existing in an open plan office in today's sanitized and politically correct world is an epoch away from the environment we all enjoyed back in the early eighties. Recent TV shows, such as Life on Mars and Ashes to Ashes achieved a decent portrayal of a working culture that was the norm back then. To be fair, even those two excellent dramas are a rather wide of the mark. The flagrant excesses, and risk taking, that was being taken all around me, was eye watering at times. I am mindful to emphasize here, by BOTH sexes! Indeed, Janice and Lainey would certainly be standard bearers!

After a few weeks of fornicating and fumbling inside Janice's knickers, she was coming to the boil very nicely. I am not exaggerating when I say, she was even becoming rather demanding. She yearned indeed! Therefore, to achieve our mutual aim, I was going to need a cunning plan. It presented itself in the form of elevation! Back then, the office elevators were still of the sliding 'scissor gate' design and used just as much for goods and deliveries as they were for carrying staff between floors. One of the maintenance lads demonstrated to me the lift could be stopped between floors if the gate was just slightly ajar. Perfect!

Even as I write this, I still can't believe sometimes how brazen the two of us had become. Without doubt, EVERYONE knew it was happening. This is how it worked. I would be nonchalantly sitting at my desk toiling away at some admin or other and then, just like the proverbial 'Bistro Kid', the beckoning aroma of Janice's secretions would waft past my obliging sinuses. Like a mesmerized vole, in front of highly poisonous snake, my eyes would start to dazzle, my throat would dry up, and my love department took on a mind all its own. Janice would rise from her seat, brush herself down, and catching my dilating eyes with just the necessary degree of her peripheral vision, she had me under her spell. She would then march toward the landing at the back of the department and wait for me by the lift. I wouldn't even look around me, as I ‘puppy like’ followed her out. Bizarrely, no one would look up, ask, or even fart?

Janice would always be standing expectantly by the lift with arms folded, legs crossed, and licking her lips. Dreamland. We had developed quite a routine and would even get to know the optimum times when the lift would be in less demand for either parcels or people.

So, in the lift we would go, press the button for the second floor and . . . we wouldn’t get there. Well, not for ten minutes or so. Where affairs are concerned there is one dynamic that will never let you down. There is never enough time! So, a well-honed technique is always worth giving that extra bit of attention to. The lift would be perfectly in situ between the two floors and then, I would pull the door open just enough to stop it ascending any further. My dalliance with Janice happened to coincide with the summer months of 1979, so we didn't have the obstacle of any tights. She would already have removed her knickers. In one well-rehearsed move, she would unzip my fly, release my manhood, and lifting her skirt she would then turn around and arch back onto a very grateful . . . me.

This little arrangement went on for about the best part of three months but then came to a juddering halt. The reason being . . . my first wife, Pamela!

CHAPTER 7.

THE STATIONERY ROOM

Before I move on to talking about the 'human hurricane' that entered my life in the form of my first marriage, it does merit rounding things off as far as Janice is concerned and taking a brief look at some of the other exploits that seemed to be perfectly acceptable behavior among the staff at Unicorn. Indeed, whenever I watched Ricky Gervais playing his now iconic role of David Brent in The Office, I can remember thinking to myself . . . Yeah that's funny, but nothing compared to the real-life happenings at Unicorn.

I previously acknowledged once Janice had crossed that line, there was no going back. Not just for me and her. Once things had reached its natural conclusion between the two of us, what happened next is just uproarious. In no time at all, I was observing a whole procession of men trooping out onto the landing to rendezvous, with an obliging Janice, indulging themselves in some kind of intimate carousel between two floors! There were all shapes and sizes too, from horn-rimmed specs wearing Ken Hornby, to twenty-stone Michael Werner, who we all called the 'incredible bulk'. Janice's accommodation of the Unicorn new recruits was almost seen as a compulsory initiation in the end. That lift saw more action over the coming years from 'horizontal jogging' than it ever did from office stationery deliveries.

My best mate Graham, was likewise, an accomplished lothario himself. His ability to think imaginatively was most impressive. Graham was a Noel Edmonds lookalike and just like his DJ double, was also a lad from Essex. As a young gun at Unicorn, he had a very important 'duty of care' bestowed upon him. He was responsible for custody of the stationery cupboard key . . . no less! There were in fact, two more sets of keys, but they were held by the underwriter himself, DF, and the office manager, Arthur Ogley.

At that time Graham had several girls within his office harem. His favorite concubine was a 'horny little sort' by the name of Kay Cronin. Even though they were really both free agents and could easily have had liaisons outside working hours, there was clearly nothing more addictive than being able to take a risk under the noses of the management. Endangering yourself is a human weakness that seems to be an irresistible temptation, especially where office affairs are concerned.

Graham devised a cunning plan of his own, so he could savor the delights of, as he would call it, 'Kay's honey pot' whilst at the same time, discharging his most important of duties. Now that's what I call proper time management! He would approach the underwriter and say he had left his own key at home, with a 'could I borrow yours please for the day'? He would happily oblige. Those two went back a long way and Derek Fairly was a personal friend of Graham's father. Having 'trousered' that particular key, he would then use the same script on the office manager. Great . . . no one else could now get access to the 'shag cupboard'.

Just as I used to be 'summoned' by Janice, Graham would call down to the computer processing department where Kay worked and gave her an all clear. Kay was not averse to high-risk enjoyment and often used to give Graham a 'hand job' under the desk. He would sit nonchalantly in front of her, with his chin rested on palms, and elbows on her blotting pad while grinning away like some kid who had found more than an 'extra sherbet' in his 'lucky dip' bag!

Ironically, the productivity during those years was astounding. Under DF's stewardship, Unicorn grew to be the largest motor under-writing syndicate in the UK. His various teams were high producers. So again, could it be sociopaths are actually a necessity to ensure the fortitude of the business hierarchy?

Graham still reminisces with great delight about those days of unalloyed pleasure. He actually celebrated his 45 years' service. He often tells me how he sadly looks around him at the 'digital world' that has engulfed the soul of the building based in Brentwood Essex, where Unicorn had moved to in 1984. He only said to me recently.

"Mate, when I look at the young members of staff around me now, I fear for the future. They have mostly attended university. They are underachieved with useless non-degrees. Barely apply any aspects of their qualification to the role they are now employed to do.

"They are scared of their own shadows, petrified of 'making a mistake' and have no sense of irony or humor. They even find Michael McIntyre funny for Christ's sake."

"But the saddest thing of all is that they show no spirit or passion whatsoever."

Here here Graham.

CHAPTER 8.

The Wrong Choice

There I was, taking advantage whenever I could, of Janice's means of teaching people 'how to use a lift in the most efficient manner possible'. Moreover, there was no way Lainey was going to be left out of the action. Between me, Graham, and several others, she would, one by one, pick us off. Invariably, alcohol was used to weaken our defenses or supply the Dutch courage depending on who was the next culprit, I guess? It was other time-honored arena for the 'office romance' to flourish would often provide Lainey with the best environment for her to swoop down on her latest victim, the office party!

Amazing when I think back, because Lainey did not really have a great deal going for her, but she was like a viper. We all played her game at some time or other. Good looking chaps who otherwise would be pulling models with high cheek bones would still be putty in her hands! Why, for Christ sakes? So, this was where I was beginning to develop my private theories, something else was at play? Surely, any right-minded bloke, no matter how pissed, wouldn't be touching that with the proverbial barge pole?

I now have definitive proof of what causes such cognitive behavior. No psychologist was ever going to provide me with the answer. Now let me share my findings with you. We always talk about 'chemistry' as the key to attraction between couples . . . but actually it's not chemistry at all. It's physics and, of the quantum variety! This is further compounded, excuse the pun, by the reality that we don't actually have the true freewill to make the choices, which would otherwise be perceived as, common-sense. How many times do we say during our lifetime, 'What on earth possessed me to do that'? Well, later in my story, you will discover exactly why?

Needless to say, throughout that entire time Lainey was, married! Anyway, I was also sowing oats just about everywhere by then, not unusual for a young red-blood of course, but all that was about to change, big style.

I happened to be sitting at my desk when the most feline figure of a female breezed past my ear. I had noticed Pam beforehand but for some reason, she seemed to be constantly doing a ‘now you see me, now you don't’ impression. Which meant there was rather a discontinuity as far as my interest was concerned. I was later to discover the reason for her continual absences from work, which would eventually prove to be both traumatising and near life threatening.

Pam worked with a team that looked after all the filing, which was extensive in back in the 1980s, because everything was on paper. The filing racks stretched for what seemed like miles on every floor. How different it is today. The filing clerks were all women, and like many in that role, they were the salt of the earth and Pam was no exception.

She was a couple of years older than me, 5’ 6” and with the obligatory feathered Farrah Fawcett-Majors hairstyle, which so many women wore back then. With high cheek bones, which were yet another penchant of mine. Top it all with a seductive mouth and THE most incredible body I have ever known on a female, even to this day. Not a single man in the office could be found to challenge that description. Even when she wore flat shoes, such was her naturally high instep, her feline form would simply glide past you and in the most seductive manner.

Pam or ‘Pammy’ as she was known by most of her family, was the second daughter born to Alf and Naomi. Her parents had split when she was only an infant. Alf was a wealthy man and had been involved with haulage all his life, but I never actually met him because he died in 1980 just after I had started to date his daughter.

As they say, Alf was as ‘tight as a camel arse in a sandstorm’ and he also had the burden of two older sisters who dictated to him just how he would conduct all his business and marital affairs. They both loathed Naomi, who I always found to be one of the warmest, loving, and most generous of souls - I ever had the privilege to know. So, their controlling influence over their brother always baffled me. As a result, he barely supported his wife and daughter; it was only as a consequence of him dying. Without leaving a proven will, the intestacy rules, meant Naomi was a beneficiary to a reasonable share of his estate.

In the meantime, Naomi would struggle to bring up her four girls (Alf was only father to two of them, Pam, and her baby sister, Jayne). She raised her impoverished family in downtown Hoxton, in northeast London. Now coming from Bow and Bethnal Green, it would be fair to say, the borough of Tower Hamlets was (as it still is) one of the poorest in the country. So, it was a stark perspective indeed, when we actually regarded Hoxton as, rough. So, you can really get a feel for the demographic I am endeavoring to describé here.

Naomi had to try and hold down a number of part time jobs whilst caring for her kids. The welfare state system wasn't the 'fiscal tit' it is today. So, nearly all her work had to be cash in hand. So, as soon as Pam turned fifteen. She no longer attended school. Pretty much cared full time for her baby sister. Together, with her three other siblings they all suffered from abandonment issues but none more so than Pam herself, which would later manifest as acute symptoms of irrational jealousy. I should know, as I was a direct beneficiary!

Like all fateful pathways, there always seems to be seminal moment when the stars line up and two souls merge to carry on a mutual journey together was. Yes, I am a massive believer all our lives are pre-programmed through a code in our 'DNA consciousness' and manifests in the pathway of our life journey. I will expand on that particular belief later, and the reasons why I know this to be true.

With regards to Pam and me, there was an added dynamic, which revealed itself in the unmistakable figure of Anthony Pager. Pamela was firmly targeted by his razor like sights. She knew it. Indeed, 'razor like' is just about the best euphemism you could ever use, to describe just about every aspect of Anthony Pagers character.

I have already mentioned how fortunate I have been when it comes to meeting naturally gifted wits and comics in the workplace. Well, Mr. Pager is most certainly at the pinnacle of those I have ever encountered. To be fair, the only reason I don't rank him above the indomitable pair of 'Ted and Albert' is because both had a heart. Now, I am not suggesting for one moment Anthony Pager was an uncaring soul, but the reptilian-like manner in which he delivered sarcastic humor was quite unparalleled in its cutting execution.

When I say that Andy Staff and Ian Ratcliffe were kindred to that of piss taking school prefects, Anthony was as near too hawkish 'Flashman' as you will ever find. Moreover, just like other men I have met who share sociopathic tendencies, he was angrily misogynistic, yet collected women with the utmost of ease, simply as he went along. It's almost as if, the sociopath cannot get enough of the very thing they detest the most. We will diagnose that most intriguing of dichotomies later.

Anthony was quite simply your classic tall, dark, and handsome man with Tom Selleck looks and boy, did he know it. Interestingly though, and yet another trait I have seen in the sociopath, there is often a particular episode or experience from their past. Where one specific female will have scored a notable victory. Which in turn, then embeds itself as a blemish in the sociopaths' cellular memory and they will then rerun that battle with subsequent partners.

In Anthony's case, it was the relationship with his first wife and the eventual failure of their marriage which did for him. He would often use quite sorrowful anecdotes, to describe how, it had all gone terribly wrong because of his self-indulgent lifestyle where he neglected his wife. However, when Anthony attempted to reconcile matters, the proverbial rugby captain 'Mike' had moved in and parked his 'size eleven's' under his wife's duvet. Too late mate!

An interesting juxtaposition was now heading my way. Not only between Pam, Anthony, and I, but at this point it also brings us back to the rivalry between Lainey and Maureen.

Like all sociopaths, Anthony Pager was used to getting what he wanted. The latest target of his want was Pam. We were to become ferocious rivals for her affections, which just happened to coincide with Anthony being transferred from another underwriting section to the one where Maureen and I, were already in situ.

We continued to report to a senior 'superintendent' John Browning, and not a more spineless chap will you ever find. John was in his mid-thirties, but his short snowy white hair made him appear ten years older. He wore thick framed glasses and had an equally thick midriff. His trademark shirking of the shoulders as he smugly guffawed at anyone's misfortune, particularly gnawed away at me. We had a pretty good rapport, but when he did his 'Mutley' impression, he had one of those faces that if I had started hitting it, I would not have known when to stop.

He was, to be fair, a man who possessed a very dry wit himself but his ability to manage the triumvirate of two other alpha men and that of the 'sugar bum fairy' was going to test him to his limits. Credit where it's due though, because manage he did through an innate ability to delegate work like no other. Good management then, I hear you say? Perhaps, but to a point where he actually did . . . nothing! Anyway, we will come back to Mr. Browning's lack of backbone later because in the meantime, I had a battle to win.

Looking back at that specific triangle of passion there have been moments when I have thought. If I could have had my time again, would I be tempted to lose out to Anthony? Pam would become the mother of my only child, so I was eternally blessed, yet I was also immature, irresponsible, and selfish, so a 'no brainer then' as they say. I do believe we all live the lives we are meant to, so we can look back with hindsight as many times as we like but we cannot change the past. We do not grow as a result of nice fluffy bits for it's the mistakes we grow by. Mistakes? Or are they all really experiences pre-determined for the growth of all the participants to that experience, whether good or bad?

It still feels like it was only yesterday when Anthony parked himself to the right of me, for the first time with Maureen opposite, and John sitting to my left; wearing what seemed like a constant 'Mutley' style grin on his boat race. At times, it was all I could do to stop myself from spanking him in the gob!

As you can imagine relationships were rather strained as we did our level best to try and get along against a background of a love rivalry, and the constant sniping at Maureen from Lainey. Maureen's powers over Derek Fairly were becoming all too apparent and unbearable for Lainey. Her own influence with DF was waning fast. At times, I was really aware of her sense of desperation as she constantly played a game of 'catch up' behind her far more attractive foe.

Then my chance came. I was determined to seize the opportunity. Before taking a few days leave, Anthony had boasted he was going to convert his flirtations with Pam into a first date. So, I knew I had to strike quickly. Every half-hour or so, she would come by section desks, and collect the files we had finished with, and I would be sitting and waiting in a cat-like manner. I had begun to warm to Maureen by then and had taken her into my confidence regarding my romantic intentions. 'Ooh isn't it exciting Luvvy', she would gush.

Fortuitously, both John and Maureen were both away from their desks when Pam punctually arrived to collect more files, so I came out with something that was an original line . . . not!

"Ello gorgeous, fancy going for a drink at lunchtime?" "Love to."

Did she really just say yes and so spontaneously?

"Errrr . . . ok then, see you at 1:00 pm in the Penny Black."

"Great, I can't wait."

With that . . . Yesssss my son, get in!

Just like all phallic combatants, as I was heading off toward the pub, I was savoring the impending victory over Anthony every bit as much as the feeling of excitement, which I should have been having about meeting up with Pam. What an immature twat!

We met in the penny black, which was the favorite watering hole for most of the staff at Unicorn. Had a lovely fifty minutes or so breaking the ice and chatting about useless non subjects. Such a banal narrative, which often goes with the 'role playing' goes on during a first so-called 'date', isn't it? She had this liking, for some bloody green liquor Crème de menthe, or as Pam would pronounce it with her Hoxton accent – 'Creem dee menff'!

Looking back with the good old benefit of hindsight there were some key expressions, Pam used in just a few moments; had I owned the level of awareness, which I have today, there would have been alarm bells ringing inside my cranium! Phrases such as . . .

'I bear a grudge' and 'revenge can be sweet' and even, 'Yeah, he is a right cunt'!

Hmmm?

What is it about that most defamatory of expletives, both my eventual wives would enjoy using so much? I can also say right now because I know what you are bloody thinking. They were not venting at me either when they used it? More analysis about that to come. Anon . . .

Anyhow, I was far too smitten. My mind was operating below a subterrain level of lust to be taking any notice of the clear warning signs. Which had I heeded, would have changed pathways forever? There we go again, freewill, or just freedom of choice? One huge amount of emotional conflict would certainly have been avoided, that's for sure.

With great irony then, Anthony returned to work 'locked and loaded', ready for an alpha duel only to discover, he had turned up on the wrong day or perhaps the right day as far as his fortunes were concerned. To be fair, he was gracious in defeat, indeed a very rare gesture for him. He used a turn of phrase that he coined 'you have chosen well young man'.

Had I indeed? Time would tell. Furthermore, the two of us became fairly good mates and together with some other great pals, like Roger, Kev, and Adrian we all played in the Unicorn 5 A-side team and won a few tournaments to boot.

It is also worth pointing out, Anthony was ten-years older than me and had quite an overt influence over my future outlook toward the opposite sex. I mentioned before that he was an archmisogynist, which is a common imperfection among male sociopaths. He would offer me what he perceived as 'pearls of wisdom' where handling females were concerned, such as . . .

"Just remember young man, if it took you thirty minutes to get a bird's knickers off, then it probably took someone else . . .just ten."

Anthony had so many like that, I would need to create a dedicated index page to fit them all in.

Throughout my early days at Unicorn, and up until my first dating Pam, there was another love triangle running in parallel, which was to become extremely complex as it would overlap into my personal life and could have upended my marriage much earlier. It involved a sappy couple, Rhoda, and Gareth Wagg. I kid you not, those are their married names.

The 'Wagg's' both started work at Unicorn a few months prior to me, had become the unofficial 'office sweethearts'. I say 'unofficial' because as with all hypocritical females Rhoda also had a boyfriend. His name was Dirk or something else very 'Essex'. Anyway, it meant Gareth, who I had closely befriended at that time was working with Graham in the 'computer department' and was getting most frustrated and stressed he couldn't get inside Rhoda's knickers.

The boyfriend eventually went west. Gareth was as happy as the proverbial 'pig in shit'. They became engaged. Over the next two years we all got along just fine doing all the usual stuff socializing couples do. But this harmony would be destabilized, in a spectacular fashion as Rhoda's interaction with yours truly, developed into a very unhealthy obsession for both parties. But Rhoda would have to wait.

Pam and I started to date. The time inevitably soon came around, where she was becoming rather persistent about being introduced to my parents. I was not altogether comfortable with this for I was only too well-aware of how Victorian both of my parents were in their attitudes and Pamela. Shall we say, was less blessed with the airs and graces would be acceptable to Harry and Marie.

I did not truly scrutinize the real reason as to why I was so uncomfortable about my parents meeting Pamela; it was certainly far more than their opinions was making me feel so hesitant. It couldn't have been anything to do with the reality we were totally unsuited of course. As is often the way, in the early days of a relationship the physical attraction and sheer mutual lust will blind side us, from the person and their flaws and by the time such a reality hits home it will be too late.

My parents had long since moved on from the high-rise tower block of flats, which my mother had sadly acquiesced to. Their new abode wasn't a great deal better for it was a second-floor council maisonette. With trepidation, I introduced my latest love. Which to be honest wasn't the reality at all because I was by now establishing a pattern of mistaking lust for love. I did not have any real feelings of love for Pam, she was simply filling the void of love in my heart with the distraction of newness and sex, which could only ever be a temporary fix at best.

Why was I not able to able to experience feelings of love to any degree of depth, which I craved for myself and from others? At the time, and due to my immaturity, I never allowed myself the time to examine what the reasons for might be. Looking back however it is now clear the lack of parental love had already caused me to build a shield around my heart so as not to be hurt. The casualty of that shield, being I suppressed my own emotions, and replaced them with a superficial air of charm. What a classic sociopathic attribute indeed!

The first meeting between my parents and Pamela turned to be quite a trauma for me. I knew what my parents' body language would be like. Especially that of my mothers. I was walking on eggshells most of the time in anticipation Pamela would not be able to control her crass and crude Hoxton upbringing. And sure enough, once she has settled in, out came a string of expletives.

"Fuck this and fucking that."

I could feel the sweat pouring down my back as my parents were clearly becoming increasingly uncomfortable with the young beauty taking center stage, who was becoming more confident by the minute.

I held an awkward cheesy grin on my face, and I could feel a warm feeling of my own anxieties for the obvious embarrassment my mother and father were feeling. I would not need to ask them both what they thought about the woman who had descended on them. Their constant frowning made that most obvious.

An hour felt like twenty-four, so I had to bring matters to an end as soon as possible, to save further embarrassment to my parents and not least of all, me!

My father wasn't present on the day that I announced I would be leaving home to go and live with Pam at her mother's house in Essex. I was relieved in a way, because our relationship had deteriorated to such a point that he had barely spoken to me other than to indulge further torturous encounters with my girlfriend. My mother was ambivalent.

"Good luck son. I can't honestly say your choice would have been mine for you, but you know I would never try to live your life for you. Please remember if things do not work out, you can always come back. I will sort things with your father."

At that very instant, I ached to my core for my mother's affection and yet, the embrace did not come. It never had before, and certainly was not going to happen on this occasion.

CHAPTER 9.

SARAH

Fast forward then. Pam and I had been staying at her mum's in Gidea Park Essex, which seemed like the 'countryside' compared to urban smoke I had been used to back in the East End of London. Pam's mum had managed to get a transfer from London in the mid-70s and was bringing up the youngest of her four girls Jayne, who was only ten years of age, when I first met her. She was a great kid and adored her 'Pammy' as if she was, her real mum.

We were all getting along really well. It was likewise a bit of an eye opener. The reason being, I soon discovered they were a family who were happy to function, shall we say not always on the sunny side of the street! When I look back what is even more perturbing, is I was not altogether aware various items which furnished our home were all. knocked off! It was a bit like the BBC sitcom Royal Family but for real. With typically immature haste Pam and I tied the knot at the

Langton's Registry Office in Hornchurch, Essex, with a few friends and my brother Terry in attendance. It was telling, however, neither of my parents attended the ceremony because they were most hesitant about the suitability of my new spouse. My 'stupid gene' was kicking in nicely. That said, despite my bravado, I was really hurting inside they had snubbed me, without so much as an excuse being made on their part.

Within just a few months of the wedding, the inevitable happened and Pam became pregnant. When the tests were confirmed, I immediately went into a state of sheer panic and even asked Pam, if she would consider a termination? I just did not feel mature enough to handle the huge responsibility that was about to befall me. Pam's reaction was both typical, and predictable.

"You total cunt, I am disgusted with you. WE are having this baby and that is that. Grow up and be a man."

Well, that was certainly that then . . .

After a few weeks, I began to calm down and my sense of terror was gradually replaced by a feeling of joy, at the prospect of becoming a father. But we were also rather apprehensive about the impending changes, which would impact on our lives, for Pam had been married previously for a brief, but traumatic period.

I never really delved too deeply into her past, but she had been subject to a fair amount of physical abuse from her first husband. So together with her childhood experiences, it did leave her with some serious issues. Neither did I have the sufficient maturity in those days to recognise the angst that she was harboring. However, I am now fully seized of the legacy that must have been imprinted on her soul and Pam, was really insecure, and as we know, acute insecurity results in one overriding emotion - which is intense jealousy!

The 'green-eyed monster' is just about THE most destructive emotion that will betide a relationship of any kind, let alone a romantic one. For my part, I have experienced the corrosive effects of this most ruinous of emotions, and from both sides! I will explore this most intriguing subject matter later and as this story unfolds and there will be numerous episodes highlighted which, for my money, is by far the worst of the 'seven deadly sins'.

The 18th of March 1981 is simply THE most important day in my life - and will remain so until the end of my days. For that was the day: when my beautiful little daughter came to join this world and graced me as one of her parents. Sarah was born at Harold Wood Hospital after a two week wait. She was due on the 4th so for each day that passed was agonising for us both - and many of the staff at Unicorn - which is quite usual of course when the two parents have met in the same workplace. Sarah eventually arrived, weighing just shy of seven pounds and I can still feel today, the overwhelming emotions, which all new parents experience for the first time. We had waited two weeks for our little angel to arrive and when Pam finally went into labor, Sarah was delivered just sixty minutes later.

I felt so blessed to be present at the birth of my first, and what would turn out to be my only child. The rotund smiley black midwife who presided over the delivery - kept both parents fairly calm throughout the labor. But nothing could prepare me for the sheer level of overwhelming emotion and love that washed over me when Sarah's first distinctive cry ricocheted around the delivery room. I walked through the door and once outside I sobbed uncontrollably as wave after wave, of a magnitude of love - I had never felt before - infused the very core of my soul.

CHAPTER 10.

THE FIRST AFFAIR

It wasn't very often I would get my own way with my intransigent spouse but as far as naming our daughter was concerned, I was determined a name I had intuitively been given was going to prevail. Unlike today, we hadn't the privilege of knowing the sex of our baby in advance, so we had obviously considered various names for both sexes, but I just innately knew Pam was carrying a girl and her name would be . . . Sarah.

Mother and daughter left the hospital after a few days. We set up home in a modest council flat in Harold Hill, Essex. As proud young parents, we naturally wanted to better ourselves. After a brief move time, we moved to a larger flat in the much more desirable neighborhood of Harold Wood. We managed to raise a deposit, generously provided by Pam's mum, for our first house. We moved 'lock stock' out to Braintree in Essex; 'escape to the country' had nothing on us. So, life was young, family-orientated and quite conventional. Well, it was for a short while. Then cometh . . . Rhoda.

There has been a distinct pattern in my life whereby things are running along just swimmingly, then for some unfathomable reason, I will press the self-destruct button once more. The only caveat to that play script is that prior to my Rhoda aberration, I was already experiencing some problems with Pam's insecurities. She had managed to keep them in check it would seem, until after she had given birth to Sarah.

To that end, I am appreciative, and not insensitive, to the plain reality many women feel less attractive to their man after childbirth.

Moreover, throw in the inescapable post-natal hormone shift, and we potentially have an explosive emotional vortex waiting to clobber any ill-informed, immature, fella - right around his unsuspecting cranium!

Pam was certainly experiencing such a potent cocktail of emotions and owned the weapons to maximize its effect. A flaring temper and repeater rifle of a tongue! Believe it or not, until Rhoda came into the mix, I had been a very good boy. I had been faithful for nearly three years, even though I had been tempted many times before Rhoda came along and strained at the leash. Nevertheless, I was dug in deep within the matrimonial 'trench'. However, such a status quo was about to be severely challenged.

That particular catalyst coincided with a decision made by the executive of Unicorn to relocate the business from the city of London to a new purpose-built office in Essex, located just inside the then recently completed M25 Motorway. There was no end of logistics planning to undertake the move. The office manager, Bill 'Roy Slater' Roberts, was going to be in his authoritarian element.

The relocation was a catalyst for many other reasons too because many of the long-term members of staff were facing a stark choice to either move to Essex or accept a generous redundancy package. One of those would be the dark destroyer herself, Lainey. This meant that she would finally lose her long standing feud with the 'sugar bum fairy' - Maureen. Anon . . .

Anyway, just a quick rewind because some six months prior to the move, the 'office wedding of the decade' was to take place. The marriage of Rhoda to Gareth. Rhoda was a Chingford girl and had the sappiest way of saying 'my Gareth', which was imitated by many and not in an altogether endearing fashion. Gareth and I were still good buddies and part of a circle of friends including Graham of course. I was asked, and honored, to be his best man.

The doting couple had invited such a high percentage of Unicorn staff to their wedding ceremony and reception. It resembled a work outing! My speech was prepared. The day had gone like clockwork. I relished the role of being best man. A sociopath would of course. The directing of family, friends, and ushers was a walk in the park for me. Then onto the reception, which was planned for the early evening . . .

Sarah was just a toddler by then and had stayed with her Nan. Pam was dressed in her best wedding finery, of course. She looked exquisite.

By that time, however, her mood swings and I hate to say this, at times violent nature. She was putting a real strain on our relationship. Within another year, I would discover the cause of those temper swings with the most stressful of episodes.

My best man speech was roundly received. It went smoothly I guess because I was so familiar with the vast majority of attendees. Coupled with the reality by seven pm I had downed the obligatory ten pints. Although the demon booze wouldn't engulf my life for another decade. And if asked, I would have made an eulogy to Gandhi himself in the biggest of stadiums, I wouldn't have given a shit. A conversation was about to take place though, that would sober me up very abruptly.

It was only when the time arrived for me to have a dance with the bride herself that one of those 'lightning bolt' moments struck home. Rhoda looked fantastic as the glowing bride with stunning brunette looks and a near perfect size 8 form. Ok, she was a bit of an Essex bird, but I am not sure that phrase had been coined back then.

So, there we were slowly dancing. The entire time I could feel daggers in my back being thrown by my own wife to the point where, I tried to look as if the whole experience was torture. Even so, I rather enjoyed having Rhoda's arms draped around the back of my neck, hold on, for one minute there, parallel universe moment coming . . . arms around my neck! Ok, the drink was flowing. We were all feeling rather 'relaxed' so to speak but there is a 'best man's' embrace and then there is draping around the neck. The latter was most definitely not on the wedding protocol list!

I continued to defend myself chivalrously, whilst at the same time coming out with all the usual pissed rubbish one does when facing such a critically emotional exchange. Unfortunately, and I am trying to be honest here, the response Rhoda gave me was to cause a chain reaction that would blight me, my career, and my marriage, until it inevitably folded.

"You look beautiful, Rhoda."

"Why haven't you told me that before now then?" "Errrr . . . not sure, I guess it wasn't appropriate." "Well, that's a real shame you know."

"Oh . . . a shame?"

"Yes, because I wanted YOU to be by my side today."

Like a complete thicko I then came out with such an obtuse reply. "But I was Rhoda . . . throughout the whole ceremony."

"NO! Not on THAT side of me, the OTHER side dopey!"

I was not as green as I was cabbage looking, but after ten pints I was sobering up fast.

"Do you mean . . . but?"

"I have always wanted you Sam . . . not him."

There was that 'fools and horses' analogy again, I was feeling very 'Rodney-like'.

Rhoda didn't waiver. I was all over the place. You know how it is when something like that happens. Despite the cacophony of 'Duran Duran' tracks playing away at mega decibels you are convinced the wife has overheard every word of that conversation! I was both anxious and elated at the same time.

"Rhoda Jeeeez. I had NO idea." And I hadn't . . .

"Yes, I know, but I have not stopped wanting you since we danced at the last year's office party."

Another 'parallel universe' moment coming - where even a Stephen Hawking sized wormhole would not have supplied a sufficient escape route. The events of the office party all came flooding back. With greater maturity and my now well-honed sociopathic radar. If Rhoda had given off the same signals today, that she had done at that previous year's office function, I would have lured her in less time than it takes to say the word . . . seduced!

Rhoda was all over me that evening. It was the last Unicorn office party I would ever attend. The reason being, Pam's insecurity and jealousy, where some three years into the marriage it was becoming really degenerative. So much so, it just made for an easier life to not even mention the annual party invites were being handed out to staff beforehand. It's strange how, when one partner is burdened with such emotions, both parties embark on a mutual level of denial. Even to the point where, excuses are made as to why 'you would love to come to the party, but Pam has been having her migraines again and she really needs help with the little one'.

Pam would have been only too aware from her own time working at Unicorn, as to the kind of inappropriate activities drunken and uninhibited staff members will be reduced to. Having seen the debauched carrying on for herself. Pam knew the annual bash was held every April, yet she resisted ever asking me if I intended to go. I certainly did not need the grief. Anyone who has experienced jealousy as a receiver or giver of such emotions, will know it is only going to end up with the same outcome.

The receiver in the end will become so suffocated the very thing the giver fears most, will be inevitable. I am not suggesting the reasons for insecurities are not justified; if they exist, it eventually is so corrosive it can only result in a destroyed relationship.

I had not heeded Rhoda's overtures that particular year. I just went on my merry way; oblivious a genie was just bursting to jump out of its bottle. But as fate decreed, again I must insist we are defenseless to avoid such an event happening if it is pre-ordained, Rhoda was to get there in the end.

Despite my endeavoring to keep Rhoda at arm's length, the fateful moment was inevitably approaching. Along with several other members of staff, we had been clearing up files, cabinets, typewriters, and telephones at the old city offices ready for the relocation to Essex. Gareth was an integral member of the computer department, which was the 1980s quaint description of IT departments. He was ahead of us at the new building where he was installing computer hardware and overseeing necessary cabling. Since the wedding, I had kept a lid on things as far as Rhoda was concerned. On this particular day, I could just sense those alluring pheromones again.

It had been a long and arduous day, as it is the norm. We all made our way to the Penny Black. Oh no, alcohol, lust, and temptation, not a good combination, is it? As it always seems to be the way, the other members of staff seemed to peel away, leaving just me and the longing Rhoda alone together. I did my regal best. I honestly did, to keep conversation as banal a level as I could, but Rhoda wasn't having a bar of it.

A female's ability to show such gross hypocrisy at the very time she is about to swoop, never ceases to amaze me. Yes, I know ALL humans do it, but its men who seem to get all the bad press. So, before you ladies reading this start reaching for 'a wok to bash my face with' if you do get to the end of this story, you will read about many more episodes, which simply underpin that stark observation, and . . . here is one prime example coming up right now.

Rhoda actually had the temerity to ask after the wellbeing of Pam and Sarah. You couldn't make this stuff up. She went on to remark on how Sarah was growing into a little beauty. At two years of age, Sarah had long blonde hair, crystal blue eyes, and would have graced any pears commercial, says her dad with no bias whatsoever. It gets even better though. As Rhoda also had the nerve to tell me how she was in awe of Pam as a mother. The syrup was oozing at this point.

As I am writing this, I can assure you I STILL didn't appreciate how things were going to escalate between the two of us. We left the Penny Black and headed off toward Liverpool Street Station to catch an Essex bound train. The carriage was nearly empty. As we sat down together, I had a distinctively visceral realization the outcome was going to be a foredrawn conclusion. Rhoda snuggled into me the whole journey home. We barely uttered a word, mostly due to the fact I was shit scared to say anything. Jesus, how that particular reluctance of mine would utterly change in the future.

Rhoda's stop off was one before mine. Just as the train began to slow, she just looked up at me and . . . what a kiss. She glided her lips so gently over my barely open mouth. Then we locked. I melted into her with a passionate and heated clinch, so much so, we were both totally oblivious to the embarrassment of the poor old lady sitting opposite. We reluctantly pulled ourselves apart. As the train halted at the platform, Rhoda mouthed . . . 'I will see you on Monday.'

Gulp!

CHAPTER 11.

I Discover Female Hypocrisy

On the following Monday morning, I arrived for work bright and early at the new Unicorn head office building in Brentwood Essex, which is a rather unappealing town located just outside the M25 Motorway. I had spent the entire weekend in denial about the looming events and all I could manage during forty-eight hours, which felt more like forty eight days, was a rather poor attempt at normal family life as Pam and I went about our domestic routines.

It may have only been a kiss on a train, but I knew the significance of that simple act was going to be far greater than any of the snatched extramarital encounters I had so far experienced. When Rhoda had closed the door of the train behind her, my emotions and physical senses were not solely restricted to lust, excitement, and desire. Something very unfamiliar had resonated within me. Rhoda had, in that one moment, managed to ignite in me an aching for her that was touching every fibre of my being. I would have to manage these feelings in a very guarded fashion for I knew there were danger signs on a number of levels. Not least of all, my own emotional vulnerability.

As with any good 'soap' storyline, the ripple effect tends to pull in many other cast members. One of the players in this particular script would be the office manager, Bill Roberts. He was about to have a dramatic episode gifted to him, whereby he would be in his meddlesome element.

I remember sitting for the first time at my new shiny desk. Although I had arrived quite early, it was soon clear someone had beaten me to it. Sat in the middle of my brand spank desk blotting pad, was a clearly 'perfumed' and 'sealed' envelope? Shit!

The rest of my team hadn't arrived yet, so I was able to read without any hindrance. As I thumbed open the letter, I can remember having mixed feelings of dread, exhilaration, and cravings. I started to read, it went on and on and on . . . my immediate reaction was, how did she find the time to write all of this and without Gareth twigging? She was in love with me or so she thought. On the other hand, if I had any cognizance, I would be level-headed and stop things right then and there to prevent matters from getting quickly out of control. Was I? Hell, I knew I wanted her too!

Rhoda's letter was effusive in just about every aspect and it really beggared belief. She had only made her wedding vows six months prior. My sexual instincts in 1984 were nowhere near as rapacious as they would later become. Rhoda actually did most of the pursuing from there on and I was most happy to oblige her. Gareth was another matter altogether. We had, since my early days at Unicorn, become really good pals. Together with Graham, we had been The Three Musketeers of the office. I was about to demolish that triumvirate completely. The sociopath lacks any sense of authentic allegiance if in the pursuit of his goals a friendship or two needs to be sacrificed, then that is what will happen. Rhoda continued to barrage me with letters. It was becoming progressively imprudent. I would have a fresh note waiting on my desk blotting pad each day. She would often ambush me on the office stairway, between the filing cabinets, and even followed me into the gentleman's toilets!

As is the way with many women, Rhoda soon confided in her 'best friend' Melanie as to just how deep her feelings for me were growing. Melanie would, of course, be the sole of discretion . . . not! The office rumor mill was now kicking into overdrive. It would only be a matter of time before the inevitable resonance of gossip and hearsay would reach the 'bat-like hearing' of our hard-bitten office manager. Rhoda, however, was determined and to achieve her ultimate aim before Bill Roberts could move into action. Being able to deploy his skills of forensic interrogation always brought a smile to his world.

As part of the Unicorn computer systems 'back up' routine, Gareth and Graham would regularly work shifts. When the cat is away, we all know what can happen. Rhoda's latest note clearly wrote down date, time, location, and her intent. The trouble being the location was no less than her matrimonial home. She clearly had every intention of ensuring the risk element would be turned up to 'max'.

What is more, she was also ensuring that the first rule of having an affair would be obliterated – 'don't shit on your own doorstep'! What was I to do? Every cell in my body desired her and I was also battling with the realisation that my feelings for her could become much deeper if I did not keep control over myself. As I have said, until that time - and despite having had many earlier opportunities - I had actually stayed faithful to Pam. Likewise, in the face of an increasingly hostile environment at home I continued to hold out and initially declined the plans that Rhoda had schemed for us both.

Sooner rather than later, Gareth's next night shift was due. I inescapably received yet another summons . . . from my 'femme fatal'.

I will never forget the day when I crossed the Rubicon, because it not only spelt the end of my marriage, it also took me to a new level of risk addiction, which is an inescapable stage of any sociopath's dysfunctional pathway. Would it end Rhoda's short marriage as well though? That remained to be seen. She appeared to be very willing to put the whole 'matrimonial apple cart' in jeopardy.

Again, she was willfully determined to bed me at her own house. I have often deliberated over her reasoning for that one? Could it be some kind of fantasy need for her to have sex with me in her husband's bed? During my subsequent philandering years that would prove to be a female liking, which wasn't to be unique to Rhoda.

I made the excuse to Pam I would be working a night shift with Gareth of all people. A reverse psychological gambit is often used by a sociopath is where they actually deploy an unsuspecting third-party to provide an alibi, whilst at the same time, betraying the very person providing the alibi. In this instance, which would be Gareth. The malevolent aspect is, such an act is much more on a subconscious level, rather than anything cognizant. It is tempting to assert the sociopath is overtly enjoying the added kick by deceiving more than one individual, but that was never the case for me. Over time, I have concluded there was a more subconscious driver behind such motives. I will explain much more as we journey on.

I drove to Rhoda's House. It was a modest little semi-detach in Cranham near Upminster, Essex. With military precision, I arrived dead on 7 pm, just as I had been instructed to do. She knew we would have the cover of darkness by that time. She had told me where to park my car to avoid the telescopic interest of the Cranham neighborhood 'net curtain' brigade. Likewise, and as asked, I sleeked through the back garden gate and headed toward the kitchen door, which I had only used less than a week before when making a contrived social visit to the happy couple. Rhoda was rather surprisingly attired in a two-piece track suit and . . . five-inch stilettos? I was soon to establish her chosen articles of clothing served both expediency and a little fetish of hers.

It took no time at all for our mutual animal instincts to overwhelm our defenses. We were soon in the kind of lithe maneuver I thought would never be realized. She tasted like nectar. I was throbbing throughout my very being.

Rhoda's track suit leggings were already unzipped so she would be able to slip them over her heels with ease. As my exploring fingers smoothed inside her waistband and over her flawless abdomen, she was clearly only wearing the garb I was looking at. Everything about Rhoda's size 8 body was a paragon of beauty. She was twenty-three, quite athletic, and sensually formed. Funnily enough, we never did make it to the bedroom. She was 'naked as a jaybird' in less than a minute of my arrival. Other than . . . those black stilettos!

The entire tryst was playing out seamlessly. I had rounded the back door less than two minutes earlier and now I had ripped off my own threads and stood 'proudly' over her - as she had obligingly spread herself apart on the sofa. Rhoda arched back and the delectable curves of her thighs, calves, and high instep were deliberately emphasized by her titillating footwear. Did we make love? Of course not, we did fuck for hours though. I had just enough conscious thought to savor every kiss, every thrust, every pulse, and, of course, every climax for it would turn out to be the only time I would ever have her.

Two hours had simply evaporated. We both knew for me to get back home in time and for her to try and remove the odor of our assignation, I would have to make tracks. Before I was to leave, Rhoda intended to drop just about the most incredulous of bombshells.

"Sam, before you leave, I do need to say something." "Ok . . . go on?"

"Well, I do love my Gareth. I want my marriage to work. You do realize that don't you?"

WHAT . . . THE FUCK!!

I didn't utter a word. I was speechless, simply because I could feel a wave of anger and disgust washing over me. Sure, we had both just been party to a lustful deception, yet the sheer level of her instantaneous hypocrisy was astounding. I mean, if she had spoken to me the next day with a convoluted level of guilt or something, I would have almost expected it, but to blurt out her undying love for her husband whilst she was still moist with a pussy full of my juices was bloody priceless! It wasn't a challenge for Rhoda to read my mind. I just pulled up my strides and stormed off without a word or even looking back.

I spent the rest of that night with my mind in a cataclysmic meltdown. For a fleeting moment, I had allowed myself to risk my emotions over Rhoda. She managed to take me to a temporary nirvana, only to deflate my ego in such an insincere manner.

I got ready for work very early the next morning. With an inevitable sense of guilt, dread, and nervous anticipation I tried to act as nonchalant as possible over breakfast with my small family. Anyone who has had the kind of experience I had with Rhoda, will know what it's like when trying to engage in banal small talk with your wife or partner whilst being convinced they can see a clear mental movie of the previous evenings entire proceedings playing out above your head.

I still managed to arrive early for work. My feeling of anger was not very far away either. I had anticipated what Rhoda was going to do next, she didn't let me down. Sure enough, as I entered the stairwell, she was already standing in wait on the first-floor landing.

"Rhoda, don't do this, I have a busy morning, so let me just get on please?"

"Sam, I love you; we can't finish now, not after last night."

"What! Do you remember what you said afterwards or are you completely losing the fucking plot?"

I didn't even allow Rhoda to reply. I brushed straight past and headed toward my desk. I can recall sitting down. I was totally oblivious to the 'good mornings' around me. Not because of the enormity of the previous night, which had been usurped by my subsequent emotions, rather because I was now realizing I had, for the first time, experienced a phenomenon I would frequently encounter during my life thereafter. Utter female hypocrisy!

Many a sociopath will have had an experience during their early life, which leaves an indelible marker in their cellular memory. You have just read about mine. That most inspirational of authors, Eckhart Tolle, speaks of this subconscious process in his many books where he coined the phrase 'the pain body'. Now, we all have a 'pain body' but for the addictive sociopath, such an effect will be exaggerated to be greater than most.

In essence, the 'pain body' will imprison you with a level of fear created by an association in the mind of a painful past experience. Where any new experience might result in the same painful outcome. In turn, we are further restricted from really growing, because an underlying anxiety of repeating old patterns remains. The massive irony being, our 'comfort zone' becomes our 'uncomfortable zone'. Thereafter, and crazier still, we continue to go for the same experience, same type of partner, same kind of job, car, boat, dog, and the like, with the same inevitable outcome. Talk about self-fulfilling prophecies. To top it all, we then have the nerve to say something along these lines . . .

"Do you know what, I always seem to attract the wrong 'type' or 'I never get any luck that's going' and 'Why don't I have any money'."

The Law of Attraction has also had much written about it and unfortunately, I believe it has been massively misunderstood. I will later expand on my own theories.

The drama surrounding my affair with Rhoda wasn't just going to go away and still had some way to go. Here was a woman who had made such a contradictory claim about her relationship and marriage, yet she continued to hound me. The pressure was incessant. Not only from Rhoda. The heat was growing elsewhere as rumor mongers around the office were naturally cranking things up for us both. Gossip is very addictive. I piss myself laughing when I observe people frowning and getting all self-righteous about other people's dalliances, but where their own lives are concerned, they always seem to experience a bout of selective memory.

"Ah, but my situation is different."

Yeah . . . right.

At the height of this particular liaison, I had a young team of underwriters working with me. One of them was a chap named, Kevin Late. Just like his name would suggest, he was NEVER early. He was another of those comedic souls who over the years, I have been very blessed to work with. He was part of another office double act supported by phlegmatic wit, a certain Roger Crossly, who despite being in a long-established relationship had for some time been playing around with Rhoda's best friend, Melanie. All good soap opera stuff. This you know I bet right now because your own workplace is just like it. Or maybe not. For the sterile 'PC' working environment, which asphyxiate the workplace of the millennial, has been conditioned over years to blunt the soul and any passionate connection, work, or relationship wise. I am actually glad to be the age I am.

Anyhow, Kevin may have been a laugh a minute but the 'Brave and the Bold' was never going to be an honor bestowed on him. So, when Bill Roberts called him into his intimidating office for his first bout of interrogation, it was like the proverbial lamb to the slaughter. Bill's management style was so conniving and underhanded it would be very difficult for someone to survive him nowadays.

In modern times we hear of stories regarding bullying in the workplace, but the kind of employment protocols and staff recourse that now exist, especially in the public sector, has at least gone some way to stemming the worst excesses of those particular characteristics. There was a constant and intense level of fearfulness among Unicorn staff back in the 1980s.

Amusingly, by this time, my old section head John Browning had been promoted to be Bill's assistant. An upward shuffle they had both enjoyed after retirement of that, 'Wiley Old Boy', Arthur Ogley. Therein, was yet another double act to be relished which very oddly, resembled those two great Hanna and Barber cartoon characters, Dick Dastardly and his sidekick, Muttely! John was such a brown nose. As I suggested previously, he even caricatured the 'Muttely shoulders' as he sneakily laughed at someone else's impending bad luck when being faced with the prospect of Mr. Roberts razor sharp inquisition. I can remember a 'Bambi-like' chap in the office named Adrian Weston, who when asked by Bill Roberts during his annual appraisal . . .

"Adrian, do you enjoy your job at Unicorn?" "Yes, I do Mr. Roberts. Very much thank you." "Oh? Well, you don't do it very well do you?" He was such a joy . . .

The sociopath's uncanny ability to project blame and culpability onto their most loyal of supporters is most disturbing, as if their own problems now belong, as of right, to their friends. You will see countless examples of this among the likes of political leaders, captains of industry, and heads of global corporations. Typically, where there is evidence of some kind of legal impropriety, corruption, or fraud, their most loyal of lieutenants will unwittingly end up on trial themselves, despite having had the naïve belief their close association with the 'Top Dog' would protect them.

They will almost certainly have been repeatedly reassured to that effect. Their sacrifice to deflect blame away from their leader / mentor is a given. Hmmm? Any high-profile cases around at the moment? A US President, or two, springs to mind?

So, it was Kevin who would be next to face the guillotine unless he broke under pressure. He then took a call lasting no longer than fifteen seconds and looking pleadingly over at me, he spluttered . . .

"Sam, which was Bill Roberts. He has asked to see me at once. I ain't done nuffink, erm . . . well, not lately, so it's bound to be about you and Rhoda? I am not sure I can take much more of all this pressure about the affair."

So, there you have a case in point, Kevin was in a real state. I could see the sweat on his upper lip as his eyes were glazing over.

"Well, you will simply have to deny everything."

"But what if he asks whether there is any truth in the rumor?"

"Well, you will simply have to deny everything, won't you Kevin?"

I was being as unsympathetic and as self-serving as ever. Kevin was expected to prove his unswerving loyalty to me, no matter how uncomfortable he might be feeling. He was in the office with Bill Roberts for less than ten minutes. I was soon to find out why. Kevin came out looking ashen faced and uncharacteristically for him wearing a grimace. Instead of walking back to his own desk, he tentatively approached mine.

"Sam, errmm . . . Bill, told me to . . . ask you . . . no . . . tell you, to go and see him. I was shitting my pants in there, but I never admitted to anything."

There you have it again. The sociopath will succeed in making a friend feel so compromised, he or she will actually apologize for misdeeds, which are not any of their own making. Next, comes the blame.
"Nice one Kev. You MUST have given the game away, otherwise
he wouldn't be asking to fucking see me would he now, you prat!"

As I leapt out of my swivel chair, Kevin stumbled backward, and in a complete rage, I stormed off and headed purposefully toward the lion's den. Theatrical outbursts are another characteristic the sociopath will deploy for as dramatic effect as possible. Both Bill Roberts and John Browning were already waiting in situ . . .

By the mid-80s, I had outwardly, at least, become a much more confident individual with a reputation in the office for being both disruptive, and non-compliant. All a mask of course. I marched toward my two inquisitors and mentally ran through my mind what would be my best line of defence. No brainer Samuel, use the age-old tactic, which had been tried and tested over millennia . . . deny, deny, deny!

I did not knock. I never did. With a facile confidence I breezed into an office, which I had never made a habit of visiting voluntarily. No end of my sycophantic colleagues would spend half their working lives trying to find pathetic excuses to drop in on Bill and John, in the vain hope they would be left alone and saved from, in particular, Bill's snarly attention.

"Gentleman, Kevin Late said you wanted to see me?"

I intentionally turned my stare in the direction John Browning with the dual intent of gauging whether my former mentor could be relied on as an ally. If not, to try and marginalize one of my assailants in their own back yard. Just like the man without a backbone, John didn't let me down. He gave me a half-hearted smirk of a smile. Then he looked down nervously at his blotting pad whilst pretending to shuffle some paperwork around his desk. He managed to maintain that nervous posture throughout the entire time I was sat there. As it turned out, his lack of confidence was so obvious, it actually worked in my favor. Bill was so baffled by John Browning's awkwardness; he initially gave far greater attention to his sidekick than his immediate task in hand.

"Do you know why I have asked to see you, Samuel?"

For that opening question, a fairly disingenuous reply was the best ploy to adopt.

"You just had Kevin Late in here. I assume this is about his poor timekeeping Bill?"

Bill Roberts was now wearing a crooked cynical grin on his puffy red face, which I had witnessed on countless occasions.

"Don't come at it with me Samuel, we both know you are screwing Gareth's wife."

There's nothing like using a subtle tactic then. Remember Sam, deny, deny, deny. So, I replied using as wounded a tone as I could muster.

"Uh? What on earth are you talking about Bill? I resent such an accusation"

I again directed my stare at JB as I tried a deflection tactic all sociopath's use when they find themselves cornered, which is to nominate a reluctant ally.

"John, where on earth has such garbage like this come from?"

Before JB could even think of not replying, Bill leant forward as if sensing what my game was.

"Look, unfortunately for you some people in this place are so indiscreet."

Yeah, and Bill was one of the worst culprits ever. He couldn't keep a secret if his life depended on it."

When a sociopath is in a fix, it's always the best tactic to draw matters to the quickest possible conclusion. At all costs, avoid a long and drawn-out defense. As Henry Ford once famously said, "Don't complain and don't explain." I gambled on a counter bluff that assumed the victim in all this, Gareth was probably either the last one to know or even if he did, he was still in such a state of that he hadn't as yet yelled about the betrayal of his wife and his best man.

"Bill what does Gareth say then?"

"Well, errrm, he hasn't said anything to me himself. No, but the rumors are rife you know."

"Oh, I see, I'll tell you what then, I will have a chat with Gareth myself. Shall I?"

This not only wrong-footed Bill because such was his vindictive manner. I just knew he would have wanted 'gloating rights' when revealing his findings to Gareth.

"W . . . what?"

"I will walk straight out of here and ask him if there is anything he would like to ask me."

After all, Gareth hadn't actually said anything to me directly. So, I further gambled Bill would habitually try to counter my gesture and he suitably obliged.

"Well, I don't think we need to cause someone any unnecessary stress, if as you say, there is no substance to these rumors?"

"Great, glad we have that all cleared up then. Wouldn't you agree John?"

JB still could not look me in the eye. "Ok then, let sleeping dogs lie."

I got my sorry arse out of that office with most haste I can tell you. Although, I would still have to bear uncomfortable moments waiting to see if Bill Roberts would be able to resist speaking to Gareth himself. However, he was quite predictable. He absolutely detested the thought of not being fully seized of all the facts. If he had the slightest inkling, he might have got it wrong and make a fool of himself in the process.

For the time being, he would hedge his bets. Hedge he did. To this day I am still none the wiser as to whether he pulled Gareth's chain or not.

Surely, Rhoda would now realize things were getting far too hot to handle and she would back off? Did she hell. She was relentless. The letters and stairway confrontations continued, virtually on a daily basis. She would even be in wait for me by the barrier at the railway station. But why? Her emotional dichotomy still puzzles me to this day. On the one hand, she made it quite clear that she wanted her marriage to survive. Yet, on the other hand, she was risking its destruction at every opportunity. Like so many women, she was becoming increasingly addicted to the drama of it all.

As you can now appreciate, I was accumulating quite a hoard of Rhoda's passionate letters. It never ceases to amaze me, how often a guilty party to an affair will needlessly hold onto potentially incriminating evidence. Almost as if, they have subconscious need to be caught. I am not an unintelligent man. Yet, with bothersome and income-prehensible regularity, I have throughout my life acted in such a reckless manner. The retention of Rhoda's letters was to be yet another perfect example of foolhardiness. I was neither discreet nor secure. I would do no more than bundle them up often without even opening them and stuff them in the bottom of my sock draw. Thus, keeping a well-trodden and traditional path of male stupidity!

Only, is it stupidity? Are we truly able to avoid such behavior through our so called freewill? Anon . . .

My life with Pam and my infant daughter Sarah had become increasingly complex and painfully strained. If Pam's insecurities hadn't already been intense enough, my unpredictable and secretive behavior, was clearly causing her ever greater anxiety.

When I was growing up, my family life had been habitually tight-lipped. It was quite acceptable behavior, not only in my immediate family but, also among my uncles, aunts, and cousins. To overhear . . . "don't say anything to your mum / dad / uncle-Tom Cobbly and all" was commonplace. 'Secrets and lies' was the name of the game, which provided the fertile ground for my 'deception gene' to seed itself. Combined with a yearning for my father's constant approval, I would create ever taller stories in a bid to win his blessing. An ingrained mindset was now well on its way to establishing a lifetime of lies, deceit, and tears.

Unfortunately, our deteriorating relationship was being exacerbated even further, because of the legacy of Pam's own upbringing, which at best, could be described as broken. An innate need to care for her two younger siblings, meant Pam was constantly called upon to help her mother out with such duties. She was then perpetually forced to lie to teachers and school inspectors, about the reasons for her constant absences. Moreover, her personality had, for whatever reason, developed into one that was distrustful, cynical, and rather aggressive at times.

My parents had never particularly taken to Pam and would tell me in private, that whenever they were in her presence . . .

"Feels like we are always walking on eggshells around her son."

I knew exactly what they mean. On many occasions I had experienced that exact same scrunching sensation under my own feet.

As I have mentioned before, Pam had indicated right from the off, she possessed such agonistic behavioral traits. She would boast as if they were a positive attribute. I failed to resonate with these early warning signs, having grown into a fairly confrontational character myself. Sociopaths naturally tend to adopt such an attitude as their default 'defense mechanism'. We were only ever going to have a very adversarial marriage.

Sarah was growing into a happy but not surprisingly, nervous child. Pam doted on her. I loved her deeply, as any father would for the apple of his eye, but she was constantly witnessing fights between her parents. Quarrels grew ever more aggressive. At times, raging. I am not for one moment trying to claim I was the victim of marital violence. Pam could be extremely abusive and possessive. A really foul mouth for any woman. I can remember on many an occasion cringing at the expletives she would use in order to simply punctuate her sentence. I did, however, have an ally through her mother, Naomi.

'Amy' as she was known to everyone, was an amiable a lady as could be and simply adored her family. She would often go without to make sure they were provided for. Amusingly, she herself, wasn't a stranger to using the 'F word'. I truly adored her. We both got on extremely well. I would talk to her at length about how things were 'tail spinning' between me and her second daughter and as one of life's great listeners, Amy always found the time to offer me very sound advice.

Amy would readily admit to me she would also feel bereft at times after being on the sharp end of a 'Pamela tongue lashing'. She was also quite a comic. She loved her bingo. Through her, I became conscious of an esoteric aspect of this world and indeed my own. That of, 'spirituality', which would eventually manifest in my life in the most profound way.

It is, to be fair, most important I must emphasize Pam had many attributes. She was extremely hard working, was a wonderful loving mother to Sarah, kept a spotless home, she clearly had an obsessive-compulsive disorder, and she was a fantastic cook. Indeed, my being indulged by various women over the years who happened to be most skilled in the culinary department, has always been one this life's blessings/

Ironically, Pam being so house proud was to be my eventual undoing. At some point, my sock drawer was going to get an airing. I had been doing my level best to put them away myself. Being the 'OCD merchant' she was, the way I was doing it was never going to be tidy enough for her. To be honest, long before my affair with Rhoda, Pam had already convinced herself I had been playing around anyway. She had, of course, been aware before we were married, I had scored with Janice Moses. When she gave up work to have Sarah, it took her no time at all to start accusing me of re-kindling things with the girl from Basildon.

No matter how much I protested my innocence, she would never be convinced otherwise. A 'jealous mind' does not behave rationally. Those who have studied the brain and the 'left side / right side hemisphere's, which dictate our thought processes, will know the left side, apparently controls our logical, analytical, and objective thinking. Whilst the right side is said to be more intuitive and visceral. Well, I can tell you right now. Pam, for a fair portion of our time together, did not have ownership of the right side of her brain at all. Her psychotic thinking had become most extreme at times, which was long before I ever strayed.

On more than one occasion, I can remember lying awake at night and pondering . . .

Well, she thinks I am playing away anyway, so I may as well satisfy her suspicions.

Pam's paranoia had become so bad, she would map out how long it would take me to walk from the office to the station, the train journey itself, and then the walk from the station to my home. I was not even allowed room for maneuver. If there were train delays or I had to work later than 5 pm, all hell would kick off with a typical 'who are you fucking now, then'?

Such suspicious intensity began to take a real toll on me. After a long day in the office, as I turned the key in the front door, I was like a quivering wreck. So, on the occasion I ended up facing the most volcanic of receptions, the sock drawer had obviously received a much closer scrutiny than normal.

"What time do you call this then?"

I was bang on time, so I pretended not to hear. "I asked you a fucking question!"

I continued to ignore my wife but that was like a red flag to a bull for a consumed jealous woman.

"Ok then, you cunt."

Pam was not averse to using the 'C' word either. The fact our five-year-old daughter was nervously peering around the kitchen door made no difference to her whatsoever.

"Let me ask you another question then . . . cunt."

Here it comes . . .

"HOW LONG HAVE YOU BEEN SCREWING RHODA . . . CUNT!"

I felt surprisingly relieved. I turned around. Before I could utter a word, a broadside of letters and envelopes, were thrown at me accompanied by Pam's fist.

Believe me, Pam was more than capable of throwing many punches in quick succession. She had done so, more times than I care to mention. On this occasion, just the one would be needed. She never said another word. She simply scooped Sarah up in her arms and ran out of the front door. I followed her outside and it then became apparent to me the back-seat and boot of her Ford Sierra was crammed with clothes and essentials.

"I am going to stay at Mum's and don't follow us . . . cunt!"

As she sped off, I could see my daughter's little face and her crystal blue eyes were glaring back at me. I felt shame at the manner of how my deception had unravelled, yet also a sense of self-pity. Sociopaths are always self-serving, even at a time when humility should be the only emotion on display.

CHAPTER 12.

Time For Change

Pam had saved me from the humiliation of slashing my clothes with scissors or throwing them in a heap on the front lawn, at least. The house though, was now lovelorn, and empty. It felt like I was diagonally parked between two parallel universes. Over the next few days, I was consumed with an agonizing feeling of guilt. If I am being really honest, those feelings weighed far more heavily with me for my daughter's sake than for my wife.

I wept for the first time since I was a child. I sat on the lounge floor in a state of shock. I pondered only one question . . . How could I have been so fucking stupid? It was the first time I would ask myself that particular question. I would need to ask that same question repeatedly throughout my life. So why indeed? I have often contemplated one specific answer to that question . . .

"I just couldn't stop myself."

The possibility of, 'Was it meant to be'? Will be examined many times throughout the rest of this story. Anon . . .

To this day, there has been one other burning question from that episode, which I have never been able to fathom. Why did Pam not confront Rhoda and remove her head from her shoulder?

A complete mystery to me. I never dared to ask her either.

On the early Monday morning train, I was contemplating both a life without my family, and what the continual struggle with the whole Rhoda state of affairs was going to entail. People who know me now, will often hear me quote, 'always expect the unexpected'. The next sequence of events was to be no exception to that well-known view on life. In keeping with habit, Rhoda was still loitering around the stairs in wait. I could tell by the frown she was wearing she had intuitively picked up something painful had occurred.

"What's happened?"

I was in no mood to either justify or explain myself. I slowly stepped into her space and through gritted teeth; I spelt out some facts of life.

"Rhoda, if I was you, I would seriously keep my head down, shut my mouth, and just pray Pam doesn't come hunting you down. She found all of your letters and walked out on me last Friday."

Rhoda glared at me . . .

"You are just saying that to put me off."

"WHAT THE FUCK IS IT WITH YOU? I'm not fucking joking your stupid cow, this is it . . . OVER. "I still can't believe Gareth hasn't said anything to you. "If you keep on, I will tell him myself I have absolutely nothing to fucking lose now."

The penny was finally beginning to drop. "So that is it then . . . I mean, really it?"

For fuck's sake, can anyone really be THAT obtuse? I just wasn't prepared to prolong the exchange any longer. I charged off. I was never to speak with Rhoda again . . .

Bizarrely, neither did I ever speak to Gareth again, until my last day at Unicorn, which incredibly, was still another two-years away. The three of us existed in parallels of denial. Eventually, the dust finally settled. We were able to get on with day-to-day working life.

My career at Unicorn most definitely suffered due to the Rhoda episode even though, I had merely conducted myself in a manner akin to the boss man himself. I did manage notable successes and pioneered the first ever 'risk underwriting', which the syndicate would undertake without need to reference cumbersome files. A forerunner indeed, to everything today being processed online. However, ahead of me, there were a few members of the sycophantic senior management team who felt both threatened and resentful of my innovative ideas.

To be fair, Bill Roberts always encouraged and embraced my creativity. His own time at Unicorn was also borrowed, as his unyielding and outdated mode of managing staff was undermined by politically correct regimes, which were now creeping into everyday work practices.

Slowly but surely, Pam inexplicably began to thaw. She and Sarah gradually started to spend more time back at home. As is often the case for couples in such a situation, they delude themselves into thinking they can bury the past and start fresh. Part of our 'reconciliation agreement' was for me to leave Unicorn, which was understandable from Pam's viewpoint; and to throw a house move into the bargain. So great, we have had no end of stress. Let's magnify things with one of the most trying challenges you can ever embark on.

Pam did the house hunting. Women always kick start things as far as that is concerned, don't they? I began my search for a new career. I had been frustrated so many times at Unicorn and despite my successfully deputizing for my senior line manager; I always knew I wouldn't be promoted. I was too much of a threat. If Derek Fairly thought you aspired to his position, you were in his sights, and out you went!

I was increasingly aware a staid office environment was encasing me too. So, when I happened to be talking to a colleague about my career options, she advised . . .

"Listen to me Sam, you have such an abundance of charisma the likes of which could charm the birds of the trees. So, why don't you go into sales of some kind?"

What appeared to be a passing observation triggered something within my consciousness, which was a desire to change direction. Indeed, it would transpire as another factor in my evolving sociopathic tendencies. With haste, I started trawling the recruitment advertisements for sales positions. I believed it would make sense for me to continue in the insurance and financial services industry.

There were a number of opportunities. One seemed to attract my attention in particular, as it was a large US Mutual company, which was starting up a new direct sales force in the UK. Hey, it is always a good idea to be at the beginning of any new enterprise, right?

I applied for the role. Sure enough, I was invited to attend an interview at the London offices of American life and Casualty Mutual Insurance Co. based in High Holborn, London. I met a most charismatic regional manager by the name of Ian Williams. He was in his late thirties. Very stylish, wore a smart pure new wool pin stripe suit, and had an amazing hairstyle cut in a shaved 'number two' on top of a balding head. Yet, he still wore a mullet at the back. We clicked instantly. I found his humorous Geordie personality easy to engage with.

Ian put me at ease. He went about outlining the great plans his new sales teams were going to have for London, and the rest of the UK. He further explained to me, unlike most other rival direct sales teams operating throughout the life assurance industry, my new position would be target driven, yet . . .

"At American Life and Casualty, we do not remunerate our sales teams by way of a commission. We will pay you a basic salary plus a bonus payment based on your sales performance. So, you can earn as much as you like. That's up to you Samuel."

No wonder I liked this Geordie chap. He had not only sold me a dream of money and success, I could also transition from underwriting to sales with a guaranteed salary to allow me time to build up my sales figures. What wasn't to like? I could not have been naiver!

It was a company requirement new recruits had to engage in a period of precontract sales training. Which seemed to make a great deal of sense. Where would I be able to figure out whether a career in selling was going to be the best choice for me? My natural abilities seemed to take to sales like the proverbial 'duck to water'. I was offered the formal position of an 'account executive' no less, with a 'basic salary plus commission', and a Ford XR2 company car. Wow! 'Bertie Big Bananas' had arrived!

My last day at Unicorn was to be the 31st of December 1986. My two pals, Kevin and Roger, had set me up in front of a packed staff-room with the obligatory 'Roly-Poly Strip-a-gram'. After the hilarity and entertainment was over, I brushed myself down as I looked up staring back at me across the room was Rhoda. I had avoided her eyes for virtually two years. We both knowingly afforded ourselves that last visual allure. She was tearful. In that minute or so, as colleagues were peeling away in the direction of the pub to buy me drinks, I felt perplexed rather than any sadness. For, even now, this woman who was living a marital charade, was obviously still holding a candle for me.

I found myself having to play 'catch up' with the crowd who had camped in the pub right next to the Unicorn building. I wound down the stairway inevitably walking up the stairs. There, of course, was Gareth. I don't believe in coincidence. Fate had again decided our pathways would dovetail a final time. Gareth's neck wound in; I could smell his state of awkwardness. He surely must have known what had occurred between me and his bride by now. I stopped halfway and allowed him to continue walking up the next flight of stairs until he was level with me.

My thoughts were crystal clear . . . Come on Gareth, here is your chance. No one else is here so go for it and shout, swear, hit me even, but for Fucks sake . . . DO something!

"Good luck Sam in your new job."

He simply held out his hand and before I knew it, we were shaking. "Cheers."

I just couldn't get another word out. What was the point? Gareth just carried on heading up the stairs and didn't look back.

After more than thirty years together, Rhoda and Gareth are still married. They have three adult children. Gareth is still under contract to the parent company of the old Unicorn business. He has achieved very little in his time there, apart from - having a protracted affair with a married woman . . . in the office! Hmm? Get your revenge then did you Gareth?

From time to time, it has occurred to me, as to how on earth Rhoda and Gareth have managed to handle that inevitable question from their kids when looking at back at their parents wedding day photos, "What-ever happened to that man who was daddy's best man?"

I would have loved to have been a fly on the wall when they were looking at my smiling face 'leaning in' for the photographer. I do need to mention however, despite the stress of the Rhoda episode, I have never since, been as happy at any time in my working life than those nigh on eight years spent at Unicorn. What is more, I must take a last opportunity to share some hilarious anecdotes, which describe the mis-chievousness, which went on at Lloyds of London underwriting syndi-cate.

Barry Copark was the office 'weirdo' make no mistake about that. I can never forget my first meeting with this Dickensian looking char-acter who had a wide face, ruddy completion, and long sideburns. The shoulders of his beige suit were smothered in dandruff. You couldn't fail to notice. His tie was tucked so far down the front of his trousers, it must have gone right underneath and back up the crack of his arse! There was a really embarrassing episode, where Barry had a private stash of 'porn mags' stuck behind his favorite trap in the gent's toilet.

Only for them to then be revealed to the rest of us when a couple of maintenance chaps were unblocking a drain. Barry hadn't quite managed to beat them to it.

'Bill Roberts and the waste bin' was a classic . . .

In the days when Unicorn was based in the centre of the city, burglars had broken in and rampaged through the underwriting floor lifting whatever they could lay their hands on. They then left their 'calling card', when Bill arrived at work the next morning, he was greeted by a massive turd, which had been deposited in his bin!

'Mad Mary' . . .

This creature worked as a filing clerk with my wife Pam. She was Irish, with a thick brogue accent. I don't mind admitting I could never understand a bloody word she was saying. Anyway, she was always absent with one fantasized excuse after another. Having had enough, Bill Roberts decided he was going to have it out with her, by paying Mary a home visit. Bad move . . .

'BR' hadn't quite appreciated the degree to which he would be out of his comfort zone when knocking on the door of her council flat in Hackney, East London. At first, she wouldn't answer. Bill persisted with his knocking. By then, several neighbors were standing at their own front doors, glaring at this awkward looking idiot in a suit. They also rather objected to one of their own being hassled. Eventually, Mary answered her door. Rather than being greeted with a . . . "Hello Bill, what can I do for you?"

Mary snatched open the door and with frying pan in hand, started swinging wildly at Bill's head and screaming "Sweet Mary Mother of God - get off my land, away with yer!"

Bill swivelled and legged it away in fear for his life! Mary never came back to work at Unicorn again.

The 'Granite Man' Terry Pearce, was a real gent . . .

He was a south London lad. He worked on one of the underwriting sections. Apart from anything else, no matter how hard Lainey O'Brien tried, she was never able to catch him out for he simply NEVER made a mistake. Terry was also married to the head of the data input operators, the lovely Maggie. They were a truly devoted couple.

Terry earned the nickname of 'Granite Man' because of his grounded, and unflinching, character. Terry feared no one. I had just a bit of a clue when I started at Unicorn. All the chaps wore Crombie's or Long raincoats over their suits. Terry on the other hand, wore a donkey jacket! The 'Granite Man' was famed for his attitude toward the Underwriter Derek Fairly. The top man was very egocentric. Every evening he would glory in crooning around the underwriting floor and wave us all 'goodnight'. In return, he would lather himself in the cacophony of 'goodnights' coming back at him. All but for a particular reply which could be heard above all the others. 'Yeah, goodnight cock'! Now this went on for an age so in the end 'DF' had a word with Bill Roberts.

"Bill, you must have a word with Terry Pearce, because it is most embarrassing hearing 'goodnight cock' every evening!"

Bill was rather reluctant to do so because he was always wary of Terry. He actually respected him like no other member of staff. And so, Bill very tentatively had a discreet word. What do you think happened the very next evening? Yeah, you've guessed it . . . goodnight cock. Waste of fucking time . . .

Terry and Maggie didn't relocate with Unicorn. They both accepted very generous redundancy terms. Not long after, they were blessed with a baby girl. But a few years later, I heard some incredibly sad news from my mate Graham. Terry had contracted motor neurone disease and still only in his early forties, passed away. Such a debilitating condition didn't seem the right way to go for the Granite Man. RIP . . . Terry Pearce.

So, I finally come back to the longstanding feud between Lainey and Maureen. As I have previously said, there was only ever going to be one winner. Try as hard as 'DF' did, he never got Maureen into the sack. She just knew exactly how to play him. This, in turn, was Lainey's undoing. 'DF' was so smitten with the chase she was often ignored. She bitched, and scratched Maureen's eyes out, and probably had a rag doll effigy in her draw. Her actions just made her appear evermore desperate. So, when it came to the office relocation to Essex, she very reluctantly gave up the ghost and accepted a generous package. She would never again be able to command the kind of position she had held and had previously enjoyed.

Unicorn at Lloyds of London; was THE most successful motor underwriting syndicate in the UK between 1968 and 1991, which was when 'DF' eventually retired. The whole dynamic, and culture, in the industry had changed over that time. Mostly, with overbearing compliance and regulation. Even Bill Roberts found himself ousted in a 'coup' only to be replaced by his 'Uriah Heap' of a sidekick, Jon Browning.

Amusingly, many of the arse licking senior managers who thought they would be in with a chance of taking over, were all systematically maneuvered out by the new regime, which was introduced when Unicorn was taken over by a Plc. RIP . . . Unicorn.

Derek Fairley had a prosperous retirement. He was a man who had most certainly lived his life to the full. Like all sociopaths, mostly self-serving, having said that, he also afforded many people a very good living, which was sustained over a long period as well. Thus, are sociopaths all bad? Depends on who you ask and whether it is someone who has been directly used by a sociopath or not.

Derek died of a heart attack at the age of 72. RIP . . . DF.

CHAPTER 13.

YOUTH IS WASTED ON THE YOUNG

The 1980s was an era, which had as it's subtext, 'Winners only please'. A culture that was perfectly epitomized by direct sales forces, which ran in that most egregious of decades. The comedian Harry Enfield launched a symbolic character of the times called 'Loadsa-money'. The mantra of 'greed is good' spoken by Michael Douglas' character, Gordon Gecko in the movie Wall Street, perfectly illustrated 1980s materialistic zeitgeist.

American Life & Casualty Mutual Insurance Company was a huge multinational financial services and investment organization founded in the west coast of the USA. It had gotten a very sound reputation, built up over a hundred years. Direct sales forces were really reaching their zenith in the 80's. With promises of an unlimited earnings potential, prestige cars, and wide shoulder double breasted suits with overseas 'conventions' for proven 'highflyers'.

Surprisingly, I had very little difficulty convincing my normally cynical spouse this was an opportunity, whereby she and Sarah could be 'richer beyond our dreams. We had both come from very poor back-grounds, so aspiring to the socially upward heights of 'Yuppies', which was a vulgar epithet given to the 'upwardly mobile' demographic who were usually denied the likes of our social class, was most appealing. However, before I could savor the promised rewards, something was about to be inflicted on my small family, which was to nearly upend any plans we had been making.

1987 clocked in. The beginning of any new year is obviously a time for renewed hope and ambition whether it is for the individual or family aspirations. The manner in which my career at Unicorn had ended, rather soured what had been a mostly happy, to say the least, eventful eight years. It had also put unbearable strain on my family because of the 'Rhoda affair'. There was also something else, a health issue, which had begun to manifest toward the end of 1986.

In the earlier autumn, Pam started to complain she was experiencing pains in both her lower abdomen and genital area. Pam was, if nothing else, as tough as they come. She would generally shrug off discomfort and go about family chores and the like with very little complaint. Thus, for that reason, it wasn't lost on me when she called me at the end of my first week's training course with an urgent tone.

"Sam, I am in really severe pain can you get home now? Mum has called an ambulance. She has gone to collect Sarah from school."

Throughout the years of our marriage, we had both experienced some real trauma and conflict. I did still really respect the strength of character of my wife. No matter the deterioration of our romantic feelings. I knew Pam never protested about being in pain. Although she would often call to check-up on me because of her insecurities, it was never just for sympathy. At that time, I was nowhere near the visceral man I would one day become. I just knew in a very intuitive way my wife was in trouble, and most likely, very unwell.

I had to make my excuses to my new sales managers and whilst being slightly taken aback, they completely understood my reasoning for having to leave early. I found myself racing down the steps of the new offices in pursuit of the nearby tube station in High Holborn. I just couldn't stop my mind from tail-spinning as I tried to fight through that afternoon's West End free-for-all rush hour.

When I arrived home, Pam's mum Amy, was in wait with my then five-year-old daughter. They were both clearly distressed.

"The ambulance has taken Pam to Chelmsford Hospital. She is in agony! You know what she is like. She doesn't ever tell you how she is feeling. I bet she had been soldiering on for a while. It has just got too painful for her now."

I scooped Sarah up into my arms and held her soft little face against mine. She was afraid and shaking. I looked deep into her forever crystal blue eyes . . .

"It will be ok sweetheart, I promise you. Daddy has to go and look after your Mummy."

I handed my daughter back to her grandmother gave them both a kiss and anxiously ran toward my car.

Mitchell Allen

It is often said, 'youth is wasted on the young'. I will readily accept that wisdom certainly only comes with age. Although I was, by that time, in my late twenties, I could still be quite naïve. I say that because throughout the whole traumatic time during, and after, Pam's stay in hospital - not one physician, consultant, or nurse, ever mentioned the word, cancer. I also readily admit, it didn't actually occur to me Pam's life was in danger until some ten years after the event.

When I arrived at the hospital reception, the usual mayhem prevailed back then, just as it is now. Nothing has changed in reality. IT systems have mostly replaced files, but the NHS was created for healing the sick rather than 'admin and protocols'! Before I could even get to see Pam, I was greeted by a rather youthful looking and nervous consultant of oriental ethnicity. His accent was quite strong, so I had to really concentrate, in order to grasp the magnitude of the news he was trying to convey to me.

"We don't have a great deal of time Mr. Kirkham. The tumors are very aggressive. We need your permission to operate immediately."

Tumors? What? I can honestly say, I had no idea what a fucking tumor even was. Most certainly, I didn't hear it really meant cancer! Moreover, I didn't ask any questions either. Not a single one, as I was in such a stupor with the speed of events?

"Oh Right? I, scc?"

I didn't see anything really . . .

"Ok then, you had better get on with it."

I had just given permission for urgent and invasive surgery, yet I hadn't seen Pam at all, to discuss the seriousness of her situation.

I rang home and called Amy. I swear, this is how the conversation went, verbatim.

"Hello girl, it's Sam."

"Hello boy, what's happening there?"

"It's all ok. Pam has some tumors or other. They are going to take them away with a bit of surgery. I will let you know then. Please tell Sarah I love her, and her Mummy is going to be fine. I will try to find out about visiting hours."

"Oh, that is good. Thanks for calling boy. Bye then."

That was exactly what I said and what I truly believed to be the extent of things at the time. A lack of awareness on my part meant I was not having any serious feelings of panic. However, my sense of concern would soon take on a new perspective.

Pam was in theatre for hours. As the time slipped by, did it begin to occur to me these 'tumors' were a bit more serious than I had initially perceived? Several hours later, I was becoming really anxious. Then, the consultant who had first greeted me returned wearing a very sober expression.

"Mr. Kirkham, your wife is now out of theatre and resting. She is still very weak. We have administered a sedative."

"Oh, right? What's the score then?"

I used such sensitive language in those days.

"The tumors were even more aggressive than we had first diagnosed. We had to take incisive action. As a result, we think we have removed all the infected and surrounding tissues. We will need to keep your wife under close observation for some time hereafter. I have to tell you now, Mr. Kirkham your wife will not be able to ever become pregnant again because we had to remove her womb, fallopian tubes, and ovaries. I am very sorry."

Not at any point did he use the words 'malignant or cancer'. It would be very different today, I guess. Well, I say that but another episode later in my story will make you wonder?

I state the obvious when I say Pam was never the same woman again. She was very anemic and remained unwell following the operation. If that wasn't bad enough, she had to endure physical and mental trauma of a very premature menopause as well. She convalesced with her mother with typical Pam resilience. She soon rallied. None of us could dissuade her from going back to an arduous cleaning job just barely seven weeks after having had major and potentially life-threatening surgery. We all continued to try and to talk her out of it, but she wouldn't have a bar of it. I offered to stay at home, but she insisted I get back to my sales training at the earliest opportunity.

Pam was a strong and very unique woman.

CHAPTER 14.

THE DIRECT SALES SCAM

History has somehow determined a 'greed is good' culture permeated throughout British society for the duration of the 1980s. With particular responsibility and blame, being laid at the feet of the then Prime Minister, Margaret Thatcher. Who it seems, had overseen a degree of unprecedented social engineering that suited her 'Neo-Enoch Powell' style of politics. Indeed, many of today's liberal minded, and 'woke' political pundits claim all of today's woes have stemmed from her stewardship of the country and her years in No.10 Downing Street. In my opinion, which is complete hogwash!

For my money she was the last true 'leader' Britain has had. I will expand on my experience as to who really runs the nation later. For a short time at least, Margaret Thatcher did manage to wrestle back control, from a faceless establishment 'elite'.

Ok. As I alluded to. The 1980s has also been characterized by the film Wall Street, Harry Enfield's 'Loadsamoney' character, the 'big bang' event in the city of London and selling off and privatization of publicly owned companies and institutions (such as British Telecom, railways, airways, airports, and aerospace), with utilities, gas, electricity, and water. However, from where I am sitting, things are now far more flagrant and conspicuous, than they ever were back then. We just don't have the 'big hair' and matching shoulder pads these days.

Back to Margaret Thatcher then. Before her tenure, the UK was in dire straits. We had barely any funds remaining from an $3 billion IMF loan, which the hapless Labor Chancellor, Dennis Healy, had to beg for due to his government screwing up the economy. People simply couldn't bury their dead and rubbish mounted on the streets. We were not JUST the 'Sick man of Europe', we were also a global laughingstock! The neo-liberal social academics and UK media can insist on rewriting history all they want, but Mrs. Thatcher restored a pride to the UK - and in the eyes of the rest of the world. She achieved this in a relatively short period of time. We all tend to conveniently forget that now.

Moreover, our 'special relationship' with the US was in real jeopardy. It wasn't until we had 'Maggie Thatcher and Ronnie Reagan love in' normal service was restored. Now don't misread me, I think that whole so called 'special relationship' thing is total bullshit. It has always been.

The Yanks indulge us as they know our hapless puppet politicians like to use the term. It suits them to play us like a fiddle. As the character 'Jim Hacker' once said in my favorite sitcom, "Yes Prime Minister . . . We no longer have any real influence; we are just like an offshore American missile base really."

Spot on Jim!

From the time the yanks 'stitched up' a flagging and terminally ill Maynard Keynes, with an onerous one-sided loan designed to bankrupt the UK after WW2, we have been their poodle. When I read the first volume of Harold Macmillan's memoirs, I was further mortified when I discovered the USA government had agreed a similar burdensome loan to the UK after WW1! I just cringed when I saw Gordon Brown acting like an orphaned beggar, as he feebly attempted to gain the attention of President Obama during his few, beleaguered, and neurotic driven years as Prime Minister.

Sales training in the 'life and pensions industry' in the 1980s, was a complete farce and very disingenuous. Life offices would use language like, 'providing for loved one's when they were most vulnerable' or 'ensuring your retirement is a safe and prosperous one'. On the face of it – it makes sense. Trouble was, and remains today, they don't mean a bloody word of it!

In the 80's nearly all life assurance salesman were simply out to win sales and generate commission revenue at all costs. Moreover, the management commission structure, which was based on an 'override' commission calculated and based on the sales of their teams, encouraged such a predatory culture even further. So, the environment was tailor made for a developing sociopath. I was about the meet others who were just like it by the dozen!

To make matters even more immoral, sales directorships of nearly all the major Life Assurance and financial services businesses, even subscribed to various 'psychology tests', used for recruitment of direct salesmen. Whereby, they would use these so called 'assessments' to determine whether the candidate was suitable for sales or management. They were simply a means of demonstrating the level of ego possessed by the applicant and appropriate enough for their agenda of 'ego driven sales commissions'. Manipulation of the ego was the real culprit. It was actively encouraged.

Not being fully seized of such an agenda back then, at that stage of my so-called growth, my own ego combined with a starry-eyed ambition for a successful life, 'success' in this instance being measured purely by generation of commission. So, I was open to all manipulation I could muster. So were numerous others.

Direct sales forces within the financial servicсs industry have invariably been replaced by desk-based and soulless sales teams, whose method is equally as immoral. But in the 80's, they had reached a peak, where salesforces working for Abbey Life and Hambro life had thousands of so-called 'associates / account executives / consultants'. Any term was used to avoid the actual word SALESMAN. Together with literally hundreds of sales managers, they all formed part of a sales 'pyramid'. Which in reality, was a glorified 'House of Cards'!

Furthermore, the immorality of the whole venture, began at the outset with recruitment long before a rookie salesman sold a single policy, investment, or pension plan. The recruitment process was nothing short of egregious cynicism dressed up as a 'golden opportunity to further your career and realize your dreams' Yuk! Still turns my guts over even as I write it.

Here is how it worked. Sales managers were obviously given sales targets for 'gross' commissions, further increasing their teams' manpower levels. The pyramid was such, no upper limit, quality levels, or retention of manpower was ever truly set. Sure, vapid language and terminology was used to make it 'appear' a professional and responsible environment was being created, but in truth, the directors did not give a flying fuck!

Looking back, the job advertisements for such positions were just laughable and extremely dishonest. The job would often be advertised as a 'basic plus bonus' (never use the word commission) with a company car, and an annual oversees convention to some sunny and exotic location or other. When the next mug would call in and inquire about the post, very conveniently they would be told . . .

"Thanks for calling about a career with the 'Acme Life'. Unfortunately, that position has just been filled. If you really like the idea of truly fulfilling your potential, we still have other exciting positions available with equally outstanding opportunities."

The inexperienced and gullible candidate then falls into the trap and sadly, agrees to an interview. Now it would be fair to say, a small percentage (out of literally hundreds of thousands, I exaggerate not) will go on to have a successful career in life assurance sales. However, the attrition and carnage that will befall the rest was, and still is, a fucking moral disgrace.

So then, Mr. 'Gullible' would go along to an interview, where he will meet a cigar puffing 'hot water bottle' of a regional manager. The manager would sit there telling all sorts of tall stories about how various chaps who used to be dustbin men, bus conductors, second-hand car salesmen, double glazing reps (I met dozens of them), and the odd former brain surgeon succeeded in becoming their top 'president high priests' or some such daft title commonly bestowed upon top producers. He would then walk the chap, with a 'beef like' hand firmly on his shoulder over to an 'assistant branch manager' who would give some 'technical information' about the role, and (this was the worst bit) play a sales video so cringe worthy syrup practically oozed out of the volume control. Finally, there would follow a 'sneak preview' of next year's oversees convention, which would only be for the 'high achievers' with

the 'ABM' as he would be known throwing in for good measure. "I can see you and your Mrs. there, right now."

This may sound like frivolous and flippant language, but it is exactly how I remember it.

The next challenge was how to deal with obtaining prospective sales. Their solution to that particular task was alarmingly simple. Raid the bank accounts of as many friends and family members you could lay your hands on! It was, of course, dressed up as 'how to obtain referrals and networking'. They would even hand out copies of sales classics, such as . . . How I Raised Myself from Failure to Success in Selling, by Frank Bettger. It was a way they could allay the fears of the recruit and most importantly, isolate the objections of his fearful spouse who would be seriously fretting as to why her idiot of a husband was about to walk away from a job that paid a regular wage, to one that was in reality, commission only!

Please remember, language such as 'commission, risk, no wages at the end of the month, stress, and dire mental illness to follow' would be knowingly averted and supplanted by language such as, 'bonus, convention, reward, hard work, and no upper limit to an ever-higher income' etc. I am afraid to say, it was and still is, dependent on the manipulation, which was presided over by many sociopathic sales directors, which was essential to groom naïve and fragile egos into 'believing' they could be the 'high achievers' of tomorrow.

Much of this mind manipulation technique came over from the USA. Doesn't it always? Back in the mid-1950s when direct sales teams were being formed in UK, our own life assurance and double-glazing industries wholeheartedly embraced such practices. Anyone who has seen the hilarious movie, The Tin Men, starring Danny de Vito and Richard Dreyfus, will know exactly what I am talking about. Equally, Glengarry Glen Ross, which stars Al Pacino and Kevin Spacey, with a brilliant performance by Jack Lemon, is another excellent example. It perfectly exemplifies the sales methods still used today. Indeed, the latter portrays another 'sin' actively encouraged by sales managers, which is envy! Yet again, divide and rule!

It didn't take me too long to witness that specific mindset, which was constantly perpetrated by the senior management teams. As for the lies . . . well . . . it was nothing short of unhealthy and pathological at times! So, sales managers would always, naturally, favor their high producers and ensure low producers knew just that. The dark art of always keeping best sales leads like a 'carrot and donkey' trick was rife. Moreover, 'referral' techniques and scripts were designed to basically exploit the circle of friends and families of the salesman. If the new recruit wasn't able to extend his circle of influence beyond immediate social groups, then the inevitable would soon follow . . . he was gone!

Did the companies care? Of course not! Logic would suggest you should recruit slowly and nurture the elite who had an ability and talent to be natural networkers. Even more importantly, could 'close a deal'. I will expand on the merits of that skill later. However, the companies did the opposite. I eventually become a branch sales manager. I will elaborate further on that eventful experience, but I recall thinking right from the off, 'this is fucking carnage'.

Before being promoted into a management role, and what an illusion that was, I was stuck firmly in first stage of three, which eerily describes the process all salesmen go through . . .

1. Starry eyed enthusiasm;
2. Complicated sophistication; and
3. Professional simplicity.

Few ever really make it to stage three. 80% drop out at stage one. 19% at stage two. Yes, barely 1% become established as so-called long term high achievers.

1. Starry eyed enthusiasm . . .

As the term would suggest, most sales managers did such a brilliant job of conning, err . . . I mean recruiting. You would see a revolving door of new sales associates sitting there hanging onto every word of the recruiting manager as if he was some kind of 'Pied Piper'. Inevitably, one or two would ask 'that question', which all sales managers knew was coming, but privately dreaded having to answer.

"How do we pay our bills, while waiting for commission to come through?"

The scripted reply was a disgrace not only because it was immoral and a gross misrepresentation. It would propagate so much pain and distress to well-meaning naïve people doomed to fail before they had started their new 'career'.

"Well, we have a great means of supporting you called, 'FEP - Financial Establishment Plan'."

Yeah right. In reality, 'FEP' was simply a means of lending sums of money against future commission paid as a percentage or 'advance' against total commission for each new policy or savings plan a new recruit sold. The problem being the advance was repayable back to the company if plans lapsed or didn't actually go into force. This could have been for no end of reasons such as a failed medical or the client simply changed their mind and opted for a cancellation, which was allowed under a 'cooling off' period.

The system was really open to abuse. The smarter or more likely desperate recruit soon figured out money was 'loaned' when the case had only been 'submitted'. It was not even underwritten at that stage. Consequently, there were no end of dubious sales going on which would never see the light of day. The implication would ultimately prove to be dire for both the recruit and his immediate branch manager. I will expand further, when I come to telling the woeful tale of my own branch manager experience.

2. Complicated Sophistication . . .

This is the period most salesmen end up being stuck in (irrespective of the industry) after surviving the initial massacre of the induction and training period. Following the inevitable early failures, they will have simply been treated as 'cannon fodder'. Of those remaining, virtually all remain at stage two for the rest of their sales career. To be fair, all salesmen actually have to endure this period. Only those with real tenacity and guile successfully join the sales elites.

I have seen an endless number of hardworking and diligent guys and the odd lady for that matter, prospecting away. Despite many sales meetings, they couldn't close a paper bag if their lives depended on it. When stuck in stage two, they would prepare endless quotes, analysis, reports, and presentations. They would even hold seminars, workshops, and buy-in 'qualified' mailing lists. Then, send out voluminous mail shots (Yes, I know, straight in the bin, eh?). Their entire sales 'modus operandi' would cost them a fortune. Even some branch managers would cough up as well. The whole thing would result in only a few very poor sales leads.

They then compound matters further by actually talking themselves out of the sale. As a sales manager, I would often accompany one of these so-called 'established' salesmen on a home visit to one of the 'orphan leads'. An orphan lead was a former client of a long gone associate, who would either have failed miserably or had 'jumped ship' to another life assurance office. Needless to say, there were lots of these 'orphans'. Remember, they would often be used as a bargaining chip overpay or support from the sales manager. It was akin to extortion really.

Anyway, I would sit there in agony most the time wearing a disingenuous smug look on my face while the associate would conduct what was supposed to be a 'hot' sales opportunity. That was based on the accepted understanding there is a greater probability of writing further business with an already existing client.

Our man would go through all the 'pre-amble' of patting the client's dog, congratulating them on the rosettes plastered all over the walls for award-winning racing pigeons, and . . .

"Hey that's a great photo of your mother." Only for the prospect to correct you.

"Errmm yes, it's the wife."

If that wasn't bad enough, after nearly two hours of bringing the prospect to 'a close', despite having ignored every 'buying signal' under the sun, our man would come out with the most priceless statement of all . . .

"Ok, Mr. Brown, I am sure you will need time to think about it?"

I have witnessed that one so many occasions. Even from people who had been in the business for years. No end of sales training and courses would include, at induction and refresher courses, how to deal with sales 'objections'. Christ, there have been countless sales books published by millions on virtually that subject alone.

Yet, despite all of that, if the salesman doesn't possess a 'killer instinct', he is doomed to eke out a painful endurance at best. At worst, bankruptcy.

Section two is totally illusory. It is a means of justifying constant, yet useless activity. In the parlance of the British civil service, it is actually in reality, 'masterful inactivity'. These salesmen may stay in the business for a long period of their careers, but barely survive. As far as their neighbors and peers are concerned, they create an illusory appearance of being a high achiever. Credit card limits, overdrafts, and mortgages will be stretched to beyond their limits.

3. Professional simplicity.

A very rare bird indeed. No doubt, since my time in the financial services industry, which came to a nasty and abrupt end in 1998; the 'CPD' - Career Professional Development - yeah, that old chestnut and so called 'compliance' has near on suffocated the genuine salesman out of existence.

Some might say for the better but as merited as that might sound, people just don't wake up in the morning with a burning desire thinking to themselves . . . I must protect my family and future retirement and buy some life assurance and a pension plan today. Therein, remains a huge future financial burden and a dichotomy for the nation.

When a salesman possesses a natural sales ability and demonstrates a studious work ethic to match then he will stand every chance of progressing his career and establishing himself as a so called 'high achiever', it was a lack of the latter that would repeatedly be my own undoing.

The key to success is as old as the hills. Yet, so few in sales careers ever really carry it off. 'KISS'!

K . . . eep
I . . . t
S . . . imple
S . . . tupid.

That in essence is what professional simplicity was all about. Sure, the salesman should put together recommendations backed up with appropriate information, but only use whatever is necessary and no more. I can rattle off more old sales techniques and clichés than you can shake a stick at. So, few ever really get to grips with them. Despite knowing all of that, however, if you couldn't master the one final sales step, 'The Close!', then you might as well pack up and go home.

With glee, I would again like to refer to that iconic Al Pacino movie, Glengarry Glen Ross. In one of the early scenes, a 'high producer' who is excellently portrayed by Alec Baldwin, is mentoring the also-ran salesman in a real estate office, whilst doing so, he uses one of the all-time iconic acronyms associated with selling . . . ABC!

A . . . lways
B . . . e
C . . . losing

The guys who master 'professional simplicity' not only have the highest levels of activity, and smart activity at that, they are indeed closing the sale the moment they engage the client because it is not just a numbers game for them. Here, I am also afraid to say, the voracious instincts of the sociopath will be heightened ever more. They will have their radar attuned to every 'buying signal' that will be subconsciously 'signposted' by their prospective client. Moreover, they will have developed a high sensory awareness that is actually more attuned to the subconscious mind than the conscious. They are almost mesmeric. They know it, too.

I will expand on my experiences and theories in this regard much later. For now, I can assure you, I have seen a number of these 'super high-producers' who clearly have a kind of sixth sense. Their clientele became akin to cult members. Their customers appear powerless to actually say the word 'no' and over time, I would become increasingly aware of how the 'collective consciousness' works and would exploit such a phenomenon to my own rapacious ends.

It was at the beginning of my 'sales / lying career' I did meet an incredible soul who was one of those extremely rare individuals. The

1% of the 1% who actually did the job 100% professionally, simply, and ethically. His name was Vahick Vardanyan.

Vahick was Armenian. When I first met him, he had been working for the company for over a year and had firmly set up himself as their number one producer. He had come to the UK after having to leave Iran following the Islamic insurgency of 1979. He had applied for over 1,500 jobs in the UK and barely got an interview. What a loss that was to the other 1,499 . . .

Vahick told me when he came to the UK, he only knew four other people, and they were his brothers! He was 5'10" with his young Omar Shariff handsome looks. He was always immaculate. I swear, he must have ironed himself every morning before setting off for the office. It was following his advice I learned to only wear 'crisp white shirts' when wearing a suit and tie.

"Samuel my friend, only EVER wear a white shirt. That way, it doesn't matter what combination of suit and tie you choose they will always match."

I have kept to that 'combo' to this day. It would be fair to say, I have received an endless number of compliments over the years about how smart and distinguished I look in a dark navy suit and tie.

On a much more sober point, it also introduced me for the first time to a uniform, which I would eventually understand its significance at a most disturbing level. The dress code of the 'Illuminati'. Anon . . .

Such was Vahick's natural appeal and generous personality. In no time he developed from a completely clean canvas, a warm client 'referral chain' that would be the envy of anyone in the industry. Laughingly, many of those businesses had refused him an interview, then came in hot pursuit offering him one lucrative package after another.

"Samuel these foolish people are now offering this humble Armenian, a 'pot of Gold' to join them. Yet, only eighteen months ago, they could have had Vahick's services for . . . free! Ha-ha!"

He would bellow at that notion. No matter how much they raised the ante, he would never join any of them. I simply adored Vahick. As I still believe to this day, 'if' I had taken his advice and hung onto his shirt tails, my life would have taken a completely different pathway. I guess I didn't have any choice, eh? Remember, no freewill . . .

Come rain or shine, Vahick would arrive at the office well over an hour before anyone else. His positive mental attitude was sublime. I have never witnessed anyone use the mantra of 'PMA' with greater effect. Tony Robbins had nothing on the charismatic and super intelligent Armenian, I can tell you. He simply oozed positive energy and was incredibly charismatic. With his spellbinding smile, he had them eating out of his hand. He most certainly was not . . . a sociopath. I must emphasize this point because many sociopaths do a very convincing job of masquerading as 'a Vahick'. I did just that for far too long, that's for sure. The real deal, so to speak, is very rare indeed. Vahick's level of integrity was peerless and every single day he would announce to the rest of the office . . .

"I love my clients."

He truly did as well. This was not just some Armenian rhetoric designed to woo the savings out of wealthy old ladies. He felt it from the depth of his soul. His 'clients' came from every social demographic imaginable. I was always rather uncomfortable with the use of the term 'client' by life assurance direct sales organizations. I will explain why I felt like that later. It didn't matter how rich or poor they were though, Vahick adored them all . . .

After normal business hours had finished, he would often muse late into the evening, proudly telling endless anecdotal stories about his childhood when he was growing up in Armenia. He insisted that he had acquired his unique style of salesmanship - many decades before - when as an infant, he had to sell baskets of trinkets at the local bizarre and wasn't allowed home until the very last bauble had been sold.

Vahick went from strength-to-strength. He mentored me whenever he could, but such was his acute competitive nature. Woe betides anyone who tried to beat his monthly sales performance. I actually did achieve that no mean feat on just one occasion. I will never forget how amusing it was to see this consummate gentleman being so compromised. As he was coaching, and encouraging me, onto greater achievements; yet he was still fiercely battling to keep his peerless position as number one.

With typical Vahick aplomb, he was so gracious when being beaten and handsomely congratulated me when the month end figures were announced. Throughout that entire handshake, he warmly smiled at me. Then, stepping forward, he said with love and no intimidation whatsoever . . .

"Congratulations Mr. Kirkham my friend. Savor your achievement for as you will surely know, it will never happen again. Ha-ha."

It never did . . .

Then the inevitable happened. Vahick's incredible performance was noticed by the powers that be within the executive force of the parent company located on the West Coast of America. So, overcame one of their hundred or so 'vice presidents'. I still find that so amusing within the US corporate world. They offered Vahick the earth to move his family lock, stock, and barrel - for him to bestow his 'love' on some American citizens.

Vahick's integrity was such, he didn't just pack up and follow their dollars because he genuinely agonized over leaving the clients, he 'loved' here in the UK. He sought their counsel, he was, of course, held in high esteem by all of them. Unsurprisingly, they enthusiastically encouraged him to take the offer so he could progress his career and the lives and well-being of his young family.

As I have already alluded to, I cannot speak more highly of that polished Armenian. I recently Googled his name. I was so pleased to see he is still out there across the pond 'loving all of his clients'. Hopefully, he might get to read this book and wonder what fate had befallen, 'Mr. Kirkham, my friend'. God bless you Vahick.

I was now proven as a 'high producer' myself. I was twenty-eight years of age, sharp suited, and had everything to play for but I was only a few weeks away from a single traumatic event that would quite simply change my life and the manner I would conduct it thereafter.

CHAPTER 15.

THE CAR CRASH

I was endeavoring to follow as closely as possible the sales strategy of my mentor Vahick. After all, if such a methodology worked for the master, then why try, and reinvent the wheel? Unfortunately, there was a real downside to my life at that time, due to the ever-increasing tensions at home. From a physical perspective, Pam had made a remarkable recovery from her cancer operation. Emotionally, she was on occasion, seriously volatile.

I didn't know which way to turn at times. My sales role invariably involved working a great deal in the evenings, which from Pam's perspective, meant I could be just about anywhere. Other than the Rhoda affair, I had kept a lid on things as far as actually bedding other women was concerned. There were an increasing number who found the persona of a charismatic salesman and newly equipped with a hypnotic ego, rather appealing.

It was early 1987. Pam's convalescence happened to coincide with the coldest winter for a decade. The UK experienced a blanket of snow that just lay frozen and stubbornly refused to thaw. So, it was on an icy very slippery morning, I took delivery of my new company vehicle, the Ford XR2. I wasn't exactly a reckless driver, but the performance of that little 'buzz box' could be quite a ripper at times. Albeit it wouldn't be the car's potential speed as the reason for my experiencing a life changing event that ultimately lead to my pathway of destruction that continued for nearly three decades into my future.

Through my mind's eye, I still replay every moment of that bitterly cold February morning as I drove off from my house in Essex. On my way to the office in Holborn, West Central London on that particular day due to frost-bound road conditions, I set off earlier than usual at 5 am. Just as it had been for over a month, the journey was slow and arduous with only a single lane with contraflows every few miles along A12 arterial road. Normally, there were two or three clear lanes. Moreover, I coveted my brand-new sparkling and glistening red Ford XR2!

As I approached the turn off for the sleepy Essex Village of Ingatestone, I was traveling a speed of 40 mph. The three-week-old frozen snow was some two feet thick. Only two of the usual three lanes were open along that particular stretch of the A12. I was cruising along in the slow lane when a lorry ahead of me happened to swerve as the driver tried to steer his vehicle around what I later discovered was a frozen clump of ice embedded with stone and Essex clay that must have rolled down an icy grass verge onto the nearside lane.

The Lorry driver hadn't managed to avoid it properly. The impact meant a football sized frozen missile ricocheted off the rear wheel and then hurled itself toward whatever would be coming next . . . me and my new XR2! What happened next was like a slow-motion horror. I can clearly remember watching this solid dark silhouette hurtling through the air directly toward my windscreen. There was no time to take any evasive action as the stone hit the target with such a force that what followed seemed to defy the very laws of physics.

I remember experiencing a kind of 'weightlessness' as my car didn't just roll; it jarred headfirst into the road and then 'end over end'. It rolled twice further onto the snow-covered verge. The whole experience felt like a drawn-out time warp with a hollow awareness of my fast-compressing cockpit and screaming noise of a tearing and twisting chassis being crushed and contorted beneath me. I blacked out.

"You were dead mate!"

Were the first words I remember hearing as I slowly regained a blurred level of consciousness.

"If I hadn't seen it for myself, I would never have believed it."

As my cognitive powers slowly reacquainted with the inside of my cranium, I became aware the excited voice belonged to an officer of law.

"W w-what . . . w-where?"

I tried to raise my head, but the traffic officer insisted I lay still. "Someone up there is looking after you, my friend. You are in one

piece. I can't see any injuries from here and I don't know if you have sustained any internal damage. An ambulance is on its way. Try and breathe slowly and keep calm for me. Good man."

The officer attempted to explain to my still muzzy brain he had been riding his motorcycle just two vehicles behind my own. He had seen my car elevate from the rear as if, as he put it . . .

"Some fucking giant was lifting it from underneath."

The officer skidded to a halt on the ice as my vehicle somersaulted in front of him and pursuing traffic. He had leapt off his motorcycle having fully expected to be greeted by the sight of my being mashed to a pulp in the wreckage.

He continued . . .

"I just couldn't believe my eyes. I could see you slumped and actually stirring. There was a strong smell of petrol, I didn't have a chance to call in the fire rescue service. I reached in and somehow your seat belt housing hadn't got damaged. So, I unbuckled it and wrenched you over the steering wheel and through the window. Your left leg might be feeling it. There doesn't seem to be any broken bones. I just had to get you away from the vehicle in case it blew. I just can't believe it. I just can't believe it."

I was becoming increasingly aware of the noise and ensuing chaos, which was surrounding me. As I lay there, I tried to glance over my shoulder. I didn't feel any noticeable pain so I craned my neck around and I could see a trail of vehicles backing up the A12 for what seemed like an endless gridlock. Had I caused this? Fuck . . .

An hour had gone by before the ambulance could eventually fight its way through the traffic snarl-up and the paramedics eventually gave me a first examination by the roadside. I could sense their amazement at my physical condition and how composed and decidedly well I appeared to be?

"You must have someone up there looking after you mate. You don't have a scratch on you."

He was now the second member of the emergency services to say that to me after being pulled from the wreckage. Furthermore, whilst it is something we might all say when someone has had a miraculous escape, that particular phrase would be said to me on numerous occassions over the following three decades. If my survival wasn't providential, then I don't know what is. Overtime, the consequence of that one single event would manifest in so many ensuing dramas. Not only relating to my life, but sadly, for so many others too.

I was driven to Harold Wood Hospital for a thorough examination. Just like the police and paramedics beforehand, the attendant nurses and doctors continued to make the same observation about my apparent well-being. A miracle indeed, and one of a definite kind I would experience on no less than a further four occasions!

So, what's all this car crash 'total loss' malarkey all about then? Nothing to it really! Regrettably, that was my initial reaction to such a death-defying event. I simply hadn't grasped at all; just how close I had come to crossing over to 'the other side' so to speak. Now, I use the term 'crossing over' as I am now fully seized of its true significance but in 1987, it held no real meaning for me.

On that same evening, and unbeknown to me, my mother-in-law was waiting in the foyer of her local bingo hall in Romford. She was waiting for her old friend 'Mitzy', the 80-year-old lady who I have previously mentioned used to read 'tea leaves' and was a bit of a 'mystic'.

Now let me be very clear here, I had only taken delivery of my new car the day before the accident. Amy, being the old East End matriarch she was, would never have had any real interest in what company vehicle I might be driving. Pam had only just told her about my extraordinary car crash.

So, there was Amy, milling around the entrance of the mecca wearing her customary cotton head turban chuffing away on a fag, when the petite and frail-white haired figure of Mitzy pushed her way through the revolving door and homed in on her expectant friend.

"Hello Mitzy girl, you, ok? You look like you have seen a ghost. Ha ha."

Mitzy didn't initially respond. Then, taking Ami's forearm in her tiny skeletal hand, she asked . . .

"Amy, has Sam had his accident in his red car yet?" "Fuck! MITZY!"

"Oh my God . . . it's happened, hasn't it?"

"F . . . Fuck! It happened this morning girl, but Pammy only told me half hour ago, but he's ok. He's badly shaken up but all in one piece! How the hell did you know?"

"I was 'told' by my 'spirit guides' on the way here Amy. I had a feeling of absolute dread. I am so relieved he is ok. That boy will always have a charmed life you know."

Amy staggered and grabbed the nearest chair as she slumped in an absolute fluster. She totally trusted her old friend's psychic ability and had seen her extremely accurate 'fortune telling' on a countless number of occasions. This time, however, it was just too close to home. She gazed, almost paralyzed, across the foyer. How Mitzy could have known and that it was a bloody RED car . . . There had been no fatality reported so the news of the accident hadn't made the local news or the TV. Moreover, the radio had only reported the traffic hold up, so no vehicle details had been given, not even hearsay.

I was discharged from hospital after just a couple of hours. Pam greeted me together with a very anxious little Sarah. She leaped into my outreached arms with my heart pounding away in my chest. I couldn't hold her closely enough. The whole day had been the most surreal of experiences. All I wanted to do was get home, bathe, and sleep.

That accident, the experience, and chain reaction that started at that point in time, will be referred to, and expanded on throughout the rest of my story. If nothing else, you the reader, will then have a much greater insight and understanding of the phenomenon of . . . 'cause and effect'.

CHAPTER 16.

WISHED ME DEAD

As my eyes opened, I not only felt alienated, I was also very aware, I could not move. I was really in shock. My mind was telling me to get up, but my body was most unwilling. Then, as my waking consciousness kicked in, the next and very unwelcome sensation almost overwhelmed me, pain! Jesus, the sheer agony as every fibre in my body was screeching out. Each and every nerve end felt as if they were being tortured over a dedicated furnace. The agony would feel like that for the next couple of days, so it was on day two of my enforced bed rest, a conversation would take place, which would not only determine my immediate future but also seal Pam's fate as my wife.

You may have heard the expression, 'careless words cost lives'? Well, on that particular day Pam would use a sentence, whilst it wasn't intended to be careless, she wasn't aware I had overheard her. She was fielding one call after another from my parents, friends, well-wishers, and work colleagues who were all asking after my well-being. I have previously alluded to the fact Pam was not known for her tolerance. She had none indeed. Whilst it may have been as a result of having had to repeatedly go over the same ground, eventually, she received a call from her younger sister, Gwen.

The call just happened to coincide. although I don't actually believe in coincidence, with my dragging myself out of bed to use the bathroom. Pam must have thought I was still fast asleep, but something intuitively told me to be extra quiet, stand at the top of the landing, and listen . . . hard.

"Yeah, what a fucking day. He's still in bed. Hasn't been able to move. Do you know what though Gwen, I came so close to being nearly half-a-million quid better off and with no bloody mortgage. Fuck me, yeah, that's how much life assurance cover he's got, and the mortgage is covered as well. Me and Sarah would have been made girl."

Those words have been embedded in my soul to this day. I was mortified, not so much that Pam could wish me dead; but she could be so grabbing for the money! She had always been very materialistic. I would become attracted to no end of women with such a flaw. Cars, houses, and trinkets were all so important to her. I lay back on the bed and can still clearly remember my thoughts . . . you are gone.

The following day, I was feeling fortified and strongly compelled to go and inspect the wreckage of my vehicle to see for myself the carnage I had miraculously walked away from. I intended to go on my own but Pam being Pam, she insisted on accompanying me. The vehicle wreckage had been transported to a local compound belonging to a loss adjuster. I was very apprehensive about the sight I was soon to behold. Upon our arrival, I produced the requested vehicle documentation. We were pointed in the direction of the sorry XR2. For what seemed like an age, we both just stood there in stillness, and gazed at the twisted metal and rubber. Pam was the first to break the silence.

"How the fuck?"

I was thinking exactly the same . . .

"You said the copper pulled you free but there is nowhere to pull you free . . . from?"

In the midst of all the carnage and the attentions of the emergency services, I hadn't actually looked back at the car, which had so nearly been my coffin. But there it was, mangled and mashed, with hardly a perceptible gap anywhere for my body to have been extracted from without the need for any cutting equipment. I approached the car, put both my hands on the dented and crumpled roof, and peered in.

"Pam, I just don't know how . . . it's all bloody a miracle?"

Yes, it was a miracle. It was also beginning to dawn on me something, somewhere, beyond my control was at work? I could not prevent myself thinking . . .

I should be dead? Nothing can stop me now. I can do what I want, go where I want, and take whatever risks doing so. A dark energy of sorts was tapping me on the shoulder. I looked up and over at Pam who was clearly pensive. It was as if she could sense what was going through my mind . . . You are gone!

Over the next few months, I began to apply my new mantra with the precise intention of releasing myself from my suffocating marriage.

Even before the car accident, things had seriously deteriorated between us, yet I kept thinking about Sarah who I adored, and Pam knew it. She was the apple of my eye. She also adored her dad. I wasn't by any means a model parent, but I did my best to provide for my family and worked long, hard, hours.

Pam's illness and battle with cancer left more than just physical scars. Looking back, whilst she couldn't have helped being so ill, her attitude and insecurities heightened to such a scale she was acting quite unhinged at times. Coupled with her lack of any trust after my affair with Rhoda, it was all quite understandable really. Having said that, I couldn't get her words out of my mind. I was no longer prepared to indulge her antics. The gloves were now off. Where I had pretty much resisted the advances of other women, from now on I was going to relish such attention, and whenever possible.

I had always assumed my marriage to Pam would finally come to an end in a fairly volcanic manner, akin to her reaction when she had discovered my affair with Rhoda. However, it just didn't happen that way. I recall our both sitting in the lounge after Sunday lunch and instinctively we both looked up at each other.

"Pam, we can't go on like this, its madness." "I know, so what next then?"

"I will move out and soon. We will have to make arrangements about Sarah."

"She is going to be so upset, she loves you so much."

We both remained surprisingly calm as we talked through various financial arrangements and the ongoing care of our daughter. It was refreshing to have a conversation that didn't end up as a slanging match along with incessant point scoring. We agreed we would both talk to Sarah together. I would move out within the week. However, before doing so there was someone who I wanted to see and discuss my plans with.

I will readily admit, whilst I was relieved to have achieved an agreement with my wife, I was still feeling great sadness. At times, I couldn't control my emotions. I had always adored my mother-in-law, Amy. I made a point of dropping in on her prior to my next evening appointment. She was usually warm, smiley, and welcoming. On this occasion as she opened the door the look on her face was one of an anxious and troubled lady.

"Hello boy, come in, sit down. Pammy has told me."

I parked myself. Before I could utter a word Amy pronounced . . . "Boy, I have seen this coming for a while now, and although I love

my daughter dearly, I want you to know I don't blame you for going. I have sat there listening to how she has spoken to you, and knowing what a fiery bugger you can be, I would not have been at all surprised if you had run away long before now."

I sat silently; she continued . . .

"That girl has suffered a lot in her life. I haven't always been able to give her the love she has needed, or to be the mum she has craved for. But I have been on the receiving end of her vicious tongue many times. It's only because I am so soft, I haven't retaliated myself."

There was still more to come from my perceptive mother-in-law. "Pammy doesn't open up to me, but I am not as 'green as I am a cabbage looking', boy. I know you have played away. You are a typical bloke. But I think you have put up with more than most men would have with from my daughter. I also know she has used her fists? Am I right?"

I couldn't believe what I was hearing. I could certainly have a real temper at times, but I would never dream of hitting a woman. Pam on the other hand, had an even sharper temper and didn't think twice about lashing out. I once saw her in a pub take a 16 stone bloke apart, just because he had accidentally spilt his drink over her.

"I would never have said anything Amy but yes, she is like a devil possessed at times. Poor little Sarah has even jumped in and stood between us."

The conversation then moved onto what my plans were going to be and the arrangements for Sarah. Amy was obviously very saddened, particularly as this signalled the breakdown of the marriage of another of her children. We were both emotional. I knew I would miss Amy a great deal. Sitting there, I truthfully had every intention of paying for and keeping a roof over my daughter's head. It would, however, happen to be just wishful thinking as the self-absorbed pathway ahead of me would become my narcissistic priority over the wellbeing of my daughter.

Interestingly, when I announced my plans to my parents, they reacted in the same fashion and without hesitation, my mother didn't pull her punches.

"Sam, to be frank, I don't know how you lasted for so long. I couldn't abide the girl. It was only because I didn't feel it was my place to say anything and my concerns for Sarah, of course, that I kept my mouth shut. Whenever you came to visit, me and your dad, were walking on eggshells most of the time just in case we said something that might start her off. I could tell from the first day you brought her home to meet us, she wasn't right for you, but hey, I do believe in fate and all that."

For that particular period in time there was a noticeable thaw in the strained and frosty relationship, which I had with my father. So, it was agreed I could move back home for a few weeks while I looked for a new place to live. Unfortunately, a combination of hedonistic desires and Pam's change-in-attitude, soon meant 'best laid plans and all that', would soon be consigned to the bin.

CHAPTER 17.

I Would Never See Her Again

My sales career was rocketing. Now that I had been unburdened from any kind of domesticity, I could really start to embrace new horizons. At first, I wanted to focus my mind on a career in sales management, yet ensuring at the same time, I would not miss out on the opportunity of conquering a whole host of very classy and alluring females. I was now thirty-years-of-age and a joint sense of maturity, guile, and an ever-growing commission income seemed to have really boosted my sex appeal. My newly discovered hubris would not however, protect me from what still is to this day, the only woman to have broken my heart . . .

The sociopath needs to always be in control; not only of his own destiny but of all those within his immediate sphere of influence as well. Therefore, a sales management career is a natural and inevitable pathway for a slick sociopathic salesman to embark on. I was to be no exception. The goodies on offer were Merc's and BMWs as company vehicles. The chance to considerably enhance earnings by means of additional management 'override' commissions, derived by creaming off a percentage of the collective earnings generated by my sales team. were luvvly jubbly!

The whole thing though, was a diabolical red-herring and one huge 'con-trick'. To make matters even worse, about 90% of the sales force, and branch and senior branch managers, only ever really got to grips with their impending plight when it was sadly, all too late. Not only for the manager but also the sales 'associate' as well. The entire financial management structure was geared up entirely for the benefit of the parasites running the company.

Before my own management career would befall such an outcome, I was all starry-eyed about picking up a brand-new Merc or BMW. So, it was with a bristling enthusiasm I set off to Wiltshire to attend a so called 'industry professionals course' for new and aspiring branch sales managers. It was during the weeklong course I would meet a fine chap who in a fairly short period-of-time would become a friend, confidante, and my best man.

As fate will often have it, we can stick a pin in our 'life roadmap' where the path of certain souls seems destined to converge with our own. Neil Follet was definitely one of the souls.

The course attendees had been booked into a hotel the Sunday night before the course started. So, as is customary, I wanted to get booked in early and go for a quick swim before relaxing with a few beers in the hotel bar. After completing a few lengths of the pool, I thought I would jump quickly into the jacuzzi as it was quite a size. There was already a dark-haired handsome chap enjoying the effects of the oversized bubble bath. He was relaxing, head back, with his arms stretched out either side of him. As I nodded an acknowledgement he smiled back, shook my hand, and confidently announced . . .

"Hello mate, my name is Neil, Neil Follet."

"Sam Kirkham . . . pleased to meet you. Here on business then?"

"Yes Sam, I am attending a management course for the American

Life and Casualty." "Hey, me too'!"

From that day on, Neil and I have been friends. As we both lazed there in that jacuzzi, I could not possibly have known what an important soul he would become in my life. Moreover, the sheer magnitude of the man with his integrity, wisdom, and forgiveness would turn out to be my savior many times over. Yet, as the flawed addict and sociopath I would become, I would use and abuse his trust on so many occasions. Jesus wept . . .

Neil was a real Nigel Havers type. He spoke with a very similar accent and even dressed like him, the suave bugger! We chatted away like we had known each other all our lives, which is a particular phenomenon that happens to me all the time. He had had without doubt, quite a colorful history of his own. Especially, where the women in his life were concerned.

Neil was several months older than me, but he had already been married twice before. He was about to embark on such a madness for a third time. Indeed, my best man skills were to be called upon again and much sooner than I could possibly have appreciated.

We clicked instantly. Neil did make me laugh when, sharing his matrimonial experiences, he told me when he was just twenty-one, he had been seduced by a much older and alluring female who, apparently, gave him such a dreamlike blow job!

"Hey, I must be in love?"

I mean, that was the only conclusion he could possibly have derived from such an experience, eh? Pah!

Furthermore, Neil went on to tell me how his 'affected and feckless' second wife - I would soon be acquiring one of my own like that, but more later - had seduced his own father and managed to completely turn the head of the retired 'Wing Commander' causing no end of family upheaval! I dunno, families and people, eh? We are all so eccentric and strange really . . . aren't we? What's that I hear you saying? That you are normal? Us homo sapiens? Naaah, never!!

Because Neil had previously been in a management position at his former company, he was earmarked for a branch manager's position once he had completed the course. Looking back, however, it was very clear that despite being as sharp as a tack and very astute, Neil had no more of an idea than me of just how much of a 'stitch up' the manager's 'contract' actually was.

We both had a ball during the week's course. Describing it as a training programme for 'industry professionals' was a laughable contradiction in terms. Simply because, the management culture was hedonistic, crass, and downright boozy. Indeed, the latter of that depraved triumvirate was just beginning to have an effect on my life and to such a degree, it would eventually become both torturous and self-destructive.

Entering the world of 'sales management' would also coincide with the introduction of a larger-than-life character who would shape and corrupt yours truly to a point where, I would cross over to the 'dark side' and remain there until the day I started writing this book.

So, enter the stage please . . . Mr. Sydney de' Brett!

Anyone who has watched that popular BBC Crime drama Dalziel and Pascoe, will know the rough diamond character Detective Superintendent Andy Dalziel. Well, not only did Syd act just like him but physically, he also uncannily resembled that terrific character actor the late Warren Clarke, who played the Dalziel in the series. To compound the likeness even further prior to having embarked on a career in the financial services industry, Syd had actually spent many years in the police as a crack driver for the 'flying squad', which we all know affectionately in the UK, as The Sweeney.

If there was one sentence, I will always remember Syd for, it was this one . . .

"What? I thought I had already told you that?"

Billy Bullshit was Syd's alter-ego. I really should have detected his nonsense from the very first day I met him when being interviewed for a position in his sales management team. Sid held the position of what was known as a group manager. He oversaw several other senior and branch managers to boot.

This was March 1988. When I rocked up outside the offices in Chelmsford Essex, there was Syd sitting astride a gleaming bronze Rolls Royce Silver Shadow. This bluff, gruff, and sandy haired almost comic figure was chuffing away on a huge Havana cigar. From ear-to-ear he was wearing a 'Cheshire Cat' smile. He looked up and bellowed . . .

"Hello Samuel, my boy. Welcome to Syd's madhouse! Ha-ha!"

If only I could have known then, what a fucking circus it was all going to be. No wonder I ended up turning to the drink!

Meeting the new sales teams based in Chelmsford, was a real eye opener alright. To think, these people were actually charged with looking after, and advising folks, about their hard-earned savings and so called 'disposable income'. I say so called, because I had already come across an early software program designed as a 'point of sale' aid whereby, the salesman could manipulate potential customers earnings, cost of living, inflation assumptions, and what his spouse would need to live on, should he die prematurely.

The trouble being, the 'skilled' salesman could learn very quickly how to influence the conversation between spouses and partners, so the wife would feel really vulnerable. Ensuring higher levels of cover with the expensive monthly premiums to match. The husband would be 'raked with guilt' if he didn't agree to ever-increasing sums of life assurance. Simple emotional blackmail!

It goes without saying any discerning couple should look to provide financial security for their loved ones in the event a bread winner dies but this particular piece of software could be skillfully manipulated and resulted in a gross misrepresentation of financial needs.

The program simply ended up being used as a means to be pressurizing the often young and naïve couples into signing proposal forms. Therefore, the salesman would easily 'close' a sale.

In turn, this would lead to no end of 'cancellations' and what was known as business 'churning' became rife. In other words, replacing policies that had hardly accrued value and then resigning new policies with an 'improved' level of cover. So, it was against this ingrained sales culture both Neil and I took the reins of the two new sales teams.

Just like my first interview with Syd, the first branch managers sales meeting was no improvement. These 'meetings' were always held early on a Monday morning in Syd's office. Indeed, picture the scene. We were herded into his swanky fortress, which was salubriously décorated and furnished with a huge dark rosewood desk, sumptuous swivel chair, oversized meeting table, and essential drinks cabinet!

Boy, did that take a hammering and so did we! Syd would chair the meeting and the other branch managers would be in attendance to supposedly plan, reflect, organize sales strategies, set up sales targets, and monitor performances with checks and balances. Like fuck we did!

There was never a meeting 'agenda'. The meetings invariably turned into a 'who shot John' session with Syd doing his utmost to bluster his way through all the adversarial banter that was being thrown in his direction. During these meetings it also began to dawn on me, just what a farce this whole sales environment was. Tragically, it was also costing careers and livelihoods.

As I have mentioned before, there was this incessant demand for manpower 'growth' the company claimed was critical for the future prosperity of all those involved. That was quite frankly . . . insane! The company just wanted to rake over, and suck out, all of the commission income - then spit out those who didn't make the grade. Such dishonesty permeated all the way down from the executive board, regional sales management, group level, and beyond.

I can even remember attending a regional sales meeting, with Syds' boss at the time. 'Reptilian-like' Jon Newland. He was the smoothest of sociopaths. He was crowing over the manpower growth figures for his region. He then had the temerity, to rebuke us for the poor manpower 'retention' figures, which were undermining his 'stats' at board level.

And so, when a naive manager flagged this could be due to the fact, we were all under so much pressure to recruit each month, and it might be leading to a questionable quality of sales recruits . . . you would have thought he had just suggested Jon Newland ate babies for fun.

The regional manager was blistering. Like most sociopaths, he went straight on the attack by pretty much threatening this guy with an immediate termination of his contract.

Thus, for simply daring to question both Jon and the recruitment strategy of the company, he would be reprimanded with severe prejudice. It is a classic trait of the sociopath; when their method is ever scrutinized, they will immediately become very angry and ensure the terrified speaker will be made to 'look the fool' in front of as wide an audience as possible. He will then, grandstand in front of his sycophantic underlings, who just like Snowball and Napoleon in Animal Farm, will, in turn, snort with smug aplomb as the sociopath brings the inexperienced managers 'soundness' into question.

Anyhow, it was against a backdrop of fear and continuous pressure I started to build my own sales team. What an eclectic group they would turn out to be. Apart from the new BMW and initial perception of a rising income, (although the financials were quite illusory and I will describe exactly why later) the management role had another benefit, it was a very effective aphrodisiac.

Also, by this time, my increasingly self-centred mindset meant I was becoming increasingly unreliable in spending time with my daughter and keeping up maintenance payments. There was absolutely no excuse either. I had more cash in my pocket than ever before. I could be as flexible as I would have liked, but I chose to spend more of both on just . . . me.

By the Christmas time of that year, I was simply paying lip service to keeping up my 'doting dad' role, whilst I adored every cell in my daughter's being, the allure of women, booze, and black-tie functions captured my soul. I ache as I write this. When recalling the very last time my eyes would see my Sarah, I wouldn't speak to her again until a brief and painful conversation some twenty years later.

It was Christmas Eve. I had taken my little girl to visit her grandparents to exchange gifts. So, needless to say, it would also be the last time they would see their only ever grandchild. After saying our farewells, we drove back to my mother-in-law's house where Pam was waiting for me. We walked to the front door and my six-year-old turned and grabbed my arm as if she instinctively knew . . .

"Thanks Daddy. I love Nan and Granddad and I want to say I love you with all my heart. Merry Christmas."

With a lump in my throat, I bent down, picked her up, and we just stood there hugging. I can remember feeling such an ache within my soul as I held her small frame against mine. She then jumped down and smiling back at me over her shoulder, Sarah skipped through the front door and waved. Father and daughter would never see each other again.

CHAPTER 18.

LOANS AND DEBT

My pursuit of hedonism was now in full swing. It was still a shock to the system when I happened to call Pam to make arrangements to pick up Sarah for a weekend stay over. The trouble being was I had not seen my daughter since Christmas Eve apart from the occasional indulging phone call, it was now late April.

"Pam, can I speak to Sarah?"

"Oh, it's you. Where the fuck have you been, and where's my money?"

"Look, don't start all of that now, I told you - the commission has been slow coming through (at that time payments were actually on time) so put Sarah on the phone please - I haven't got long."

"Yeah, fuck you too. Wait, I will get her."

I waited and waited and, just as I was about to check the line wasn't dead . . .

"She doesn't want to speak to you. Let's face it, it's not hardly surprising."

"What? Don't try that one Pam, she WILL want to speak to me."

But before I could insist further, I heard a high-pitched voice shouting from over Pam's shoulder . . .

"Tell him I don't love him anymore and I never want to see him again."

"There you go Samuel, now fuck off and sort my money out or you are going to end up in court I can promise you that."

Phone goes dead . . . purrrrr.

I am ashamed and disgusted to admit, I actually felt a sense of relief I would no longer need to interact with Pam. How shameless to be lacking a backbone. So much so I would sacrifice my daughter's relationship with her father rather than face further contentions with her mother.

As far as the courts and child maintenance was concerned, I had by then, a much higher cash flow. Now, I say cash flow and not income. I will explain that cunning company 'con-trick' later.

Furthermore, I had also become 'self-employed' and as most of us know, 'Schedule D' income can be mitigated in no end of imaginative ways when disclosure to any court was needed.

So, there I was, glumly sitting in my office. Even had my name plaque on the door by then. When I happened to peer across the open plan area in front of me, a new receptionist was being introduced to all the administrative and sales teams. She had that slightly bewildered look people often have on their first day in a new job. This new object of desire was around 5'5" and very red headed. I have always found reds and strawberry blondes most alluring, full-figured in all the desirable ways, she had such a delicious mouth that looked like it had been created for one purpose only - to suck me dry! I just knew she was going to be . . . trouble!

Kate Dumfey was the name of this desirable and voluptuous redhead. It happened she was the mother of two young daughters and was recently divorced. It's always most amusing to watch the 'bees around the honey pot' when a new attractive member of staff arrives on the front desk. Not forgetting of course, the feline jealousy directed at their new colleague. Unlike the other guys in the office who had made it so obvious, I would nonchalantly hand in paperwork and knowingly, I avoided catching her eye. My instincts just told me Kate wasn't used to men ignoring her. As always, I would play . . . the long game.

Kate wasn't backwards in coming forwards either. So, I didn't actually have to wait very long for her approach, which shall we say, was direct to say the least. She had to bring me some 'lie sheets', which is what us managers cynically called sales associates activity records. I was quickly aware she had made a point of closing the door behind her. She slinked across the room and in an overtly feline manner, sat cross legged on the sofa next to my desk. Kate purred . . .

"Hello Mr. Kirkham, I have something for you here."

"Of course, you have Kate, are they this week's lie sheets then?"

I was hedging ever so slightly because I wasn't completely sure where the conversation was heading at this point, but matters were soon clarified for me . . .

"Fuck the lie sheets Sam, I have a very wet pussy and I want to come over there and sit on your cock right now."

"Errrrrm . . . do you now?"

Kate's desire might not have been satisfied at that very moment, but as she stood up to leave, her serious intent was made clear as she handed me her home number and address. I was obviously in a heightened state of lust, but I also had a nagging feeling it just all seemed rather . . . too easy?

It was to be on a weekday afternoon my fate would be sealed, when Kate had taken a half day's leave. She lived just a stone's throw from the office. She gave me a quick call to let me know she was 'ready' and had a couple of hours before she had to collect the kids from school. So, I jumped into my new champagne colored Jaguar XJ6. I couldn't flick the automatic 'J gate' into the drive gear quickly enough.

I arrived at her house; the front door was already ajar – convenient - so, without hesitation, I wandered through the hallway with an expectant air for the scent of my favorite pheromones. I was thinking "basque, stockings, lacy knickers" . . . Nope!

I pushed open the Kitchen door and there was Kate standing at the sink up to her elbows in washing up and marigold gloves.

"Oh? Hi, how are you . . . doing?"

"Helloos yooo, mmwwaaaah. Come here and kiss me."

I moved in and we clinched. Ok, I was slightly perturbed the anticipated erotic undergarments were not on offer but that would surely come when we moved upstairs, right? Wrong! I was just coping with her soapy rubber gloves around the back of my neck, when she pulled her succulent mouth away from mine, and gazing back into my eyes with her own deep blues, she came out with a very different line to the one I was expecting.

"I have to do the weekly shop shortly, so is it ok if I just bend over the sink and you fuck me from behind? I will get my tits out for you to grope as well if you want . . . yes?"

Now, who said the art of romance was dead eh? Despite a reputation to the contrary, this just wasn't my style at all. I am very passionate and just cannot engage in frivolous sex. Never could and never will. She was clearly being serious as well so stepping back, I protested . . .

"Kate, I am not just here for a bloody 'Quickie' you know." "Awww . . . better than nothing? Ok, I can give you blow job and a wank as well, if you prefer?"

"What! A fucking wank! Look, big mistake . . . so you just piss off to Sainsbury's and I will get back to the office. I am supposed to be running a fucking sales team!"

"Hey . . . Sam, please don't be like that. Have you ANY idea how many men I could have had here today? You even know a few of them. You will regret this if you just go now."

"Yeah right, this didn't happen, ok! Well . . . nothing fucking did anyway, did it!"

I was steaming, so I spun around on my quarter tipped heels and stormed off. I jumped behind the wheel of my Jaguar and as I was reversing off Kate's drive, her parting words were reverberating inside my head . . .

"You know a few of them and you will regret this."

I was shaking with a seismic outrage as my knuckles turned white with the pressure of my clenching the steering wheel. I was feeling both angry and even humiliated for being taken for granted by this ginger temptress.

"You know a few of them."

So, who were the few exactly? I knew which hapless fellas Kate had been flirting with in the office. She had wasted very little time with her sultry seduction technique on my male colleagues. I would also 'regret leaving'? Surely this was just an ungracious female reaction to my having rejected her. How wrong could I have been? So cometh the first - and by no means my last . . . stalker! Anon . . .

Until the fallout from my decision to refuse Kate could really manifest; I had to try and concentrate on steadying what was becoming a rather unwieldy 'monster' of a sales team. No matter how much ongoing sales training you try to impose, one simple rule always prevails, which is the '80/20' rule. In other words, 80% of the entire sales production will always be produced by just 20% of the sales team. My team verified such a rule. My gross commissions were invariably derived by four or five stars 'associates' out of the 20 or so who made up the whole team.

Now I say 'or so' simply because, manpower recruitment and so-called retention has remained a game of musical chairs and revolving doors. The madness of branch and group recruitment targets continued unabated, and while the company continued to make egregious profits despite the perpetual burn rate. It was never going to change. I attended no end of useless 'management courses' where the fashionable term of the day was 'added value'. What a fucking joke that was! It was used from the top down and permeated the course notes, overhead slides, and PowerPoints of just about every training course in the land. There was just one problem though, no fucker really knew what it meant!

I will cover much more about this illusory bullshit later. As my understanding and awareness of psychological manipulation continued to grow, it never ceased to amaze me just how gullible and sycophantic people in senior management could be. Even worse, they were supposed to be the up-and-coming brains of the outfit!

I previously mentioned 'lie sheets', because these were the weekly 'sales activity monitoring sheets', which were completed by associates and management alike. Needless to say, they were also complete fiction. Moreover, to add insult to injury, everyone knew it. Therein was the underlying problem that would financially screw so many. The majority of desperate sales associates would bullshit their manager so he would be hoodwinked into sanctioning further 'FEP' cash flow checks. Then, in turn, the manager would feed this crap up to his superiors to ensure his own monthly cash flow payment would be sustained, and so forth and so on.

The whole 'House of Cards' would lurch from one month to the next. Where that particular financial paradigm, if we can call it that, would be replicated in my life over and over throughout the next three decades. What is more, I would eventually become so conditioned by that particular method of funding; it would have a calamitous 'knock on' effect for so many others.

A year into my management contract, things were just about keeping on an even keel with a revolving door recruitment strategy retaining the status quo, as far as the size of the team was concerned. Around this time, Neil had been offered the opportunity to take-up the reins of a much larger 'city' branch, he was fast becoming a favorite of the regional manager, Jon Newland.

We had become firm friends. I was again invited to play the part of 'best man' at a simple registry office wedding ceremony when Neil took the plunge for the third time with his new bride, Edna. She was, shall we say, a rather rotund Scottish girl with a very a direct approach to life. I know I am not one to talk, but even I found her Glaswegian tongue both crude, and at times, her dialect was impossible for this cockney to understand.

Neil and Edna soon became parents for the first time when a beauty-ful baby girl arrived. They called her Lorrie. Whilst Neil appeared to be extremely proud and happy on the surface, I would find out some twenty years later how he had been entrapped into the whole marriage. To be fair, even at that time, something about their union just didn't feel right. What with Neil's cultured and refined manner, contrasting so glaringly with his latest wife's somewhat crude and discourteous character.

So, it was on a rather sobering moment when, just before he was about to say his farewells to his admin and sales team, Neil pulled me to one side and gave me a quiet yet concerned warning about a certain redhead.

"Sam, just before I go, I wanted to mark your card about something mate."

"Uh? What about?"

"Tell me, have you been poking that Dumfrey bird?"

"I nearly did but to be truthful, when it came to it, I found her a bit cold and err . . . weird actually."

"You were right to think that as well son. I have had some rather disturbing feedback from Caron (who was another stunning brunette of a receptionist). She told me Kate can be quite unhinged. Caron knows her ex-husband who might be a bit bias of course but has alluded to some very 'specialist behavioral traits' on the part of his ex-wife. If you know what I mean, son?"

"Errrrm . . . Yeah, I think I do."

I didn't have any fucking idea of course. Looking back, I would often display a rather naïve side to my character and that naivety has never really left me. Over the years, very few of those close to me would have ever believed that one, but I can assure you, it is quite true.

I did, however, take the time to reflect on the first time Kate had wandered into my office with the intent of declaring her 'interest' and the rather clinical attitude she took toward me when I visited her at her home.

"Well Neil, I have had my own thoughts on that one too, so I will keep 'em peeled mate. Thanks for the heads up."

Neil was to run the Haymarket Branch for the next eighteen months. He had a very successful time there. He would eventually return to the Chelmsford office due to the demise of a certain, Mr. De' Brett. I will tell you about that very episode soon . . .

I was still trying to juggle the branch finances, which would become a 'juggling skill set' I would have to get used to over the next three decades. Now whilst some of the commission generated by my four 'star players' was rattling high at times, due to the built-in disadvantages of the financial establishment system, that insincere term still makes me cringe. I was constantly being hit with 'financial losses'.

How this stitch up worked was whenever a salesman left the company for another rival - the poaching and churning of sales staff was rife amongst various life assurance offices - if the advanced commissions that had been paid out to the salesman were greater than any future sums to be accrued by the policies which he had sold - then the deficit was 'clawed back' from the manager. The 'con' didn't stop there though. The company benefited from a 'double bubble' by then, relentlessly pursuing their former 'associate' for debt. They couldn't lose but the manager certainly did . . .

Such a ruthless approach would inevitably lead to conflict, and a culture of fear.

Here we go again, the 'divide and rule' strategy of executive management never failed. When there was an air of mistrust prevailing throughout the entire organization. Managers never trusted their salesmen because they could never know when a team member would manipulate onc final paycheck from the system before he 'jumped ship'. In turn, the associate never trusted his manager, because they always believed he favored his best producers, which he did of course by keeping 'hot leads' away from him. That Glengarry Glen Ross culture again. I beseech you, watch that movie.

In the end, I thought 'Fuck this for a game of soldiers' and went to seek the wise counsel of my group manager Syd. Wise counsel? My arse!

"What do you mean the system is a stitch up Samuel m'lad. Didn't I tell you that?"

That fucking line again . . .

"No, you fucking didn't Syd. What's even worse, you must have come across this so many times over the years. The system is totally geared in favor of the company. Let's face it, the commission payments are not really commission at all, are they? THEY ARE FUCKING LOANS!!"

There you have it . . . loans. A term that would become a byword for the way I would derive an income for years to come. To be totally corrupted by it as well.

"Now tell me something else Syd, how come the entire direct sales team are all taxed under 'Schedule-D' and classed a self-employed status when in reality, they are all working for just one company eh?"

"Www . . . hat? You're not supposed to say that, shut the fucking door you little prick."

"Why? Every cunt in the office knows it. The entire industry is taxed by the same method. There is some huge stitch-up going between the 'elite' of these businesses and the bloody tax man! Is that why our great leader Sir bloody Marcus Weinstein got his fucking knighthood then? He wouldn't have managed to pull a sodding actress of a wife, if he hadn't!"

"You are really treading on thin ice now son. Anyway, all sales associates are allowed to do other business to confirm their self-employed status?"

"Oh, what a load of bollocks Syd. You know full well it is all we can do to get the idle bastards to turn up for a weekly sales meeting. For sure, those who are 'moonlighting' would never tell us anyway just in case we withheld their cash advances. The whole system stinks and lower ranking managers are getting it in the arse!"

"You don't know the half of its Sam; even I get hit with claw backs."

"Yeah, like hell you do."

I stormed out of Syd's office with a definite feeling my time as a sales manager just might be nearing its end. Interestingly though, toward the end of my time at American Life and Casualty I actually discovered Syd was not entirely 'gilding the lilly'. So, you see, the method of advancing 'loans' was how the elite kept getting away with it, and basically still do to this day. As you will read later, the same sharks at the top of the company back then, would become the same sharks who colluded to create another company . . . 'The Rosenberg Group' with no less than a Lord of the Realm acting as its so-called vice chairman.

CHAPTER 19.

Unnerving Bitch

After my separation from Pam, I had bought a property of my own with a mortgage organized by the wife of one of the other senior branch managers, Les Broomer. He was yet another bull shitter of the highest order. Les and his wife Kay had a real little 'cottage industry' going on because Kay had previously worked for the biggest mortgage provider in the UK, The Halliford Building Society. Between them, they used to organize loans and mortgages for all the other sales associates and managers within the Chelmsford Group. In return, they would take a percentage of all the commissions . . . nice. Today, you often hear a great deal of criticism of the manner by which mortgages were arranged in the late 90's and the early 'noughties. I can tell you now, it was far worse in the late 80's.

The mortgage lending criteria had become a farce. A far cry from the previously accepted careful practices. When I think back, I had to save for two-years with Abbey Nations Building Society to raise a deposit, which was topped up by my mother-in-law. Only then, was a mortgage offer forthcoming after a stringent interview with a branch manager, who would apply a strict 'three times' income multiple for the largest amount that could be borrowed.

Anyway, Les' wife was processing mortgage applications like there was no tomorrow. The lending criteria was a complete farce. Fake wage slips, company income references, confirmation of earnings from accounts. The entire environment was a lie. A huge fraud. In fact, every group up and down the country had a 'Les Broomer'. It became an acceptable and even necessary business standard. Did the company executive know? Of course, they did!! Ask them now if they were aware of what was going on and we all know what the reply would be. Life assurance and pension contracts sold off the back of mortgage loans was huge business. All they really cared about was an immoral means to an immoral end.

I saw countless presentations and sales techniques, which were specifically designed to demonstrate how to sell more pension and endowment products by simply coupling them to mortgages contracts. Company sanctioned 'product training consultants were conveyed to over eager sales teams. So, the greed was actually company sponsored! Let us be totally clear on that one!

The whole 1990s 'pensions mis-selling scandal' came off the back of that very strategy and no end of salesmen were reprimanded. Some were even imprisoned. Yet, in the vast majority of cases, they were actually manipulated by so called 'executive management' into doing their bidding.

Matters were then compounded by the overt encouragement by UK governments of the 80' and 90's to 'opt out' of the State Earnings Related Pension Scheme (SERPS) and 'Stealth Tax' raid by the then Chancellor of the Exchequer, Gordon Brown, on the UK Pension schemes. No wonder we have an old age pension deficit that looks like it can only now be solved by a Logan's Run style cull at age of 30! Yes . . . for all those liberal minded snowflake readers out there I AM joking!! The practices that were perpetrated throughout that entire period of time were a disgrace. In many ways, it is now worse than ever.

The 'financial services industry' now operates under an illusion known as, 'compliance'. We will revisit that particular charade later when we consider how an already unsustainable model has been exacerbated beyond any imagination, by the so-called Coronavirus pandemic. My new dwelling was a modern 'link-detach' three-bedroom 1980s built house, so utterly boring by design. All the same, I was feeling very pleased with myself for escaping the shackles of my marriage. When I should have only felt absolute shame for abandoning my daughter. My financial support for Pam and Sarah was dwindling by the month. Inevitably, it would result in only one adversarial outcome, court proceedings.

It would turn out to be another year before I would be bought to account. Even then, I somehow managed to squirm out of making any maintenance payments for Sarah. Much to my surprise, my divorce from Pam finally came through without her putting up any real fight. Most strange, I thought. Subsequently, I was now going to indulge my passion for female company with ever greater zeal. Before I could do so; however, there was going to be a much more formidable obstacle to overcome, Kate Dumfey!

I had just assumed her threats had been no more than hot air. I was about to go to bed, when my newly installed phone rang. I had only been in the house for a week. Hardly anyone had been given my new house number. As this was 1990, mobile phones were only really used as a permanent fixture in the car. I picked up the receiver and before I could actually reply . . .

"Hellloooooo . . . you." "Errmm . . . who is this?"

"It's Kate . . . are you busy?"

Fuck . . . it was Kate! How the hell did she get this number?

"Kate? Hi . . . errrrm, how did you get my new number I haven't even given it to my PA yet?"

"Oh, is this a NEW number then?"

What the fuck is this bird going on about?

"Kate, I only moved in last week you know that, surely?" "Oh, have you recently moved, then?"

This was all now getting extremely weird.

"You didn't fuck me when you should have Sam. I don't handle rejection very well. I have left you alone, but you did promise me, and I can tell you I would really love you like no other. Go on, tell me right now you don't want me. I will drive over right now. If you tell me to my face, I will leave you alone. But I want you now. That hard cock of yours. It is throbbing . . . I can tell."

Love me like no other? She was clearly as brainsick as Neil had warned me and how the hell did, she get my new number?

"Kate look, it's very late, I have to be at the regional meeting early tomorrow. I really need to get to bed now."

"Oh, I know you are. I shall be there as well tomorrow taking notes for Syd. Shall we travel up together? You will feel great after having me. I know you do want me, don't you? Right now, I am playing with my wet clit. I so need you to fuck me right now, Sam. I will get in the car shortly; it only takes thirty minutes to get to yours."

"What d'ya mean thirty minutes?"

"I already have your new address; I was teasing you earlier and I want to tease your cock as well."

I was really feeling quite unnerved by this point. A very uneasy visceral sensation was hindering my ability to appear insouciant by Kate's ambitions to fuck me . . . in my own bed! She pressed me further . . .

"I am lying here naked on my bed and thrusting my vibrator deep inside me and wanting it to be your cock darling."

I thought . . . Lying there naked?

As I allowed myself just a few seconds for clearer thinking, it occurred to me that she had two fairly young children and she couldn't leave them on their own. I quickly decided 'indulgence' was the best way forward . . .

"Kate, just imagine I am lying behind you and you can feel my hot breath on the back of your neck. You look over your shoulders and into my eyes. Our mouths lock and my hand snakes around your waist over your abdomen, and down between your wetness. I take your swelling breast into my other hand and pull you into me as your hand feels behind you to stroke my proud throbbing cock. You arch back and slide yourself back onto my hardness as I pump my hot cum deep inside you."

"Uuuuhhhhh aaarrrggghhh fuuuuck I'm cooommmming now!!!" Silence . . . click . . . prrrrrrrr. That seemed to work . . .

The next morning, I found myself milling around the George Hotel foyer in Colchester, as the waitresses served coffee to the mingling managers and their personal assistants. I did actually enjoy these monthly regional sessions, even though very little was ever really achieved. It was during such gatherings, the usual lip service was paid to that latest burgeoning management imposition, known as Career Professional Development (CPD) which was even more of a farce than the previous waste of time . . . added value.

I was just about to dunk my early morning chocolate finger, when I was caught by the mesmeric gaze of a certain Mrs. Dumfey glaring back at me across the noise of matching ties and handkerchiefs. I just thought to myself . . . Let's get this over with now, and I glided up to her.

She was well aware of my intent. She pretended to engage with another administrator. What a cheeky cow, I wasn't having any of that obtuse behavior I can tell you.

I stepped into her space, firmly taking her arm, I turned her around to face me. The rapacious redhead then incensed me further by having the nerve to look me up and down.

With my hand pulling on her arm, I pulled her into to me . . .

"Good morning, Kate!! I must say, you were rocking last night, and I will now ask again, how did you get my fucking new home number."

She characteristically replied in such a manner so as to gain maximum attention . . .

"Oh, good morning, Samuel! I'm sorry, I am sure I don't know what you are talking about?"

Through gritted teeth . . .

"Don't pull that stroke Kate! What the bloody hell was that all about last night. You are some head fuck I can tell you."

Kate then calmly insisted . . .

"Look, you are going to embarrass yourself in a minute. Really? What is it with men? They can be soooo immature at times. Did you get out of the wrong side of bed this morning? You need nurturing by a good woman Sam. Living on your own doesn't seem to suit you at all."

A horrible sinking feeling came over me as I became aware the cacophony of sound which had been drowning out our aggravated exchange, had dissipated in favor of a circling wall of senior managers who were all gazing at yours truly.

"Everything ok, with you two?"

Boomed a smiling and less than convincing, Syd De'Brett.

Kate never said a word and her prolonged icy stare - just momentarily - appeared to be somewhat pleading. So, I withdrew my hand . . .

"We are all ok here Syd. All ok."

Due to the day's distractions, I didn't really take any further notice of Kate. After the meeting had finished, we all inevitably folded back into the hotel bar, which was quite the norm for such meetings.

Until my incursion into management, I had been no more than a 'social drinker'. Although I now laugh at such a description and for sure I had on occasion drunk more alcohol than was sensible. To be fair, up to that point in time, I could take or leave alcohol and never drank at home.

This was all now changing for me. The whole drinking culture was very much part of the management scene. Together with peer pressure, self-important egos were constantly trying to 'drink each other under the table'!

I had my usual skinful and by 11 pm. We all started to disperse. Picture this scene, a dozen or so pissed up 'gobby Cockney and Essex' types, all stumbling through the hotel foyer revolving doors and staggering toward what resembled a 'premier league footballers car park'.

Brand new Porches, Mercs, BMWs, and any other high end prestige marque you care to think of were all spoils paid for by the unsuspecting policy holder's premiums.

To make matters even worse, we all drove home! Most disturbingly, it was an almost accepted practice back in the 80s and most of the 90s. I can even recall remarks like, 'come on you light weight, one more for the road'. 'I actually drive better after eight pints'. It was a miracle we didn't kill anyone. Incredibly, until I finally stopped alcohol over seventeen years ago and counting, I was never once stopped or cautioned for 'drink driving'. For sure, my luck was to run out by alternative means.

I managed to get home in one piece. After eventually negotiating the key in the front door, I staggered into my hallway. I slouched onto the bottom stair and was just kicking off my hand made Italian loafers, yeah, I know, when the phone-sitting on top of my antique card table started to ring. It was by now, well past midnight. No, surely not?

"Hello, who . . .?"

"Hellooooo . . .I hope you didn't think that your little outburst today was going to change anything?"

"For fuck's sake Kate, what do you want now?"

"Do you really need to even ask; I want your cock inside my wet pussy right now. I am coming over there to get it."

"Yeah, yeah, yeah, we had all of this last night. Kate, you are just looking for a cheap thrill, now please piss off and go to sleep."

"Oooh, I love it when you get objectionable like that, I want you to get angry with me when I am sucking your swollen cock and then make me so wet and aching for you to . . ." Click . . . prrrrrr.

I slammed down the receiver. Kate had played me in front of everyone earlier that day and she was bloody far too convincing as well.

Then . . . ring ring . . . I was determined to ignore her, but as stalkers do, they just keep on dialling; so, in the end I had to leave the phone off the hook.

I was obviously determined to bring matters to a head with Kate and as I pulled into my parking space early the next morning, I had decided to simply wait downstairs in the atrium before she could even enter the office building. This was going to be, 'confrontation city'.

Sure enough, Kate soon came breezing up to the building entrance and wearing her habitual wide-eyed grin, she gushed out an ear-splitting "Good morning, Mr. Kirkham!" She had some serious front; I would give her that. This was 'grab the right arm time' again and on this occasion, I wasn't going to let up. I bellowed . . .

"Kate, you are a total head fuck. I now realize the rumors about you are all so true. You are like that fucking bird out of Play Misty for Me and you would give Glenn Close a run for her money as well! So, I will ask you for the last time, how did you get my new house number? No one here has been given it yet. It won't show up on any phone directories for a month or so."

She just stared at me and was now quite stone faced. She pouted her lips and thought for a moment . . .

"Sam, I am a most resourceful female and woe betides ANY man who rejects me. I did try to warn you but look, I will now leave you alone; well . . . maybe? It will be great fun toying with you and watching you squirm. Just never knowing when I will strike next. Oh, and by the way, how is that Trudi lady you are seeing?"

"What! How the fuck do you know about her?" "I did say I was most resourceful Sam. Ta-da!"

Kate pirouetted on the pavement and let out a high-pitched hysterical laugh, which startled the early morning office workers who were milling past. She blew me a kiss and walked off toward the office entrance. I just stood there . . . stupefied.

To this day, I still don't know how Kate had obtained that phone number. Of course, this was also at a time when access to such information was not easily available as it is today. There was also that parting shot about Trudi? How on earth did she know about her? Trudi was actually a girl I had known from my days at Unicorn. From time-to-time, she had become a 'plus one kind of girlfriend'. However, she had no link whatsoever to the office. When bearing in mind Kate had only been at the company for a few months herself. She just could not have interacted with anyone else in my social circle.

By this time, I had begun to adopt a particular 'modus operandi' where I would compartmentalize various elements of my life, so that, more than one relationship could run in parallel. This is another very typical lifestyle choice of the sociopath. An overconfident practice I believed would protect me from the machinations of, a girl like a Kate. I was also rather concerned about her getting her claws into the rather naïve Trudi.

I found the whole 'Kate episode' really unnerving at times. Ok, there were not any 'knife attacks in the shower' or 'bunnies getting boiled' but she had this ability to keep me second guessing as to just what her next move might be. The other problem being she continued to work at the same company and was still there right up until I finally left for pastures new. On virtually a daily basis it could clearly be seen just how much she was enjoying teasing me. I later discovered I wasn't by any means the only one! So, it isn't just the boys who engage in such behavior, I can assure you.

Neither was it to be the last time I would experience such conduct by a woman. Many of us would have seen movies like, sleeping with the Enemy starring Julia Roberts. I have experienced and personally observed extreme, possessive, and unhinged activity from BOTH sexes! Men often get all the 'bad press', which is appropriate when it is deserved. Women blame men, and men blame women. Guess what? Both sexes are human beings! So, we had all better start to wise up to the 'gender blame game'. Men and Women are, of course, ALL flawed souls! What is more, our behavioral differences are far less marked than we would care to admit to ourselves. It has been that way over centuries.

We have been manipulated into believing the differences are greater than they are in reality!

It actually suits the manipulative 'forces' on this planet to condition us all. From the time of the cradle, into believing our genes and chromosomes are so different. We 'think' and 'behave' opposite to one another. Then, a social discord runs as an undercurrent throughout the rest of our lives. That old 'divide and rule strategy' again. It never fails. Even worse, so many buy into the numerous 'life coaching and self-help books', which are sold to conditioned masses who are so psychologyically damaged by the time they become adults, they invariably end up eternally searching for the 'key' to that elusive harmonious relationship. No wonder Rhonda Byrne's The Secret and Ester and Gerry Hicks, Ask and it is Given have sold so many bloody copies!

CHAPTER 20.

Julie Clarkson

I previously alluded to the fact only one woman has ever truly broken my heart. Certainly, there have been others who have left a mark of unhappiness or bittersweet memories but in June 1990, I was left reeling, devastated, and utterly bereft. The woman responsible for the worst emotional experience of my life, was Julie Clarkson.

Now bearing in mind, Mrs. Dumfey was constantly monitoring my every move, looking back, it makes the Julie episode all the more intriguing. Especially when considering, how she arrived in my life, and who Julie would have to navigate past in the first place. Yes, you've guessed it . . . Kate!

The recruitment process continued to be relentless. As managers, we were expected to constantly run recruitment advertisements, all at our own expense I might add, and the responses would be gathered by the branch administrators. Most inconveniently, Kate being one of them. They would collate the responses, and in many cases, filter out those applicants who appeared to be unsuitable for the madness of a career in direct sales. I often think back with envy at all those lucky buggers who had been instantly rejected!

The great irony was when Kate happened to be appraising the latest candidates, she happened to find an application from a woman who was thirty years of age, had two young children, and was apparently looking to return to career in financial services having had a five-year 'baby break'.

"Ooh, look at this one Sam, she WOULD suit you!"

Kate had no idea, just how much.

"Ok Kate, turn it in. Just hand it over, haven't you got some stalking to be getting on with?"

After recent events, I was on constant guard whenever Kate was around and every conversation we had was bejewelled with sarcasm.

"There you go Mr. Grumpy, take a look for yourself!"

I thumbed open the full application and started to scan the contents. I had read so many by then, trying to apply any level of real interest was increasingly difficult. Julie Clarkson, had indeed just turned thirty, had two young boys, and lived fairly local to Chelmsford in the rustic picturesque village of Coggeshall. Her application revealed she had previously worked for the large 'Unit Trust' group, Merchant and Guilds for several years before leaving to start a family. Intriguingly, the application said she was married to a guy called Rolph Clarkson. Hmm. That name seemed familiar somehow.

I just was not sure about taking on another woman in the team. Now any ladies reading this, please don't react to that statement because I can assure you I did far more than many of my colleagues in trying to encourage and recruit women into taking up a career in sales positions. Hey, there were even dedicated campaigns to attract the fairer sex into the fold. I had, over time, really persevered with the equal opportunities' mantra of the day. All the same, I have to admit, they just didn't succeed. There was one middle-aged Scot lady named Eileen, who did alright, but the rest just found it much too hard going.

So, what was I to do with Julia Clarkson? My logical mind told me to just ask Kate to call her back with an early 'sorry' but my intuitive right side of the brain just nagged away persuading me to at least give this particular lady a chance. You see, upon reflection, the Julia decision wasn't mine to make. I am absolutely convinced, 'something above' dictated the next roller coaster sequence of events, and the traumatic experiences that were soon to unfold. As with all things they were predetermined, and no matter what my rational and cognitive processes were telling me my fate was already . . . sealed.

Kate, of all people, had made the appointment for Julia to come to the office for a first interview and I can still remember that particular fateful morning, as if it were yesterday. It was a 10 am appointment and I was preparing myself a fresh coffee in the office kitchen when the hawkish Kate craned her head around the door and poked a sharp finger into my rib.

"Hey, you . . . your 10 o'clock appointment, Julia Clarkson, is here."

Kate just glared. I did think it rather odd, she hadn't just phoned through to my office - as the front desk girls usually did - to inform me that the next one off the 'conveyor belt' had just arrived. It was also most clear; she was somewhat agitated as well.

"Kate, steady, I am just making a sodding fresh percolated coffee here can't you see that? I will come through when I am good and ready so can you give her a bloody company brochure or something to read . . . yes?"

"Errmm . . . ok then, but I think you will want to come through pretty soon Mr. Grumpy!"

What was she bloody banging on about, and why did Kate come through personally to hurry me up? I had previously interviewed hundreds of hopeless candidates and she had never egged me on like this before? And why was she so worked up? I was soon to discover exactly why . . .

I left my fresh cup of black coffee on my desk and passed through the open plan office space and as I did so, I happened to jut into a 'young gun' of an associate, Kenny Beazle who had just arrived (yeah, they were all so keen and it was 10am remember). He just grinned at me. I stopped to quiz him . . .

"What the fuck are you laughing at you little prick. What fucking time do you call this? Did you close that pension deal I gave you last night?"

Kevin completely ignored my question and was now grinning even wider.

"Hey, I just came through reception boss, is THAT your next interview?"

Now the way he expressed his question and the manner of his smile, kind of suggested to me I was about to interview a 'female hippo, wearing a grass skirt'!

"Oh no . . . she's pig ugly then, is she?"

Kenny was about to reply but I was such an impatient and arrogant sod in those days I already walked off toward the reception area and was thinking to myself . . .

Jesus let's get this over with and send this 'Doris' off packing.

As I turned the corner into the reception area, I didn't actually focus on the woman who was sat there in anxious anticipation, simply because my attention was caught by the glare of the three 'admin girls' sitting behind their desks. They were all looking rather expectantly and Kate, in particular, was giving me a very 'knowing' look. I then glanced back in the direction of the visitor's sofa and just . . . froze.

Now I could try to conjure up as many adjectives as I can muster in order to describe the woman who was about to turn my world upside down, but two words will achieve that much better than any others I can think of . . . a young clone of, 'Brigitte Bardot'!

Julie Clarkson was browsing obligingly through a company brochure. I must have looked such a moron - just standing there 'statue-like' - as I was simply in awe of this 5' 4" bronzed and perfectly formed blonde, who was dressed in a classic navy suit with tight knee length pencil skirt and white blouse. Her deep blue stilettos were crossed, which further accentuated her toned and stockingless calves. She then peered up and as our eyes made contact, she nervously grinned, yet with a radiance that is normally only the privilege of . . . an angelic being.

"Oh hello, are you Samuel Kirkham?"

To be honest, I was so utterly paralyzed in that moment, I had no idea who the fuck I was, where I was, and what the year was either. My first thought being . . .

This must be what nirvana is truly like?

I continued to stare and again, it was Kate who broke the awkwardness of my 'schoolboy' emotional state.

"Mr. Kirkham, shall I get Julie a cup of tea or coffee?"

I simply couldn't acknowledge Kate, as my entire universe had become consumed, and gaslighted in just one moment by this most enchanting and delightful young woman. I think even Julie was beginning to wonder whether my trance would be broken any time before the dawn of the next millennium. Indeed, as I write this, the lightness of that one instant still pervades through me. Anyone who has experienced being touched by that unique other soul who instantly aligns and connects with your own DNA will appreciate what I am waxing lyrical about. So please, just forgive me this brief moment of retrospective and heartfelt indulgence.

She then stood up and offered her silky delicate hand, which I gratefully accepted. I proudly gestured for her to follow me back to my office and when doing so, I couldn't avoid catching the eye of the ever-watchful Kate who was wearing a very unfamiliar and pensive frown.

With an extra sense of purpose, I kicked my office door stop away just as Julie glided past me and sat down. I looked back with an arrogant intent across the open plan office. I could almost visualize the collective speech cloud above the heads of thirty or so - testosterone fuelled salesmen - who were all thinking just one thing . . .

Who the fuck is . . . she?

Well, SHE, is in MY office pal!

Julie was sat opposite me. I quickly picked up on her nervous and childlike demeanor. Even though this was supposed to be a serious job interview she leaned forward, balanced her elbows on the table, and rested her sweet, beautiful, smiley face between her palms. This lovely woman possessed my pre-requisite liking for high cheekbones, a full sensual mouth, long honey blonde hair, with a cute fringe resting perfectly on her crystal blue gaze. I was simply transfixed by her radiant aura.

Now, I know all you cynics will simply be thinking she was using her female guile on me. Maybe she was, but over the coming months I would experience just what a beautiful heart Julie possessed.

Because of my hopelessly amorous state, there was absolutely no chance of me being able to conduct a conventional interview, so it promptly turned into something tantamount to a first date! We laughed, joked, and in a naturally tactile manner just didn't feel inappropriate for a job interview.

Julie went on to tell me her marriage had failed due to the constant philandering of her husband (yes, I know, I know). He had walked out on her for another woman, who unsurprisingly, was 'fat and ugly'. Her words not mine remember, but here, yet again, was another example of a phenomenon I would witness many times.

The blonde of my dreams went on to tell me her husband also left her with two very young boys to care for. I remember listening to her plight with great insincerity, sociopaths are just brilliant at feigning such empathy as part of their manipulation process. I even had the temerity to 'tut' when she said she was now being forced back to work because her ex 'Rolph' was not 'paying his way'.

It also happened the object of her venting, actually worked in the same industry as a 'sales inspector'. I am not sure if such a role still exists today, but it was one of those 'non-jobs' guys did in my business when they were failed salesmen.

A first interview would generally take about thirty minutes, or an hour if the candidate was an especially strong one. However, this particular interview took over two hours. We had barely discussed any of the sales role itself. The three Witches of Eastwick sitting in reception, obviously knew the protocols. Kate in particular, was having no more of the threat being posed by this gorgeous blonde interloper. Just as she did when Julie first arrived, she actually came through to my office, knocked, and without being invited, opened the door. The cow then used one of her best well-rehearsed tactics, which was designed to antagonize with maximum effect.

"Oh, Mr. Kirkham, so sorry to disturb you, but your GIRLFRIEND Trudi called about an hour ago, she sounded rather anxious. I did tell her you were in the middle of a meeting with Julie, and she then called again about ten minutes ago. I just thought you would want to be told. I hope you don't mind my interrupting you both. Oh, hello Julie . . . how did it all go then?"

How did it all fucking go then?

Kate's front was amazing on the one hand yet confirmed her contemptible envy on the other. Sure, she was a most attractive woman in her own right, but she had quickly realized competing with this tanned and lithe blonde was going to be an extremely tough challenge.

I am also ashamed to confess, the hapless Trudi, wasn't going to stand a chance either. Although a loyal and sweet girlfriend, from the moment my gaze had finally come into focus on Julie, it was simply going to be game over for any woman within my sphere of influence. Trudi had been a friend, lover, friend, and lover again. I got on great with her parents and I will recount later an incredible supernatural encounter, which I experienced whilst being with her father.

"Errrm thanks for THAT . . . Kate. Can you let her know I will call in about twenty minutes?"

Kate was still blazing at me as she reversed and closed the door. There would yet be more meddlesome behavior to come from her, no fear of that. I now had an inconvenience to explain away.

"Aha, Trudi is actually an 'ex' who kinda hasn't let go yet, you know how it is?"

"Oh, please, you don't need to explain anything to me it's not any of my business, is it."

No, but I had every intention of making her my business and real soon.

I walked Julie through the admiring vanguard of salesmen who were conjointly in a . . . 'tongue hanging out' condition. I then, pathetically, offered to be most chivalrous and escorted Julie to the downstairs foyer. I was absolutely determined to steer her out of the glare of the gawking sales associates, and to be on my own with her as soon as possible. For the past couple of hours, I had simply been spellbound by her and not just by her obvious form. Julie's sheer angelical presence was awesome. I was solid gone!

I can recall Julie standing there in the foyer. Her awkwardness was unmistakable as she turned to say goodbye. Needless to say, she had no real idea how she had faired during the so-called interview. Neither did I really.

"Julie, thanks for coming in and telling me all about yourself. I think it would make sense for me to ask one of the girls to make contact with you again to arrange a second interview . . . if you are still interested?"

"Oh . . . gosh, yes . . . thank you, that would be just great."

She was clearly very relieved. It was all I could do, not to maneuver her into a clinch with me. She turned, gave an artful little wave, and sauntered off toward her parked Ford Capri. I watched her admiringly as she drove off. I decided right then and there, no matter what it took Julie Clarkson was going to be my woman.

As I meandered back up the two flights of stairs, I decided on one other matter . . . I would not be offering her a job.

I plainly expected some rib-digging but even I couldn't have anticipated the broadside that greeted me as I walked back through the reception doors. Blimey, you would have thought I had just said my farewells to an 'HRH' or three? Even Syd had got in on the act and was huffing away like a 'hot water bottle' at the front of the mass ensemble.

"Hey, sounds like you have pulled a right little sort . . . m'lad?"

"Pulled a right 'little sort Syd'? Who said professionalism was a dying art, eh?"

I could barely push my way through an impatient scrum of crowding associates who were hectoring me to find out so much more about the sweet and beautiful girl who had been the center of my attention for two hours. I eventually managed to get back to my office, closed the door behind me, and propped myself back against it in order to prevent anyone else barging in. My next thought turned to Trudi.

Bollocks, I am going to have to dump her . . . again.

CHAPTER 21.

I Finally Fall in Love

The effervescent mood hanging over from the proceeding day's events had just begun to abate when I arrived at the office, having visited a client earlier that morning. Driving into the office car park, I kept playing through my mind how I was going to somehow avoid Julie taking up a sales position yet maintain enough contact with her to achieve the ambitions and aspirations I harbored for her.

The frothy reaction of my team had made me even more determined to follow my instincts. I knew having a woman with such an allure working amid a hotbed of 'testosterone' would be a massive distraction for both of them, and me! Furthermore, any romantic pathway I would wish to pursuit would be massively compromised. Office dalliances can be fraught at the best of times. This one would quickly 'redline' if I did not control events. As fate has often decreed, that conundrum was soon to be resolved for me.

When I walked into my office, I could see one of the receptionists had left a note on my desk. I instantly recognized Kate's handwriting.

"That Julie tart called and wanted you to ring her."

What a joy Kate was, em?

I was slightly uneasy about making the call, but I didn't hesitate in doing so.

"Hello Julie, its Samuel from American Life and Casualty here . . . you called this morning. How are you?"

"Oh, hello Mr. Kirkham, thanks for returning my call I wanted to speak to you, because I don't think I am going to be able to take things any further. I do hope you don't feel I have wasted your time?"

"Hey, please don't worry, what happened to change your mind?"

"Well, I had a chat with my mum last night and we both agreed the hours I would need to put in, just won't make it practical for her to look after the children. It just wouldn't be fair because they are only both very young (two boys, aged just eleven months and three years). I am so sorry. I feel awful now after all the time you gave me yesterday."

This was heaven sent and it was all I could do to maintain an impression of disappointment yet laced with a false and empathetic tone.

"Julie, please don't take on so . . . these things happen all the time. I would only ever want what's best for you and your family (and me of course)."

"Oh . . . Sam, thank you so very much you really are most kind. I was quite worried this morning. I felt I was letting you down."

Such obligated language is just wonderful to hear for any alert sociopath and my rapacious instincts were now ready pounce.

"Well, Julie, you could make it up to me you know?" "Oh, how?"

She would now feel obligated.

"By meeting me for a drink this evening?" "Gosh! I errmm, oh no I can't tonight."

As Julie's voice tapered off, I began to feel a sense of wounded rejection washing over me, but she then quickly interjected . . .

"I can't get a babysitter tonight, but my mum would have the boys tomorrow night. So, if you could make it then, I would love to . . . very much."

Another of those 'parallel universe' moments instantly descended upon me; the second one in the space of just 48 hours indeed and, it just didn't get much better than that. This must have been exactly how the young King Arthur would have felt, as he was pulling the sword Excalibur from the stone.

Julie had clearly bought my pathetic explanation about Trudi the day before. So, I didn't wait any further to confirm the date while keeping as nonchalant an appearance as my state of euphoria would allow me to pretend . . .

"Hey, that's great Julie. Shall I come and pick you up at 7:30 ish?"

A good 'closer' never leaves any loose ends, and whether a sale or a date, the same imperative always applies . . .

"Oh right, I thought you meant meet in town, but if you want to come here that would be great, if you really don't mind Sam."

Me? Mind? Perish the thought!

For the rest of that day, I was doing 'cartwheels' around the office. No matter what bad news I was hearing about the sales figures or the lack of confirmed attendees for the next planned recruitment seminar, I couldn't have given a damn. I did, however, have to tell Trudi before the end of that day's play she was to be kicked into the long grass . . . yet again. My overriding desire for Julie consumed me. I did feel a pang of guilt for Trudi who was a well-meaning and kind soul and did not deserve to be treated with such disrespect.

Looking back, how I dealt with so called 'serial monogamy' was very different then to how I would later behave. I used to skip from one relationship to another. Often, already having the next girl lined up. Classic sociopathic behavior of course, but to be fair, over the years I also witnessed numerous women doing . . . exactly the same!

It is a basic insecurity of all humans, where they feel it is a MUST to always have a partner.

I made my excuses to Trudi. Woefully, she had become almost accustomed to losing out when something better was on offer. Remarkably, we remained close friends over the years and have discussed my philandering pathway on countless occasions. She did then meet someone and had a child, Alison who has turned into a fine young woman. We are all very proud of her. Trudi didn't actually marry Alison's father. They eventually drifted apart but she did later marry a guy some ten years ago and guess what? Yes, he is a serial sociopath. Patterns, bloody habitual patterns! He is an extremely arrogant bastard and the parallels between him and me are uncanny. He was also convicted of fraud and ended up inside. Trudi does at least, have the grace to afford me one significant difference between her hubby and me, something she now recognizes is I do have a conscience and have many regrets for my misdemeanors. She tells me her husband has neither. He still blames everyone else for his demise and is constantly on the attack. Abject denial is, indeed, another habitual trait where 99% of sociopaths are concerned.

Julie lived in a 1980s built detach property with her two young sons in the rural setting of the Essex Village of Coggeshall. To be honest, the house was in an ever so slightly sorry state because her estranged husband had neglected the property, which had been their matrimonial home for nearly a decade. Rolph was a few years older than me. I am afraid to say, yet another rampaging sociopath. Moreover, he was a guy who shared my increasing dependency on booze.

Such was my high hopes for this lady; my stomach was churning with a nervous fervor. For I just knew something was going to happen between me and this heaven-sent woman. I pulled up onto the drive and before I could even get out of my car the front door had opened and a beaming blonde greeted me, accompanied by a very refined looking middle-aged woman who was, no doubt, her mother. Julie was holding a wide-eyed blonde baby boy and her mother was holding the hand of a very shy toddler who was doing his utmost to bury his face into his grandmother's skirt.

Mr. Charmer himself got out of the car and I just walked up to Julie. As I pecked her on her gleeful cheek, I instinctively ruffled the baby boy's fine blonde hair. Julie's mother was hesitant, yet most warm with her greeting. After exchanging a few pleasantries, Julie handed her youngest to her mother and we both hopped into my Jag. I then slipped the 'J gate' into 'drive' and off we headed back toward Chelmsford.

Even as I write this today, I can still feel the sense of almost disbelief that in the space of just a few days the Gods had sent me a beautiful angel, who was actually sitting right there beside me. I was solid gone. Now you can call it being besotted, enamored, infatuated, or just plain old smitten, whatever it was, I had it in spades as every cell in my body ached for her. Love at first sight? Yes, it most certainly was, and what is more, over the subsequent years I have NEVER been able to replicate or have experienced such magical emotions as those that were to be embedded in my soul by Julie Clarkson.

I state the obvious when I say how heavenly the evening was to experience in Julie's company. We simply melted into each other as we chatted away and laughed over many drinks at my most frequented wine bar, which was conveniently found just a few minutes' walk from the office. Julie was both tactile and amorous in the silkiest way imaginable, and it felt like I was 'bathing in chocolate'.

We left from the wine bar just after 11 pm and most conveniently. The last words Julie's mother said as we drove off earlier that evening were . . .

"Don't worry about the time. We will be fine here."

Julie had actually arranged for her mother to stay the over for the night - what a little tinker, eh?

As we walked back to my car we still hadn't passionately kissed; such was the delight of just being in her captivating and auric presence.

We were naturally chatting and holding hands. As we approached the Jag, I turned and suggested . . .

"Julie, I have the office keys so shall we have a coffee upstairs then?"

"Why not?"

I deactivated the alarm system and only the night security lights provided any illumination as we made our way through the dimly lit reception and toward the office kitchen. I actually had the intention of making a freshly percolated pot of coffee. As I set two coffee cups on the kitchen work surface, without further hesitation, Julie turned me around and palming the back of my head planted her full lips warmly over my own. As I pulled her tiny waist into me, the sweet nectar taste of her hot tongue was already deep inside my mouth with a feverish yearning. Forget the coffee then . . .

It had been a mild evening, so her garments were sparse. This was 1990 Essex remember. Julie was wearing a scant white boob tube, stretch denims that had only the tightest of fabric covering her bronzed, and shapely 'pins'. Julie may have recently become a mother for the second time, but her curved size 8 form was just perfection. By the way, her stilettos were NOT white!

I didn't need to make any of the running for she kicked off her heels as I peeled her top up and over her gorgeous face. Her breasts were pert and swelling as I expertly released them from behind the small of her back. Our mouths would barely part for the rest of the evening, and I gently glided the tips of my fingers over the rounded contour of her breasts.

My throbbing enveloped through my every cell as I picked Julie up and carried her from the kitchen and through to my office. I can still visualize to this day, her seductive pout as her long blonde locks cascaded over her face. She arched back onto my desk and rolled her denims down and over her tiny ankles. She was then perched in front of me wearing only a white lacy thong . . .

Our lovemaking was aflame with passion and the next few hours took on a sensation, the likes of which, I have only ever experienced with Julie. It was, as if, we were both taken beyond our physical senses, and this was truly a divine state of hieros gamos. I pulsated deep inside her for an hour of sheer rapture and my feeling of complete love for this girl was the first time I had experienced such a unique and unparalleled emotion.

As I drove Julie home in the early hours, I honestly believed I had found the woman who I would be with until the end of my days. How wrong could I have been.

Over the next few weeks, we became inseparable and even the scowling Kate, seemed to show a degree of graciousness as far as my newfound happiness was concerned. Kate had been such an unsettling bitch toward me at times, but she was just beginning to thaw and would ask after Julie’s wellbeing . . . without too much sarcasm!

I adapted well into domesticity again and Julie seamlessly integrated me into her young family and readily introduced me to her three brothers. Furthermore, as was a pattern I would later develop, I got on very well with my new ‘pseudo-other-in-law’. Sociopaths quickly align themselves to their woman’s mother and in order to curry favor, they will regularly flirt with them.

There was obviously the tricky task of dealing with the shenanigans of her estranged husband Rolph who, to be fair, maintained fortnightly access to his children. However, like all sociopaths, he created as much chaos and disruption along the way as he could. I was also being hopelessly hypocritical myself, as I would loyally listen to Julie's criticism of Rolph's carryings on, despite my obvious abject failure to contact and support my own daughter. That particular contradictory pattern would be another I would further repeat - several times. God only knows why. I would parade my new trophy lover at every opportunity and ensured she had the best of everything to accentuate her ‘Barbie-like figure’. Cozy foursomes with other ‘corporate couples’ were the order of the day. Being one of the four branch managers within the group; whenever there was a ‘black-tie’ function, I would proudly puff out my chest as I sat on ‘high table’ accompanied by my new ‘Queen’. I simply adored her very being. She demonstrably felt the same about me but there was always a lurking demon ready to destroy my blissful life. Alcohol . . .

Ironically, one of Julie's constant gripes about Rolph was his inordinate drinking and how it had been having an adverse effect on their marriage for quite a while. Although they had been married since Julie was just twenty, they had only started a family when they had been together several years. She readily admitted to me, she hadn’t really noticed his unhealthy levels of alcohol consumption while she had still been at work. However, once she had become a housewife and a young mum, the shift in parental priorities and responsibilities was only being made by Julie. Rolph simply wanted to remain, ‘one of the lads’.

Rolph's own predatory inclinations meant he spent a great deal of time on the road, and in the beds of other women. Such a practice was one I would eventually adopt with relish. I have often attributed my eventual 'female addiction' to having observed Rolph's 'modus operandi' and previously, the likes of Anthony Pager, Derek Fairly, and all. It also may not have been lost on the reader here is yet another example, where a man cheated on a stunning and beautiful wife in favor of a woman who, shall we say . . . is not! This theme will reappear countless times in my story, and not restricted to my own exploits.

My imbibing had also gained some real momentum. It was both acceptable and even fashionable for all the managers to keep their drinks' cabinet well stocked. Whilst I never became an outlandish drunk, I was by this time drinking pretty much every day. When, thinking back, it was only because Julie was so in love. She did not recognize I too was on a slippery alcoholic slope. Denial, eh?

Being in love may, for a while at least, defer any underlying problems but the gradual and corrosive effects of alcoholism on both an individual and their partner; always result in an inevitable outcome. My relationship with Julie would befall such a fate.

In the meantime, however, we had an extraordinary 'family thing' going on and quite unusually, even my parents took to Julie and her boys, Jamie and Adam, despite having lost contact with their only grandchild. Julie had lost her father a few years earlier and she clearly still pined for him.

Coincidentally, it was at this time my good friend Neil Follet had been transferred back to Essex to take up a new and more senior management post. I for one, was most pleased to be reporting directly to him. We had lost a fair amount of contact because of our mutual management demands, so we took no time catching up about my new love life. Neil was naturally wary, but at the same time he was really pleased for me.

On a more serious note, we also had other things to discuss, which was regarding my underperforming sales team. I could have said this was largely down to my romantic distractions, but that would actually be unfair on Julie. In truth, I was becoming increasingly disillusioned with the whole management culture and the recruitment circus that seemed to be getting ever worse. Neil was both appreciative and sympathetic to my views as he had also suffered massive financial losses but was buoyed by a wider financial support package due to his new position. Although I hasten to add, still largely supported through loans. I can remember revealing to Neil, how I had conducted an interview with a really pleasant chap who had enthusiastically watched all the recruitment videos, swallowed the bullshit about the financial support, and had then brought his wife along to a final interview to confirm his

appointment.

The young and discerning couple; were both sat there. Despite their nervousness about surrendering a regular wage, had mutually decided to take the plunge. They had savings to supply a further 'cushion' (which they were encouraged to place in a bond to give them a little extra commission . . . fuck me).

So, the date was set for this new and gullible recruit's weeklong sales induction course. Here is the even worse bit though, I smiled, shook both their hands, and said with utter insincerity, "Welcome to a bright and prosperous future." As they walked out of my office, the smile was instantly wiped from my face only to be replaced with a disturbing thought of . . .

He will fail.

I may have become self-serving in my ambitions, but the manner by which these lambs to the slaughter were being exploited and put upon by an uncaring corporation was leaving me with both a sense of depression and failure. Only to be compounded even further when they were coldly discarded and thrown on a slag heap once their usefulness had become redundant.

I was not on my own either. For I had attended no end of so called 'management workshops' and when comparing notes with colleagues they were nearly all feeling the same way. This just couldn't go on. There would soon be a catalyst bringing matters to a head. Something indeed, that will sound quite comical when looking back, but at the time, was treated with the utmost seriousness, which further confirmed just how cynical and ruthless the 'corporate psychopath' can be.

My blissful world with Julie had truly blossomed. It was only a matter of weeks when inevitably, my adorable Julie and her two young boys moved in with me. For the most part, it was a utopian existence. Considering the pace of it all, it felt at times as if we had always been together. Even Rolph was becoming more compliant. It was as if by my being in Julie's life, the heat had been taken off him. That particular 'social paradigm' would re-surface on many more occasions.

CHAPTER 22.

Destroying My Dream

So, here I was in a loving Shangri-La. Well, so it seemed. But as it is often the case, matters are fated to implode our world through a destructive sequence of events. During the summer months of 1990, I would endure a level of pain and emotional heartache, which would take decades to heal.

As this story continues to unfold, you will read how my pattern of 'self-sabotage' actually worsens over the years and how I began to spin out of control. With egregious necessity, the level of destruction had to be intensified to destroy an ever-greater sense of potential happiness. Almost as if, I was never worthy of the very thing I craved all of my life, to be capable of giving unconditional love.

What is more, the demands a sociopath will make on his woman also become impossible to satisfy. If anything goes wrong, she will get the blame. The pressure at my workplace to deliver results was growing and I inevitably began to take home the stress with me. Julie and the kids were in the firing line.

Anyone reading this, who is or has been in such a family paradigm, will know the 'step-parent' role is one that is virtually impossible to get right. If you chastise the bad behavior of your own children, this can, at the best of times lead to an adversarial relationship with your spouse. So, when it happens where step-children are involved, the additional dynamic of 'you are not my dad or mum' helps create further conflict.

Julie, bless her, tried to accommodate my increasing mood swings. I only defended her children when I was being particularly assertive. I still harbored a great deal of guilt about the way I had abandoned my daughter and I was paradoxically resenting any fondness I would afford Julie's offspring. Despite this, our own passions had intensified but with hindsight, we were both rather 'needy' at times. Julie's was understandably, as a result of her experiences with Rolph. Mine was caused by a continuous legacy from the unemotional experiences of my childhood.

No matter the undercurrent of the relationship, I was still as deeply in love with Julie as the moment when I first set eyes on her. It was an all-consuming emotion, which prevented me from foreseeing the devastating meteor hurtling toward me.

To this day, I am still baffled as to how, and why, my relationship with Julie ended so abruptly. How could I have prevented it happening and prevent losing the most perfect love I could ever have been blessed to behold?

We had been together for six months. I could not have been prouder to have Julie as my consort and lover. Yes, there had been certain tensions at times but that was not unusual given the circumstances, surely? While I may have drunk more than was healthy for me, I was never physically aggressive. Anyway, compared to my years with Pam, my life with Julie and her two boys, was bliss.

We decided to take the children on a short family break to Centre Parcs together with Neil and his family. We all had a most pleasant time in each other's company. We had adjoining family chalets and the children were clearly in their element embracing the unique atmosphere provided by the leisure complex.

On the final evening Neil and I went for a few beers, leaving the ladies to have a bottle of wine and 'girlie' chat. I was later to discover, Julie actually revealed to Neil's wife, she had never before been so in love, felt so loved, content, and fulfilled. Julie also told Neil's wife . . . I am going to marry that man. Within just two weeks, however, she would be gone.

Once we had come away from the holiday 'bubble', it was back to the reality of sales and management meetings together with the entire charade, which accompanied it. Fair enough, our relationship was being tested but not to such an extent as to be able to predict Julie's next decision. We were beginning to experience some cash flow problems as my management pay packet was being repeatedly affected with losses from failed sales associates.

Julia had also started to dip into what little savings she had and used some of it to pay for her preferences of furniture, music, and decorating the house. I had also bought her a brand-new car, which of course, was

on finance. My lavishing of women with gifts I couldn't really afford,
Mitchell Allen

was now becoming a pattern that would repeat itself many times over the coming years.

On the morning of the worst day of my life, Julie and I had actually made passionate love before I headed off to the office. I was in high spirits and basking in the clear blue skies of early spring. Hey, I even had a new enthusiasm for the sales challenges facing me for that coming week.

Just ten minutes into my journey and my car phone rang. As I answered, Julie's shaken voice greeted me . . .

"Hi, it's only me."

"Hello sweetie, you, ok?"

"No . . . not really, Sam."

"Hey, what's wrong?" Silence . . .

"Julie, what's the matter, tell me? You are worrying me." Still silence and then . . . click . . . prrrrrrr.

I had this horrendous sinking feeling. My visceral intuition was screaming loudly at me. I could feel I was about to have my world completely blown apart. I knew I would not be able to concentrate on anything, so I called the office and told Kate to cancel the interviews for that day.

I was in the fast lane of the A12. At the first opportunity, I took the Jag into an acute U-turn and kicked down in the direction of home. I don't know how I managed to drive and keep control, because my hands were actually trembling. No matter how firmly I gripped the steering wheel the fear and anxiety that was threatening to overwhelm me was getting even worse.

Pulling up outside my house, my feelings of foreboding quickly changed to 'anxious confusion' as I was prohibited access to my drive by a . . . REMOVAL VAN? I flew from my car seat just as the broad silhouette of Julie's younger brother Matt came anxiously running toward me. With a look of, What the fuck are you doing back so early'? "Hello mate, look, I am really sorry about this . . . but Julie insisted.

I have always really liked you mate, b . . . but she is my sister you know. I tried to talk her out of it. We all did. I don't think she even knows herself what she is doing."

I was so confounded and bewildered, the words would not come to my lips. Julie and the kids were nowhere to be seen as I powerlessly observed Matt and two of his pals loading various items of furniture into the van. Grabbing Matt's arm, I finally spluttered . . .

"Matt please. Stop! For fuck sake! WHERE IS SHE?"

Matt pulled my arm away and whilst he clearly wasn't threatened by my actions, he was most uncomfortable himself. I had really befriended Julie's younger sibling. I knew he wouldn't bullshit me. Since my return, he had also determined something else . . .

"Jesus, I thought so. I now know why she wanted us to get this done so quickly and before you got back home. You don't know, do you?"

"Noooooo, I don't . . . know what? Fuck, tell me man!"

"Sam, I am so sorry to be the one to tell you this, but Julie has gone back to Rolph."

CHAPTER 23.

No Woman Will Ever Hurt Me Again

That evening, I just lay on my sofa in a state of paralysis and isolation, with my face buried in my hands. I remained in that position the whole night long as I was simply feeling to hurt to move. The pain I was feeling in my heart and my soul was of such a magnitude it has never been equalled in my life since. Not even in the dark times fate still had in store for me. Indeed, when you have finally ploughed through to the end of my story, you will have read about many crazier, and at times, really frightening experiences. However, I maintain right here and now, Julie Clarkson's name has left a scar on my heart like nothing else.

In the midst of the emotional hell, I did afford myself just one brief moment where my thoughts found clarity.

No woman will EVER hurt me like this again.

They have not been allowed to . . .

CHAPTER 24.

Goodbye Syd And Laurie

I barely slept and had no intention of attending the next day's sales meeting. They could all go and fuck themselves as far as I was concerned. I was 'sloth like' around a house that only twenty-four hours earlier, had been host to the cacophony of noise that always goes with the energy created by toddlers. I was feeling just hollow.

The phone rang. Although I didn't want to speak to anyone, my intuition told me to pick up the receiver and I barked.

"Yeah . . . who is this." "Hi ya, I heard."

It was Trudi; I never deserved her caring loyalty. "Fuck me, how are the vultures?"

"I won't ask how you are, it's bloody obvious. Neil knows as well. He is as baffled as the rest of us. I really mean this Sam; I am so sorry things didn't work out. We all knew you believed you had finally found . . . the one. Anyway, I am here when and if, you need me."

I didn't wish to appear disrespectful to Trudi as she had yet again, humbled me with such unconditional caring and generosity.

"Trudi, you are amazing, and your words mean so much to me, but I just want some space right now, if that's ok?"

"Oh yeah, of course. Chat later, eh?" "Ok sweetie, by then."

I really did just want to curl up and die, but yet again fate interceded in such a manner; whereby someone else's misfortune distracted me just enough, to prevent me from jumping off the nearest bridge. Hardly a minute had passed after Trudi had rung off, and the phone rang again. I picked up the handset and deliberately just listened and to see who it might be, before I might have to commit to a tortuous explanation of events. This time it was Neil.

"Hello . . . you there Sam?"

"Hello mate, sorry I am in a real state here."

"I do know that son. I was going to leave you alone, but some serious shit has hit the fan here."

For fuck sakes, this is all I needed on top of everything else. I knew my month end figures were due in at any time, so they must be really dire, and Jon Newland was probably going ape?

"Look Neil, I will deal with the figures in a few days or something." Neil just spoke straight across me.

"Fuck the figures Sam, Syd's gone! He was fired an hour ago, so you had better get over here right away."

Some three seconds on, and Syd De' Bret's demise is going to read as rather comic. However, I can assure you, at that time, he was treated by the executive management as if it had been revealed all along, he had in fact been a Russian spy!

I was so mentally and emotionally drained I didn't have any protest left in me, so I threw on some casual clothes and headed off to the office. What on earth could Syd have done to have antagonized the 'Top Brass' so much, that they would have axed him? Sure, he had a real Mr. McCawber style of management at times, but he had always been very loyal in his own way and had followed Jon Newland from the police and into the life assurance business.

When I arrived at the office it was bedlam. Even the usual super cool Kate looked very unsettled indeed. Despite the noise and crossfire, Kate touchingly came up to me and just mouthed . . .

"I'm so sorry."

I intuitively know when an insincere gesture has just been made, after all, I have done it enough times myself, but my former femme fatale, truly meant it.

The office 'gossip mill' had seriously shifted into top gear and to be honest, it was all quite chaotic and rather unbecoming of a so-called professional sales outfit. My own break up and Syd's sacking, fed the 'piranhas' like never before.

Neil peered out of his office and anxiously beckoned me over. "Shut the door behind you mate."

I sat but really wasn't interested at all by what Neil had to reveal, but looking back, it was quite hilarious really.

"Listen, Jon Newland is in Syd's office going through files and God only knows what else, but Syd was sacked on the spot this morning and told to clear his desk."

Neil then went on to explain - you might have to read this twice - Syd was fired because he had bought a 'boy's bike', using his 'gold' company credit card. WTF! Now technically, I guess that's fraud, but EVERYONE used their business credit cards for personal usage, and it was deducted from their pay at a later date anyway. Talk about a sledge-hammer to crack a nut. They (the reptilians at the top) had clearly been after Syd for some time and needed an excuse to get rid of him. It never ceases to amaze me how an intelligent man will try to explain it away with an excuse so pathetic and stupid, it just beggars' belief.

So, when the 'audit police' in accounts had finally snaffled Syd, they hauled him down to their regional office where Jon Newland, who was supposedly his best pal, was gleefully in wait. Sociopaths have no loyalty whatsoever. Even less so for another of their kind. Syd was about to have that one confirmed.

Neil went on to then relay a priceless anecdote . . .

"Anyway, when Syd was being carpeted, 'JN' asked him what the reason was for buying his son a bike and meriting the use of company funds? Syd's reply was a fucking gem. He actually told Jon the bike wasn't for his son; it was for and wait for it . . . fucking branch deliveries! Ha-ha."

I actually laughed out loud. Light relief indeed. "So where is Syd now then Neil?"

"No fucker knows mate. He just cleared his desk and had to piss off.

Guess that means I will get his job now?"

Even Neil, a man of immense integrity, had the instincts of a real 'raptor'.

We were then eventually called into the staff meeting room where JN and his sycophantic sidekicks, held court. He then came out with a load of disingenuous 'claptrap' about how Syd had been a great and loyal servant for the company, but it was time for him to move on, and

. . . fucking out!

The vultures were soon circling the carcass of Syd's office belongings. It was all quite flagrant to watch at times, what with pouring over 'Edinburgh cut crystal' drink cabinets, high back swivel chairs . . . it as a bloody feeding frenzy and very vulgar. Even Neil handed a few unopened boxes of cut crystal to me, but quite frankly, I was in no mood to indulge.

When the dust had settled, Neil walked into my office sat himself down, and asked me . . .

"This is the first chance to really ask how you are mate? I still can't believe it you know. My wife was stunned because Julie had only told her a couple of weeks ago, she was going to, I mean . . . really wanted to, marry you?"

This was where I had first heard this almost incredulous of anecdotes.

"What? Do you really believe that she meant it mate?"

"I asked the wife that same question last night mate. She is adamant Julie meant and believed it."

"Fuck . . . in many ways, I could handle it better if I thought she hadn't meant it?"

I wasn't prepared to discuss it any further, not even with Neil, who ironically, within just twelve months would be my best man at my second wedding. Jesus!

As far as the life expectancy of my management role was concerned, Syd's departure actually heralded a short-term reprieve. A few members of Syd's sales team were transferred over to me, so my sales figures were artificially boosted for a while and the sacking aftermath also helped to distract me from my romantic woes. However, and as I strongly suspected at the time, Sydney de' Brett was not the type to just go away quietly and lick his wounds. Indeed not. The former 'Sweeney' driver would be most pissed off at the manner by which he had been stabbed in the back, by his so-called friend. The acrid stench of 'revenge' was in the air. It would soon turn to being most sweet.

Throughout the 60's, and through to the 90's, the life assurance industry was akin to the 'wild west' only with far less integrity. To be fair, friends and associates who are still in direct-sales tell me it is hardly any different today. In many ways, so called 'compliance' has simply made matters worse rather than better. The smart 'sociopathic reptilians' at the top, just exploit the glaring holes in the numerous and suffocating protocols to further their own ends.

Consequently, rival companies were constantly on the lookout for unsettled managers and sales associates, which was practically all of them. My own team, proved to be no exception. Rival offices would 'tap up' the sales teams of their competitors during the many industry forums and conferences, with offers and counteroffers, to those who were open to seduction in either direction. I also see the many comparesons today with professional footballers and the devilments carried out by their clubs and parasitic agents.

Syd de Brett had no intentions of hanging about either. Despite the abject flaws in his sales management style, he had a fairly good track record by the low industry standards. It wasn't long before he was approached by another leading life office - Guardian & Legal Exchange. Bloody fools!

Needless to say, they were just as predatory in their recruitment practices as any of the other life offices. So, they cobbled together a management package, which needless to say was based on yet more loans. Syd had only one real aim, which was to recruit as many of his former sales associates as possible. Which would have been a sizeable enough threat on its own but when your sales team are disgruntled, feeling disillusioned, it leaves the sales manager extremely vulnerable. I discussed the menace of Syd with Neil. We both agreed he would go for the low-hanging fruit, my North Essex branch!

There was by now, a torrent of lies coming from various members of my team who were intent on extracting evermore money from the massively flawed payment system. They were desperate, and so was I. Two notable episodes occurred in unison, which was no coincidence and hammered the final nail into my managerial coffin. The mass exodus to Syd's new 'madhouse' and an ex-policeman. So, enter Lawrie Conran.

Before I relate the story around the mass abandonment of both mine and Neil's sales teams, it is worthwhile recounting the story of arrogant Lawrie for a number of reasons. Firstly, as a prime example of the ludicrousness of the recruitment culture. Secondly, the lack of any real support for the exposed managers, which then resulted in the desperate lengths people will go to in order to keep their heads above water and keep their pride intact.

Lawrie was one angry young man indeed. He was then in his mid-twenties. He was engaged to a little nymph named Nicky, who was already a member of Syd's sales team. It is worth mentioning here she was wholly unsuited to a career in sales, no matter the sector. Syd's own predatory and opportunistic instincts had persuaded her to join his outfit simply because she was an heiress to a family that owned a hugely successful department store. Syd clearly believed, wrongly as it would turn out, she would have influence and be able to introduce the services of the business to the extremely wealthy family that owned the store.

Anyhow, the 'pyramid' style of recruitment rampaged on. Nicky, like all existing associates, was constantly being manipulated . . . errrm,

I mean encouraged . . . to 'recommend' a 'career in sales' to their family and peers. She stupidly and naively then tapped up her own boyfriend, Lawrie.

Lawrie had joined the police force as a raw 'Hendon recruit'. He became disillusioned with the job very quickly. I think the posting of this Essex lad to a station in impoverished Bethnal Green in East London had not really helped matters! There had been quite a long tradition for former services personnel to have joined our company and some had even made a decent fist of it. Let's look at Syd and his boss John Newland, both being a case in point. I mean, throw enough shit against any wall and some is bound to stick, eh? Well, Lawrie was well, and truly on Syd's radar. The only problem being Syd decided with misguided intent, Lawrie, should join my fucking team!

I can vividly remember interviewing the lad. Whilst there was quite a likeable side to him, the arrogance . . . well, it actually made mine seem quite pedestrian. He was a rather brittle character. Physically, he resembled the actor, Charlie Sheen. So, he was a handsome chap and boy, did he know it!

He also had a massive problem with any 'authority figures'. To be fair to him, I made the early mistake - as sociopaths can - of designating him as one of my sycophantic favorites, as opposed to making him work his 'way up' just like everyone else in the team. Then, the classic pattern of resentment from established colleagues kicked in, and an undercurrent was created that would inflict untold damage on yours truly. Such a chain reaction is often referred to as 'karma', which it actually isn't at all. The phenomenon of 'reaping what we sow' is in reality, 'cause and effect'. I will clarify the dynamics of 'karma' later.

Lawrie was also both wooden and completely lacking in empathy. He lacked fundamental skill sets for selling. He was so brittle, he couldn't even fake it. To really compound matters, I allowed him to persuade me to recruit his younger and rather naive brother, Adam. I saw no end of nepotism in the sales industry, which often resulted in the destruction of sales teams. I was readily stoking up real trouble for myself; that was for sure.

Likewise, any genuine sales support and coaching was pretty much non-existent. Yet, despite the company spending literally millions on sales brochures, marketing, and promotional material, it was all a monumental red herring. No matter how glossy the sales ad, if the new 'associate' had been recruited for all the wrong reasons, he would be doomed to fail!

Lawrie readily fell into this category and so did his brother. His girlfriend Louise, who was still in operating in Syd's team, was struggling herself. Yes, she had finally discovered, mystery of all mysteries, Syd had hoodwinked her totally. Therefore, when the three of them failed, so did their collective commission payments, or should I say, the lack of any further loans! The pressure to survive then mounts and the back biting, snitching, and heaping the blame for their woes on their manager; really intensifies . . .

He is clearly feathering his nest at my expense.

I bloody wished. The losses were seriously mounting for me also. It was all I could do to persuade Neil to support me. The blame, and the pleading, escalated as far up the scale as you could possibly imagine.

The real dilemma being, if you failed to continue to support the associate with yet more 'loans' they would constantly threaten to leave; thus, crystallizing debts further which would be borne by their manager. If you did continue to pay them, then of course, the debt just grew and grew. Damned if you did, damned if you didn't! It would have been laughable if it wasn't so potentially damaging. They all lied when asked the obvious question . . .

"Before I pay you again, are you thinking of leaving?"

An absurd monthly game of 'cat and mouse' followed and the stress, for all parties, was absolutely unhealthy. So, the associate was eventually forced to either making evermore dubious sales. They became so desperate; they would be tempted to take desperate risks. Lawrie was about to cross that particular Rubicon!

I was about to take my first sip of percolated coffee and the phone rang; it was Kate . . .

"Morning Mr. Grumpy, I have the manager of Lloyds Bank on the phone. He wants to speak to Lawrie Conran's Manager. I must say, he is sounding a bit agitated."

"Okay Kate. Put him through. Fuck knows what Lawrie's been up to."

"Good morning, Mr. Kirkham, this is Lloyds Bank, Chelmsford here. We have one of your employees, Mr. Lawrie Conran, who has applied for a personal loan. The reason for my calling you is he has provided an income reference, we would like to have verified, if that's okay with you?"

Employee?

"Mr. Conran is not technically employed by us, as all associates are contracted and taxed as self-employed. May I ask who has signed off the 'income' reference?"

"It's signed off by you, which is why I have called you personally."

"Has it now?"

The bank manager continued to explain Lawrie, had made an application for a $10,000 personal loan. I perfectly understood his reasons. Lawrie's sales performance was dreadful. As with everything else, when the confidence ebbs away, inevitably so does the commission.

Similarly, when bearing in mind Nicky wasn't bringing in any sales either, their situation was becoming rather dire. Desperate people do desperate things. Lawrie was about to become another example.

"Ok, so what does the reference actually say? What does the official headed paper look like?"

I asked such a question because for reasons of status and ego, the official stationery of managers and 'senior sales associates' were all personalized. What a load of old pretentious bollocks that all was. Nevertheless, it really gave the game away and also made me realize; Lawrie must have had an accomplice within the administration team.

In my absence, only my personal assistant Pam, or one of the receptionists, would have had access to my stationery. Indeed, this bank manager went on to confirm the reference was typed on my personalized company stationery. The wording of letter had confirmed Lawrie was employed and on a SALARY!

"Ok, may I ask what raised your suspicions? Was it the appearance of my forged signature?"

Even at such a serious moment, the bank manager still found it in him to quip . . .

"Not at all Mr. Kirkham, it was the fact Mr. Conran, had actually misspelt salary as . . . celery!"

You just can't make up priceless anecdotes like that!

I thanked the 'man from the bank' and asked him to send me a faxed copy of the offending letter. I would have just loved to have been a fly on the wall when Lawrie was informed, he would not be eligible for the loan and even worse, he was to report immediately to his branch manager.

I phoned through to Neil and jested . . . "Houston, we have a problem."

I definitely detected from his response Neil was going to enjoy this confrontation, as he had never really taken to Lawrie, and had found his attitude to be both arrogant and obtuse. Neil had proven to be absolutely correct in his reservations. He recognized my being so friendly with Lawrie was about to cost me dearly.

Lawrie's potential financing losses on his account was also well in excess of the $10,000 loan amount, which he had been endeavoring to 'con' out of the bank.

Neil decided I had allowed Lawrie to become far too familiar within my personal social group, so it would be for the best if I just sat in on the disciplinary and observe proceedings. I wasn't going to argue because despite his flaws, I always liked Lawrie. I identified a number of familiar traits in him. However, the major difference being I was a half decent salesman.

Even now, I maintain my management style, whilst being far from perfect, was really quite effective. Had I been allowed to develop with genuine support, I would have become quite successful. The problem being was, I could not reconcile the method of recruitment and the virtual nonexistence of any real help.

Many of my detractors will assert, to a certain extent understandably, I was void of any conscience. I have to disappoint on that one. Whatever my flaws and my poor way of showing it, I do actually care about the misfortune of others. Especially, if it was as a result of my reckless and selfish behavior.

A most anxious and sheepish looking Lawrie craned his neck around Neil's office door. My boss, and friend, then beckoned over the 6' 2" former London Bobby, who despite being 'banged to rights' was still very capable of cutting his nose off to spite his face. I remember thinking, Lawrie, just show some humility because, right now, Neil is holding all the aces. My telepathic skills clearly hadn't evolved properly and before Neil could utter a single word Lawrie just went for it . . .

"D-Don't fucking start you two! If you pair of cunts didn't hold back my money each month, then I wouldn't have been forced into doing this."

Lawrie, just like the majority of associates, could never quite seem to fathom, despite their sales figures being virtually 'zilch', they somehow had an entitlement to a monthly check. It was down to 'them managers' who were holding back 'my money'! His whole posture resembled a coiled spring. There was a noticeable bead of sweat on his upper lip. It was at this point, where I saw Neil at his best, especially when bearing in mind, he was no admirer of Lawrie's.

"I am sorry you feel like that Lawrie. Surely, as a former officer of the law I need not point out to you trying to obtain funds through fraudulent means, is an extremely serious matter. What do you say to that?"

Neil then skilfully and assertively, continued with the dressing down before Lawrie even had the chance to respond.

"I have a fax copy of the letter you forged. Luckily for you, the manager at the bank agreed to destroy the original and leave any disciplinary matters to us. Now you are the ex-copper, so what should I do now?"

It was a rhetorical question. Neil pressed on regardless . . .

"I have taken advice from Jon Newland. Don't forget he is also a former senior police officer. So, it was most fortuitous his guidance was at hand. Jon advised me we will need to terminate your 'sales associate contract' with immediate effect. You should consider yourself a very lucky young man because we have decided not to report the matter to the police, despite our being perfectly within our rights to do so. To that end, we will not be taking any further action against you."

I was rather perplexed . . . When exactly did Neil have the opportunity to speak with JN?

Lawrie's defensive expression then changed somewhat. His biggest being should the matter be referred to the police. As a former copper, there would be serious ramifications for him.

"Clear your things and fuck off immediately."

Lawrie muttered some inaudible expletives under his breath and snarled at the pair of us as he stormed off, out of our lives. The sheer nerve of the guy was just priceless though. Within less than two weeks of his departure, I received a 'job reference request' from of all organizations, including Essex Police Department! Apparently, Lawrie had the audacity to rejoin the force. As far as I am aware, he remained in the job. I toyed with the idea of being circumspect with the reference, but I just thought, hey, we all make mistakes, so give the twat a break?

So, for all those who have been judging me recently, there you go. I am just an old softie really.

"Neil, you didn't speak to Jon at all did you?"

"No. Of course not. We don't need that arsehole interfering with this believe me. I just knew Lawrie would put up very little resistance if he knew 'JN' being a former police sergeant was hovering in the background. Just let sleeping dogs lie, Sam."

"Neil, that's ok for you to say, but within two months upstairs will reconcile Lawrie's account, and shaft me for the losses."

As it would turn out, I wouldn't even need to wait a week for the final axe to fall on my management career because Syd de Brett would soon see to that. I first had an inkling about my impending management demise when I held my next branch meeting where attendees were distinctly thin on the ground. When I posed the obvious question to those who had turned up, I was met with a rather collective 'blank' response. Neil's subsequent branch meeting took on an equally sparse resemblance. So, it was becoming fairly obvious our former master was being more than just meddlesome, he had been very active indeed.

To manage expectations, Neil conveyed his fears about Syd's interference to Jon Newland who, with an unsurprising lack of sensitivity, just brushed the whole matter to one side with a 'Syd is past it' gesture. As far as being a long-term serious player again, yes, Syd was most certainly a busted flush, but in the short term, he was still capable of inflicting untold damage on both mine and Neil's manpower count. That old bastard didn't fail in his objective either.

All the classic signs were there. With sales associates avoiding calls, nonattendance in the branch, although still expecting their commission advances, of course. Endless rumors. My stress levels were going through the roof! Syd had planned his attack with nigh on military precision, and on a particularly gloomy Monday morning, I started to receive call after call from gutless associates.

None of them had the courage to tell me to my face they had decided to 'further their careers' and join Syd's 'new band of merry men'. Even my top producer, Adam Dickinson, who was also supposed to be a 'pal' had the bloody nerve to turn up that morning and present me with this little gem . . .

"Good morning, mate, have you got a minute?"

"Always for you son. I guess you have heard what all those idiots are doing and falling for Syd's bullshit, eh?"

"Errmm . . . w-well . . . that's what I wanted to speak to you about." "You ARE kidding me, right? I have always looked after you, made sure your money has always been there, and even on those occasions where your figures have been, shall we say, somewhat on the low side." "Oh yeah, mate, I do know that, but Syd has made me a very tempting offer and guaranteed me an extra $500 a month 'cashflow'. But I will tell you what I will do for you, if you can make sure I can have my check today, with the extra $500, I will tell Syd I won't decide for another month. Let's then see how we go from there. I can't say fairer than that now, can I?"

"Son, I always knew you would be upfront with me but that still makes you a total cunt! No extra, no check, just . . . fuck off! I can't say fairer than that now, can I?"

"What? You can't stop my last paycheck before I go, that's my commission!"

Even my top producer never understood his pay was, in reality, a series of loan advances.

"Well, read the small print in your contract. You will find I can. And, I have done just that. Good luck with Syd. You won't last very long."

Adam jumped out of his chair through gritted teeth . . .

"That's just sour grapes. Syd is gonna fuck over this office big-time!"

I guess, when faced with a situation like that one, it is easy to be accused of being churlish, but I wasn't actually. In many ways, it gave me the excuse I had been looking for to resign from the madness of sales management.

Back then, I may not have become quite the intuitive soul I would eventually evolve into, but my prophecy about Syd and his new crew, transpired to be right on the money. If you can forgive the pun. Just like the Pied Piper he had enticed no less than two dozen or so sales associates across to his new outfit, and as is often the reality, most of them were wretched failures who were still just bouncing from one commission paycheck to the next. So, Syd was stoking up huge potential losses, all over again.

That old definition of 'insanity'.

Albert Einstein: "The definition of insanity is doing the same thing over and over and expecting different results."

Hey, I should know. Regrettably, whilst being fully seized of that famous quote a long time back, I would continue with such a folly for another twenty-five years!

Within six months of the launch of Syd's new operation, the whole operation had blown up in Syd's face. Not only did the majority of the team 'jump ship' (again), but Syd was also unmercilessly thrown to the wolves.

This larger-than-life character, who once boasted he had been an elite driver for the London Metropolitan Police 'flying squad', enjoyed a high-flying group management position with two company cars, and massive annual override commission, was now finished. What is more, to add insult to injury, he had also owned a monumental residential nursing home in Essex, which had to be sold at auction in a 'fire-sale' as part of his inevitable bankruptcy, which soon followed.

I recently looked him up online. There he is working for a 'bucket shop' insurance brokerage and barely 'eking out' a living. Syd is not, by any means, on his own in that regard, having befallen such a fate after a so-called illustrious career in financial services.

I was not prepared to endure another single day of this torture. So, I informed Neil I wanted an audience with Jon Newland at the earliest opportunity in order to discuss 'my future'. Neil totally understood. Neither was he overly happy about the number of associates who had left his own team to join up with Syd. As it was fated, JN had a planned visit the very next day, so he came to see me in my office, and I told him straight about how disillusioned I had become with the whole management structure. Or should I say, lack of. JN was clearly rather embarrassed about getting it so wrong regarding Syd's effectiveness and his successfully coercing many of our vulnerable sales team.

Jon readily conceded I had had enough of the management foolishness and readily accepted my resignation. Fortunately, I had always kept up a very healthy level of personal sales, so it was agreed, I would go 'back on the road' so to speak, and as soon as possible.

The most galling aspect of it all though, was Jon still expected me to cover any future financial losses incurred by defecting associates. So, he 'very kindly' devised a financial package for me (yes . . . yet more loans) whereby, my future commissions would be 'discounted in order to offset losses'.

What a generous man he was. If I wasn't already being blockheaded enough, I would in the foreseeable future again allow this lizard to recruit me into his latest 'opportunity'! Nevertheless, moving on from a management role, did allow me a much greater level of freedom. So, I soon set about putting this newfound liberation to great use and I don't mean the selling of insurance, investments, and mortgage products.

CHAPTER 25.

PLATE SPINNING

I have previously mentioned how it isn't always the best-looking chap who will win the hearts as well as beds of the most attractive women out there. There will also never be a greater example of that contradiction in terms than me!

5' 9" in height with a completely shaven head, and until recently, I spent the majority of my adult life carrying far too much weight, especially around my waistline. Even so, I don't care who my record is compared to, for I have always been extremely effective in the lothario stakes. This has, I believe, also been down to the fact I have always adopted a very ubiquitous approach and could never be accused of having a 'type' so to speak.

You see, I genuinely find 'beauty' in some of the most unconventional looking women, which in turn, has blessed me with many women who could readily be described with adjectives such as . . . glamorous, beguiling, enticing, vivacious, tempting, seductive, elegant, stylish, tantalizing, exquisite, alluring, beautiful, and extremely sexy.

I was absolutely determined to avoid repeating the agonizing pain of my experience with Julie. So, I began to protect my insecurities with a 'safety in numbers' approach. What I mean by that is my anxieties and bruised ego would not have been able to deal with any further sense of rejection or abandonment. So, I would create a 'harem' of women around me who would in turn, feed my ego. Therefore, if any of them either moved on, or I ended the relationship myself, there were always several others 'waiting in the wings'. This is a classic relationship 'blueprint' of many a sociopath. Once firmly established, they will most probably never have relationships in a 'linear fashion' ever again. Their 'addictive gene' will become insatiable.

This is where I also began to develop the skill set of 'plate spinning' and 'juggling' of women. I had first observed such a dynamic, when it was expertly deployed by my old boss at Unicorn, Derek Fairley, who was most certainly an arch exponent of the 'craft' himself. At first, I started gradually with just a couple of women 'on the go'. Over a period of around twelve months or so, my 'harem' evolved into a revolving and workable number of between five and seven women at any given time.

Now, I am fully seized, any feminist who might be secretly compromising their principles and reading this story 'for research purposes' - will probably be looking to tear their 'kitchen sink' away from its fixings, so it can be launched in my direction with severe prejudice! I am afraid to say however, not once, have I ever had to force a woman into ANY situation. Indeed, in many cases, they were themselves in relationships, married, or embarking in multiple dalliances too! For sure, manipulating and compelling a woman into bed was the order of the day, but again, I have seen no end of women, doing exactly the same!

CHAPTER 26.

THE ONE THAT GOT AWAY

As my pathway headed into the year 1991, I had no idea it would be such a tumultuous one. I would enjoy many female encounters. Marry for a second time and end up leaving American Life and Casualty to become a 'founder partner' for a new financial services group, being set up by a 'Lord of the Realm'.

I was 'playing' a number of ladies from early on that year. One in particular, had become the focus of my attention . . . Judith Fanshaw. Judith was a lawyer I had developed a working relationship with. She had been in a fairly steady relationship, albeit one that did not seem to be without its problems. Apart from being a classic 'English Rose' she was also an uncanny 'Princess Diana look-alike'. Surely, you must have worked out by now, I always managed to punch well above my weight! Anyhow, I had a number of women on the 'firm', which is yet another trait of the sociopath who will always be prepared to play 'the long game' if, and whenever, it was necessary. I just knew, from what this tall classically dressed, and elegant lady had shared with me over the umpteen lunch 'appointments' I had connived to win her over, that sooner rather than later, her boyfriend 'Steve' (yes, you've guessed it, he was yet another sociopath) would surely slip up leaving Judith in a vulnerable place.

'Super Steve' did not disappoint. He pissed Judith around no end. It would appear, as with so many sociopaths, he also had real 'anger management' issues. I totally associated with that mindset. As the levels of my alcohol intake increased, the tendency to 'blame and strike out' rather than accepting any responsibility for 'one's own cock ups', worsened. Judith had had enough. Whilst Steve was looking to upend the relationship anyway, Judith moved out and recoiled straight into . . . Moi!

Most will have doubts or at least question marks, as to whether someone is even ready for another relationship or being caught on the rebound. I am now ashamed to admit I didn't give a shit, as all I desired, was to get Judith into bed. I would not have to wait awfully long, but I did have to negotiate my other distractions as well.

For in the mix at that time, was a very alluring brunette who would be very instrumental in playing 'cupid' between me and my future second wife. Although, I am not sure she necessarily intended to be in such a role. Moreover, Rowena Beacon, was to be the next in a very long line of women who were older, married, or in a long-term relationship. Throughout the entire time they would be bedding me. More of the delicious Rowena to come . . .

It goes without saying, I wanted Judith to be my latest conquest. Afterall, I had been much more patient than I would normally have allowed. It wasn't just about bedding her either. Judith was truly one strikingly attractive, very classy woman. My ego was boosted to no end when we started to date. We would both spend time staying at each other's houses. On the first occasion we made love, I was honored to have yet another stunner who was blessed with one of the most fantastic figures I have ever been pleasured by. She wasn't just a young woman in her prime, twenty-seven at the time. She was also naturally athletic too. Her full breasts were a simply sensational '38 DD' and perfectly shaped and weighted. If I had not known they were natural, they almost looked too perfect, which 'implants' can often do.

Accordingly, I saw a great deal of Judith whist plate spinning with a several others. One in particular, was some fifteen years older than Judith and about a foot shorter! Valerie Caed, a hornier little blonde you could never find. She was a lover of mine for the next eight years or so. It is quite remarkable, how a sociopath will keep such loyalties from many women all at once and over a period of some considerable time too.

Thus, many women seem to just turn a blind eye. Val knew all about my other women. Throughout the entire four years of my second marriage, she was a committed and loyal member of my first 'harem'. However, just like all the others, she was brutally discarded in the end.

In the meantime, I was very happy to have Judith as my 'Queen Bee' so to speak. The majority of sociopaths have a 'Pharaoh-like' mentality, and at any given time, they will always have their 'favorite'. Unfortunately, Judith had other ideas. Despite not being privy to the existence of my other lovers she wanted me for herself.

Enter . . . Rowena. I was introduced to this most voluptuous of woman, who was 39 at that time by a 'Spiv' type of character, Gavin Howe. He was one of those sales associates who spent nearly all of his time working so hard at having to not work very hard, if you get my drift? Gavin was a real 'Essex wide boy', who had also survived a horrendous car crash and literally bore the scars to prove it.

Gavin was a loveable rogue and staggered from one sales disaster to another. He happened to jointly own a property in France with his older brother, which was so dilapidated, I would be stunned if the great renovation plans, he had for the building were ever completed? That did not stop him, however, from claiming he was some kind of 'international property dealer', which sounded hilarious and very, Walter Mitty. So off he went in hot pursuit of other like-minded property magnates. Where did it lead him? To the south of France, Spain, and Channel Islands even? Nope! Burnham on Crouch in Essex!

Those who are already involved with the sailing fraternity will be very familiar with that odd and most quirky little Essex town, located along the edge of the 'Crouch Estuary'. Incredibly, for such an outpost, Burnham Regatta week is second only to Cowes's week in the domestic yachting calendar. Furthermore, not a more eccentric community will you come across. Most bizarrely, where I would eventually end up living, under great protest, with my eventual second wife. I have already alluded to my theory; our lives are simply pre-programmed (much more of that later) and the fated pathway which would lead me to 'Burnham' will clearly demonstrate this very point.

Rowena ran a tiny estate agency in partnership with a lovely blonde called Sue. Who by the way, only just avoided my seductive charms herself. The two of them were scarcely making a living.

This was 1991. Remember, the UK was in the depths of, yet another recession. The property market was seriously on the floor. We have, of course, experienced two more housing recessions since, with another on the way, which will most probably be the worst ever, as a result of the elite globalists Coronavirus 'pandemic'. I often wonder, when are the masses going to finally wake up to the reality, 'a house is for nesting.

Not investing'! There is not a more financially astute nation on the planet than Germany. Are they wedded and addicted to personal home ownership? Nope! They are not that fucking stupid.

You do not need the economic acumen of a Maynard Keynes, to work out that the UK lurches from one 'boom and bust' cycle after another simply because of the generational 'con-trick' that we are somehow lesser beings if we don't 'own' our own home? Moreover, the whole concept is delusional anyway. The vast majority are not homeowners. In reality they are mortgage owners! That rather changes things, don't you think? Sure, if you own the last brick then you are indeed a property owner, but if your portfolio is largely propped up by loans, then your so-called assets can look very illusory indeed.

In turn, the nation is piling on evermore personal debt. Therefore, unlike our Bavarian cousins, we are so sensitive to any interest rate fluctuations. Even with the near zero interest rates which the Central Banks have manipulated on the back of so called 'quantitative easing', a cynical name given to obfuscate the reality of printing money, which ironically is not a reality at all, is a complete illusion. The egregious levels of debt which are being created to solve the so called 'Covid-19 crisis' will inevitably result in a planned global economic crash, raising of interest rates to combat hyperinflation. and plummeting value of money. Together with implosion of the housing market, no end of repossessions our perfect storm is inevitable . . .

Nobody has learned anything from the economic crash of 2007/8, other than the globalist bankers, billionaires, and tech giants, who will be the ultimate winners. With nearly all printed money propping up their balance sheets, 'Big Pharma' is making zillions on the back of 'vaccines' aided and abetted by the State who have weaponized fear against citizens and designed to offer a solution to millions of 'grateful sheep' who have had the shit frightened out of them and are screaming to be 'saved'. So, they can enjoy their ever diminishing 'freedoms'.

Where the average German might have some car finance or other, he isn't going to go into a seizure every time his 'Central Bank' starts murmuring about rate increases. So much of our UK national debt is on a psychological knife edge because of the disproportionate number of mortgage owners with the incessant misguided belief, you can only be someone of merit if you are on the property ladder. The sheep have become self-imposed economic slaves.

Back to Rowena and Sue. The lightweight joint proprietors of Equitable Estates. Things were so financially tight for their business to make ends meet; they somehow came up with the brainwave of 'marketing French properties' to the UK wide market no less. The only flaw being, they didn't have a fucking clue what they were doing.

So, it was by browsing their 'ad' in one of the local classifieds, where Gavin had spotted them on his radar. He approached them about using his re-mortgaging services to finance French properties. That financial model was not particularly innovative but there were not going to be too many takers based around the river Crouch area either!

Gavin had somehow managed to get an appointment with 'Ro and Sue' to discuss his latest hair-brained proposition. He asked me to accompany him during a meeting at their little estate agency, which was located in the main high street of Burnham. I wasn't convinced for one moment Gavin's ideas would be remotely successful. He was always good entertainment value, so I agreed to join him for no other reason than for an afternoon's fun. Why did I have to tempt fate like that?

I had lunch with Judith and picked Gavin up in my new Mercedes 190E, which had a factory fitted full Mercedes Cosworth body styling (Yuk!). Needless to say, I thought I looked the # 'dogs' bollocks'! Gavin loved all that 'being large' rubbish and was really in his element. Then, we drove into the sleepy estuary town of Burnham. I can remember thinking what a twee place it looked. I had absolutely no idea, of course, that in a fairly short space of time, it would become my hometown, and it wouldn't be with Judith.

Equitable Estates, traded from a tiny shop front, which was in truth, was a converted front room of a Victorian house with a boatyard at the rear belonging to Rowena's partner, a salty old sea dog, 'Tubs' Leeson. Tubs was famous the world over as a Helmsman. He had competed in just about every international ocean race or regatta of any repute. He and Rowena had been together for a while. He was bankrolling his lovers losing battle against a housing recession, and in the face of stiff competition from nationwide chains of estate agents.

We rocked up outside their tiny trade outlet. As I got out of the vehicle, I consciously peered up and down the high street of this quaint parochial town with its rows of tiny shops and Victorian built fishermen cottages on either side of the high street. I was still completely oblivious to the irony that the next matrimonial home I would buy within less than six months was actually standing no more than 100 yards away.

Gavin marched in through the Vert de Terre colored front door ahead of me. We were greeted by a real 'Ying and Yang' of a couple. Rowena was mid-height strikingly dark, attractive, curves, and heaving boobs and Sue, was blonde, tall, thin, and haughty. Rowena certainty had an air of Mrs. Bouquets about her, despite a great sense of misplaced snobbery. She just couldn't hide her 'Luton' roots. I remember shaking her hand and my intuition immediately kicked into a high resonance. I just knew we would soon be lovers.

I deferred to Gavin and allowed him to sit there just like a 'King Canute' spouting on and on about his delusional foray into the French property scene. It was bloody hilarious. You could see the two ladies didn't believe a word they were hearing. I didn't believe a word either. Gavin probably didn't believe his own bullshit. So, I allowed him to make a fool of himself for half an hour or so but then, I could stand no more . . .

"Thanks for that Gavin - I am sure the two ladies have found your presentation most enlightening."

I then took over the dialogue. We all chatted about the many other conventional ways we could assist by arranging mortgages, life cover, and such like. To be fair, despite the reality their tiny business was not much more than a housewife's whim, we did start to receive a trickle of leads that converted into mortgages. As I also suspected once Gavin had finally realized the 'French Connection' wasn't really going anywhere his enthusiasm waned. He left it to me to manage their account.

I haven't seen or heard from Gavin in over twenty years. If he only knew just how much influence he would have over my future pathway by introducing me to two other people in particular, I would like to thank him now . . . the cunt!

Having intuitively detected Rowena's amorous response during our first meeting, I took it upon myself to visit her business at every opportunity. I was determined to get closer. I was also introduced to 'Tubs' who looked just like his name suggested, which was a cross between Captain Birdseye and David Bellamy. He was an affable enough chap on the surface. From various anecdotal accounts, he had one hell of a temper. Indeed, it certainly wasn't lost on me, that one does not get chosen for the prestigious crew member of helmsman on a British Prime Ministers Racing Yacht by being a shrinking violet.

Rowena would eventually reveal to me how Tub's smashed a beer glass into the face of a mercurial local property developer. A certain Jon

Hardy, who had been trying to strong arm Tub's into selling his ramshackle boatyard to the man who known as the 'entrepreneur of Burnham'. Jon needed the land occupied by Tubs yard, which happened to be the last of the numerous boatyards, which had once occupied a mile of promenade with myriad moorings and jetties. Abbott and Hardy Developers Ltd had gained planning permission for a 'yuppie style development' of trendy apartments and townhouses with much sought after 'marine views'. In reality, they were looking out over the dirty brown and silted river Crouch. Jon had been delayed by the maverick and obstinate yacht repairer for far too long but by overstepping the mark, he very nearly lost the sight in his left eye.

Tub's reaction to being hassled was appalling and left Rowena mortified her partner was even capable of such a violent act. Intriguingly, had Tub's not had such high-level contacts, a former Prime Minister indeed, he would, no doubt, have received a much tougher sentence than the tariff warranted for the common assault conviction handed out by a 'friendly judge'. So, bearing in mind it only took a few shots of rum for Tubs to erupt it made my six-month affair with his woman, even the more daring or stupid indeed!

The 'fickle finger of fate' would play its hand yet again in my story for Jon Hardy's second wife, Demi, would eventually occupy my bed, my home, and the most traumatic of times in my life.

Of course, there was also Judith and the other members of my thriving harem to consider. Whilst I was clearly indulging myself on a 'conscious' level. Julie Clarkson was always embedded within my 'sub-conscious heartache'. That very level of our 'being', which in truth, is who we really are, not the 'mask' or 'veneer', we portray to so many others.

It is as if we are all constantly role playing, using our egos to portray a superficial 'self' to create an image we think is more acceptable to the other person than that of our true selves.

I knew I was in real trouble, when Judith made the rather unnerving move of introducing me to her very middle-class parents who invited me to her sister's wedding, still some three months hence. Which to me, very much showed her longer-term intentions.

During an evening meal, Judith gave me a heartfelt look . . . "Sam, I have fallen in love with you."

She hadn't of course, but in her head, she was looking for someone to usurp 'Super Steve'. Judith was a serious case of 'rebound'. Whilst I was really embracing her company and enjoying the most fantastic sex;

my heart was still far from being over Julie. Thus, I was not in the commitment business, or even close. All the same, I was content to indulge her and to see how things played out.

It is funny, no matter how crass or pathetic the excuse when a woman actually decides she wants to be seduced, a man can tell them just about any old crap and they will still come running. Whether it is the pheromones, the subconscious mind, or just plain old-fashioned primeval behavior. The outcome will always be the same.

So, I came up with the very thin excuse I needed to discuss sales opportunities with Rowena. It would be best if she 'popped over' to my home to 'ensure we wouldn't be interrupted', pathetic or what. She then contributed to the whole charade by responding with,

"Oh ok, I can bring the dog over for a walk as well".

Jeeeez, it couldn't be more of a farce really. She obviously wanted to use that little ruse to throw Tubs off the scent. Now call me cynical, but I could be forgiven for thinking it was a fairly well-rehearsed ploy of Rowen's as well. Perish the thought?

Rowena pulled up outside my house. As I answered the door, I could see her furry accomplice, a nervous red setter, perched on the passenger seat. She confidently breezed past me with an air of a woman who was purposeful and expectant in her aims for the next hour or so.

She wasn't to be disappointed. So began a fairly short but extremely passionate affair, which ran in parallel with Judith, Valerie, and many others who were now all firmly embedded into my harem. The sheer exhilaration and adrenalin rush of taking on a high-risk lover, was also becoming quite addictive. A particular habitual practice, which would become a key driver for the next three decades.

Typically, I can recall inviting both Rowena and Tubs to a black-tie function, knowing full well Tubs would decline what would have appeared to him to be such a stuffy evening. He loathed social events. I just knew the reverse psychology would pay off, where predictably, Tubs would insist Rowena go with me.

Skilled sociopaths are just brilliant at using the dark art of psychological manipulation. Just as I had done with Gareth and Rhoda, I made an unknowing ally out of one of my lovers' partners. Let's be clear here, it 'takes two to tango'. Throughout the entire time I was philandering the members of my harem were always very willing. In many instances actually perpetrated the deception with relish.

Sociopaths are known to be highly promiscuous. On the face of it, I 'appeared' to fit such a profile. Despite the reputation I acquired over the years, I have never quite demonstrated stereotypical behavioral traits. Anon . . .

My plate-spinning technique was now becoming extremely well honed. I was actually being inspired to write more new business than ever. Therefore, all was going extremely well, but in keeping with my self-destructive pattern a new woman was to enter my world who would be unfortunate enough, to become my second wife. A matrimonial outcome which would juxtaposition with my joining just about the most prestigious and elite families in the world of financial services . . . 'The Rosenbergs'.

CHAPTER 27.

THE GREEDIEST MAN I EVER KNEW

Whilst there never seemed to be a dull moment in my life, there have certainly been periods of time where events have come together with an even greater intensity than even, I had become accustomed. One such period, descended on me between 1991 and 1992. Whereby, my risk taking would be taken to ever greater heights.

My sales associate Gavin, was again, to be the catalyst for introducing me to someone who was to have an extremely destructive and manipulative impact over me, for the next several years. Gavin's sales ability was limited. He was always looking for ways to improve his production levels. So, he forged a working relationship with a chap who was prolifically involved in the 'secured loans' business. By that, I mean second mortgages secured on people's homes in addition to any formal first mortgage. The man's name was Tom Coward. Not a more egregious and pathological character would you ever find. It's amazing how, when many people mature, they actually begin to look like their personalities. In Tom's case, we are talking of only one possible description, 'Weasel-face'!

Tom was a thin and wiry man in his early thirties with mousey wavy hair, angular screwed up features, and the most penetrative eyes that were noticeably far too close together. So, not just 'Weasel looking' but bloody intimidating to boot! Gavin had assured Tom, he could introduce him to his 'manager'. Despite my being in the process of resigning because 'we could all make use of Tom's services'. So, a meeting was set up for me to engage with a man who would feed my thriving ego and indulge his own pathological flaws at the same time.

My own levels of arrogance were also reaching a 'zenith', which would prevail for many years yet. When a silver long wheelbase S class

Mercedes smoked up outside the office, my superficial thought process quickly concluded . . . Well, he must be doing really well for himself'. That's how mem and many of my peers, simply measured success in those days. Oh, ok then, nothing has changed really. Might be worse even?

Without being invited, Tom burst into my office and flopped himself down with wide and smug look his face.

"Ello Pal, I'm Tom. I am here to earn you 'loads of dosh'. Can I suggest we start right here and now?"

Tom's forward attitude and boorish tone would become a familiar one I would hear for nearly a decade. At that time, I had become rather unrefined too. So, I was all ears and wanted to understand precisely, how this 'rat-like' character was funding his lavish lifestyle?

Tom would perpetually use the term, 'bolting-up the client'. It was as crass and immoral as that. In a nutshell, he would receive sales 'leads' from a company advertising loans for 'home improvements' and such. Tom had 'agencies' with various loan companies and finance houses who were offering high interest bearing 'secured loans'.

His poor clients would then be subject to an 'evening appointment' and he would deploy just about every underhand sales technique akin to a sharp 'double-glazing' salesman. Tom would actually brag he would never leave a client's home, no matter how late, until he had a signature on a loan application form

I am now most ashamed to admit in those days, I actually found myself becoming ever more impressed by his sales 'closing' abilities. Tom was a 'sociopath extraordinaire' and a pathological liar who would do and say virtually anything to secure a deal to fuel his self-serving craving for money. He wasn't, however, promiscuous, which is most unusual for a sociopath. He proudly claimed he was a 'very happily' married man. Well, that's what he might have purported to be and believed. I was soon to discover someone had forgotten to tell that, to his wife!

I began working in tandem with 'Tom the Weasel'. We were 'bolting deals' left, right, and center. The 'con' being he would go and visit all of his loan clients and persuade them to 'consolidate' their various loans, which he had 'bolted' in the previous twelve months. Having already earned an eye watering amount of commission from the original deal, he would then persuade them to re-mortgage and consolidate, yet again.

"A 'double bubble' on the commission then pal!" He just loved that crass expression.

Tom's brash and creeping influence over me would eventually, severely antagonize my second wife who, in turn, would despise him. So, time to introduce . . . Chasney!

I had become most familiar with Rowena. Shall we say, on many 'levels'. Somehow, we were both managing to stay under Tub's and Judith's radar. During my time spent in Rowena's most 'pleasurable' company, she would regularly refer to a young friend of hers, called 'Chasney'. Rowena was obviously very fond of her. Chasney had apparently been sailing under Tub's tutelage and mentoring since she was a very small girl.

Rowena often suggested to me her immature friend was more than just a tad on the 'spoilt' side, which would turn out to be the fucking understatement of the decade! Despite their mutual affection however, she was quite clearly exasperated by the over-indulged and juvenile attitude Chasney habitually demonstrated. So, the said young lady, was beginning to appear most unappealing, but it later transpired Rowena had a vested interest in describing Chasney to me in such unflattering terms. I was soon to discover why.

Rowena and Chasney had recently been guests at their mutual friend's wedding. I arrived at Rowena and Sue's office for my latest 'visit' and could hear the two ladies chatting to Tubs at the rear of their building. I happened to notice several recent photos strewn across Rowena's desk. When she appeared from the back of her shop, I couldn't help but notice her awkward glance between me and the snaps which were lying on her blotting pad.

"Hello sweetie, you and Tubs all well?"

How insincere eh? The sheer gall of most sociopaths can be priceless at times. They will readily ask after the well-being of the very people they are currently deceiving.

Before Rowena could even remark . . .

"Hey Ro, they look like 'pics' of the lovely couple, you don't mind if I have a gander, do you?"

She took a deep breath, in the manner of someone who was resigned to an inevitable outcome . . .

"Oh yes, please do." She said with zero sincerity.

I started to thumb through the photos and feigned my interest and barely holding back a yawn, until . . .

"Oh . . . errrm, who is THIS?"

With her worst fears about to be realized, Rowena leaned over and confirmed . . .

"Samuel . . . that's Chasney, you know, the young lady I have been telling you about."

I was looking at an extremely attractive and curvy girl in her mid-twenties who was garbed in her best finery for her friend's wedding. Elegantly carrying off the wearing of a hat, which would have done any 'Ladies Day at the Ascot Races' very proud indeed. Rowena just knew the game was up . . .

"Samuel do not even think about it. I am not going to introduce you to her under any circumstances."

"Why on earth not?"

"Because . . . because she will fall in love with you, and you will break her heart."

At the time, I was convinced Rowena was understandably protecting her own interests regarding our ongoing clandestine and steamy encounters. But upon reflection, I readily acknowledge her main concern was truly the future well-being of her young charge. But as with all sociopaths once they have a new target in their sights, they will not be denied.

The events leading up to meeting the young lady who would become my second wife, even by my standards, ran at quite a pace. I had arranged to take Judith down to Burnham for a drink. Coincidentally, she happened to be very keen on the sport of sailing. Brinkmanship brings with it an adrenalin rush sociopaths simply cannot resist, for they will become ever more addicted to the epinephrine hormone. So, I had decided to disrespect both Judith, and Rowena, and at the same time, hoped to encounter this Chasney chick.

It all ran like clockwork. I took Judith into the White Hart Hotel, which was the public house most frequented by Burnham's sailing 'in crowd'. No matter how long an 'outsider' lived in that incestuous place, you would never be regarded or accepted as 'one of us'. So, I used to quite relish shoving my snout into the faces of the 'salty old sea dogs' and yachting prigs, who most nights would be habitually drinking themselves into oblivion.

Rowena's face was the proverbial 'picture' as she came swanning into the lounge bar and saw me sitting on a stool chatting away with . .

. Judith. Ro was accompanied by a fresh faced and very attractive girl

who in the space of less than six-weeks I would become wedded to . . . yours truly. You just couldn't make it up.

It was to be one of my finest hours. The upbeat demeanor Rowena was wearing upon entering the bar, quickly evaporated as she clearly didn't know whether to 'stick or twist'. She made a rather silly attempt to shield Chasney from me, whilst having to deal with her own awkwardness due to her being confronted by the beautiful Judith. This was going to be very interesting indeed . . .

"Hello, Ro, fancy bumping into you. Hello? And who do we have here then?"

I was being so insensitive to Judith, but I pressed on regardless . . . 'You must be Chasney, right? I recognize you from the wedding

photos'?

Chasney appeared from behind Rowena and beamed at me. I instantly connected to the deepest of blue eyes . . . ever. She wasn't tall, barely 5'3", and wore a highlighted 'Suzi Quatro hairstyle' with a perfect set of brilliant white teeth. She was very curvy. The cleavage was, well, in abundance. She oozed charisma. The self-assurance of a young woman who just knew most men desired her. She stepped into Rowena's space ignoring Judith completely, she held out her hand . . .

"Hi, I am Chasney. So, you must be Ro's Cockney 'interest' then?"

Rowena noticeably cringed. Her very apparent body language was one of . . .

"I fear the worst."

Without further ado, Chasney snuggled in between me and Judith as if she was being re-acquainted with two dear old friends who she hadn't seen in an age. She assumed a posture; I would become most familiar over time with annoying frequency. Which was, for her to be sat crossed legged, with a cigarette between the fingers of one hand, and a gin and tonic, in the other.

Chasney then 'held court' in a manner which was obviously very well-rehearsed. Her many sycophantic followers soon gravitated toward us. They took on many different guises. From chaps who had previously fucked her and still couldn't let go, to 'yachtie' types and local businessmen, who all aspired to be the next in line.

As with many of the mistakes I have made with women over the years, I allowed the needs of my ego to get in the way of my heeding any early warning signs. Chasney was to be the next lady to be added to that flourishing list of errors. They were all there on full display.

In keeping with a sociopath's inability to pay attention to anything for more than one minute - other than the next object of his desire, which is - I obtusely ignored this girl's numerous and obvious flaws. She insisted on using sarcastic and self-absorbed banter and blatantly flirted with me right under the unfortunate Judith's nose. Despite the ignorance and disrespectful manner by which she was being treated, Judith maintained a regal dignity with a gracious and polite countenance throughout.

My ego was just loving the contest. I happened to glance over at Rowena, who had conveniently slipped away and was chatting with some friends. She returned my glance with a rather forlorn expression I read as . . . What the hell have you just done you fool? I can recall trying to justify my actions to myself, as just 'a bit of fun' but on a visceral level, Rowena's scornful grin, resonated with me in a less than joyous manner.

The evening came to a close. I just already knew I wanted the curvaceous Chasney to be my latest conquest. She had been chirping away all evening and interrupted Judith whenever she tried to spark up any kind of conversation.

Such rude behavior was already beginning to grate, so here was yet another example. I was setting up my future marital demise as early as the first time of meeting my next spouse. We all said our disingenuous farewells with a round of hugs and 'kissy cheeks' and as I pecked Chasney, I purposefully left my hands around her waist for far longer than I ought to have done.

It was only at that point, when Judith demonstrated any degree of jealousy. I felt her firm hand on my arm as she intently pulled me away. I turned with a . . . What me? expression on my face. Judith was clearly becoming increasingly uncomfortable with the amorous affections being exchanged between myself and her new adversary.

What is more, it was crystal clear Chasney operated in a like manner. Her ego was enjoying 'getting one over a rival'. At the same time, sending a distinctive message to her other admirers in the pub of

. . . 'you still can't have me'.

The drive back home was barely ten minutes. The silence and frost-filled atmosphere made it feel more like a couple of hours. I had both insulted, and embarrassed, Judith in front of a number of people she didn't even know. I also offended Rowena's pride in the bargain. My ego had been fed its latest fix but today, I just wish I could apologize to Judith for my shameful and self-serving behavior.

Despite the tensions, Judith still slept at my house that night. I did not realize it was to be the last time she would ever stay with me. But we 'kissed and made up' making passionate love all night and again, early the next morning. By the following evening I was to be doing exactly the same with my future wife.

I made a call to Rowena. Not unexpectedly, she was most unimpressed by my shenanigans of the previous evening.

"Oh, hello you shit. I know we haven't known each other that long but my bloody suspicions about your conniving character were seriously confirmed last night."

"Rowena, don't you dare try that line of wounded disapproval on me. I mean, are you really getting all indignant on me? You haven't exactly been covering yourself in glory these past few weeks either, have you now? Oh, and by the way, how is Tubs, then?"

Touché or what! Women and their 'selective memories', eh? Their sheer hypocrisy! They never let you down.

"Look Ro, I just wanted to thank you for not letting on about anything last night. I know you would have felt compromised, but you could have caused me no end of problems if you had been so inclined. Surely, we can still be friends, eh?"

"Yeah, I guess so. But don't you dare play Chasney. She didn't shut up about you on the way home. She was very susceptible to you charms . . . you smooth bastard."

Funny isn't it. Again, that same old phenomenon of, 'female hypocrisy' in full swing. Rowena had been deceiving her long-time partner and then she actually had the nerve, to lecture me about my intentions in respect of her little friend Chasney. A girl, who despite my clearly being with another woman, readily made her own intentions most clear that she was going to do everything in her power to come between me and Judith. This was a 'moral vacuum' all right.

I was never one for 'letting the grass grow'. That same evening, I made my way to The White Hart with great purpose and expectation. I made certain I was early. Sure enough, Chasney popped her smiley face through the door and judging by her nautical clothing she had clearly just come off the river. Despite being windswept, she was looking fresh faced, and most radiant. I could instinctively tell she was looking for her new 'Cockney interest'.

"Why hello there Sam. So, you are not with the lovely Judith tonight then?"

Her sarcasm was all part of the early banter and, over time, Chasney's liking for it would be something that would seriously piss me off about her. Here was yet another aspect of 'relationship madness' whereby, the appealing mannerisms we initially find attractive become the very same traits which irritate the fuck out of us, once the 'shine goes off the gold block'.

Yet again, it is all about the relationship 'role playing'. In other words, we all 'wear a mask', which we believe to be the version of our ego most attractive to the object of our desire. 'Role playing' eventually becomes demanding work though. When the mask inevitably slips, the contention increases. It would not take very long for this particular mask, to slip.

We sat there point scoring. It was our adversarial style of flirting, which would be our eventual undoing. Drinking, and driving, was commonplace back then. Whilst Chasney owned a place of her own locally, most sociopaths prefer to lure their latest conquest back to their own 'bolt hole'. So, we left the pub with as high a visibility as possible; thus, feeding our egos and titillating the local gossip mongers with as clear a message as possible.

I drove Chasney back to my new house. The sequence of events did not initially go quite as I had anticipated, which is why I often use the term 'always expect the unexpected in life'. We actually sat and chatted for quite some time before retiring to the boudoir. There was none of the obligatory tearing the clothes of each other's bodies. The conversation took on some unusual twists and turns and not once did either of us mention Judith. Although, it was soon pretty obvious Chasney certainly had her suspicions about my previous interest in her best friend Rowena, which I speedily rebuffed with a very unconvincing . . . 'Perish the thought'!

Chasney quickly opened up to me and gave a rendition about her parents and her difficult relationship with her very domineering father. Have we heard that one somewhere before? Likewise, the very strained relationship with her sister (who within just twelve months of our marriage, would become yet another lover of mine), and her adoration for 'Tubs'. She described various other past events in her recent life whereby she had moved to Los Angeles where she 'au paired' for one of the biggest 'pornography motion picture moguls' in the USA! Hey, when she started on that one, even I was happy to defer any bedroom action for a while.

All succulent background information despite coming from her loose alcohol basted tongue, I still had a feeling she was being just a tad 'economical' with the truth regarding her experiences when working for the movie magnate's family. Moreover, she alluded to but didn't ever expand how matters had seriously deteriorated. She apparently ended up in such a state of stress and ill health, Tubs was sent to the States as a one-man rescue party charged with bringing her back home.

Over the coming years, I never quite got to grips with what really happened to Chasney while she was in the States. The fact it was Tubs and not her father who eventually brought her home did not really ring the bells it should have at that time. Rumor and innuendo were rife about her time spent in the States within the Burnham gossip machine. Not least of all, when speaking about it to her so called 'BF' Rowena. What loyalty, eh? Even Rowena never seemed to be fully seized of the facts, but she did speculate with some really juicy morsels, and always insisted Tubs knew far more than he was ever prepared to let on. So, Tubs was keeping secrets from Rowena too. You couldn't make it up! Much more about Chasney's own colourful past later . . .

I couldn't help noticing how Chasney was knocking back my Remy Brandy, with such consummate ease. Thus, began yet another pattern whereby my own excessive drinking became further magnified by a succession of relationships, with women who drank more than was going to be good for them or indeed . . . me!

So there came a point in the evening where I was no longer going to accommodate her overemotional reminiscing. I just wanted to get her upstairs. I already knew she wasn't going to resist, but she did something else that kind of wrong-footed me. I hadn't actually even so much as kissed her yet, but as I moved in . . .

"We are not going to do any 'rudey dudey' stuff are we?"

Now, I am all up for a bit of 'playful teasing' before the main event, but it was the manner by which she said it. Even allowing for half bottle of Remy inside her she was using a most odd and childlike tone?

"Errmm sorry? Come again?" "No 'rudey dudey' . . . he he he!"

That was enough of that! I wasn't prepared to listen to this anymore. She was attempting to play the 'little girl' role. To be honest, I find all that stuff to be quite affected. As it turned out, Chasney had many partners before me, but as time went by, I realized she was really quite repressed sexually. She would use 'childish language' as a cognitive means of dealing with and deflecting it. Again, it must have had something to do with her experiences back in Los Angeles. Hmm? More speculation on that intriguing little plot line later.

Now this is the real paradox. Our lovemaking was extremely passionate. It lasted virtually the whole night long and was very fulfilling. Yet, we never made love like that ever again! What?

The following morning, I dropped Chasney off at her home. Before I set off for the office, she looked back at me wearing her most soulful 'lost puppy look' and she pleaded with me.

"I have had an enthralling night my little 'Teddy Boo Boo Bear' (yeah . . . I know) please choose your 'Chazzy Wazzy' over that Judith . . . pleeeeeeez?"

I still wasn't heeding the warning signs. I just smiled and blew her a kiss - ffs! - and slipped my Jaguars 'J-gate' into the 'D' slot and sped off. I had just five more weeks of so-called freedom. What a total Wanker!

So, how was I feeling about the choice that lay ahead of me? My attraction to Chasney was purely ego based. I had little sense of the visceral aching, which should have at the very least been necessary for someone who would I contemplate marrying. On the other hand, Judith was tall, elegant, classy, and reliably loyal. I did not feel any true love for her though. I had resisted making any further commitment to her because of my still yearning for Julie Clarkson. In any case, there were the other female cast of characters who were sharing my stage and it would be most unlikely, I would forgo the attentions of any of them in favor of a monogamous marriage.

A collective set of karmic events were now contriving. I later discovered such a juxtaposition is never truly just a coincidence. This would shift my life up a few more gears to an entire new level of intensity. In those days, Chasney was employed in the world of telecommunications. She was playing the 'corporate sales game' herself. I was somehow impressed by this. She clearly knew how to present herself as a 'corporate wife'. Hmm? But then again, so could Judith. In many ways as a young and ambitious lawyer, Judith was even more refined, gracious, and suited to the role when attending for example, a black-tie function.

So, despite the reality I was far from over Julie Clarkson, for reasons purely egoic I found myself being led by the nose into marrying again.

CHAPTER 28.

THE ROSENBERGS

Needless to say, there were many other women who were playing out the 'subplots' of my insane life. For instance, I was still keeping up my regular dalliance with the little vixen Val. Whenever I happened to be passing by her modest flat in Braintree Essex, I would treat myself to a cozy little breakfast goody on my way into the office. But a new girl had arrived in the mix who would afford me with the most amazing loyalty, affection, and lovemaking. Laura, my new personal assistant.

Laura had been married to a desperate and hopeless drunk. He had systematically destroyed her self-esteem by violently abusing her and their three children. Matters eventually came to a head and she finally found the courage to give him his marching orders. Soon after, filed for a very liberating divorce. After joining my team, Laura went through an amazing transformation from being dumpy and 'mumsy' to losing some forty-eight pounds in weight and rediscovering her carnal mojo! I enjoyed her support and loyalty, underpinned by our mutual desire, which only came to an end when the inevitable happened and someone new came along. Throughout that time, Laura vied for my affections with a second member of my 'support team', which at times felt like sexually driven musical chairs.

My ability to plate spin was becoming well-honed. I was developing an enviable reputation among my male colleagues. Most sociopaths will develop this characteristic to support their ubiquitous and promiscuous, way of life. Our lives do not run in a convenient and linear fashion. Life-changing events can converge in a very short period of time. I would later have such a phenomenon explained to me, which is known as . . . 'A Collective Karmic Event'. Anon . . .

If the arriving in my world of the 'Weasel' and Chasney, was not already enough to contend with, the final player of a life altering triumvirate was about to descend on me and bring with it an extremely hedonistic lifestyle. Together with a much unexpected insight into who really runs our country, and indeed, the planet. Enter . . . The Rosenberg Family.

But before I get into the dark influences of that highly manipulative dynasty, there was still one further plot twist to come. Neil Follet had become somewhat secretive. He kept disappearing from the office and was not even briefing his PA, about his whereabouts. He was certainly planning something which must have been ultra-sensitive for him to not have kept me in the loop. Apart from being a very close mate, he was at the end of the day, also my immediate boss. I remember one particular evening I was trying to reach him at his home and on his car phone (yes, the cellular revolution was getting into full swing by 1991), but despite leaving several messages, nothing . . .

We would all soon to be enlightened. Sure enough, it was all over the financial press the following morning. It was announced, 'Mr. Neil Follet was to be leaving American Life and Casualty and joining a new financial services group to be Chaired by Lord Rosenberg'. It had all been planned in such a covert manner, Neil's old employers had been caught out, and with their pants down!

Neil had been sworn to secrecy because a few months earlier, a number of directors had left American Life and Casualty including our regional Director Jon Newland, to throw their lot in with Lord Rosenberg and entrepreneur, Sir Markus Steinberger. 'Sir M', had been our old Chairman. He was a Jewish entrepreneur who had landed in the UK in the 1950s with a team of creative and manipulative intellectuals who set about successfully building two 'cowboy' direct sales outfits in the 1960s. Then, had the nerve to repeat the formula again in the 1970s.

They pioneered a new investment fund management model known as 'unit-linking', which flew in the face of all the staid and traditional investment models, such as 'with profits' funds that had served us all so well over the previous hundred years or so. Moreover, the old ways were of course, very robust and most importantly, secure. This sociopathic joker, linked fund management directly to the performance of the stock markets. Need I say any more?

And . . . guess what? He was even knighted for creating such a financial illusion that has contributed massively to the nature of the 'debt mountain' that befalls the globe today.

So yet again, he was about to do the same thing in the 1990s, by hijacking the so called 'elite' name of one of the world's most powerful families. This time though, he was going to dress up his latest enterprise as a business, which apparently aspired to only service the investment needs of 'high net worth' individuals.

The trouble was, I was about to be seduced by this new brand confidence trick, and like no other. Jon Newland was busy doing a 'Syd De Brett' by systematically targeting all of our high producers and inevitably, I soon appeared on his radar. But before he could make a call to me, he and the other directors were dealt an early body blow with a very serious plot twist. The 'pink financial press' had barely a chance to become 'fish 'n chip wrapping paper' when no sooner had they a fresh story to salivate over, so it was all change again.

Before I could even 'tap' Neil for some advice, who had actually left his desk in situ and gone into hiding, a virulent chain reaction of a rumor had begun to spread around the office my pal was now, in fact, coming back! It was just like Wayne Rooney's turnaround when he was about to leave Man Utd. You couldn't make it up!

Jon Newland's replacement as regional sales director, was one of the smoothest and slippery operators you could ever meet. He was an Arab gentleman by the name of Marif Yewani. Ironically, he was a year older than me to the day. He had breezed into the hierarchy of the company less than twelve months previously. Marif had all the necessary sociopathic and manipulative traits, despite Neil's usual level of acute discernment, he was always quite in awe of the guy. I have never to this day, been able to learn why. In any event, it transpired Marif was determined to get one over his old boss Jon. Hilariously, they tried stitching each other up over other business transactions as well, which ended up in expensive court actions . . . such professionalism.

Marif somehow managed to track Neil down who had been hiding in his 'bunker'. He swiftly offered him a king's ransom to reverse his decision and decline the offer made by Rosenberg's. Disappointingly for me, Neil acquiesced. Before we all knew it, a contrived meeting was held in front of our entire sales group so they could herald the return of the prodigal son. I had to attend, of course, and together my other colleagues, we all had to sit there and go through the charade of welcoming our 'glorious leader' back to the fold.

When the numbers had thinned out, I waited for Marif to be distracted and then grabbed my opportunity to collar my mate . . .

"Neil, what the fuck are you doing turning your back on Rosenbergs? Surely, it's not just about the cash? I mean . . . you would have been the Regional Director. And why all the secrecy, you know I wouldn't have said a word."

Neil's reply was very perturbing to say the least. Yet again, I was to ignore his stark warning . . .

"Sam, I was under all sorts of pressure to sign, but despite the claims in the papers I hadn't actually agreed to anything. We both go back a long way with Jon Newland, so when the call came, I just thought . . . What the hell, let's just see what's on the table?"

He then revealed just how conniving 'JN' could be . . .

They made an eye watering offer mate, but despite them refusing to put anything in writing, they insisted on a signature all the same. I naturally said I wanted to think about things and that cunt said it would not be a problem. The next thing, I read in the pinks that I had already joined them for fucks sake! So, I went into hiding until I could think straight. I was actually relieved Marif managed to get hold of me. And hey, I at least found myself with a chance to leverage a deal. You know the score son, both sides are shameless, and I just took the view . . . 'better the devil you know' and all that.

He then pressed home his feelings and advised me . . . accordingly. "Sam, I well aware that you are about to talk to that reptilian bastard, but after the way he has handled this, I beseech you not to be taken in. Sure, he has a very prestigious brand but that old peer who is lending his name to the project, will regret it big time I can assure you of that much."

I just wasn't having any of it and found myself indulging my friend without any level of conviction. Anyhow, I would be asking him to carry out a 'special duty' for me in just a matter of weeks

I had the inevitable conversation with Jon Newland and agreed to meet him at his home, which was a 17th century, full moated manor house. I stupidly felt very privileged to have been invited to such a stately abode as I rocked up in my newly purchased 7 series BMW. I noticed Jon raised an eyebrow as he scanned the vehicle. I wanted to impress.

Jon had barely indulged me with any chit-chat before launching into an offensive about my friend. He was fully seized of the fact we were close pals if nothing else. He needed to embark on a quick damage limitation exercise just in case I also decided to stay put.

Jon made a rather pathetic attempt at trying to convince me how disappointed he was Neil had decided not to join the Rosenberg elite. He then went into 'bullshit overdrive' when describing how my new financial package would be structured.

It was then, I encountered a whole new spin on how I would, in reality, still be paid on a 'commission only' basis and my funds would yet again, be advanced by way of loans. My stupid gene had now fully developed to its most destructive best. Indeed, a continued means of deriving an income would both entrap and condition me for decades to come. The new 'con' was to avoid describing payments as commission, for they would now be called . . . 'Turnover'. Clever, eh?

And to think, the new sales team were supposed to be so bright and astute. Yet, they were still treated as if they were not supposed to notice there was not an iota of difference. Fucking hilarious!

Another really interesting aspect to the contractual arrangements was that rather than being called 'associates' or the more svelte title of 'account executive', the new sales force was to be given the even more cultured and credible status of 'partner'. So, we would be called something along the lines of . . . Joe Soap, Partner of the Roseburg Partnership.

Now the Rosenberg marketing department would go to great lengths to clarify the new sales team were not strictly 'partners' in the legal sense or as one might describe 'partners' in a firm of lawyers or accountants. But the sales force was allotted a very handsome share option package and clearly printed on all of my personalized stationery, business cards, and monthly financial statements. I would very clearly and unambiguously be described as a . . . 'partner'!

Therefore, coupled with the fact I might and did eventually derive a very significant number of shares in the partnership - should anyone decide in the future to legally challenge they were actually a 'partner under the Partnership Act would probably have a fairly good run at it. Much more of that little conflict later . . . . . .

Unfortunately, I was so far up my own arse in those days I would use very little discernment (none in fact). So, I would continue my well-trodden path of ignoring all the obvious warning signs in my pursuit of further egoic glory. So 'JN' put together the finishing touches to my next, and most ridiculous, sales contract wearing his famous 'reptilian' grin. This tall, and lanky, ex-police sergeant, shook my hand, and hissed . . .

"Welcome to Rosenbergs."

CHAPTER 29.

CHASNEY

A number of life changing characters and organizations were now aligning in the guise of Tom, Chasney, and Rosenbergs, together with ever-expanding supporting cast of my labile reality. As with all good 'soaps', certain cast members are dropped and then, inevitably replaced by characters who will hopefully enrich the plot. So, fate decreed whilst the likes of Val, Rowena, and Tubs collectively continued to play their part, it was time for Judy to depart the stage, just as Laura entered the cast to replace her.

I could not hand my resignation in quickly enough. Despite Neil's reservations, I was off. We were all apparently supposed to be self-employed. So, why should we even need to resign? To this day, I always felt we should have been classed as 'employees' as very few had outside business interests, so the scam perpetrated by the life assurance companies to avoid 'Employers National Insurance' and 'PAYE schemes' continued unabated!

Whilst I am on my high horse about such a fraud, the UK courts recently ruled Uber workers were actually 'employees'. In my view, if there was a retrospective appraisal of the tens of thousands of so-called 'self-employed sales associates' who 'worked' for life assurance companies galore, there would be a huge windfall for the UK Treasury with considerable reparation for many individuals as well. Anyone fancy an epoch changing 'class action'?

I packed up my things and sat down with my new PA, Laura, to explain my plans. I reassured her I would like her to continue working for me in my new role as a 'partner'. What a fraud that professional description would turn out to be. I was really delighted when she quickly agreed to join me.

Now, to be fair, Laura was a very grounded girl and as I have already mentioned. She came for her initial interview only seeking part-time work to support her young family. Her alcoholic husband had basically ruined all the family finances. An undoing I would become only too familiar with myself, I am ashamed to admit, and she was quite desperate to find the hours to suit.

I had already been given a 'heads up', by another member of the sales admin team who was a personal friend of Laura's, who had actually recommended the dark brunette for the position. Apart from providing me with a sound character reference, her friend had also gone to great lengths to describe one of Laura's physical traits, and in no uncertain terms it was made most clear, Laura was also very . . . fat!

She had come to work for me just a few weeks before I joined Rosenberg's. She quickly proved to be both an efficient assistant and most popular with all the other staff members. Sure enough, she was seriously overweight. However, I can recall thinking during the interview . . .

"What a lovely countenance and very attractive face and smile you have."

I was taken by how much Laura was very much akin to a certain renowned actress 'Dawn French'. So when I came to tell her about my new role, I was so made up with everything that was going on that I had failed to notice even in the few weeks she had been working with me, Laura had already and as she would reveal to me during our first intimate encounter, lost over twenty pounds in weight.

So, as far as the admin and support was concerned the new assistant was now in place, but I needed something to give me an edge in my new prestigious sales role. A 'top notch' sales assistant would be needed as well. I then made, what would eventually prove to be one hell of a stupid move, I recruited Tom.

For reasons that I still can't fathom, (that lack of any true 'freewill' theory again) I decided Tom could add a much-needed sales production to impress my new 'employers'. Unfortunately, I simply ignored all the warning signs of the extremely sharp sales practices Tom would regularly brag about, as if it were a real talent. I would not only regret the decision on a professional level but also on a very painful personal level as well.

So, the final piece of the jigsaw would be down to which women would be my 'trophy' as far my professional expectations were concerned. The executive management were not over enamored by my attending various functions with a different girl on my arm on each new occasion.

For sure, they were invariably very high calibre and classy females but the new powers that be, liked to see a stable and 'acceptable' relationship. In their language, this only meant one thing, marriage! What hypocrisy, when you consider many of them were also . . . 'At it'!

The two women who had been vying to be the unlucky winner, were of course, Judith and Chasney. This is yet another example of the infuriating and clear 'choices' where my left sided and logical thoughts screamed at me. There was only one suitable candidate and that was obviously Judith. Tall, beautiful, intelligent, professional, very discerning, and would enhance considerably the stock of any an aspiring 'partner'. Judith was lovely in every sense, and for some inexplicable reason, she also adored me. So, did I choose her? Did I hell . . .

I was being relentlessly pursued by Chasney. My ego was simply soaking it up. To be fair, she was very attractive. I have previously alluded to, she certainly had a huge number of admirers. Nonetheless, although she was short, curvaceous, and certainly lacked Judith's lithe class and style, she possessed something Judith did not, which was a most charismatic and alluring appeal.

Thc way I treated Judith was an utter disgrace. This beautiful woman, who was the object of desire for no end of handsome lawyers and professionals, wasn't only dumped, I just simply . . . ignored her. Embarrassingly, some six months down the line I had a meeting with a few of her colleagues at the same law firm who all expressed in no uncertain terms, that I had been insane to turn her attentions down. They mused, initially, Judith had been telling everyone I was her new love interest and she had great plans for the relationship. Only for the next occasion when they inquired, she sheepishly had to reply with a . . . "Oh, I never heard from him again."

If it wasn't bad enough making such a glaringly stupid choice. I then compounded the insanity by actually marrying Chasney in a less than five weeks from our initial introduction!

So why did I do it? Why choose a girl who was so vain and incomepatible, rather than, choose someone who was both beautiful and, safe? For many years I was so self-absorbed I gave very little time to even pondering such a question, let alone finding the reason behind it? In recent times, however, as my life has unravelled and I kept on repeating

George had got himself proudly pumped up for the long night ahead. 'Ladies nights' are supposed to be one prolonged Masonic tribute by demonstrating an appreciation for the members' wives and women folk. At the same time, raising funds for various charities. Ok, a fair amount is raised for needy causes at such black-tie bashes, but as far as 'indebtedness' to their women are concerned. It's all complete hogwash in my view. In fact, it appeared to be rather insulting to the intelligence of women who were invariably kept in the dark regarding their husband's lodge meetings and secretive activities. If they want to truly honor the fairer sex, then why not let them become bloody members?

I had purchased a new 'monkey suit', cufflinks, wing collared white shirt, with a matching bow tie and cummerbund. This was the 1990s and whilst the fashion was very much for outlandish designs and 'paisley's', I have always had a much more conservative preference and didn't really care much for such expressive tastes. So other than a discreet flash of crimson on my bow tie, I turned up at the then named Swallow Hotel in Waltham Abbey, Essex, with my new fiancé (still feels weird writing this even two decades later). Before I knew it, we were posing for the obligatory 'cheesy couple' shots with Chasney wearing her new 'little sequined cobalt number'.

The pompous protocols at a black-tie 'knees up' are all rather familiar but, at a Masonic thingy, I still couldn't get on with all that 'presenting of couples' to the wife of the 'Grand Master' whose turn it was next . . . 'to be in the chair' or whatever they call it. The ego, eh?

I had already sunk five large 'scotch and cokes' at the free bar. Chasney's older sister Shelley, and her partner Raymond, had been matching me 'drink for drink'. So, by the time we had sat down to listen to the many insincere speeches introduced by the elderly 'Master of Ceremonies' and his well-worn gavel; we were already very pissed!

Chasney sat next to me, of course, and would she shut up? Nope! She just droned on and on about the wedding. Even though my senses were rather numbed by alcohol, I had developed a knack of picking up body language using my peripheral vision. There was already a definite air of 'wedding fatigue' among the other family members. Bearing in mind Chasney had only announced the bloody engagement a few weeks earlier, it was a poignant sign of just how much she loved the sound of her own voice.

Her self-absorbed and childish demeanor was in full swing. She was knocking back plentiful amounts of red wine, on top of the several gin and tonics, she had guzzled earlier at the free bar. In my early days of hefty whiskey consumption, my mood would soon darken (although in later years, no matter what levels I consumed it barely had any impact). I was about to prove, by just how much. It didn't seem to matter whether a speech was in full flow or when anyone else attempted to engage her in alternative conversation, Chasney was having none of it. It was 'her way, or no way'. She just kept ploughing on while she cranked up the decibels.

On the other hand, I was actually getting quieter and darker, until. . .

"Why don't you just shut the fuck up!"

Despite the Ray McVeigh band performing ever blaring jazz numbers, everyone heard my outburst . . .

There was an inevitable pause, followed by a stunned bewilderment among the other eight guests on the table. Chasney stood up. As she turned toward me. With one rotation of her arm, she slapped me around 'the kisser' and within full view of all those now bopping away on the dance floor. As she stormed off, her mother chased her in the direction of the ladies bathroom. I tried to gain some composure but found myself glaring back at the many cringing and embarrassed faces. Not least of all, the grimacing expression belonging to her outraged father. This was going to be fun . . .

If everyone had heeded those early warning signs, a great deal of pain could have been avoided but (as I have observed in so many other marriage miss-matches since) we all allowed ourselves to get swept up in the momentum of the 'wedding juggernaut'. I would have liked to have said money could have been saved as well, but such was the pace by which Chasney, and her mother, were emptying George's bank account. It was all rather too late for that one. When two feckless and superficial souls collide, the stroking of their mutual egos overtakes all other logical and reasonable thought processes.

I can remember my 'stag do' so vividly. I was standing outside a wine bar in Chelmsford with my old pal Graham, despite the booze flowing, I was having a pre-wedding 'sobering' moment . . .

"I am not sure I can go through with this, pal. Quite frankly, she really gets on my nerves."

Graham then repeated some advice, he had been directing at me since I had first informed him, I was going to marry again. He was one of the many who had thought I had been crazy for dumping the elegant Judith, in favor of Chasney.

"Sam, mate, you don't have to go through with anything. It is not too late to back out. Much better to do so now, than regret it all soon after?"

My spineless response was so lightweight and no doubt, typical of so many who try to justify to themselves regarding the lunacy they are about to embark on.

"Yeah, I know what you mean mate, but her dad has forked out a small fortune. I will be letting down so many people if I go all flaky now."

I reached into my jacket pocket and took out a 'studio picture' Chasney had given me of herself when we first met. She was ever so modest like and holding it under Graham's nose, I even had the gall to say . . .

"How many chaps would give their right arm to be with THAT pal?

Yes, I did say 'that' and not 'her'."

In time, I would discover yet again, I did not really have any . . . choice.

The big day arrived, things didn't bode well right from the off when I received an early call from my brother Terence who expressed in no uncertain terms, he was not prepared to 'wear a bloody top hat and tails'! My brother's protest was duly noted. I was not in the frame of mind to insist he wear the desired dress code, which had been hired for him. He wasn't an usher or anything. So, I let the matter drop much to the disapproval of Chasney's parents.

Now to be truthful, I was far from enamored at the prospect of wearing such formal wear. It was really compounded for me when I saw the color of the cravats . . . they were a bright shimmery 'emerald'! Chasney had a bloody fixation for emeralds. The engagement ring she coerced me to buy had such a colored stone placed in the centre. On top of that, she revealed another of her childish attachments, that to this day, I still have pals asking me 'what was all THAT about'? You see, Chasney was crazy about FROGS, albeit the decorative, rather than the amphibian variety.

Like every other eccentric thing about her, which I initially disregarded; I failed to notice her house was full of pictures, ornaments, and figurines of the little green gits. It was only when we eventually set up house together, where my space was invaded by a vanguard of emerald knick-knacks, did the real extent of her obsession register with me.

As I had been divorced, I hadn't counted on having a 'white wedding'. As such, Chasney and her mother were going to have their 'church do' no matter what. So, the compromise was a registry office service followed by a 'church blessing'. All a load of bollocks as far as I was concerned, but hey, my opinions counted for . . . zilch! After the church service, it was then onto the reception and an evening knee up at a very large country pub, near Bradwell-on-sea, which was organized by another so called 'best friend' called Deborah Brekon. Chasney had many 'best friends' who would invariably be disloyal to Chasney by sleeping with her new husband, but more about the reasoning for such betrayal on my part, and theirs . . . later.

Credit where it is due though, Chasney looked utterly sensational as she stood by my side in front of the registrar. Although his uncanny resemblance to the 'spitting image' puppet of 'Roy Hattersley' meant neither of us particularly flowed when making our vows. But then again, despite the humorous distraction, we both managed a clear enough an 'I do', which would be capable of inflicting adequate mutual pain over the term of our ill-fated union.

Neil Follet moved into his best man highest gear. He smoothly pointed our joint family members, who together with Graham were the only other attendees at the registry office, in the direction of awaiting cars and the white Rolls Royce purring away outside waiting for 'bridezilla' and her groom.

It was while we were sitting in the back of the Rolls, Chasney decided to drop another surprise on me . . .

"Ooooh, this is all sooooooo exciting, isn't it? By the way, you just wait until you hear my speech darling."

For one moment there, I thought my new wife had just informed me she had a speech prepared. Naaaah . . . I can't have heard that correctly. Surely? My worst fears were soon to be realized.

"I have been preparing it for some time. I don't know why it's only you men who get the opportunity to be center stage."

"Chasney, what the fuck are you talking about? The best man, your dad, and me are all sorted and primed. The timetable, and protocols, are prepared with the 'Master of Ceremonies', so we can't have you interfering with things . . . ok!"

The Master of Ceremonies was a car dealer pal of mine named Marc Levi, who I knew to be a long time Freemason himself. So, we had arranged for there to be a 'Masonic style' reception, which kept my new father-in-law very happy. Marc was a real 'cheeky chappy' who was a director of a business at the time called 'Matrix', which symbolically at least, will have a marked significance later in my story. He eventually went on to play a 'Spiv' character on Breakfast TV. Unfortunately for him, he ended up being, errrm . . . murdered!

Marc was murdered under the noses of police officers who had been tailing his killer when he was dragged into woods and killed, despite NCA officers watching a nearby farmhouse. They had earlier followed another drug dealer unaware Marc had been lured to the murder scene on the pretext of a business meeting and was then beaten and bundled into the boot of a car . . .

Police followed the car to a farm where Marc was taken to the nearby woods. They did not know he was being murdered because he had fallen out with the dealer who they had been following. Two weeks later, when an empty shallow grave was discovered, the body of the 43-year-old father of four had disappeared and has never been found.

My berating of my new 'bridezilla' was like a red flag to a bull. "Well, I am not going to be put off. I have put so much thought into the planning of this performance, so you can just lump it. All my friends can't wait!"

My God, she just said, it is going to be a bloody 'performance' as well now. This will be the embarrassment of the sodding year!!

By the time the rest of the wedding guests had all rocked up, the church blessing went surprisingly smoothly. In the 1990s, you couldn't have a wedding service that wasn't videoed, of course. One of my old sales 'team', a drunk named Alan, was charged with being cameraman for the day. Thinking back, it was all rather amusing. When, at a time a steady hand is crucial, the bloke thing to do is to pick the shakiest hand you can think of for filming the most important of events. Knowing full well he is going to get uncontrollably pissed as the day progresses.

The group wedding photo was a sham on the one hand, but quite prophetic on the other. As a whole bunch of Chasney's so-called friends and sycophants, smiled away for the hired 'Masonic' photographer. Who was also a pal of my new father-in-law.

In the center of the group was my new wife with her friend Rowena standing directly behind her, who only a few weeks before had been in my bed. On her right, were her two bridesmaids. An old school friend Tonya Coin, and Chasney's sister, Shelley. Both would take me to their beds (and I do mean 'their' beds) within months of the lovely day. To round it off, the organizer of the days catering, another of Chasney's 'lifelong friends' Deborah, who would also soon be very keen on visiting the spare bedroom at her friends' new matrimonial home.

So, what was it about my new wife, which motivated all four of them to deceive her so quickly? As events unfold, I will reveal how a number of other ladies who also claimed to be trusted friends, would similarly betray her.

Neil was still doing sterling work as the best man. He ushered everyone toward the motorcade and sent them off in the direction of the reception venue. As I previously mentioned, it was a somewhat unlikely wedding venue and isolated out in the middle of the 'Essex sticks', surrounded by boggy marshes. Who said the art of romance was dead eh?

I was not particularly looking forward to this bit. Not so much because of the expectations surrounding the groom's speech, but largely because I knew 'bridezilla' was just desperate to get stuck into her 'performance'. Despite my angst, the speeches of the men went down extremely well and were majestically introduced by Marc Levi who delivered his jokes and anecdotes with masterly aplomb. For a 'spiv second-hand car dealer' he certainly did us all very proud. RIP . . . Marc Levi.

Then, as like any kid at a school nativity waiting to get on stage to deliver their only line, 'bridezilla' could wait no more. Without further ado, up she jumped. Jesus, this was going to be bloody painful. But, before we could all get into full cringe mode, she snapped her fingers to her friend Deborah. Clearly a sign for some pre-planned speech prompt. We didn't have to wait long to find out. Deborah came walking over to my new spouse with a . . . flip chart and stand. WTF!!

I wheeled around and was met full on by the toothy grin of a Bedouin wearing black sunglasses. By his side, was a young helper who had a 'one humped beast' tethered behind him.

"Yes Mister, just ten dollar and my boy will help your wife up . . . yes?"

Chasney was insistent . . .

"Oooh . . . Can't wait any longer, help me up then."

The camel knelt down. Before I knew it, I had peeled off ten dollars and Chasney was up on board and whooping away . . . the stupid cow.

I couldn't bear it any longer so without further ado, the lens cap came off my newly purchased Nikon SLR. Off I went, snapping away at the surrounding wonderment. As I did so, I again marvelled at the three main pyramids. I reflected on the theories I had read by authors such as Erich Anton, Paul von Däniken, and Zecharia Sitchin. They suggested these huge structures may have been fashioned by alien-beings, which were later understood to be 'Polytheistic Gods'. Such deities were subsequently - and unsurprisingly - worshipped by an ancient slave race . . . mankind! I will expand on such theories later, but it was beginning to become clear in my mind at least, that the 'ancient Gods', whether Greek, Sumerian, Roman, or Egyptian were all actually the same beings and just labelled with different iconography, according to the culture you read about. Hmm . . .

My theorizing soon came to an abrupt end though, as my shallow wife had already become bored of riding on the back of the spitting dromedary.

"Ooooh . . . daaaaarling, can I get down now pleeeeeeez.?"

I signalled toward the Bedouin and instructed him to deposit my consort back on the sand. The Bedouin then grinned and further gestured by rubbing his finger and thumb together before using a sarcastic 'honorific'.

"Of course, Effendi, which will be ten dollars." Uh? I must have misunderstood . . .

"Sorry pal, I think you have already forgotten I just paid ten dollars to stick her up there, so I ain't paying anymore to bloody get her down again!"

"You pay now Mister . . . Pip ip Eeenglish or I put a curse on you and your wife."

Chaps from Tower Hamlets don't care much for being cursed . . .

"Is that so? Well, let me tell you right now Effendi, if you don't let her down, I will put a curse on you. So, I will say again, you ain't getting another penny out of me so you can leave her up there for all I care."

I spun around on my sandals and stormed off in the direction of the Great Pyramid with a clear intent of maximizing the use of my new telephoto lens. Chasney wasn't . . . impressed.

"Pah!! You bastard! Pay him right now or I will scream this fucking place down!"

I just 'cocked a deaf one' whilst at the same time, being most impressed by the capabilities of my new SLR camera. Then it all kicked off because 'Mr. Effendi' was getting seriously pissed off by now. He marched up to my face. Spitting with rage, he started wailing all sorts at me in 'Arabic'. Hearing all the commotion a lady guide came up and warned me . . .

"Excuse me sir, but the Bedouin is quite insulted. I would advise you to pay the money to allow your wife to get down."

I was by that point, sweltering in the desert heat and quite incensed myself, so I only had one reaction.

"Bollocks to that love . . . I ain't coughing up another penny."

I walked off and left them all to it. As I did, I could hear Chasney behind me going completely mental from high up on the back of the humped beast. So much so, the Bedouin eventually had enough and signalled to his boy to let her dismount. She then made one beeline for yours truly . . .

"You fuckin bastard!"

"Look . . . he let you get down, didn't he?"

"You wouldn't pay a miserly ten dollars to get me down though.

What does that say about this marriage?"

A very good question Chasney, a VERY good question indeed.

Before we would finally leave Cyprus and head back home to marital reality, another incident occurred, which was a foreboding of things to come. It was on the penultimate day of the 'perfect Moneyspoon'. We were both sitting by the pool in near 100-degree heat. I had smoothed some coconut oil on Chasney's back, so my hands were still quite slippery, when I decided to take a dip in the pool for a welcome respite from the searing temperature. As I dove in, I could feel the water pressure, splaying my wedding ring finger apart and as it did so, my ring dutifully slipped cleanly off. It headed toward the bottom of the deep end. Oh dear.

Despite the remonstrations of my wife to the hotel pool supervisors, the ring was never seen again. Although I feigned my distress at losing it. I knew Chasney was never going to buy my synthetic anguish.

"Well, if you think that is some kind of omen then you can forget it right now and by the way, I will NEVER divorce you."

Thankfully, she did not keep that promise . . .

CHAPTER 31.

CHASNEY BETRAYED

I did a fairly sterling job of staying faithful to Chasney for all of . . . ermm . . . six months! The lucky girl who would break that duck, was certainly the most surprising and unlikeliest of all. Her name was Tonya Coin. She had been a 'friend' of Chasney's since infant school. I describe her as a 'friend' not only because she would stab my wife in the back, but also due to the fact Chasney, hilariously, could not really stand the sight of her!

It is another of those weird 'woman things' whereby, they will derive the greatest of pleasures by inviting another long-time friend to 'share' in their happiness. Albeit they just want to rub salt into the wound and highlight just how unappealing and still 'on the shelf' that poor soul really is. Inhumane or what?!

Tonya was a native of Stevenage in Hertfordshire. One of London's many overspill towns, such as Basildon, Harlow, Croydon, Crawley, etc. They were mostly built shortly after WWII. The old towns gave them their names and were systematically ruined in the process. Ok, I may have been raised between 'the gasworks and the cemetery', but in nearly all those instances, such places were looked down on by both Chasney's snobbish parents as . . . 'that council house dump'.

Poor Tonya didn't have a great deal going for her. With her dreadfully sour attitude and a mouthful of wonky teeth. She had hair that always looked greasy. Her dress sense was pretty much non-existent. Capitalizing on this off-putting portrayal, Chasney would treat her with never-ending disdain. Yet, despite such treatment, Tonya would show endless gratitude for being included among Chasney's feckless associates. So, it would be with enthusiastic relish, Tonya would exact revenge on Chasney for belittling her so much, for forcing her to wear such a distasteful emerald bridesmaid's dress, no doubt!

My new wife had been suffering from severely impacted wisdom teeth for over forty-eight hours. Despite the agony, she inevitably milked it for all it was worth and persuaded her mother to pull some strings with a 'Freemason dentist friend' who booked Chasney into a private clinic for surgery with a one night 'stay over'. Chasney had the surgery. I dutifully visited her in the afternoon.

As I departed, I artfully kissed her cheek and assured her I would pick her up the following morning. I then sauntered off in the direction of my favorite bar, where several pals were waiting for a night out. Even I, could not have predicted how that evening was going to conclude and the particular Rubicon, which I was about to cross. A line I did not return from until I started to write this book.

After a disorderly evening, during which I had guzzled a dozen bottles of Becks lager, I drove home. Yes . . . drove . . . for what I still thought was going to be a night of blissful kip and an early start before collecting my convalescing wife. Wrong!

At that particular time, we were still living at my house as we hadn't quite been able to decide between the two of us where we wanted to live. I was keen to get away from the Burnham area. Chashey was being very obstinate about leaving the town she loved. The main reason being, of course, her lifelong addiction to sailing. Before I could even think about climbing into the sack, the phone rang. Who the fuck is that? I need to get some sleep.

"Hi Sam, it's only me, Tonya. How is she doing?"

Bloody hell, why did she of all people have to ring now!

Tonya was a complete pain in the arse. Chasney hardly ever said a nice word about her. I always thought it strange how certain people who have pissed us off all our lives, never seem to get the hint. They will endure endless disapproval, sarcastic comment, and are never invited to anything just to keep a fruitless loyalty. As I already alluded Chasney had only asked her to be one of her bridesmaids to laud it over her. Tonya, however, was about to get her own back, and some.

I had consumed quite a large amount of beer. The alcohol made me feel strangely amorous toward a girl, I would not normally have given a second look. Tonya was a brunette with buck teeth and very pale skin. She had a half-decent figure with an ample cleavage, but absolutely no style or dress sense. Even so, in response to Tonya's insincere inquiring after her friend's well-being, I artfully updated her on Chasney's progress. We then started to banter, which in turn, led to unmistakable . . . flirting.

"Are you toying with me Samuel?" She was obviously hoping . . .

"You might say that, Tonya. Well, yes . . . actually."

"Oooerrr . . . well, I am with you too. I have always been attracted to you, even though I could tell you were a bit of a rogue."

Women can rarely resist a 'naughty boy'. Time and again, they will repeat that choice only to then complain . . . "Why do I always end up getting used by men?"

I then found myself suggesting something I mistakenly assumed was never going to cause me any real problem, simply because of the unforgiving hour . . .

"Well, if I called your bluff and said I will jump in my car right now and come and fuck your brains out, you would run a million miles."

"Best you do just that then . . . MISTER!" "WHAT?"

"I will leave the door on the latch. You can come straight up to my bedroom. I will be waiting for you."

The phone went dead. I just lay there in disbelief. I might have had a few beers, but I had not misheard her. It had barely taken half a dozen sentences for one of the bridesmaids at my wedding to invite me to her bed.

Furthermore, a girl who repeatedly claimed to be my new wife's oldest and most loyal friend. I pondered for a couple of minutes to try and decide if Tonya was just teasing. I obviously did not want to make a huge twat of myself, but hey, there was only going to be one way to find out.

I hadn't changed out of my suit despite it being 2 am. I jumped behind the wheel of my car and headed in the direction of Stevenage. The drive seemed to take an age. I was bursting with anticipation. Not because I fancied her, I didn't really. The buzz I was feeling created by the fact she had been a bridesmaid and so-called lifelong friend of Chasney and the betrayal from both our sides added to the adrenaline rush.

Chasney and I had only been married for a short while. We had already experienced a great deal of conflict. I can say without any fear of contradiction, Chasney was, by a country mile, the most spoilt little mare I had ever met. It would also be my inability to say no to her impulsive demands that would be our undoing. Indeed, my unmistakable pattern for indulging women was now well established. Yet another indicator of the sociopath feeding his addiction and ego.

I could not help thinking Tonya's come on, wasn't quite as spontaneous as it at first appeared. You could smell 'sweet revenge in the air'. For what, I wondered. A modus operandi a number of Chasney's 'best friends' would replicate when conniving behind her back.

I arrived at Tonya's grubby flat. Sure enough, the door was left on the latch. Rather promising! I could hear her giggling from the bedroom. It was so dark, I had to fumble my way past furniture, and then flopped onto the bed in what seemed to be one motion.

"What kept you?"

"Tonya, are we really going to do this, have you no guilt?" "Well, what about you then? I won't tell if you don't?"

That was good enough for me. Before I knew it, we were in an erotic clinch, which lasted for quite a few hours. To this day, I still do not believe Chasney ever discovered one of her oldest friends had fucked her husband, while she was convalescing. Which was just as well, because her other friends would, one by one, systematically betray her in a similar vein. However, none would stab her in the back with more relish, than the other bridesmaid at Chasney's wedding, her very own sister, Shelly.

By the time I became entangled in a very passionate liaison with Chasney's elder sibling, I had already helped myself to a number of the other female guests who had adorned our group wedding shot. Not least of all, another of her many 'long-time friends', Deborah Breckon, who you might recall was the landlady who hosted our wedding reception.

In keeping with Tonya's lack of conscience, Deborah didn't bat an eyelid when she first tempted me in the confines of my own home. A few hotel encounters followed, but after we predictably became bored of each other. Deborah would continue to nonchalantly chat away to Chasney who was still none the wiser.

Chasney's sister, however, was to raise the bar to very heady heights. Not because she was more attractive than her sister, for she was quite the opposite in fact. No, it was because, just like Tonya, Chasney had lauded it over Shelly for many years.

Shelley was a couple of years older than my wife. She was a flaming redhead with freckles, and rather prone to a glass of wine or ten! Chasney by contrast, was a glamorously attractive high-flyer, could attract virtually any guy she wanted, and appeared to be very vivacious. She was always putting her sister down as 'a loser' who was always envious of her younger sister. So, it was even a surprise to me, to eventually discover how 'hot' she was.

Shelly had worked in the hotel industry all of her working career. Like so many in that sector, she would 'job hop' with alacrity. By the time the 90th birthday came around of Chasney's grandmother, I had been fairly integrated into the Bowland family and quite understandably, the birthday venue was organized by Shelly. She was working as head housekeeper at the Hendon Hall Hotel. The same venue that had hosted the England World Cup winning squad of 1966. Although the establishment was by now looking somewhat tired, it's 'labyrinthine corridors' were about to serve me well.

The party was predictably laborious. I was becoming increasingly agitated. I had agreed to drive. Therefore, I was unable to have a drink. Normally, I wouldn't have been so mindful but as all the family were in attendance, I knew they would not approve. So, when Shelly suggested giving me a guided tour of the iconic venue, I was more than glad for the respite. I looked over at my less than sober wife who gestured she had already seen the best the hotel could offer, and tersely nodded her blessing.

I yawned my way around my personal tour only to be somewhat awakened when Shelly stopped by the laundry room and made a caustic remark about the 'Jewish Orthodox wedding night consummation'. She then grinned and poked her index finger through a hole in the sheet, indicating that there must not be any 'skin to skin' contact. That was a new one on me!

Shelly threw the sheet in a large basket. I continued to follow her as she twisted her way through the corridors. For the first time, I found myself appreciating her curves and the manner by which the particular dress she had chosen for the occasion, actually 'creamed' the contours of her rather 'peachy' shaped rear.

Shelley approached an adjoining door that was being particularly stubborn and as she tried to push on through it . . .

"Here let me help you." "It is rather stiff, eh?"

She looked right into my eyes as she suggestively smiled through the innuendo.

As I leant forward to push on the door, my other hand conveniently rested on her hip. I allowed it to remain long enough to decide if there was any awkwardness on her part. Tellingly, there was none . . .

My sister-in-law turned out to be a surprising sensation as a lover. She may have lacked the charisma and charm of her sister, but she possessed one particular quality in abundance . . . passion! In no time, I would regularly drive over to the hotel, often into the night. When Shelly wasn't working, we would spend many erotic hours between the sheets. We became closer than I could ever have envisaged. Shelly would often write to me at my office and share her fantasises about the two of us. She barely showed any sense of guilt for betraying her sister. Our lovemaking became more regular. The pillow talk was most revealing. We would discuss a great deal. She would often vent her frustrations, about how her younger sister had always been spoilt and was clearly her parents' favorite. It was most apparent she had a dependence on alcohol. A bottle was always open. Indeed, by this time my own imbibing was heading skyward. It wouldn't be long before such an intake was to be become a full-blown addiction.

Our affair lasted a good six months. Shelly became ever braver and would visit her sister just to have closer contact with me. Apart from an isolated occasion when Chasney happened to walk in on her sister talking rather closely to me, we would snatch moments when Chasney would go off sailing. The exhilaration we felt when alone in my house was off the scale. I would fuck Shelley on the kitchen work top, in front of the fire, on the stairs, and she particularly enjoyed riding me in her sister's bed. I know, I know . . . again, why did so many women, take such pleasure in betraying Chasney?

My risk taking was hitting new alcohol fuelled levels. Sociopaths have a dysfunctional penchant for doing so. I would leave my Shelley's flat at all hours.

Despite often coming home approaching breakfast time, Chasney would never interrogate me about my whereabouts. Only once, did she half-heartedly ask me if I was having an affair. I just 'shrugged my shoulders'. No more was ever said.

Inevitably, sociopaths become disinterested in any previous conquest and its then time to move on. Shelley knew we could not go on for too long. When I drew things to a close, unlike many lovers who I simply dismissed, I stayed friendly with Shelley. I did have a soft spot for her.

Denial, especially for women, is a most bizarre phenomenon. No doubt, many who are reading this will associate with such repressed cognitive behavior. Indeed, a male sociopath will seize on a female's inclination to bury their head in the sand. Even convince their partner they are acting in an unfounded and neurotic fashion, should they ever dare to challenge or question the suspicious activity of their man.

No other women; would better illustrate betrayal and hypocrisy, than my two PA's Laura Texeira, and Lyn McGlone. Laura you will recall, had joined my team as a PA and as for Lyn? Well, what can I say . . .?

I remember first setting eyes on this most seductive and sultry of women when I was invited to a black-tie function hosted by a business associate, property developer, Jon Hardy. This in itself was a game changer. I would also meet another woman who I would eventually end up leaving Chasney for, no less than Jon's own wife, Demi! Serendipitous, eh?

CHAPTER 32.

HYPOCRITE LYN

Lyn McGlone was quite simply pure temptation walking on two incredibly shapely legs. She was blessed with deep 'Anglo-Indian' eyes, high cheek bones, and a mouth with the fullest delicious lips. On and off, we would be lovers for the next six emotionally conflicting years.

I say conflicting, because despite having been married to Max, a chartered account for decades, Lyn somehow, just never seemed to fathom she couldn't always have her cake and eat it. As I have previously asserted; whilst I do appreciate men often receive a much-deserved bad press for cheating and serial infidelity, it does, as they say . . . 'take two to tango'. Over the years, I have met more than my share of women who were nothing short, of contemptible hypocrites! What? Me a misogynist? Perish the thought.

Hence, for a couple of years - I bizarrely had both Laura and Lyn, working in 'rotational shifts' as both my personal assistants and lovers. Even more humorous, was the fact Laura was aware throughout, she was sharing me with her colleague. But Linda was completely unwitting I had ever had an affair with her close colleague. Yes, you know, another 'friend'.

I will never forget the occasion when Lyn pulled me into her 'pheromone soaked' web of allurement. I was developing the relationship with Jon Hardy. He was looking to develop a new golf course on the site of a dilapidated former stately home in Hertfordshire. Jon was not really one for spread sheets and financial forecasts. So, he suggested I call in his consultant Max McGlone, to 'go over the figures'.

I had met Max at Jon's offices on a few occasions. To be fair, I found him to be a smart chap and most amiable. Conveniently, Max lived nearby in Burnham. I called ahead to ascertain if it would be convenient for me to call by and chat about the finances of Jon's project. It was the dusky Lyn, however, who answered the phone . . .

"Oh, hi Sam, Max is out at the moment. I don't think he will be too long though. You can always pop by and have a cup of tea, while you wait?"

I did not need to be asked twice . . .

Don't come home Max, don't come home . . .

I must have played those words non-stop in my head as I pointed my Mercedes in the direction of the accountants' large 'Georgian' style detached house, on the outskirts of the town. Max owned a 5 series BMW, which he informed me had previously been owned by the great Spurs and England footballer, Jimmy Greaves. I was praying his vehicle would be absent from the drive.

Max's house was only a ten-minute drive from Jon's office, but the journey seemed to take an age. I was feeling such a sense of anticipation to be meeting up with such a horny woman. I would have been seriously gutted if Max had come home before my arrival. I turned right into Mill Road and . . . bingo!

As I pulled on to the gravel drive, my heart was beating away inside my chest. Indeed, only Lyn's Ford Escort sat on the drive. As I climbed out of my Merc, the front door quickly opened. The sensual 'Anglo Indian', beamed back at me. Such a brilliant white smile was accentuated against Lyn's dark skin and white midi skirt with a black, skintight V-neck. It was simple but looked exquisite on her perfect athletic form. Lyn was seven years older than I, so that made her forty years of age. I can remember thinking . . . Your body would put most twenty-year old's to shame.

"Come on in Sam, the tea is in the pot. I do hope you like Darjeeling tea?"

As Lyn directed me to the lounge, I took stock. Max and Lyn's home was immaculate. Typical of the 90s with 'swags and tails' in abundance, Floral design sofas, deep pile Axminster carpets, and expensive reproduction dark oak furniture. Lyn was smiling as she placed the bone China tea pot, cups, and saucers on the marble coffee table.

"It is always tea, rather than coffee here I'm afraid. It is my Indian heritage on my mother's side that has stayed with me. Milk and sugar, Sam?"

Lyn poured the tea through the strainer but did not take her stare off me for a second as she then poured the next cup. How dexterous of her. A sign of things to come?

"Sam, I am glad I have you to myself before Max comes home, for I was hoping to ask you something?"

Wow, this was happening far more quickly than even I could have hoped for.

"I know you will think I am being forward, but . . ." "No way Lyn, just be as forward as you like."

"But I was wondering if there were any job opportunities at Rosenberg's. Your regional offices are in Colchester, right? So, that is not so far away to drive?"

Fuck me, Lyn was certainly being forward, but she was driving down the wrong fucking highway!

I had to think quickly here but made a call I would so later regret. Especially, as later events would reveal, I had no need to do so to achieve my carnal objectives.

"Oh, umm . . . Lyn? Well, I certainly was not expecting to be asked that question?"

"Sam, I am so sorry if I have compromised you in anyway. I just thought I would ask. Never mind."

"No, not at all Lyn," I lied.

"Let me think now? You see, my personal assistant, Laura, is only able to work part-time these days (not exactly true) so the timing could be most fortuitous."

This was mad. I had absolutely no idea, whether Lyn had the appropriate skill set to be an effective personal assistant yet here I was, practically offering her a position. And why? Well, you know . . .

Lyn sipped her tea. As she crossed her svelte and smooth calves, there was most definitely a self-satisfied air about her.

When was Max coming home? Not . . . yet . . . please?

Despite the chances of a BMW pulling up outside any minute, Lyn and I bantered away in a more than familiar manner than would be normal for an initial meeting. Lyn did not need alcohol to loosen her tongue.

"Sam, I wasn't exactly being honest with you."

"Aha? I, see. Actually, I don't know why I just said that Lyn. Come on then, how do you mean?"

"Max isn't coming home anytime soon."

"Is that so? Now why did you tell me otherwise?"

"Because I am so bored at home being left alone so much. He . . . is always out. Mostly at the damned golf course club house with his big buddy Jon. So, I thought there might just be an opportunity at your place? We haven't really spoken much. I promise I have always admired your swagger and self-assurance. These are very attractive qualities in a man."

No alcohol was ever introduced at any point in the proceedings. The high-octane sexual energy between the two of us was unmistakable and did not need fuelling. The opportunity for another sexual encounter at the home of another man always added to the risk appeal.

We both gravitated into the kitchen. In one slinky feline movement, Lyn pulled herself up onto the black granite work top. Lyn's smouldering stare did not flinch.

"Sam, do you want me to suck you?" I feigned ambivalence . . . "Suck me?" "Yes, your mouth and your cock."

All at once, I was glowing and throbbing, then Lyn unveiled her party piece. With the tip of her talon-like fingernail resting on her pulsating bottom lip, she slowly parted her creamy dark thighs, which clearly revealed she was not wearing anything underneath.

Before I knew it, Lyn had both of her super soft hands palming the back of my head, as she pulled my mouth deep into her soaking pussy. She gyrated and tightened her legs around my shoulders. She was instantly pleasured. I then straightened my back and our eyes and mouths locked. Lyn wasn't joking when she said 'suck'. We melted into each other and kissed for what seemed like hours.

"Now, I want you in my mouth."

Lyn just knew instinctively, how to use her tongue on me.

It goes without saying; I was now fully expecting to make the next move by raising Lyn's tight peach butt so I could fuck her hard in her own home. But then . . . that fucking BMW!!

"Oh, my God! No!! Sam, take a piss in the downstairs toilet, be quick . . . go!!"

I slammed the door of the downstairs bathroom and holding my ear close to the door, I listened . . . hard!

"Hello Luv, where's Sam?"

"He's just in the loo, he has been waiting very patiently for you Max. Why are you so late? As if, I didn't know!"

"Come on Lyn, you know how it is in my profession. Anyway, I'm here now."

I took that as my cue to flush. I washed my hands as theatrically as I could for an exaggerated effect, just to prove only a few moments before my tongue had not been buried deep inside Lyn's sweet pussy.

As I walked nervously into the lounge to my relief, Max was all smiles and he swiftly offered me his hand.

"Sorry about the wait Sam, couldn't be avoided I'm afraid. Anyway, my wife is always the perfect host. She never lets me down."

You can say that again, you fool.

Lyn was quick to interject.

"Yes, I have indeed. Do you know what? Sam happened to be telling me he has been looking to add an administrator to his team. So, I was quick to reveal I have been keen to get back into that environment."

Max was grateful for the conversation switching away from his lack of punctuality.

"So, have you offered my wife a job then Sam? That would be great."

Again, Lyn kept control of the exchange in order to guarantee I had no chance of casting any doubt on the prospect of her working for me.

"Sam was really pleased his search was over Max. I am starting next Monday. I will be working afternoons with an hour overlap with Sam's part-time PA, Laura. I am really excited and looking forward to meet Laura. It will be fun too. Right Sam?"

The boldness of the woman! Over the next few years, I would witness Lyn's sheer audacity and daring, more times than would be healthy.

Both Max and Lyn smiled back at me with clear expectations. "Aha! Monday it is then Lyn. Those elegant fingers are just made

for typing, eh?"

To this day, I still find it incredible Laura would be so complicit. She would regularly reserve a hotel room for the two of us to rendezvous in the mornings. We would make hot and fervent love before she left to do her stint in the office. I would then, rapidly remake the bed and await Lyn's arrival for a 'lunchtime of sex'. She was completely oblivious her work colleague had just been making love to me between the same sheets and barely half an hour prior. To avoid raising any of Lyn's suspicions, Laura was always most considerate, and would refrain from wearing any perfume until she left for the office. Neither did Lyn ever did notice how warm the sheets still were.

The best bit though, was when Lyn became so paranoid about what I was up to, she began to ‘confide’ in Laura, of all people, she had suspicions of . . .

“I think Sam might be screwing someone else.”

Lyn persuaded Laura to drive her and follow me about in the vain hope of catching me out! Laura would constantly give me feedback about all these shenanigans. So, we would plan bogus appointments with alternative routes, to take Lyn off the scent. Laura took as much pleasure as I observing Lyn getting evermore agitated and jealous about my movements. You couldn't make this stuff up!

Lyn was quite obsessed at times and would constantly interrogate me about what I might be getting up to. I would simply use the same riposte every time . . .

“Lyn, what is it with you? You are fucking . . . married!”

Lyn constantly bemoaned how boring her life had become over the years as a ‘golfing widow’ of the hard-drinking Max. So, I would goad her, asking why she simply didn't just leave him, if her life was so bad? Lyn loathed that question, simply because she enjoyed all the financial trappings which Max provided, but by far her biggest flaw was her hypocrisy.

With arms folded, Lyn would gossip about anyone who she suspected might be having an affair yet would not think twice about accepting Chasney’s hospitality just to glory in the deception. She also had the sheer temerity to invite Chasney and I to her home for cozy evenings hosted by her and Max. I am ashamed to admit, my audacity was just as egregious, because I accepted the invites with relish.

My dishonorable behavior was further compounded by my personal dealings with Lyn’s husband, about various business matters. I had developed a buoyant relationship with the property developer Jon Hardy, and Max was also his business consultant. Accordingly, I would regularly meet with both of them as they were chairman and vice chairman of the local golf club, which had also been built by Jon's company. Over the entire period when I was in a dalliance with his wife, Max did not once, give any sign he was suspicious of anything. I don't believe he was ever in denial. He was just too self-absorbed with his own world of golf club socializing and drinking as much as he could and whenever possible.

So, the ‘Laura and Lyn’ dream ticket continued in tandem for the best part of two years. Linda was such a lush creature and Laura was certainly motivated to compete with her. Over that time, I witnessed a girl reduce her dress size from being a 22, to a very lithe, size 10. Her image was transformed. She ended up looking most stunning in her own right. Laura eventually tired of competing for my affections, but we did part company on really good terms. A rarity for me, that was for sure.

My relationship with Chasney was in a continually adversarial state. Apart from my two PA's, there were a number of further indiscretions including another of my wife's so-called friends from the sailing scene. Matters really came to a head, as a result of two episodes that coincided to seal the fate of our beleaguered marriage. One was Chasney's behavior during a Rosenberg 'overseas convention' and the other, the demise of yet another marriage, which was that of building developer Jon Hardy and his wife, Demi.

I had enjoyed a particularly successful year in 1992. So, it was off to Monaco, with a number of the other 'partners' accompanied by Rosenburg 'Top Brass'. As was often the case with my wife; we were first to arrive at the airport 'duty free' but we were always the last to leave. Her shopping addiction was in full flight - excuse the pun. I became increasingly irate as I could hear the airport address system asking for the two remaining passengers to 'board the flight for Nice without further delay'. So, it was with a real sense of exasperation, I grabbed my wife's arm and dragged her through the boarding gate.

As we boarded, a 'camp' flight attendant was clearly unimpressed and brusquely ushered us along the flight deck toward our seats where most of my colleagues were impatiently waiting. I was obviously embarrassed and in one of those bizarre, serendipitous moments, sitting at the front of the plane was the most debonair of actors 'Sir Roger Moore'. I sheepishly met his eye and nervously reacted with a . . .

"Alright . . . Rog!"

There was uproarious laughter from the other passengers. He very graciously smiled back. I didn't think it was appropriate to delay matters any further by telling him he was 'my favourite Bond actor', so I sauntered off to the rear of the plane. RIP . . . 'Sir Rog'.

Despite staying at the Hotel de Paris, situated next to the iconic Monte Carlo Casino, I thought Monaco was overrated. Chasney was most certainly in her element. For days I had to me endure her constantly banging on about 'Monte Carlo this and Monte Carlo that'. By the end of the week's convention, I had had enough of her. Matters were to come to a head on the final evening when, after an alcohol-soaked dinner, my wife did what she was prone to do – she spiralled off somewhere. I was becoming increasingly agitated because we had an early flight the next morning. It was already well past midnight.

I eventually caught up with her at a wine bar. There she was, in her usual pose, crossed legged on a stool, gin and tonic in one hand, cigarette in the other, surrounded by numerous male sycophants. I breezed past her admirers and grabbed her arm.

"Come on you, we have an early flight, and you are fucking pissed . . . again!"

Before she could even think about protesting, I dragged her past the surprized black-tie wearing assemblage, and we headed off back toward our hotel. I was seriously fucked off with her. When we had finally arrived back to the room she was barely 'conscious'. Yet again, she was doing her 'newborn foal' impression. I shoved her onto the bed and as I walked onto the balcony to calm myself down, I could barely hear the . . . 'fuck off you miserable bastard'.

I leant over the balcony and just as I was contemplating finally getting some sleep before the early dawn start, our room doorbell rang. As I tried to anticipate who might be outside at 2 am I had not noticed Chasney was no longer lying on the bed. I promptly opened the door and found myself staring back at the concierge and a hotel security officer?

"Monsieur, is everything . . . ok?" "Err . . . yeah, of course, why?"

"Really? We have had a call from your wife, and she was claiming you were trying to murder her?"

"What the fuck?"

I pivoted around and sure enough, Chasney was nowhere to be seen. My mind tried to collect itself and I did not need to invite the two visitors in the room, as they had already bowled straight past me. It was the security officer who tried the bathroom handle. It was becoming apparent to all, the shower was on, and that bitch had called 'security' by using the bathroom phone!

"Madame, this is hotel security - is everything ok in there, we have received your distressed call?"

Distressed, my arse, pissed more like!!

The door was locked, so the concierge used his master key to get access. I was most intrigued to see what kind of state my lovely wife was going to be in. I couldn't actually see past both of the two six footers, but their reaction and body language said it all. The concierge then appeared from the steamed-up bathroom with his security colleague standing behind him, who was wearing the proverbial 'grin of a Cheshire cat'.

The concierge looked much less pleased . . .

"Monsieur, I think you will have to attend to your wife. We will not be taking matters any further; you have enough problems to deal with already. We will wish you a goodnight and a safe journey in the morning."

I gestured a 'goodnight' and tentatively craned my neck around the bathroom door. I do not think I could have been met with a more undignified sight. Chasney was slumped, fully clothed in the shower basin, and still clutching a miniature vodka bottle. Her mascara was running over her cheeks as the torrent from above, cascaded over her head on full power. It was about the most unedifying episode I had experienced with her. I had had enough.

We had barely a few hours' sleep, Chasney nervously came down to breakfast, wearing the proverbial 'dark glasses', having to endure the inevitable sniggering coming from various other breakfast tables. Word travelled fast. I would soon be facing the wrath of the 'executive' for attracting such unsavory attention.

For reasons that would only become clear to me some two decades later, I was still indulging a new spouse who, and worse luck for me, was running into issues at her workplace. As was so typical with Chasney, her catastrophizing was beginning to catch up with her. Her next move was quite predictable, especially as it coincided with the sailing season.

"Do you know how much happier I could be as a housewife, if I was able to spend more time at home and sailing with my friends?"

What the fuck? She was being quite serious though. I now found myself in a situation which was becoming all too familiar. Whilst I had a number of long-term lovers such as the ever-hopeful Lyn, not forgetting Valm and Chasney's sister, I did not want to be with any of them. Yet, I couldn't see a way out of the marriage as I had become hamstrung, both emotionally and financially.

This was the early 1990s. The UK was experiencing one of the worst economic recessions since the war, with the level of house repossessions running at a record high. An eye watering 300,000 homes being seized in the courts. John Major and his conservative party had been in government over the entire period. Against all odds, he had somehow managed to be victorious at the 1992 general election by defeating the labor party and its 'Welsh windbag' of a leader, Neil Kinnock.

The vexing outcome being, Kinnock manoeuvred himself into an unaccountable commissioner's post at the European Union in Brussels. While Major had to suffer the plotting of the so called 'bastards' among his own cabinet colleagues, finding himself up to his neck in the 'Maastricht Treaty'.

So, what did I do? Well, the stupid gene was about to excel itself by my allowing Chasney to persuade me we should finally buy a property in her beloved 'Burnham'. At the same time, allow her to give up work so she could spend more time with the 'sailing fraternity'.

I was already overstretched; what with my two other properties and spiralling outgoings. Yet, Chasney still colluded with her friend Rowena, for me to purchase a newly built, four-bedroom, timber-framed house, which due to the recession, had been stuck on the market for over eighteen months.

Thus, against every sensible instinct, I stupidly agreed Chasney could resign her position to become 'a lady of leisure'. The problem being Chasney didn't for one moment expect she should compromise her lifestyle. My Rosenberg income would 'simply have to suffice'.

My practice income in those days was some twenty thousand pounds a month, but what with me funding Tom's monthly cashflow, my two P. A's, and spiralling debts, our finances were in constant deficit. To make matters worse, losing Chasney's salary meant our borrowing ability was just shy of the required amount needed to buy the new house. Consequently, I negotiated a deal with the property developer, whereby they agreed to defer an amount valued at twenty thousand pounds of the original purchase price if repaid within twelve months of the agreement. Like so many men, I kept all of this away from Chasney simply because I could not contemplate the usual 'hysterics' she generally greeted any news that did not give her what she immediately demanded. Indeed, even when a troublesome planning issue gave me an opportunity to pull out of the purchase, she just screamed down the phone at me.

"Get me into that fucking house; and right now!"

The twelve months flew by and before I knew it, I had to come up with the twenty thousand pounds. Needless to say, I did not have the cash readily available. I put everything at risk by pledging my Rosenberg shares, which totalled some 180,000 and borrowed money from my slippery lawyer Steve Bannon in return for a large lump of interest.

So, I had paid off the developer only to then, leave myself exposed to the jaws of a very aggressive law firm. To compound matters, Steve did not inform his two partners he had transferred the funds. Once they had realized what had occurred, they demanded the return of their funds. Most embarrassingly, I then did what I probably should have done from the outset, which was to go to go 'cap in hand' to my father-in-law and beg for the money. Like the gentleman he was, he resisted judging me out of concerns for the well-being of his daughter. He contacted my lawyers and paid up.

I was obviously most relieved; but I had now clearly established a pattern, where I would 'rob Peter to pay Paul' to save my stupid male pride and prop-up my finances. Indeed, my false sense of security came from the value of my shares, which at the time, were valued in the region of $400,000 (the same shares today are worth in the region of $10 million . . . fuck) and therefore, I always believed that no matter what the level of debt; if 'push came to shove', I could settle up. With that said, if my father-in-law was prepared to indulge me, rather than my cashing them in, then so be it.

CHAPTER 33.

CHASNEY'S NEMESIS

The catalyst that would prompt me to end my relationship with Chasney, really began when I received a call from the charismatic property developer Jon Hardy. He informed me he and his wife Demi were separating.

Jon had previously been introduced to me by yet another pathologyical sociopath, Jed Cowen. He had known Jon for over twenty years. It is worth mentioning here, Jed could put most sociopaths in the shade and his influences over me, would seriously manifest later in my story. Demi Hardy was just about the most desired woman in the 'Dengie Hundred'. The marshy Essex peninsula where Burnham on Crouch is found and Demi was employed as the 'head of technology' at the local high school, 'St Peters'. She was a striking brunette in her mid-thirties with the most vibrant and vivacious of personalities. Ironically, she had first become involved with Jon through an affair, and deception, which she would eventually suffer from herself. Not only by Jon, but also from me! Pre-determined? A very good question indeed.

Like so many alpha-male sociopaths, Jon appeared to be a most charming and 'likeable' guy. He was also a serial philanderer. His prowess was legendary throughout the area. He and I became more acquainted. He would recount his many conquests and how he had pursued Demi. Because of his reputation, she resisted him for quite some time. As we all know by now, a sociopath is never more determined than when he is rejected by his latest interest.

Demi and Jon met in the mid 80's. She would eventually succumb to his charms. After a chaotic divorce from Jon's first wife Marilyn, Jon and Demi married. They soon had two daughters. This was all in parallel with Jon embarking on a flamboyant housing development project that would, prove to be his financial undoing.

The recession of the early 90s finally 'nailed Jon's financial colors to the mast of receivership'. Although he tried to keep an air of 'Mr. Successful', as most arrogant sociopath's do - the piling up of financial obligations eventually overwhelmed Jon's ego and inevitably his business folded with massive debts.

The company Jon inherited from his father, then managed with his four brothers, was no more. This must have been emotionally crippling for his parents because they had created the business decades before having earned a reputation for high calibre housing developments providing many jobs with lucrative contracts for local suppliers. Most of those same suppliers, many from small firms, likewise failed because of non-payment of invoices.

Many sociopaths will use furtive affairs as a distraction from such pressures. With Jon's propensity for extra marital activity, he again found solace in the form of a much 'younger model'. Needless to say, there was no end of female detractors who piously felt Demi was getting her comeuppance. For my part, I had always been one of her biggest admirers. Chasney had always found her rather intimidating. While she was with Jon, Demi always seemed out of my reach, and despite their impending financial woes, the 'high flying' couple kept the fairly convincing charade all was well in their relationship.

I just knew she would now be courted by all. Being a 'high functioning sociopath' myself, I was determined to beat the opposition and win over Demi's affections for my personal indulgence. I had previously been as decided with my first wife, and well, we all know how that one turned out.

I had married Chasney for all the wrong reasons. I most certainly did not love her. Our 'intimate' life never really started. I found her rather sexually inhibited. That doesn't excuse my philandering of course. Upon reflection, I still find it most intriguing a dozen or so of her 'friends' did not think twice about cheating behind her back. Some, including her sister, even relished the deception. What had she done in the past for so many of them to readily seek revenge when they were offered the opportunity?

I had overstretched myself financially to indulge her and had purchased a house that was so unnecessary. Especially, as we already owned a property a piece.

As with the world that surrounds most sociopathic womanizers, there are many examples when comparing the destruction that follows them around, their impact on former loved ones. So, it will come as no surprise both Chasney and Demi, would initially savor a victory and then, suffer in the same way as the woman they had replaced. Classic 'cause and effect'.

They truly believed they could prevent their new man from continuing his adulterous and illicit ways. The subject matter of how so many women have such a belief, they alone, have the ability to change the roaming ways of their man could fill the pages of a voluminous book on its own. But as we reflect on the subsequent events in my story and especially, the past ten years, there will be ample opportunity to observe, analyze, and arrive at various conclusions regarding that most emotive of topics.

As I became evermore spellbound by Jon's charisma and his speculative ambitions, his gorgeous spouse soon began to show up on my wayward radar. In keeping with the kind of superficial showboating that was Jon's trademark by being associated through a business relationship, it inevitably meant we would be socializing a great deal. I would be able to enjoy the company of the vivacious Demi more often.

By this time, my imbibing had increased substantially. The fact Jon happened to be a huge, big drinker himself, did not really help matters. My daily liking for several pints of Guinness, was now being aided and abetted by my propensity for consuming ever larger quantities of whisky.

I mentioned before, how one of Jon's most devoted disciples was his account, Max McGlyone. Max was most certainly a qualified professional and practised as such. The only 'accounting' he ever seemed to be involved with, was reconciling the bill for his and Jon's monthly spend on booze.

Max was also drinking heavily on a daily basis. As the treasurer for the local Golf club, along with John being the club captain, they never needed an excuse to frequent the 'nineteenth hole'. Indeed, like many a golf widow, Demi would come to despise the place. Not only because Jon neglected her in favor of the club's appeal, but she was eventually, to lose out to the attentions Jon received from his next femme fatal, Cora. Who most annoyingly, happened to also be ten years younger than Demi.

This then set the stage for a very intriguing juxtaposition, where both Chasney and Demi would soon both be thinking intuitively . . .

She is going to be trouble.

Demi was having such thoughts about Cora. Chasney would ironically be thinking about Demi. What a wicked web we were all about to weave.

This was also a period in time, where my addictive dysfunctions were beginning to take on unhealthy proportions. Although I hadn't as yet, become knowingly self-aware of such a pathology. Certainly, my alcohol consumption was increasing incessantly along with the greater levels of attention from women. I was cheating on Chasney with her sister Shelley, Lyn, Laura, Val, and even an 'ex' of the rabid Jed Cowen, a certain Susan Browning. Chasney either didn't have a clue or she was demonstrating another female foible, that of utter denial!

My self-esteem was being fuelled by a combination of alcohol and ego, which was about to be worsened even further when I was asked by Chasney's father to organize guests for a table at one of his umpteen 'Masonic ladies' nights'. The evening was held under a marquee in an Essex field, which must have been the most ill-conceived invitations by a lodge Grand Master, ever! For the best part of day, the weather had been atrocious. It had pelted down with rain leaving the field resembling something like 'Grimpen Mire' from 'The Hound of the Baskervilles'.

So, by the time the guests came rocking up in their black ties and sartorial elegance, I couldn't help chuckling away to myself at the sight of the various felines doing their level best to retain a modest degree of dignity as their stiletto's sunk ever deeper into the sodden and swampy morass.

The function managed to salvage itself by the reliable, obligatory, excessive imbibing of booze. I can remember having a most sanguine moment, where I scrutinized the guests sitting around me. Out of sight under the table, Lyn had wrapped her shapely calf around mine. As she did so, I couldn't help musing every lady sitting there whether with their husband or boyfriend was sleeping with me. There was one exception. I sure wasn't sleeping with my own wife any longer. You couldn't make it up!

Chasney had known of Jon and Demi Hardy for a number of years before she had even met me. But hadn't engaged with either of them by anything more than making the occasional acquaintance at a yachting regatta. It was obvious from the off, Chasney was more than intimidated by the effervescent and vibrant Demi, which certainly amused me to no end.

In no time, we were regularly socializing as couples. I have to say, it was a constant source of smug gratification, when seeing the struggles of my wife endeavoring to compete with her superior and far more sophisticated, nemesis.

Although I found Demi lusciously attractive, at that particular time, I naturally assumed she and Jon were inseparable. I just mentally tuned her out of any reckoning. So, you can imagine how I was rooted to the ground when I happened to call Jon one morning for a routine business update. Jon's hesitant response to my, "Hello mate how's things?" - would indeed, turn out to be a very fateful reply.

"Hello Sam, well errmm, actually a bit unsettled really, you see, me and Demi are ermm . . . splitting up."

As the words ricocheted around my cranium, I could feel the sense of yet another 'parallel universe' moment coming on. Did John really just tell me his wife was now . . . available? In keeping with my cyclical behavior, a distinctive characteristic of most sociopaths, my propensity to own what was 'off limits' would yet again surface. At times, such as these, a disingenuous response was the standard pathological reaction.

"Jon, I'm mortified."

Faking concern and sympathy are trademarks of most sociopaths. Jon being one himself, would have readily used such a line in his past, and no doubt, probably done so many times since.

"Yeah Sam, I just don't feel that Demi understands me anymore . . . you know?"

"So, what was the tipping point then Jon?"

"Sam, we all deserve to be happy, don't we? I have met a ravishing girl at the golf club. We were meant to be together mate. She is most definitely the one who I have been searching for."

Yawn . . .

I wonder how many women readings this have heard that one before, whereby, to justify their philandering, womanizers always make self-serving claims. Most unnerving of all, unless they eventually raise their levels of self-awareness, they will continue to believe such rubbish, and repeat the same emotional errors, over and over again.

Jon further explained how he wanted to . . . "Divorce Demi, but not my two young daughters."

He hadn't let the grass grow either. I was actually taken aback when he informed me, he already vacated the matrimonial home and had shacked up with this 'Cora'. A girl who just happened to be more than twenty years his junior. Yes, that classic anthropological pattern, of the aging alpha male.

I was instantly bored by Jon's diatribe. To avoid sounding impatient, I then used the well-worn excuse to wind up the conversation of . . . "Jon, sorry mate, I have another call coming in." As soon as I had finished feigning my 'sincere regrets' at the demise of Jon's marriage, I hit the receiver.

Demi was going to be mine!

My emotions were indistinguishable to those I had experienced fifteen years prior, when I committed myself to denying Anthony Pager and winning the affections of my first wife, Pam. I simply had to get to Demi before any other potential suitors came sniffing around. For there would be many of those for sure.

Demi was just about the most desirable woman in Burnham. So, I knew time would be of the essence. Even leaving it for just one day, might supply some other opportunistic predator an opportunity to swoop down on the vulnerable and well-endowed brunette. I had a fairly busy schedule, with pre-arranged appointments, and client meetings that day, but as with all addicts I immediately discarded any such priorities from my thoughts and usurped them with the only one that now mattered to me, getting Demi's thong off!

With my renowned impatience, I charged through the door of my office. Without even looking back, I barked instructions over my shoulder in the direction of hapless Lyn, sitting in bewilderment behind her desk.

"Lyn, cancel all of my appointments today, something extremely urgent has come up."

I skulked behind the wheel of my newly purchased E class Mercedes and couldn't select the 'drive' gear quickly enough. I often drove past Demi's substantial pile on the way to my office, so I drooled at the prospect of pulling up onto gravel drive of this most alluring of women. When a 'sociopathic addict' has a prize in his sights any consideration for potential risks and implications that might befall either his, or the wellbeing of others, can vanish in an instant. I lacked the level of self-awareness in those days to realize I was not only becoming an alcoholic, but a full blown 'addict'. Whether it be the booze, having my ego stroked, or craving my next 'excitement fix', all the classic behavioral traits and dysfunctions of an addict had become firmly established within my psyche.

In my eagerness to pursue Demi, I hadn't given the slightest consideration she might even be at home. So, my relief was palpable when I saw her convertible black BMW parked on the drive outside the immense six thousand square foot house.

I knew the doorbell didn't function properly because Demi was always taunting her husband, so much remedial work was still needed to the house two years after they had moved in. I always assumed; such oversights were typical for a builder's own house. I would soon discover, the real reason for Jon's reluctance to finish the work. It was just that his attentions were elsewhere.

As I have already alluded, Demi was a true stunner. A real head turner. So, I was amazed when, after a good few minutes wait the front door, it suddenly unlatched and sharply opened wide.

"Gotcha!! Hahahah!"

A set of perfect white teeth and crystal hazel eyes, beamed back at me.

"And WHAT . . . are you doing here Mister Kirkham? My God, the gossip mongers don't hang around, do they?"

I staggered rather, not so much because of Demi's bullish and self-assured greeting, but more so, the sheer delectable charisma of the woman. And she knew it! So, I did my level best to stammer a reply, as I tried to recalibrate my brain.

"Actually Demi, Jon told me himself, this morning. You know I often use this route, so I thought I would call by to see how you are dealing with things and if there is anything I can do to help?"

"Awwww Sam, so sweet of you."

She paused and then . . . another raucous outburst! "Hahahahahahahaha! What DO you take me for?"

Demi was not easily going to be taken in by my insincere bullshit; that was now most clear.

"Oh, did I sound THAT phoney?" Still grinning.

"Yes Sam, you are so bloody fake! Come on, what are you REALLY doing here?"

I had to quickly regroup, and trying to sound remotely genuine . . .

"OK Demi, I have always been fantastically attracted to you, and being the opportunistic hunter, I am I thought I had best monopolize your attentions before some other huntsman did so. So how does that sound?"

Demi, was still grinning . . .

"YOU have got some bloody brass neck Sam! The trouble is, I actually believe you. Yet, I can't think why I shouldn't be seriously offended right now? But I'm not. So, would you like to come in for a drink . . . you utter bounder."

Stepping through the porch, I found myself in awe of the cavernous atrium, which could have readily accommodated a 'first time buyers' home within its vast cubic space. Demi's slinky hips swivelled as she beckoned me through to the sumptuous and lavish lounge. Despite my enthusiasm for the pursuit of this curvaceous feline, I was astonished at the amount of weight Demi had lost since I had last seen her only a few weeks prior. It is incredible how weight can fall off people when suffering from emotional stress and anxiety.

It was barely afternoon, but Demi reached for a gin filled 'Edinburgh crystal' decanter and poured two very large measures into the tumblers bearing the same trademark. It soon became apparent; this was not Demi's first drink of the day.

I seriously loathe the unmistakable aroma and taste of juniper but before another word was uttered, Demi had already polished off her drink, and was pouring another. The smiling and spirited mask that had greeted me at the front door was now morphing into a pained and snarly grimace.

And so, without so much as an offer of any 'ice or a slice', Demi pressed the glass into my hand as she purposely quaffed the neat Gordon's.

"So, what has that prick told you then?"

I hadn't even taken a sip from my glass, before Demi denied me a response to her obviously rhetorical question. She then went into a diatribe, which was about to bring me swiftly up to speed.

"Sam, that fucking jerk doesn't have any idea of the mess he has left me and his kids in. He's got no fucking backbone. Do you know what the final straw was?"

"Ermm . . . no?"

"I will tell you. So, please sit down because you are going to like this. I remember thinking from the first moment I set eyes on that Cora . . . She is going to be trouble and I need to keep a keen eye on her."

There we go again . . .

"Oh, really?"

"Yes Sam. Let's face it, why should I have been so surprized? After all, Jon was cheating behind his first wife's back with me. So, I guess it must be some kind of karma, right?"

Demi then revealed a real gem.

"It all came to a head at the weekend. My friend Gill had been trying to tell me for some time the gossip mongers were in full 'chinwag' mode. The entire golf club membership was aware something was going on between Jon and that fat tart. Over the months, my intuition was telling me he had been up to his old tricks, but like a fucking idiot, I just stuck my head in the sand. All the classic signs were there. If nothing else, he was mirroring his behavior when he was knocking me off. I suppose . . . denial, eh?"

Demi then lit a cigarette, which was so unusual for her. As she poured another stiff measure, she took a deep drag, and exhaled . . .

"Anyway, Gill called me last Saturday afternoon just as I was serving up a late brunch for the girls they had come home late from brownies. I didn't even have a chance to say hello, before she blurted out that I needed to drop everything straight away because I should drive to the old station where Jon was cavorting with his tart in the lay-by near the sidings."

I remained silent, as by now, I was really engrossed, and I was even beginning to enjoy the bloody Gordon's.

"Sam, my mind was like 'spaghetti'. I had difficulty grasping the reality of what Gill was telling me. I told her I couldn't just leave the girls as they were about to eat. But Gill accused me of being afraid to confront reality and screamed at me to go straight away, and that she would be here to look after the girls in five minutes."

The Gordon's began to really take its effect on Demi. She was shouting by this point.

"Do you know what I then did Sam? I told the girls to eat their lunch while Mummy had to go out and Auntie Gill would be here for them in a few minutes. My God, I left the girls on their own, before they could even ask where I was going. What has that fucking man done to me?" I was so absorbed; I didn't really care whether Demi was again being rhetorical or not. She was now relentless in her ranting and about to reach fever pitch. Even in the middle of an emotional outburst, I found her utterly captivating. Her sexual allure was overwhelming me. "Anyway, the red mist came down, and I drove to the sidings. Typical

Jon. They were only five minutes away from this house. He just loves the thrill of 'shitting on his own doorstep'. He is so predictable. I'm ashamed to admit, he used to park up with me in the exact same spot when fucking me in the back of his car. What a creature of habit."

I couldn't agree more, for I shared Jon's habitual idiosyncrasy. Take it from me, so do the majority of men. It's not only typical of sociopaths, who have that particular flaw.

I couldn't have stopped Demi from raging if I tried. Neither did I want to, for this was all too riveting. She was now in full 'I fucking hate Jon' mode.

Demi was coming to the final act . . .

"I was quite traumatized as I drove to their little rendezvous spot. You know how it is when you are in such a state. So, I couldn't even remember having driven there. The prick's new Porsche 928 was parked up. I turned off my engine to allow me to quietly ghost up behind them. I was trembling with anxiety as I walked toward his car. I could see them both in a clinch. As I tapped on the window Jon jumped and with startled eyes, he glared back at me. I was so distressed I could barely speak. So, I stepped back as he opened the car door. His bloody tall frame climbed out. Can you believe what the fuckshit then said to me?"

Demi's body language was so contorted that her questions were obviously still rhetorical, and she was sobbing hard by this point.

"He bore down on me. Then, turning back toward that whore, he said, errmm . . . sorry about this Cora, I think my wife is a bit upset! Can you fucking believe him?"

Best to just keep drinking Sam . . .

"I then fucking lost it with him. I was shouting and screaming so much, I can't honestly tell you what I was saying to the pair of them. Jon just stood there, arms folded, as he looked down at me, as if I was fucking demented or crazy."

I was actually wincing inside for this was classic Jon. Even in the most contentious and combative situations like no other, he could remain unruffled and smooth. Knowing Demi though, such emotional ambivalence would have simply antagonized her even more.

"There was a brief standoff between the two of us. Then he just huffed and without uttering another word, turned, walked back to his car, and calmly sat next to his new plaything."

I was still trying to appear as neutral as I could, but privately this was all music to my ears. Despite my attempts at doing so, the sheer level of my thankfulness at Demi's misfortune, would have been rather obvious to anyone with a clear mind. But Demi wasn't finished yet.

"Before he could fire up the ignition of his new car, which he couldn't fucking afford by the way, as I walked off, I was able to compose myself just enough to score my key as deeply as I could along the entire wing of the car, leaving a lovely deep gorge in the gleaming metallic paint. The prick soon reacted to that. Ha-ha! He sprung out from behind the wheel calling me every bitch under the sun. Did I give a fuck!"

While she was ranting, Demi had still managed to pour two more large measures of Gordon's. She became increasingly loose tongued and progressively more furious. This was all aiding and abetting my own opportunistic aspirations, but at the same time, I did hope I might be able to keep her fairly sober? No chance.

Demi's two young daughters Gemma and Isabella were still at school, not due home for another couple of hours. Hence, by my slide rule calculations, this gave me a couple of hours before the shrill voices of a nine- and five-year-old would be raucously heard charging through the front door. Demi's friend, Gill, was apparently picking them up from school that day as another favor. I think Demi knew she was not going to be fit to drive that day and spent most of it 'on the lash'.

I somehow needed to delay Demi's gin consumption and try to ground her emotionally. It is always a good idea to demonstrate empathy at moments like this - with a sense of 'dignified understanding' of an inebriated woman's grief'.

"Demi, come, sit down here with me. Let's talk. You are getting far to upset. Cora would just love it if she knew she had had such an effect on you."

This distressed lady might have been feeling exceedingly unsettled, but it was the first time I had ever been in Demi's company on my own. She clearly hadn't quite finished with her grumbling. So, apart from the occasional indulgent utterance of . . . 'quite' or 'is that so'? I had to be content with allowing her to continue her outpouring. I mean, it never ceases to amaze me how a woman will feel a man has understood her, simply because he never said a word and simply allowed her to do all the bloody talking!

Here was yet another clear example of a quixotic encounter. Where 'playing a role' is invariably adopted by both parties to create a perception in the other person's mind that you are 'the kind' they would wish you to be. Therefore, appearing more attractive and appealing. In other words, it is one big act and all so bloody superficial . . . 'I will play who you want me to be, and you will play who I want you to be'.

Eventually and predictably, the potent cocktail of Gordon's; angst, and depleting emotional energy finally caused Demi to start sobbing. So uncontrollably, this usually so gregarious of women, struck a most dejected and sad figure. Devastatingly for Demi, barely three years would pass when she would again experience the same anguish, due to the dishonorable deeds of another womanizer.

"Demi is there anything I can do? You know I will always be here for you."

Fuck me, how could I come out with such bile.

Whether a sociopath, or a regular person, keeping up the pretence is really hard work. Inevitably the mask will begin to slip. When it does, what is revealed can be extremely sobering. The real person behind that mask can be the complete opposite to what you initially believed them to be. 'Wanting and needing' can so easily be mistaken for 'falling in love' which is extremely rare in reality.

For most, it is simply the craving of mutual egos needing to fulfil self-gratification by becoming infatuated with the other person's mask. True and profound love has nothing to do with it. Therefore, when 'the shine goes off the gold block' so to speak, most of the characteristics the mutual egos were initially attracted to become the very same traits that inevitably piss them both off about each other.

Demi was, fairly-predictably, laboring all those same annoying traits about her estranged husband. How she had, at first, believed Jon to be her 'knight in shining armor' only to later discover, he was no more than a 'shallow and feckless fraud'.

I was now able to study Demi close up as her uncontrolled rendition, ebbed, and flowed between acute anger and a sense of deep sadness. Her fairy tale union with her daughters' father had amounted to, in her own words, 'fuck all'!

I was struggling to keep up, both with the emotional rollercoaster, and the level of Demi's gin intake. Then again, Demi's sheer glamor meant I could be distracted enough from her vexations to still appreciate her appeal. Indeed, she was aged thirty-seven and in her absolute prime. Which illustrates no matter how stunning a woman, when a sociopathic womanizer becomes bored, and they always do, she will not keep their loyalty.

Demi was tall, brunette, and with exquisite angular features. Her sparkling green eyes and most 'dirty laugh' portrayed a stronger sense of self-confidence. I was now discovering wasn't quite the reality, that damn mask again! No end of rapacious men had been seduced by her sheer outwardly effervescent and vibrant personality.

Demi had recently returned to work as a teacher. At the very same high school where she had trained as a young tutor. At the age of twenty-one, she had indeed, disgraced herself by having a steamy affair with a rampant seventeen-year-old! Demi had been fortunate to survive that particular episode, which was made all the more ironic, due to the young man concerned being a close friend at the time with Jon's eldest son! As they say, the truth is always better than fiction.

Demi continued to pour out her heartache to me as her lithe form writhed and shifted from one side of the sofa to the other. Her evocative gushing was being projected through her 'talon-likc' fingernails. Even at the worst of times, she was always very animated.

"Sam, again, you are so sweet, I just need to lick my wounds. One day, Jon will so regret what he has done. All he ever does is let people down. He bullshits everyone. Even his family, friends, work colleagues, and lovers are all eventually disrespected in the same way. I even think he actually believes his own crap. I just know that tart will go the same way as all those before her."

I really wished Demi hadn't just said that.

Such was my fascination with her. I still had some gin left in my glass. I purposefully resisted giving her a peck on the cheek as I motioned toward the door. Just a brief and knowing touch of her arm, was all that seemed proper as I walked toward my vehicle. I mouthed a concerned, 'you take care' as I climbed behind the wheel of my Mercedes.

As this was 1995, mobile phone technology was now moving apace and had quickly proven itself in the business world as part of the 'must have' tools. An unhealthy dependency hadn't quite taken hold back then, as it has nowadays with the digital revolution spawning the absolute explosion of smart devices. I tis hard to imagine now, brands such as Motorola, Siemens, and the then global market leader Nokia would, within just ten years, be wantonly usurped by Apple I-Phone and their rival Samsung with their Galaxy range.

Despite the limitations of mobile technology back then, what with their bloody annoying 'flip' design and useless aerials, 'Caller ID' had recently come into service. This I could see there had been several missed calls, while I had been conducting my counselling session with Demi.

All but one of the calls had been made by my soon to be erstwhile wife, Chasney. So, what the fuck did she want? It was actually quite unusual for her to call me during the day. Largely, due to the fact we had reached a point in the relationship where, at best, our communication levels had been reduced to a strained minimum.

I was ambivalent about calling Chasney back, as I mulled over my encounter with Demi trying to make some sense of what my next move should be. The woman was of the highest appeal and desirability. Although I was under no illusion, serious competition would soon appear over the horizon. My wolfish instincts were telling me, whilst I should not delay; to be too keen, might also result in Demi feeling rather ambushed.

So, I would have to resist my pre-dispositions, which was most rare for me and trust in fate I would win the day. In time, I would see increasing evidence if something is fated to be . . . or not, no amount of manipulation or pressure will influence the outcome.

In a matter of ten minutes, I was pulling up on my drive. It wasn't until I focused on Chasney's parked car, I was reminded, I hadn't called her back. "Fuck."

I would have lost count how many times I dreaded turning the key in my front door. This was another of those occasions.

"Hey, I tried to call you . . . where have you bloody been?" "Nowhere in particular, my battery was low - look!"

Fortunately for me, the battery indicator on my Motorola was sufficiently low as to be convincing. Phew!

Chasney had been enjoying her favorite alternative activity and rather than undertake any domestic duties, a large Gordon's gin and tonic was evidenced by the tall glass resting on the coffee table. Chasney had been a complete waste of space where doing any household tasks were concerned. Believe it or not, I seriously support the view couples should share such chores whenever possible. Chasney never touched an iron or vacuum cleaner in four years. She had spent the final two years of the relationship messing around on boats or shopping. To be fair, she was however, an excellent cook.

"I was trying to call you with some serious gossip. The best bit of scandal I've fucking heard in years."

"Really, and what might that be then?"

"You would just love to know who has been caught cheating on his wife, go on, guess?"

"Dunno, who?"

"Only 'Jon the big swinging dick, Hardy' that's who." "Naaaaaah never, you are fucking kidding me?"

"I know. It is fucking great, isn't it? I bet that stuck up cow Demi is pig sick. She rubbed Jon's poor ex-wife Marilyn's face right in the mud. Now, justice has been done - big time! So, it's 'karma' if you ask me."

There was that 'K word' again. It is always used as a meaning for 'what goes around comes around'. I now know that simplistic interpretation is incorrect. It is something quite different. Far more complex, both spiritually and scientifically.

"Chasney, is this really the right time to gloat? Remember, there are two young children caught up in all of this. I will call Jon tomorrow and see how he is doing."

"What the fuck are you talking about? He is a fucking cheating slime ball. I could never understand why you liked socializing with him and that Cruella DeVile, anyway?"

I simply ignored my emotive spouse as she was clearly relishing the prospect of there being further updates from whichever scandal monger had enlightened her. To think, social media platforms supply the forum for all the gossip these days. Why don't just call it 'gossip book' or 'misinformation book' and be done with! Society is increasingly becoming addicted to just that - gossip! It was now my turn to pour myself my preferred tipple. A very large whisky indeed.

I still had a dilemma though. Demi's emotions would obviously be very raw. It was hard to imagine she would seriously entertain the notion of any kind of new relationship. Yet, we all know someone who has jumped from one relationship and then rebounded into another. Often in face of such wise advice as, 'to take some time out and get your shit together'. Only to ignore said advice and steam straight into another relationship with all the potential disastrous consequences. Hey, I was contemplating and planning such a folly for myself. That stupid gene again!

Accordingly, Demi was bound to be feeling very exposed and emotionally susceptible . . . right? Wrong!

Whether the motive was revenge, or sheer bloody determination (I'm still not sure to this day) I couldn't have been more mistaken, regarding Demi's resolve and apparent emotional steadfastness. If she was going to come out fighting, then I was going to be a very willing accomplice.

From my perspective, Demi's grand house was conveniently located. Her own feelings about the property and its location couldn't be more contrasting. The house was in a rather remote spot. It sat upon about the highest point between the two arterial rivers running through South Essex, 'the Crouch' and 'the Blackwater'. Her persuasive husband had convinced her to relocate their young family to this isolated place because the 'near derelict' property offered a 'fantastic investment opportunity'. Little did Demi realize, at the particular time Jon's development company was experiencing dire financial problems.

Jon had been 'robbing Peter to pay Paul' for a number of years prior. Demi later informed me Jon had mostly ran under a financial charade for most of his adult life. Jon's father, who started the company in the 1950s, had run a sound business for decades before being convinced by his eldest son he could 'grow the company to a whole new level'.

It also happened, the house move was only a ruse to release equity capital from their existing home, to then, re-direct the funds into the ailing company's balance sheet. Of course, being a sociopath, Jon's pride was so misplaced he would not admit to anyone and especially Demi that for some considerable period of time the business had been trading insolvently. He was facing the distinct prospect of bankruptcy after some forty years of trading.

Demi had been most reluctant, acceding to such a move, but the tumbledown farmhouse had been originally built in the 1920's. It obviously offered a great deal of space for a growing family. The main structure needed extensive and costly remedial work before any modernization could even considered. An embarrassing irony for Jon and certainly something I experienced later myself, was despite portraying himself as a 'high flying businessman' he was invariably, and almost habitually, skint!

Demi found it incredibly galling, having to watch Jon parading his ego as 'the Captain of the Golf club'. He was hosting functions, which he could ill afford. All while funding large scale developments he had little prospect of finding potential buyers for, during the seriously depressed housing market of the 1990s.

CHAPTER 34.

ACCOMPLICE AND ALIBI

I took the 'bull by the horns' and would regularly visit Demi when driving home from the office. This would allow me an hour or so before the kids needed collecting from school. I wasn't imagining either, Demi was soon beginning to look forward to my calling by her house. It allowed her to open up evermore about her feelings and past experiences of love, life, and Jon Hardy.

She continued to vent. On one occasion, when she must have been mulling everything over, she sat me down with a drink, making sure everyone concerned, received a lashing of her tongue.

"Image and perceived status are everything to Jon. He is so fucking insincere. What's more, his so-called best friend and accountant, arse licking piss head Max McGlone, is so two faced. If you could only hear how disloyal he can be to Jon behind his back. As for his four useless brothers, well . . . they run him down all the time. They truly believe Jon owes them all a bloody living."

Demi was in her stride . . .

"Jon's pride would often get the better of him. He would readily deprive himself and his family, before ever allowing his brothers to go without. They all draw bloated salaries and dividends the company could never afford and quite frankly, none of those fat lazy tossers deserve to draw one penny. Jon was always, 'gravy tomorrow' and that 'big bonus' was only just around the corner. It was ALWAYS, only just around the corner."

It sounded to me, when the ship would finally come in, it would be more like a 'battered and rusty trawler' than the promised 'ocean liner'. I wonder how many wives of so-called entrepreneurs are told something akin to Demi's denunciation, just about every day?

With a tone of abject resignation, Demi concluded her frustrated peroration.

"I finally realized just how bad things had deteriorated, when Jon came home and told me we could no longer send Gemma to private school. My God, the conceit and smugness Jon had gloried in when he sent his eldest daughter to a private school, was something to behold. I promise you Sam, I genuinely want my kids to have the best start in life and being a teacher, their education is paramount to me. But Jon merely basked in the snobbery of it all. What made it all the more exasperating, was he barely demonstrated any real interest in their educational development. Never attended parents' evenings. He couldn't have even told you the name of his daughter's teacher. Such parental duties were always down to me."

When the going gets tough for a sociopathic womanizer, what does he tend to do? Well, he has yet another affair of course! Sociopaths, and addiction, will often go 'hand in glove' once the habitual cycles have become well-established deep within their psyche. They will use their next fix as a kind of grotesque coping mechanism, to alleviate any feelings of guilt.

Demi certainly wasn't a naïve woman. She was well aware my level of 'concern' for her wellbeing was most likely scheming, and disingenuous at best. Despite her knowing my wife, neither was she discourageing my attention. She was clearly aware of the obvious state of my own marriage. I have seen on countless occasions, the phenomenon of female hypocrisy. This was developing into yet another classic case in point.

By this time, I was beginning to seriously develop the art of 'relationship plate spinning'. Whether it be womanizing, socializing, business. or consuming evermore copious amounts of booze - the demands on my time were becoming increasingly difficult to manage. The two most potentially damaging aspect, of course; being my alcohol fuelled philandering.

Demi had clearly become my latest obsession. As is often the case with a sociopath, my interest in the other members of my 'harem' instantly faltered. This invariably brings a number of unwelcome consequences. Not least of all, the displeasure of a former 'favorite', which in this particular instance, it was Max McGlone's horny spouse, Lyn. If the probable ramifications of any affair with Demi were not going to be explosive enough; Lyn McGlone was obviously well-known to Demi. Not surprisingly, the two women were not too keen on one another.

During that sequence of events, I had built up a friendship with a local fella, who had been introduced to me, via one of my clients. Submarine Commander, Gerrard Neilson. Gerrard's younger brother Kerry was loud, brash, and built like a bull. Not a more indiscreet young man could you ever meet. He was a struggling salesman in those days and was just about managing to pay his bills and mortgage. He was also, another alcoholic.

Kerry enjoyed drinking, sailing, drinking, partying, and . . . drinking. Indeed, just about anything that meant he did not have to take any of his responsibilities seriously. Much to the frustrations of his mousey little girlfriend, Sara.

For some considerable time, it had also been plainly obvious to me, Kerry, had serious designs on my wife. As such, I knew I could use his ambitions against him by cajoling him into being my alibi. It was becoming increasingly difficult to find even the slightest of plausible excuses to meet Demi in the evenings. So, Kerry, you will have to do the honors.

By sheer luck - or perhaps not - Kerry called me to ascertain how things were moving and attempted to sound as if he had my well-being in mind. What rot! Kerry's attempts at trying to sound like he had genuine interest were pathetic at the best of times. All he wanted to hear were updates on my many affair(s)? He would not be the last friend of mine, who would be titillated by hearing about my conquests.

He was also the worst of gossips. He had been struggling with his own very dysfunctional relationship for some years. So, he wanted to hijack mine and escape from the entrapment of the wretched Sara, as early as possible.

"Master Kirkham, how the devil is you old boy. What's happening with that new filly of yours then?"

"Hello mate, yeah all going to plan, fancy a beer later?"

Kerry could not say yes quickly enough. What I did not share with him, was I had every intention of having some fun at his expense. In fact, I had every intention of spending some more time with Demi. So, when I met up with Kerry in the White Hart, I made sure I was driving. This achieved the double objective of preventing Kerry from later nipping around to see Chasney, while I was nipping around to see . . . Demi. Kerry jumped into the passenger seat of my Mercedes, which he always enjoyed. He just loved the panache of a prestige car. As I mentioned previously in those days, he drove around in a beaten-up old Honda. I guess he has since owned a Merc or three himself. So, bearing in mind Kerry could barely read or write, there is hope for you all. Anon

. . .

We quickly sank our first pints before Kerry could order the next round, I put my hand over my glass.

"Right mate, come on then."

"Uh? I'm happy to have a few more here first mate." "I'm not though; come on you can be my chaperone." "Are you fucking kidding me?"

"Thought it was time I introduced you to a very horny female, mate."

In the normal scheme of things, I would have bragged to Kerry by now about all of my latest conquests and any potential lovers. He already knew about Demi of course. As far as his own intentions where my wife was concerned, he would have liked to have been equally duplicitous.

Kerry gestured with a token protest. Like all gossips, his curiosity would get the better of him. He had heard about Demi's reputation and the vanguard of men who desired her. So, he would not be able to resist checking out my 'new bit of stuff'.

Part of a sociopath's many behavioral patterns, is to 'fly by the seat of their pants'. Relishing the myriad 'highs' risk taking brings with it. So, fuelling the ego with a new member of the harem, then showing her to one of his so-called pals, achieves just that.

We swept onto the gravel drive of Jon Hardy's former matrimonial edifice where Demi was already outside the front door nursing a glass of white wine. She wore a curious expression on her face because she had no idea, I would be bringing company with me. Any questioning thoughts she might have had, did not stop her from greeting me with a gushing embrace. Demi absolutely 'sucked my face off" and when she eventually came up for air, she was grinning. She turned to Kerry.

"So, who do we have here then? A little friend of yours?"

Kerry was just about the loudest and most expressive 'foghorn of a fella' who I have ever known. He was rarely embarrassed. Nonetheless, Demi had an innate knack of being able to intimidate even the usually most confident of men. Kerry just stood awkwardly and wore a sickly smirk.

Demi reverted her intense gaze back to me, pecked the end of my nose, and then grabbing my hand, led me through the door. It was a good job Kerry just followed, because he was clearly not going to be officially invited in.

Demi directed us both toward the lounge and offered us the obligatory drink. We both asked for a large scotch. The delicious feline then minced off in the direction of the booze store.

I gestured to Kerry, seeking his approval.

"Fucking hell Sam, she is sooooooo horny. She is sex on legs pal. I can tell you all the reports about her have not been exaggerated. Jon must be bloody mental mate."

Therein, we discover yet another conundrum. Why does a sociopathic man abandon his beautiful and desired spouse or girlfriend; to be with a far less attractive woman and one that has a markedly less appealing personality to boot?

Demi breezed into the lounge holding two large glasses of scotch and a bottle of Famous Grouse tucked under her arm. Then Demi did what only Demi could and floored the pair of us with a typically brazen pronouncement.

"Right then, young Mr. Kerry or whatever your name is, here is your large scotch and the rest of the bottle to keep you company."

Bewildered glances were exchanged between the two of us.

"You can work your way through that, while I take this man upstairs with me. Long overdue if you ask me."

I looked at Kerry, who was wearing the broadest of dumbfounded grins. I just shrugged my shoulders with an air of 'well, someone's got to do it mate'.

Demi did not allow Kerry any time to wipe the astonished expression from his face, as she thrust the glass tumbler and bottle into his thunderstruck snout. A firm hand grabbed hold of mine and wearing the widest of beaming smiles, Demi led me up the stairs and in the direction of her boudoir. Kerry was just going to have to make the best of it . . .

"Hey, Demi, have you got any snacks?"

"There are some Pringles and Crisps in the first cupboard on the left. Enjoy."

"Errmm . . . Yeah, you too."

Demi was in her prime. Regardless of her being rejected by Jon, she showed little sign of any lasting damage to her esteem. Lust can be so overpowering it can often prevent a chap from taking the time to appreciate the beauty and form of a ravishing woman. For my part, I have always been blessed with sufficient control over my desire and compulsions, to take that split second to scrutinise true loveliness when it presents itself.

Demi had confided in me Jon had not been intimate with her in over a year. So, Jon's loss was about to be my fortuitous gain. Demi's desire to satisfy her hormonal frustrations was now being matched by a rapacious determination. Yet, despite the show of bravado Demi would later admit to being incredibly nervous when we first had sex. She appeared anything, but as she slipped out of her pure silk bedroom attire and stood naked in front of me like a poised siren.

I had become very accustomed to gliding between clean white sheets with a beautifully formed woman. Demi was certainly most beautifully formed. Yet here again, was a prime example of my need to win the prize. Far outweighing my lustful desires. I recall reading, one of history's most iconic sociopaths, President John F. Kennedy, once claimed that . . .

"My womanizing is not about the sex. It is about knowing I could, if I wanted to."

As with many sociopaths (and so many world leaders), it's all about power, and the chase.

You see that's the fundamental flaw of sociopaths. Their all-consuming requisite, to achieve their next conquest, always negates any moral concern and a discerning consideration of others' feelings.

Thus, my aims needed to be satisfied there and then. So, I gave no thought whatsoever to the eventual impact my actions might have on Demi, and the lives of her two young daughters. Beating the competetion was everything, whether it was real or imagined.

However, I was soon to discover the ironic reality, Jon's attitude toward the new relationship of his 'estranged spouse' would be one of 'Thank God for that, Sam has taken Demi off my hands'. Equally, I would also take such a similar view where Kerry and Chasney were concerned. What a bloody merry go round!

We devoured each other for the best part of two hours. It was only a sheepish knocking on the bedroom door that disturbed our intimacy.

"Jesus Kerry, what the fuck do you want?"

Taking a couple of hours for Kerry to polish off a bottle of scotch was about par for the course. He was sounding a bit hangdog and slurred his speech.

"Shoreeee mate, but I need to be getting home now."

"Kerry, you have no fucking sense of discretion. I will be there shortly."

Demi was dreamy and clinging onto me. I kissed her forehead, apologized and left her to sleep. It would not be long before I was able to be stay.

I dropped Kerry off outside his tiny, terraced house. A situation that would not be staying that way for long and then made my way back to the home which I shared with Chasney for some three years.

CHAPTER 35.

GOODBYE CHASNEY

finally bought the axe down on my relationship with Chasney. Once I had found enough courage to write to her father. I had always admired George. After all, he had bailed me out when I was in seriously deep shit. So, I felt somewhat obliged to explain my reasoning for leaving his daughter. I knew his 'Freemason conditioned thinking', would acknowledge, and appreciate my taking the formal approach. Surprisingly, George contacted me by phone. He was very gracious about my decision. Even more astonishingly, he even wished me well. He would not; however, maintain such an accommodating attitude toward me . . .

When I arrived home from work that day, I found Chasney in her usual position of lying on the sofa, cigarette in hand, with a large Gordon's and tonic on the go. She made for an untidy sight. The degree by which her standards had fallen, was most apparent. The stink of smoke deposits, and carcinogenic residue was everywhere. Including Chasney's long wavy hair and skin. You may not feel it, but it is there releasing a smoky odor and her disgusting habit was ruining a home we had heavily invested in. Madness!

Buoyed by the consent of her father, I was in a sarcastic frame of mind.

"Had a tough day then?"

"What the fuck are you talking about?"

"I see the vacuum cleaner is stuck in the middle of the hall?" "Oh . . . I tried to vacuum, but Henry was . . . sick."

Chasney was referring to 'Henry' an iconic brand of vacuum cleaner, which had a cheeky infantile face on the front. She hardly ever did any housework. I also did all the ironing, which included 99% of

Chasney's ever-expanding wardrobe. Somehow, she had still managed to blow the entire contents contained in the dirt bag all over the lounge carpet. I have no idea how she had achieved such a feat, but her childish riposte was her final death knell, if ever one was needed.

"Is that so? Chasney . . . I do need to tell you something."

She raised an eyebrow and took a long drag on a newly lit cigarette.

"I am sure you will have seen this coming, but we can't go on like this?"

"Go on like what?"

Chasney's ability to be intentionally obtuse had become a real art form.

"I really don't know what you mean. Spell it out?"

"Ok then, how can I put this crystal-clear? I am fucking leaving you and, right now!"

She tried to splutter a response but before she could explode, I just got up and headed to the bedroom to grab some clothes. I had quickly organized a short-term house rental in the nearby sleepy town of Maldon. So, I rifled through my belongings and grabbed a few suits and essentials. Chasney stormed up the stairs behind me and howled . . .

"No one EVER . . . leaves me! You CUNT!"

There we go again, that adorable 'C word'. I just pushed past her as I descended the stairs. I countered . . .

"And THAT, is actually the reason why I am leaving you. So goodbye, I will come back for the rest of my things next week."

As I slammed the front door behind me, I remember thinking . . . 'Demi, here I come'. I had no guarantees of course, Demi would even reciprocate but I just instinctively knew she would be the next favorite Queen of my harem.

Chasney would no doubt, try to portray to anyone who would listen, she had been betrayed with a false sense of loss and abandonment. But as it would soon be revealed, her powers of recovery were admirable. Within just four weeks of my moving out, a 'friend' of ours had moved in! Anon . . .

Many among the Burnham gossip mill would try to whisper in my ear 'this or that' had been going on, but quite frankly . . . I didn't give a shit! What made it even more hilarious, was I knew all along the chap in question, yes, Mr. two face himself' Kerry Wilson had been besotted with Chasney for years.

As we know, he would often cover for me, when I was cavorting around. Kerry would never admit his own duplicity to Chasney and demonstrated yet again how those who were supposedly close to her - did not think twice about deceiving the spoilt bitch.

During that period, Kerry was a failing car warranty insurance salesman. He could barely pay his bills. He and Chasney were eventually together for a few years, but inevitably, things didn't work out. I have no idea to his day what my ex-wife's pathway has been. Kerry on the other hand, went on to be the co-founder of a travel insurance group that eventually netted him multi-millions when he sold the business to a bigger competitor. Not bad for a guy who could barely read and write and had battled with the disadvantages of dyslexia most of his life.

So, you can imagine my reaction when I recently discovered Kerry had succumbed to cancer, aged just forty-eight. He didn't have too many years to enjoy his millions, eh? RIP . . . Kerry Nielson.

Upon reflection, despite her superficial, and insincere personality, I had treated Chasney and her family with terrible disrespect. I should never have married her. Sure, she was mercurial and spoilt. Her heart was always in the right place, and she could be very generous at times. Which again, I have to labor the point the level of betrayal and deception by her many 'friends', including her own sister remember, was quite staggering! I have no idea to this day, if Chasney ever became aware of the sheer amount of treachery that went on, which was virtually throughout the entire four years we lived together!

It has only been in fairly recent times; I have been able to determine the real reasons behind such levels of collective deceit. An explanation which will unfold, as I journey on, and my story becomes ever darker in the second and third volume of this story..

ABOUT THE AUTHOR

MITCHELL ALLEN

A true Londoner, Mitchell Allen has witnessed a great deal during his lifetime. His writing and storytelling draw from challenges and near-death experiences he has experienced, which also framed his outlook on living.

Formerly employed within the financial world, Mitchell has developed an indepth understanding of how the world's financial alchemists truly operate. His belief is their influence over global policy making affect all of our lives.

He is a double stroke survivor, and passionate supporter, of the stroke survivor charity www.stroke.org of the United Kingdom.

VISIT THE AUTHOR

SOCIAL MEDIA AND WEBSITES

PUBLISHER:

- DonnaInk Publications, L.L.C. – https://www.donnaink.com
- Mitchell Allen's Page - https://www.donnaink.com/mitchellallen
- Nocturnum's Muse - https://www.donnaink.com/nocturnumsmuse

SOCIAL MEDIA:

- Facebook – https://www.facebook.com/Author-Mitchell-Allen-101004648440628
- LinkedIn – https://www.linkedin.com/company/2989409/admin
- Pinterest – https://www.pinterest.com/donnaink/_created
- WordPress Blog - https://authormitchellallen.wordpress.com

www.donnaink.com
THE SPIRITUAL SOCIOPATH
MITCHELL ALLEN
available at
amazon

EDITOR

STEVEN KAY

Steven Kay was born in Lancashire, and he grew up in Hambleton close to Morecambe Bay and the Forest of Bowland. His father introduced him to the great outdoors and his mother showed him how to make the most out of his life. His education started in mathematics and at university transitioned to languages. Steven leads a simple life as a health-food enthusiast, he loves to go lake swimming, cycling, and camping. He maintains fluency in Dutch, and he intends to retire in Austria where the landscape reminds him of Cumbria but without the continual rains. In Austria he communicates fluently with the locals, and meets up with many flying Hollanders, who also appreciate the Low Countries rather than the Alps. Finally, without a car and TV, Steven values love of a bygone era and the peacefulness it allows him to enjoy.

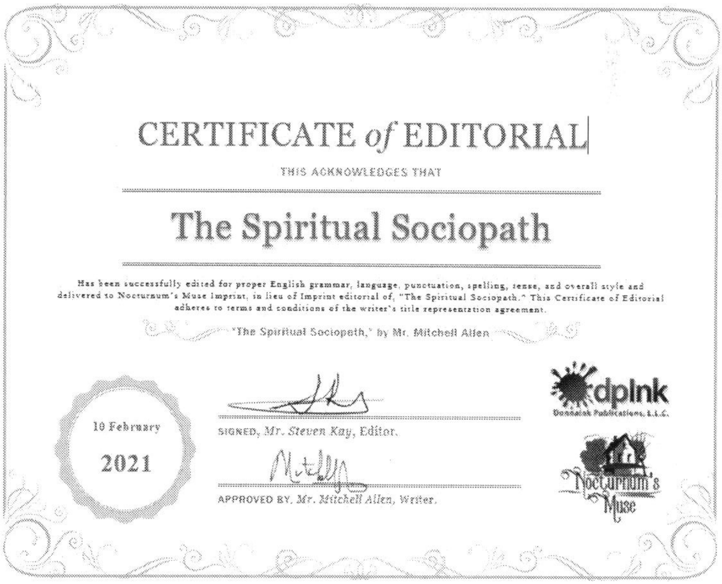
CERTIFICATE *of* EDITORIAL

THIS ACKNOWLEDGES THAT

The Spiritual Sociopath

Has been successfully edited for proper English grammar, language, punctuation, spelling, tense, and overall style and delivered to Nocturnum's Muse Imprint, in lieu of Imprint editorial of, "The Spiritual Sociopath." This Certificate of Editorial adheres to terms and conditions of the writer's title representation agreement.

"The Spiritual Sociopath," by Mr. Mitchell Allen

10 February 2021

SIGNED, *Mr. Steven Kay*, Editor.

APPROVED BY, *Mr. Mitchell Allen*, Writer.

dpInk Donnaink Publications, L.L.C.

Nocturnum's Muse

MERCHANDISE

THE SPIRITUAL SOCIOPATH

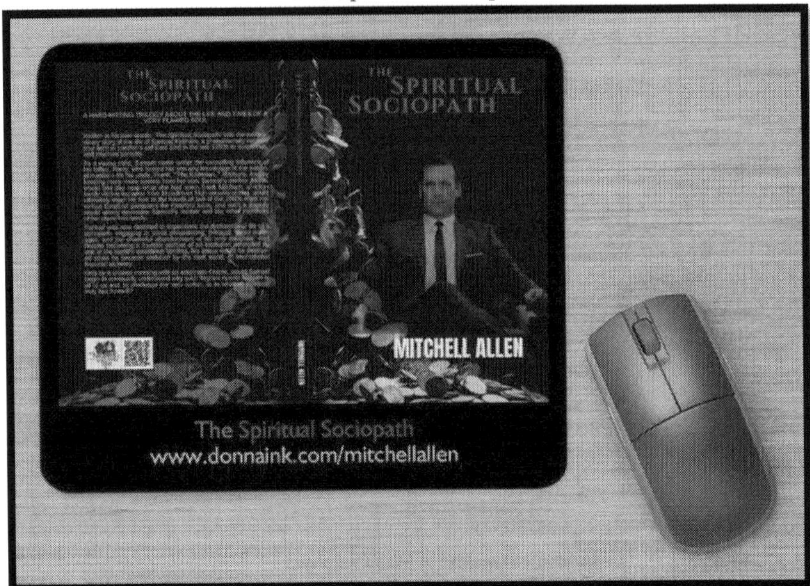
THE SPIRITUAL SOCIOPATH
THE SPIRITUAL SOCIOPATH
MITCHELL ALLEN
The Spiritual Sociopath
www.donnaink.com/mitchellallen

SPIRITUAL SOCIOPATH
MITCHELL ALLEN

COMING SOON – PART TWO
OF THE SPIRITUAL SOCIOPATH SERIES

"A Fool's Paradise"

"Religion is for people who are afraid of going to hell; spirituality is for those who've already been there."

Vine Deloria Jr.

THE
SPIRITUAL
SOCIOPATH
MITCHELL ALLEN

Nocturnum's Muse

dpInk
DonnaInk Publications, L.L.C.

Nocturnum's Muse Imprint
Publishers Since 2012
An imprint of **DonnaInk Publications, L.L.C.**
601 McReynolds Street
Carthage, NC 28327
or
1390 Chain Bridge Road, #10029, McLean, VA 22101

Printed in Great Britain
by Amazon

82913576R00188